only
copy 01/07

D0926559

CEREMONY OF INNOCENCE

CEREMONY OF INNOCENCE

Humphrey Hawksley

HEADLINE
FEATURE

Copyright © Humphrey Hawksley 1998

The right of Humphrey Hawksley to be identified as the Author
of the Work has been asserted by him in accordance with the
Copyright, Designs and Patents Act 1988.

First published in Great Britain in 1998
by HEADLINE BOOK PUBLISHING

A HEADLINE FEATURE hardback

10 9 8 7 6 5 4 3 2 1

All rights reserved. No part of this publication may be
reproduced, stored in a retrieval system, or transmitted,
in any form or by any means without the prior written
permission of the publisher, nor be otherwise circulated
in any form of binding or cover other than that in which
it is published and without a similar condition being
imposed on the subsequent purchaser.

All characters in this publication are fictitious
and any resemblance to real persons, living or dead,
is purely coincidental.

British Library Cataloguing in Publication Data
Hawksley, Humphrey
Ceremony of innocence
1. Thrillers
I. Title
823.9'14 [F]
hardback ISBN: 0 7472 2113 8
softback ISBN: 0 7472 7628 5

Typeset by
Palimpsest Book Production Limited, Polmont, Stirlingshire
Printed and bound in Great Britain by
Clays Ltd, St Ives plc.

HEADLINE BOOK PUBLISHING
A division of Hodder Headline PLC
338 Euston Road
London NW1 3BH

For Christopher

Turning and turning in the widening gyre
The falcon cannot hear the falconer;
Things fall apart; the centre cannot hold;
Mere anarchy is loosed upon the world,
The blood-dimmed tide is loosed, and everywhere
The ceremony of innocence is drowned;
The best lack all conviction, while the worst
Are full of passionate intensity.

W.B. Yeats

Chapter One

Spring winds blew down from the deserts of northern Asia.
They swept along highways throwing up stinging dust, so
that those still out and awake walked along hunched and masked.
Cyclists were buffeted, and gales blew around the edges of the high
buildings, pushing away the dome of pollution which had hung
over Beijing for days.

In his nineteenth-floor hotel room, Mike McKillop turned restlessly, unable to sleep properly, partly because of the noise but also
because of the anger which had been eating away at him for a year
now, returning as it always did at night. Whisky had eased it a bit,
but his dreams were jumbled and confused, of children screaming
at him, of women running from him, of gunfire on a river bank.
Then as violently as the images swirled before him, they would
stop as the window rattled and woke him, the wind howled and
a coal truck from the provinces changed gear and lumbered past
far below like an old freight train.

The hotel had given him a room with twin beds and he hadn't
complained. Tonight was the anniversary of Sally leaving him and
it was apt that he lay awake alone in a strange room for single
people which smelt of disinfectant and stale air-conditioning.

Mike McKillop was in the heartland of the world's most powerful
one-party state and tomorrow he would represent Hong Kong at
the opening of an international conference on corruption. He had
to chuckle when he thought about China teaching the world about
clean administration; and about himself, at forty-two, in a job he
hated, working for a government he despised and loving a wife
who had left him.

It always went like this: whisky, failed sleep, gunfire on the river,
Sally, the kids, revenge, insomnia, more whisky.

McKillop got out of bed to pour himself another drink in the
hope it might blur his thoughts, quieten the wind and allow time
for the phone to ring with Sally's breezy voice on the other end to

1

say it had all been a mistake and she was in the lobby waiting for him.

He went to the bathroom to splash water on his face and carry out a ritualistic check that he was still in good shape and unbowed by the catastrophes of the past year. His eyes were still alive and curious, the same brilliant piercing blue which had coaxed Sally into falling in love with him. He combed his dark hair back to reveal a high forehead and thick, bushy eyebrows. His stomach was flat, despite wild bouts of drinking. The grief lines on his cheeks and crows' feet from his eyes showed experience more than age.

It was twenty years since he had left Inverness in the Highlands, straight from university, to go to Hong Kong as a young policeman, planning to stay for only one two-and-a-half-year contract until they offered him a transfer to the Special Duties Unit, Hong Kong's equivalent of the SAS. He learnt to speak Cantonese like a local, busting immigration and drug rackets. Then he took up Russian so he could track the Soviet agents moving through Hong Kong during the Cold War as merchant seamen. Sally did not want to leave when the British flag was lowered. So Mike stayed on and watched as the Communist Party broke its promises, put its men in place and eased him into a desk job far away from the action he loved.

McKillop lit a cigarette and looked through the window at the garbage and dust swirling around outside. The ringing of the telephone made him jump. The hotel clock said it was just past one in the morning. In a ridiculous hope, he always associated the telephone with Sally. But he took a sip of whisky, answered it and heard a voice from the past: 'Mike, it's Clem. Clem Watkins.'

McKillop drew hard on the cigarette. Clem kept talking: 'Put on a shirt and come for a drink.'

'Clem?' McKillop managed.

'I need a hand, old friend,' said Clem, his voice softening. 'It's like Maekok.'

'Of course,' said McKillop.

Clem told him the bar and McKillop turned on the bathroom tap to shave and give himself time to think. The Maekok River had just been in his disturbed dreams. Never would it go away and leave him in peace, not for one night, although it was almost thirteen years ago, the last time he had worked with Clem.

He ran his hand down the stubble on his face. He fumbled for a bar of soap, whipped up a lather and spread it first around his chin, then high up on the cheekbones. So Clem would be thirty-seven.

2

He had been a friend, a genuine friend and there weren't many of those left. He flinched as he drew a blunt razor down his face and wondered if the years had taken Clem's youth. Whether there was a runaway wife who had drained him of emotion. Whether Clem knew whom Mike was now working for. And whether he would understand, even forgive.

Mike threw a sports jacket over his shirt, and wrapped a scarf around his mouth as he stepped out of the hotel into the wild winds. A cyclist passed him. At the traffic lights, more coal trucks, linked together in a road train, rumbled round the corner.

Beijing tonight was like Maekok, Clem had said on the phone, meaning it was a dangerous city and they should know about the men who were against them, who might follow them onto the streets. Automatically, Mike spun round to see if he was being followed. But no one vanished into the shadows. No one scuttled away. The sidewalk was empty. No one was there.

McKillop walked into the haze of a bar that was getting tired with the night. A light swung like a cradle above the pool table, blown back and forth by blasts from the huge air-conditioner in the corner. Bulbs in the ceiling shone towards the centre of the room. Smoke spun through their beams.

Clem sat in a lightless corner. He looked fit. His hair was thick and tangled. His eyes were sparkling and keen. He waved, kicking a chair out with his feet for Mike to sit on. 'So how you keeping, Mike?' He took a long, slow drink from his glass, keeping his eyes on McKillop.

'Not bad,' Mike sat down. 'It's been a few years, though.'

'Not long in the tapestry of life,' said Clem. 'You're still earning a crust, I hear.'

'Not the way a man would want,' said McKillop cautiously. His work and personal life were so closely entwined that Mike didn't want this sort of conversation so soon. So he turned it: 'And you?' he asked.

Clem grinned boyishly: 'I've been working here and there. They sent me to Central Asia to keep an eye on the Islamic fundamentalists. Now I am back in the Far East here. Still single, childless, itinerant and irresponsible.'

'Still getting shot at?'

Clem laughed. 'Not so much. But I keep my hand in. You know, after the Cold War, there are no real sides any more. It's

3

becoming so fucking complicated that no one has the capacity to identify evil.'

'Talking of which, you know who's the Party chief in Hong Kong?' said Mike, having to raise his voice above the music.

'I heard,' said Clem. His words trailed as if he wanted to avoid bringing that night at Maekok into the conversation.

A waitress wiped her forehead sulkily. She looked at her watch, impatient for the night to move on so she could make the transition from waitress to prostitute and earn a respectable income.

'So why's the great Clem Watkins seeking out an ageing policeman in a hooker's bar?' said McKillop.

'Not ageing, Mike. In your prime,' said Clem. 'But hooker's bar?' He looked around the room. 'It's definitely got potential.' He moved his chair round the table closer to Mike so they didn't have to shout over the music. He lowered his voice. 'You can step back over that thin line from collaborator to resistance fighter if you want.'

'Go on,' said Mike softly.

'There are people I've been working with who are getting very dangerous and I need your help.' Clem paused and picked hardened candle wax off the tablecloth. 'Have you heard of a place called Heshui?'

'No,' said Mike.

'What about Happy Family?'

'No.'

'Remember the spring of 1996, China conducted high-profile missile tests off its eastern coastline?'

'Threatening Taiwan,' said Mike.

'Right. And the missiles worked well. Better than expected. Everyone became terrified of China's superpower ambitions. We wanted to avoid an arms race, so decided to bring the Chinese alongside. We gave them some low-grade technology. They kept us across what they were doing. It seemed a perfect answer.'

McKillop took out a cigarette and rolled it back and forth along the surface of the table while he listened.

'We also had a genuine desire to help them. Their navy and airforce were junk. And that was causing friction with the generals at the top. We wanted China to feel at ease with itself.'

'Some hope.' Mike lit his cigarette.

'It was called Operation Happy Family.' Clem waited for Mike's reaction.

'Like I said: Never heard of it.'

'I was up at Heshui for nearly a year.'

'Was?'

'I've been moved. They want me on some project in India like by yesterday.'

'Take me back,' said Mike. 'What is Heshui?'

'It's a deep covert operation researching missile technology and delivery systems, so secret that it is covered layer by layer so that in the end I guess no one would be accountable.' Clem paused and squeezed his temples, revealing his tiredness. 'And you've never heard of it.'

'Should I?'

'You had your ear to the ground, Mike. You were the best intelligence agent on active duty in the Far East. You took on the Soviets, the North Koreans, the Vietnamese, then when the Cold War collapsed you headed straight for the drug traffickers and busted their operations from Thailand to New York to Amsterdam. You didn't need a file to come across your desk to find out if something was happening.'

'That was before China ran Hong Kong.'

'Understood.' Clem paused for a moment. 'Now listen to this. Heshui must have been set up by a very tight group. Missile scientists, right-wing pro-defence people from the CIA, the armed forces, maybe Congress. They didn't like the idea of America weakening its armed forces. They didn't like what was happening with the democratic process in Russia. Gangsters. Nationalism. Brushes with Nato. They wanted to keep China cohesive and friendly.'

'OK,' said Mike. 'But why tonight? Why tell me? Why such urgency?'

'I'll come to that,' said Clem. 'Heshui's a dreadful complex of low-rise concrete huts, way up in the mountains. I was there for the winter. Sometimes we were snowed in for weeks and our only transport out was a Chinese military helicopter. In the summer, Chinese officials flew in like dignitaries. They had a banquet and got a limited tour. Earlier this week, the guest of honour was Li Tuo.'

On hearing the name, Mike dropped his cigarette on the floor and crushed it under his shoe.

'He wore a general's uniform,' described Clem. 'Medals down his chest. He was armed, with two pistols, the same ones probably.'

'As Maekok?'

Clem nodded and Mike pictured it just like he had every day for

5

the past thirteen years, not just one image, but the whole sequence playing itself back again and again.

A light flickered on the river bank, so faint and so quick that Jimmy Lai's signal could be taken for a firefly. Then when Mike and Clem were out of the water and ashore, they watched four men at a trestle table, drinking together. Kerosene lamps hung from an awning and their faces glistened in the evening heat.

Jimmy Lai was one of the four. He had been up there in the Golden Triangle for three months, flush with money and posing as a buyer to take heroin from Burma to New York. Brave Jimmy. Slipped off saying he had to piss in the river, then guided them in with his signal.

The northern military commander of Thailand sat across from Jimmy in an Adidas sports shirt, his eyes red with cognac. Opposite was the head of Burma's secret police whose junta lived off handouts and weapons from China. And next to him Colonel Li Tuo, recently appointed head of security in the southern Chinese province of Yunnan: 'No longer should we refer to this as the Golden Triangle,' he boasted. 'A new age has dawned in Asia. There are four of us now – Burma, Thailand, Laos and China.' He drained his glass, holding it upside down to prove that it was empty and with that elevated the heroin trade to a level of regional politics.

'Li was at Heshui for about three hours,' Clem was saying, pushing ahead, not wanting to talk about the river, the past, the violence which was bringing them back together. 'The next day, that was three days ago, the military unit which guarded Heshui was changed. Troops have been posted outside every building. Not the unkempt sort you see here, but in deep olive green, pressed, polished brasses and webbing. Helmets. The same elite units they use in Tibet. A wide, straight asphalt road, well built for China, runs through the place. At each end now, there's an armoured car.

'The day after Li Tuo left, my swipe card stopped working. I went to change it and they said it would take a week. I walked out of the office and was told to go back to my quarters. My meals were brought there. I needed to send some E-mails so I logged on. But I was frozen out. Nothing wrong with the computer. I checked. Someone had pulled my access. Then for two whole days, I was living under house arrest. Soldiers outside my door. Until I was ordered down to Chengdu and was put on a commercial flight to Singapore.'

'Who exactly threw you out?' said McKillop.

'Depends how you look at it,' said Watkins. 'Do you know Warren Hollingworth?'

'CIA head of station and head of intelligence gathering for the Asia-Pacific. I've never met him.'

'I report to him and only to him because he told me that Heshui is not technically a CIA operation. There's only him, me and a handful of people at a place in California where we work from. The cover is a company called Geotechnologies.'

Clem drummed the fingers of his right hand on the table. 'Hollingworth ordered me out. He rang two days after Li Tuo was there. He wanted me to go straight to Bombay via Singapore. I know the project in Bombay. It's dull. It's beneath league, Mike. For beginners. Did he want me to do a debrief on Heshui? I asked. Later, he said. He didn't even want me to overnight in Singapore.'

'But you disobeyed him?' said McKillop. 'You came to find me?'

Clem smiled and took a sip of beer. 'That's right, Superintendent. You see, in Singapore, I called Hollingworth on the secure line in the office. He picked up the phone on the first ring. Why are you moving me, Warren? I asked.'

Clem's eyes darted around the room looking for the signs of danger. The smoke, the airlessness and the confines of the corner Clem had claimed as his own made the place hot and stuffy. Mike took off his jacket and loosened his shirt.

'Hollingworth was surprised to hear from me,' Clem said. 'He wanted to know where I was. Who was I with? Alone, I told him.'

Clem paused. 'Give me a cigarette, Superintendent.'

'Fifteen years ago you said you were going to give up,' said Mike, dropping one out of the box and handing it to Watkins.

'I have,' said Clem, lighting it and drawing deeply before he continued. 'Hollingworth was flustered. Usually he doesn't panic. He's cool. He's good. He's in command.'

Watkins coughed, unused to the smoke, then drew on the cigarette again. 'So I tell my story, then he tells me the Air India flight to Bombay leaves at six twenty in the morning. He wants me on it. OK, but shouldn't I come up to Hong Kong for a debriefing? No, he says. Not now.'

'Maybe he's been busy. Juggling a dozen balls in the air.'

'I rented a PC and a private booth for half an hour. I paid cash. No

7

names. I logged onto California using my private number which I couldn't do in Heshui. Our office there had closed down. I put a call through. The lines were disconnected. Our cover company, Geotechnologies, does not exist any more.'

'California time?' interjected Mike.

'Out of hours calls were transferred to a central switching area. Direct lines had answer machines. Read my lips, Mike. The lines have been cut. I rang John White at home. He was one of the guys in Geotech's administration. I woke him up. He said everyone had been suspended on full pay. It was something to do with the upcoming congressional hearings on the CIA and budget allocations.'

'Had he spoken to Hollingworth?' said Mike.

'He wouldn't know him.'

Clem was talking now with his eyes looking down at the table all the time. 'Next I called Martin Hewlitt. He was the agent posted to Heshui before me.'

'A policeman answered the phone. Wanted to know who I was. Then he put Joyce on, Martin's wife. I don't know her well. Martin and I had coffee at their place after a handover session. He didn't like Heshui and missed Joyce desperately. He even cut short his tour there.'

Watkins pulled toothpicks from their holder and broke them up, piling them in front of him like tiny bits of firewood.

'Joyce told me Martin's car had been crushed by a truck. Happens every day, doesn't it? Road accidents. One hell of a coincidence that I get marched out of Heshui; my data access is blocked; California's closed down; Martin gets killed.'

Both men fell silent. Songs from the band were becoming indistinguishable. It was late, even for the Redwood Bar. The waitress dozed, her head on her arms on the table. The manager did the accounts, sitting on a stool on the other side of the bar. In fluent Mandarin, Mike asked him for two whiskies and two coffees.

'I didn't tell Joyce he had been murdered,' said Clem.

'You had no evidence.'

'Then I called Bombay, to a guy I know, Dr Satish Krishnan. He's the office administrator. I told him I wasn't coming any more. Plans had changed. There's a long silence. I could hear him tapping the computer keyboard to check my schedule. Then he came back to me. I was never due to arrive in Bombay, Mike. There was nothing in their records about Clem Watkins being rushed in to work with them.'

'Different project?'

'No Mike. I wasn't on their books. I wasn't expected.'

The drinks arrived, prompting both men to fall silent. Then McKillop asked: 'How much technology did you give them at Heshui?'

'I know only two things, Mike. They're a damn sight better than they were in 1996, much more advanced than they would be if they had done it themselves. The Russians gave them a lot, but not the sort of high-tech information warfare we're into. The second is they're not anywhere as good as us yet.'

'Is that the sum knowledge of Western intelligence efforts?'

'Give or take a few thousand specifications on smart, stealth technology . . . Yes.' Clem grinned. He got up, pushing the table back a bit and picked up his bag. 'I'm going for a leak,' he said.

'I'll watch that,' said McKillop, pointing to the bag. But Clem kept it with him, walking to the washroom without answering.

Chapter Two

There were only two tables of people left. The manager closed the door and swung the sign round to 'closed'. The waitress sat with customers. One was playing guitar on the podium. He had long black hair, kept back with a bright red headband with the five rising stars of China.

'I heard about Sally,' Clem said when he sat down again. 'I'm sorry.'

Mike just nodded and waved his hand, not wanting to talk about it, but glad that Clem cared. 'How are the kids holding up?' Clem continued.

'They're with her. I haven't heard anything at all from them,' said Mike. 'Charlotte's twelve and Matthew's eight. So how did you hear?'

'Tommy Lai still sends Chinese New Year cards. He just said you had separated.'

Mike didn't want this conversation and he didn't know why he opened up then, probably because Clem was an old friend, a man whom he trusted and who should know about it. And Tommy was no longer a friend because he had been clawed into the recesses of the Chinese Communist Party by the same forces which had taken Sally from him, of nationalism, power, race and culture. Suddenly Mike found himself telling Clem about Tommy, Maekok and Jimmy.

'Do you two still keep in touch?' Clem was asking.

'We were very close. But since '97 the local officers have been banned from fraternising with foreigners,' said Mike. 'Tommy asked me to tell the family about his brother's death. I took the lift up to Jimmy's flat. Agnes and the kids were doing homework together and the kids got excited and started showing me their computer game. Then I just said that Jimmy had died. Agnes listened,' Mike laughed bitterly. 'She even asked me if I wanted a cold drink.

10

'I didn't tell them how he died. What else was there to say? In the States you would say that he gave his life for his country. But it didn't work like that in Hong Kong. No one knew then what country they belonged to. Not Jimmy. Not me. No flag over his coffin. No coffin, because they never got the body.

'I didn't tell them we left him on the river bank.'

First they had crawled to the hut. Inside was a heroin refinery and Watkins took only three minutes to collect the evidence, exactly the amount of time Mike needed to lay the charges. As soon as Clem came out with samples, they blew it up, first a dull thud and a few sparks, then a ball of fire which leapt out of the jungle.

Clem got into the boat. Mike pushed off, then climbed in himself, lying flat, looking back towards the silhouettes and the fires. He saw Li Tuo on the bank, his back to the river, Jimmy Lai on his knees in front of him, the pistol levelled at his head and Li's voice carrying easily across the water.

'You think I didn't know,' Li sneered. 'You think I'm stupid. You think you are not going to die.'

Jimmy didn't respond. Li Tuo struck him and he fell to the ground. Clem passed Mike a revolver. But they were too far, the boat too unsteady to take an accurate shot. Blood ran down the side of Jimmy's face.

Mike saw the pistol buck before he heard the shot which killed Jimmy. McKillop fired. He sprayed the river bank in fury. Clem started the motor. Return fire hit the water around them. The boat was underway, soon out of range. They travelled downstream to another part of Thailand before putting ashore just before dawn.

They said goodbye on the river bank. Mike was ponderous, reflective and maudlin. But Clem said: 'Men die in our business. Men die in wars.'

That was the last time Mike had seen Clem, now Watkins leaned across the table and put his hand on Mike's shoulder. 'You didn't kill Jimmy, Li Tuo did. Don't hate yourself. Hate him.'

'You ask me why I'm still there,' said Mike. 'That's why. One day I will avenge Jimmy's death.'

'I heard you were given the big freeze after the Brits moved out.'

'They segregate us now like a bad smell.'

'So is it worth sticking around?'

'They launched a Chinese family culture campaign,' said Mike.

11

'There was one at Sally's hospital. It started off by offering to track people's ancestry back to their home village. The government paid for trips and it seemed harmless enough, like an American tour to Scotland to find out your clan. Sally came from a village in northern Guangdong. We went up there as a family and that's when I started sensing that things were going wrong. I was in civvies. They didn't know I was with the police and didn't think I could speak Cantonese.'

'So what did they say?' asked Clem.

'We were sitting at a huge banquet table. These bastards were serving me garoupa and lobster, smiling like the sun shone out of my arse, and at the same time saying stuff to Sally like: 'How can you stay married to a foreigner? Your children must understand the Chinese race. We've neither forgiven nor forgotten what the Europeans did to us.'

'And Sally was shaken up, too. We'd talked a lot about it in the past. People just didn't realise how the Party used the race card. She was getting insults at work, not just from the cleaners, but from the consultants, for Christ's sake.'

'Why didn't you . . .'

'Leave. You don't know how many times we talked about it,' said Mike. 'Sally thought about setting up her own gynaecological practice in Edinburgh. Her qualifications would have been accepted. Charlotte was just beginning to show her musical talents and it was when we were just finding out about Matthew's problems that I thought we should quit.'

'What problems?'

'Sally had a difficult birth and there was some bleeding to Matthew's brain which ended up with mild cerebral palsy. Between us, that was fine, but the remarks from medical staff and neighbours were hard to live with. One nurse told Sally that if she let Matthew die, she could always have another healthy baby. Then a neighbour told her in the supermarket that the Chinese race would be better off without crippled babies.'

Both men were quiet for a while, then Mike picked up: 'If I leave, I abandon my family. Sally's flighty, imaginative, patriotic. I think she got sucked into all the racist crap. I don't know where she is now. But I have to see her again, just to ask her if she really wanted to go away. Or whether she was forced. Or if she'll come back to me. If she says "No", fine. I'll go back to Scotland, become a car park security guard or something.'

Clem moved forward to touch Mike's shoulder, nodding his head: 'What a perilous path you've chosen, old friend.'

'You know, every time I see Li Tuo up there making a speech, opening a hospital or something I think of the ugly compromises I've made. I wear their uniform. I abide by their rules. Each document I sign with my British name gives the regime international credibility. I look the other way when charges and convictions are rigged against political activists, like the good citizens of France when the Gestapo kicked down their neighbours' doors.'

'That's why I want your help.'

Mike leaned forward and took a handful of peanuts from the bowl. 'Clem, she left because of the Party. It wasn't us. Our marriage. It was the fucking Party and its racism and nationalism which tore us apart.'

He washed the peanuts down with cold beer: 'And I'm going to get them back. I'm going to kill Li Tuo and get my family back. And that's why I'm staying.'

The band was winding up. The musicians squatted down, unplugging wires from amplifiers. They drank beer and smoked. Friends chatted to them around the stage. The coffee was cold, but McKillop drank it anyway.

'Sorry,' he said. 'We got sidetracked. If I can help you, I will.'

'We'd better get out of here,' said Clem, 'before someone turns up the lights and gets a clear look at us.'

Mike left money on the table. Outside the air was cool. The streets were quiet except for the roar of the wind and the rumble of city sound.

They turned left and walked towards the big crossroads. A taxi drove across the junction. They automatically kept to the edge of the pavement. McKillop estimated there were seven yards to the left before the cover of the undergrowth, then the railings of the diplomatic compound which they were passing. To their right was the expanse of a Maoist boulevard, a six-lane city highway with a bicycle track on each side.

'Something's going on in Heshui,' said Clem. 'Hollingworth knows about it. Li Tuo knows about it.'

McKillop saw the same directness in Clem's eyes as he had known all those years earlier: 'What do you need me to do?' He asked.

'You're going to the corruption conference tomorrow, right?'

'Today, I think,' said Mike, glancing at his watch.

'A Burmese general will make contact with you. I used to run

13

him as an agent and he's about the only man in Asia apart from you I know can be trusted. He'll try and get onto your table. But don't tell him anything there. When you get a chance, afterwards, walking out or something, just say that I told you that Heshui had run out of control. He won't ask you more. Use my real name. Doesn't matter.'

'That's it?'

'For now. He might get back to you somehow.' Clem grinned. 'Li Tuo isn't unbeatable, Mike. Powerful people are working to get rid of him and thousands like him. They killed Jimmy. They took Sally from you.' Under the flyover ahead, Beijing's homeless huddled in rows, burning fires to keep them warm. Clem stopped and swept tangled hair back off his face. 'You can be damned sure she wouldn't have left without that pressure. You had a great marriage.'

Mike looked at his friend. They were conspicuous on the pavement. It was almost four in the morning. Pockets of dawn were breaking through. 'Thanks,' he said.

McKillop tore a sheet of paper from a notebook which he carried as a habit left over from when he was a real policeman. 'This is my hotel direct line number. No switchboard. This is my private mobile number for after I leave,' he said. Mike folded the paper and pushed it into Clem's top pocket. 'Remember it. Don't ring, fax or E-mail. There'll be a trace. Page it and leave your number – but run the number backwards, with the first and last digits inverted, like we used to before. It'll be safe for one contact.'

They were at the end of the flyover, with the trucks tearing down too fast for the obsolete conditions of the vehicles, kicking up dust and blowing out filthy exhaust. The road widened for hundreds of yards like the meeting tributaries of a great river. Bicycles moved slowly and purposefully in their allocated lanes as the city came to life. In a nearby army compound, troops shouted in a workout routine then hoisted the Chinese national flag to a pole that rose above the secure walls. Embassy guards in green greatcoats and with cold red cheeks marched in a messy formation to take over the morning shift, their eyes ahead, ignoring the two tired foreigners saying goodbye on the pavement.

Mike watched as his friend walked, almost ambled north along the Third Ring Road. In ten minutes he would be up by the Great Wall Sheraton and the Lufthansa Centre. The night clubs would be disgorging themselves, not scruffily like the Redwood Bar but of Beijing's beautiful people, bedecked with the designer labels of

Europe and America which had become the hallmarks of a great Asian society. The neon colours shone hazily through the pollution. These were the aspirations and resentments of modern China.

Mike waved. Clem, by now a distant figure, was made distinctive by the bag slung over his back. A truck struggled past, three men in the cab. The driver smoked. The cigarette glowed onto his face. The trailer, stacked high with coal, swayed and bounced in and out of potholes.

McKillop covered his face against the grit. He didn't notice anything was wrong until the black Audi saloon was only a few yards in front of Clem. The window was down. A hand held a machine pistol. He could see it clearly. Clem carried on. Mike shouted. Then he shouted again. But the distance was too much. The wind was against him and another coal truck reverberated down the flyover. Mike broke into a run. The Audi slowed to walking pace. Its wheels first brushed the kerb, then bounced onto the pavement. The tyres screeched and spun. The pistol bucked and fired.

But Clem was ready for them. He turned and in one continuous movement threw himself over a low fence. He landed softly on grass and rolled twice. Shrubs and small trees were planted everywhere. The grass was long and unmown. Three yards further back was the wall of an embassy, covered in weeds and ivy. The area was out of range of the street lights which illuminated the Third Ring Road, giving Clem an advantage. His movements and the shadows were erratic. As he finished his second roll, he released the bag from his shoulder and took out his own weapon. He fired twice. The first shot hit the windscreen.

The second caught the front left-hand door. A line of return fire embedded itself into the wall behind him. Leaves were cut from their branches and fell to the ground. Clem rolled again and emerged from behind a fruit tree. He fired two more shots, both through the back window. The Audi accelerated, bumping harshly back onto the road. Clem's last shot smashed the right rear light.

The driver was clumsy. The car speeded up, then began doing a U-turn under the flyover. It moved into the underpass filled with street sleepers. There were horrible screams as if someone had been run over. The people rose up with their squalid bedcovers. Some scattered. Some attacked. They threw bottles and cans. The Audi came out heading north, chased by the homeless people of China, but only for a few yards before they retreated back into their sanctuary with the sullenness and anger of people used to humiliation.

15

Mike looked first to where Clem had been. But he had melted away. Then he turned to the junction where the Audi had just gone into a diplomatic compound. It was so close, just a hundred yards beyond the Redwood Bar. Mike looked back again. Still there was no sign of Clem Watkins.

Mike broke into a jog. Each step jarred his body, his shoes kicked up dirt on the track which ran close against the wall, hidden from the road by darkness and trees. He side-stepped people outside the Redwood Bar. He recognised the singer and something different in his look as he ran by him. Suddenly, the musicians, the manager and the waitress seemed alert and orderly. Maybe Clem had picked the wrong bar. Maybe Clem hadn't realised what it was like in Greater China. Everyone worked for the Party. Everyone was a spy. Or maybe he was going mad, the paranoia eating away his reason and his judgment. Maybe there wasn't a right bar to pick.

He ran on, jumping over a bicycle which had fallen onto the path. The pollution and wind burnt into his throat, making him cough. He kept going until he saw the gate to the diplomatic compound and inside a long, ugly building with cars parked in front. The building was seven storeys high and appeared to have been built in the Seventies after China signed a communiqué with America and tore down its bamboo curtain. Lights were strung down each side, making it look impressive from a distance, but as Mike came closer he noticed broken bulbs and the stains from leaking pipes. At the gate itself, there was a guard, upright, stationary, eyes dulled with boredom.

The compound was secured by high, green railings. The Audi was parked bonnet-first towards them. Three men talked in the dialect of the south-east coastline. Laughter, like in a locker room, with no effort to conceal the noise. They slammed shut the doors and walked towards the front of the building. So arrogant, so close to the scene of their attack. So certain there would be no retribution.

The men were inside the foyer. The lift door was open. They got in and McKillop gave it a full two minutes before he followed. The gates of the compound were open. Red and yellow plants in dozens of small pots decorated the driveway. A smile from Mike's white face took him past the guard. Once inside, he would have no interest in Mike: foreigners may do what they want behind these gates. The Audi was between a maroon Chrysler Cherokee jeep and a white Mercedes van, used by a German construction company. On the railings were the signs of the diplomatic missions inside: Slovenia. Macedonia. Croatia, Mozambique, Peru and

16

Ecuador. Two steps went up to a revolving door in the centre. On each side were floor-to-ceiling glass doors, framed in a light and varnished wood.

McKillop caught his breath. His heart raced with sudden exercise and nerves no longer used to unexpected danger. Clem Watkins didn't have a family. He was as alone as Mike had ever been. Tonight even more so, somewhere in Beijing, trying to escape, with a hidden gun and powerful men hunting him. The foyer ceiling was high. The floor was stone. It echoed, empty and ghostly. To his left was a padlocked shop with signs on the dark windows saying: 'You are welcome. Wine & Cigarettes.' To the right were rows of numbered letter boxes painted in a faded, light green, each one framed with a brass rim.

Three of the bulbs for the lift lights were broken. The figure Seven was illuminated and that was where the lift had gone, and where it was now stopped. The lift didn't move. There were more Embassy plaques on the wall. Ecuador 2nd; Peru 8th and 9th; Uruguay 3rd. But no seventh. No register of tenants. Mike pressed the call button. Machinery high in the building whirred. The lights moved from sixth to fifth floor. McKillop moved out of sight into an unlit corridor as the lift car halted and the doors slid open.

He revived instincts of observation which had lain dormant for years. He waited again to make sure that the lift was empty, then he worked his way across the vast foyer, avoiding the main sweeps of light, moving in arcs which kept him away from lines of fire, from the road, from the lift, from further down the corridor. His first destination was the far corner, the window ledge near the letter boxes by the revolving door. Without stopping, Mike picked up three envelopes of newspapers, put them under his arm and walked out through the swing doors. He turned right so that he could leave the compound from a different entrance under the eyes of another guard.

Mike slowed himself down, catching his breath, walking as if on a contented stroll back from a good night out in a strange city. He pushed his hair back to tidy it up, brushed down his jacket, and walked briskly through the lobby of his hotel with its loud vacuum cleaners, floor polishers and sleepy waitresses laying out the buffet in the coffee shop. His room was untouched. Nothing was out of place and it would have been if they had decided on a search. There was a stink of recycled smoke from the air-conditioning. Mike looked at the newspaper envelopes.

One was addressed to the Bruneian Embassy. The other two

17

bore no name – just the address Seventh Floor, Sanlitun, Bang-yu. Mike slipped the newspapers out of their envelopes. Today's – or yesterday's as it was now, and the preceding day. There were no markings on the front page. Mike looked for some kind of identification. On the back of each envelope, the newspaper vendor had marked up the name of his customer in English and with Chinese characters.

The seventh-floor apartment's tenant was Lance Picton, a diplomat at the American Embassy.

Chapter Three

Mike lay exhausted on the bed, fully clothed. He took a cigarette from his shirt pocket and lit it. He felt filthy. The whole grimy environment stood as the monument of the enemy. He closed his eyes and images of Sally as he had known her, and of their imaginary home in Scotland, tried to fight their way through. He always talked to her in his head, even now, as lonely men often do. He told her about Clem wanting his help and his friend being attacked. He replayed the whole conversation about a man killed by a truck in California, a spymaster in Hong Kong whom Clem didn't trust, an intelligence pact between America and China which officially didn't exist in Congress, the Pentagon, the CIA, or the White House, but had a home in an inhospitable wasteland of a place called Heshui. He told Sally he had to pass a message to a Burmese general and was surprised by a wave of nostalgia and excitement that passed over him. Clem had come back and asked him to work again. After all these years. Proper work. His mind drifted between sleep and memories of his wife as she had once been, all in the messy room with its foul air. Until the phone rang again on the direct line and he heard Clem's voice from a payphone: 'Made it,' he said so quickly that they might trace the call, but not his voice.

An old Boeing Air India airliner rose into the sky from Singapore and climbed to thirty-nine thousand feet above the Andaman Sea heading north-west towards the Indian Ocean and eventually Bombay. The passenger in First Class seat 1A had finished his meal, but kept the table open in front of him. Anyone who looked at what he was doing would have seen tables and figures outlining the troubles of a multinational company working in the developing world. The components for his company's new notebook communicator were manufactured in China, Bombay and England. The Indian-made mother-board was causing a delay to the launch. If it wasn't ready by Christmas, his rivals would take the market, and he could be looking not at share options but at redundancy.

He switched on his laptop and watched the batteries jolt it into life. He tuned the plane's headphones to the rotating selection of classical violin music. There were only two other passengers in the cabin, seated at the back and sleeping. A hostess refilled his coffee. Then she brought down a cushion which she said should be put just above the small of his back for maximum relaxation while working. He was grateful. The hostess returned to the galley, drawing the curtain behind her and fastening it. The cabin lights dimmed.

The first tip of an elongated and reinforced hypodermic needle pierced the cushion cover when he leant back to stretch his back muscles with the full force of his torso. Sodium pentothal shot into his body and by the time he had realised the sharp pain of the injection he was drifting into unconsciousness. A second syringe pumped in pancuronium bromide which paralysed his diaphragm and stopped his breathing, followed by potassium chloride which stopped his heart.

The one slight cry the passenger let out went unnoticed. He took just over thirty seconds to be executed with the same cocktail of drugs which gushed into the arterial system of prisoners on America's death rows. Ten minutes later, the hostess checked that he was dead. She lifted his body gently forward to remove the cushion and the needle. The captain notified air traffic control in Burma that he would be diverting to make an unscheduled landing at Rangoon.

Mike didn't sleep. In the morning, he showered and drank coffee. A car had been sent to the hotel to take him to the Great Hall of the People. The waitresses, with red blouses, stood expressionless in a line, bearing pots of tea and coffee. The hall was without windows, but illuminated by lights, fixed high across the high cream-coloured ceiling, curving like curtain folds. Behind the head table, ten bright red flags hung on poles, forming an arc over the national flag of the Motherland, and displaying the date of 1949 when the Communist Party took power in China.

A fanfare from the military band exploded through Mike's head. A dull and delicate ache was taking hold in the aftermath of the alcohol and a sleepless night. He sat down, took two Panadol from his pocket and swallowed them. He looked at the name badges of the other guests. Across the table was a stocky and beaming Thai General Vichit Moolasartsathorn. For years, Mike had tracked the general's career from lean anti-communist fighter in north-eastern Thailand to owner of hotels and golf clubs in the south. Next to him was Cambodia's superintendent of Interpol, Chea Banh, whose wealth originated from kidnapping Western tourists in the Nineties and cutting deals to share the gem and logging wealth of his Khmer Rouge enemies. Next to him was a young Singaporean, Lim Yok How, whom Mike didn't know. They shook hands and McKillop noted approvingly that Singapore had downgraded its delegate to Chief Inspector. Throughout East Asia, only Singapore had managed to avoid the grip of the Party and its conglomerates, clinging to its reputation of being a clean island state.

'So you have a headache? Or is it a hangover?' A Burmese sat down beside McKillop, pointing to the packet of tablets on the table. He spoke in the soft and fluent English which Mike immediately associated with a British education. 'As a matter of fact, I do,' answered Mike curtly.

The Burmese offered his hand: 'Brigadier-General Win Kyi, Mr McKillop. The Chinese have borrowed yet another idea from the Americans. The working breakfast. And they turn it into a banquet for a thousand people.' He paused as Mike shook his hand, then added: 'You wouldn't remember me, but I attended one of your courses in Hong Kong. It was on narcotics.'

'Sorry. I don't remember.'

'No need for you to. It was a big joke.'

'Oh?'

'Because we knew and you knew that we were all up to our eyes in the trade,' explained Win Kyi.

Mike put his hand to his mouth and coughed, quietly promising himself no cigarettes until midday.

'I suppose your honesty is meant to impress me.' McKillop poured himself a glass of water.

'You wouldn't have bothered to look me up,' Win Kyi continued. 'But then I never had your professional stature. I found your biography on AsNet, and learnt about the break-up of your marriage. I was very sorry to read it. You see, I married an English girl. I met her at Oxford. We studied medicine. For a long, pleasant time we lived in England. Quiet lives, in Suffolk in a joint country practice. We had three children. Of course, to outsiders it looked like an idyllic life.'

Mike picked at peanuts in a bowl with chopsticks and Win Kyi continued: 'For many years, though, I had this crazy desire to live

21

in Burma. The winter flus were becoming repetitive, Burma was becoming more open and my patriotism appealed to Elizabeth.'

The general, bedecked with medals, looked at Mike: 'As you know, the openness didn't last long.'

'No it didn't,' said McKillop. He laid his chopsticks on the tablecloth.

'The children and I had to stay, because we were of Burmese blood. They physically took Elizabeth to the airport and put her on a plane to Bangkok. That was seventeen years ago.'

'And you?'

'The children have just finished university and are beginning work for the regime. I assume they spy on me.'

Abruptly, the band stopped playing. The guests rose, heads turned to their left towards the red-carpeted entrance from which the leaders of China were about to emerge. They ambled in; their military green uniforms and dark black suits contrasted with the bright red carpet which led to their tables.

'Asia is a dangerous place, my friend,' whispered Win Kyi.

Mike looked straight into the unwavering, concerned eyes of the general, the only man Clem said he could trust except for himself. The dignitaries separated to take seats at the four tables below the flags. A voice came over the public address system. Mike shifted in his chair. He knew the voice, like the winds which blew into Beijing from the Gobi desert, like the grit of northern China, and the filthy humidity which clung to him during a Hong Kong summer. He was an expert on it. The voice of the enemy with whom he collaborated. Of the Communist Party. Of his employer: 'Welcome foreign guests to the Great Hall of the People.'

'The building you are in now was constructed in just ten months between 1958 and 1959. It was the inspiration of our Great Helmsman Mao Tse-tung who liberated the Chinese people from colonial aggression.'

There were more military men on the top tables than Mike had seen before. The People's Liberation Army and the Communist Party had become one institution. On the far left, thirteen out of the seventeen officials were from the armed forces.

'The Great Hall of the People covers seventeen thousand square metres. The auditorium which is used by the democratically elected National People's Congress can seat ten thousand people. The red star of China is embedded on the ceiling in a galaxy of lights. Thirty rooms run off the reception hall . . .'

Taking advantage of the noise from the public address system,

Win Kyi leant forward to speak to Mike: 'It was I who hid Clem's weapon in the washroom,' he said. 'And an American was murdered on the Air India flight from Singapore to Bombay this morning.' He edged his chair out, bringing him closer to Mike.

'The plane put down at Yangon to off-load the body. India is not under their control. But my country is, so the post-mortem is being done there. Our enemies are brutal, but inefficient.'

The voice of the Party faded to applause. 'And now, ladies and gentlemen, I present to you the President of the People's Republic of China.'

'The assassin was looking for Clem,' said Win Kyi, clapping. 'But he didn't board. The man who died was Christopher C. Watson. An innocent. A cock-up.'

The breakfast guests were rising to their feet. The President of China, Kang Guo-feng, smiling, bowing, left his table to walk to the podium. He had wisps of grey, dishevelled hair, a small man who moved nervously as if his mind was on other matters. With his little, rounded glasses and a nervous twitch in the left eye, he looked like an academic keener to shy away from the spotlight. Kang's speeches and books had been widely translated in the West. His argument over the pace of democratic reform in developing countries had been embraced in America and Europe. Even the State Department admitted there was now a man in Beijing with whom they could do business. Kang shuffled papers on the podium. The hall became quiet. Kang adjusted his glasses. He looked back over his shoulder at the symbols of the country emblazoned above him, against which he was dwarfed.

Kang had devised a slogan: 'Love China and love your contract. It is the word of the Motherland.' He had freed the legal system from the whims of the Communist Party. Political prisoners were being released from labour camps. He had been televised in meetings with Amnesty International, Human Rights Watch-Asia and other pressure groups.

Foreign money was flowing in and America had stopped pushing for faster democratic reform.

'I think you all have my opening speech in front of you,' he said with a smile. A theatrical pause. A rustle of papers. 'In many languages. And those of you who have not found engaging conversation with your breakfast partners, might even have looked through it.' Laughter. Scattered handclaps. 'So that's the speech and as we all are busy people, I won't waste time by reading it out.'

Kang took off his glasses and chuckled: 'For the television

producers needing a soundbite, I hope there'll be something in what I have to say now.' He put his glasses on the lectern and clasped his hands in front of him.

'This conference is about corruption,' began Kang. 'It is about policemen taking bribes to let off a traffic offender. About a railway clerk getting rich by charging too much for a ticket. Corruption is about tycoons paying money to politicians like me so they can build a bridge or a skyscraper. Why would I do it? Because the salary of the President of China is 8526 Renminbi a month. For our foreign guests that is about seven hundred American dollars. The British prime minister, on the other hand, gets 13,000 dollars and he's about the worst paid of Western leaders.' The audience laughed. Kang paused and brushed his hair off his forehead: 'No, ladies and gentlemen, I am not seeking a pay rise. I have a roof over my head which comes with the job. I have enough banquets like this not to starve.' Kang's hands clasped the edges of the stand. He shook as if with anger. 'But the policeman and the railway clerk do not. And until we pay our people a decent wage they will continue to be corrupt.'

To this there was loud, spontaneous applause. Kang waited. 'China's foreign reserves are the highest in the world. We have more than two hundred and fifty billion US dollars in the bank. Doing what? Gaining interest? Giving foreign brokers our wealth to gamble on their stock markets?' Kang stopped as if he was expecting an answer. The banquet hall echoed with silence and when he spoke again his voice reverberated with a new strength: 'So as from today, right now, I am authorising a pay rise for all public servants. We will pay them what they need to live on; to feed and house their families and educate their children. From today there will be no excuse for taking bribes and anyone caught doing so will be sacked and sent to jail for a very long time.'

Kang drank from the glass of water in front of him, waiting for the applause to end: 'That's all, ladies and gentlemen.' He smiled again. His eyes were bright and playful.

Chairs shuffled back as the audience rose to give Kang an ovation. Half of them were on their feet. Half were still sitting, when the President raised his hand: 'Just one more point. Corruption breeds through unaccountable institutions,' he said. 'So I'm putting out another document later in the week outlining my plans for limited direct elections to the National People's Congress. Let our Western critics not be deceived. We are not being copycats to their political system. That has already been rejected by the Chinese people. We are merely streamlining our institutions to make them credible in the eyes of the people. Our great helmsman, Mao Tse-tung, noted at the beginning of this long struggle: '*Our countrymen have only known how each man could manage his own private interests in such a way to maximise his own personal profit, while minimising social benefit.*'

'Today,' finished Kang, 'we are making another tiny step in his vision to create an equal China for all.'

Kang walked down from the stage. The whole audience, from one hundred and eight tables, more than a thousand people, were on their feet, applauding. Waitresses and waiters moved along their designated lines to pour coffee and tea.

'Very clever,' began Win Kyi. 'Did you notice how he brought in Mao at the end.'

'Clever perhaps,' said Lim Yok How, the Singaporean. 'But look at the generals. They don't think it will work.'

'It won't,' said Vichit Moolasarthsathorn, the Thai general. 'We tried it. We got rid of opium growing. We got rid of military rule. We got rid of Communist insurgents. But corruption? There is not the will. What do you think, Superintendent?'

The Chinese Communist Party in Hong Kong employed McKillop to explain its police activities to the outside world. His response was automatic: 'Corruption is an international disease. It isn't just confined to Asian cultures.'

Win Kyi pointed to a young aide who had approached Kang and was whispering in his ear and handing over papers: 'That man is the great ideologue of China,' he said. 'Zhang Ding is the brilliant and daring pupil and Kang Guo-feng is the wise and steady professor.'

'I've heard he signs documents Tony Zhang, with a Western name, instead of Zhang Ding, and gets away with it,' said Lim Yok How.

Movement was slow. Delegates crammed against each other to get out. The lift made creaking journeys back and forth. A queue stretched into the corridors which linked the chambers of the building. Mike stayed with Win Kyi. The others dispersed into the mêlée. 'Let's take the stairs,' suggested Mike. The two men broke away and found the stairs in the corner. A few others had the same idea and as they mixed with them, Mike said softly: 'Heshui's run out of control.'

Win Kyi slowed his pace. It was barely noticeable, but gave him time to react before reaching the vast foyer on the ground floor.

He turned, looked straight at Mike and held out his hand to say goodbye: 'It's been a pleasure meeting you, Superintendent. Please look me up if you're ever passing through Yangon.' He paused. 'And we must keep in touch,' he finished.

His release of McKillop's hand was an indication that Mike must move on. He walked quickly down the remaining flight, aware of the man still behind him and grateful for the architecture of the Great Hall which allowed for high ceilings, generous voids and time to think.

Mike walked out into brilliant sunshine. Red flags flew forcefully in the wind all around Tiananmen Square. The sky was clear and blue with wisps of clouds. The western hills were visible. For a day, perhaps two, the pollution had been blown away. Coaches and limousines were parked in line along the Square. Policemen stood at intervals between the portrait of Mao Tse-tung above the Forbidden City to the north and his mausoleum to the south. They marked the area which was closed off to the public. From the steps of the Great Hall of the People, there was nothing so stunning, so ideological, so blatantly patriotic anywhere in the world. It made Red Square look like a suburban baseball park. Mike remembered Trafalgar Square and Hyde Park Corner as badly designed roundabouts. Washington was peppered with memorials and monuments, but none as arrogant as this.

Suddenly, shouting and running disrupted the order of the Square. Mike spun round. Footsteps quickened pace behind him. Men ran in front of him, ignoring the delegates streaming out onto the steps. A scream from a woman. Violent sounds above the roar of traffic. People stumbled in panic down towards the Square, a scattering of black suits. Three more men, more dangerous, appeared. Mike didn't move. They weren't after him. They were all at the top of the steps, now. Two had earpieces. There was the crackle of a radio signal. Inside the Great Hall, through the glass doors, images confused by reflections from the sun. But people moving quickly in different directions. Mistrust. Uncertainty. A chase. The glass from the huge door shattered and flew out. A man hurled himself through. Curled up to protect himself. His clothes tore on the jagged edges.

Win Kyi's hands and face were cut on the broken glass. Blood ran down onto his clothes as he fell forward. He landed on his knees. His hands were stretched out in front to stop the fall. He looked up. His hair fell over his forehead, soaked in sweat. His eyes were of a hunted animal, trapped, searching for an escape. They locked onto McKillop. He picked himself up, bloodied, panting hard, his hands grazed on the concrete. The distressed man lurched towards Mike. He fell, his head crashed on the top step. Mike dropped to his knees, reaching out to help.

A bullet cracked, striking Win Kyi's chest, throwing him backwards. The gunman was thirty yards away, his weapon ready to fire again. 'Stop,' shouted McKillop. Win Kyi's head lay in the crook of his arm. McKillop had known the anxiety of guns pointed at him before. It took a psychopathic mind, even for a trained assassin, to kill someone not on the list. McKillop wasn't. The attacker was a policeman, his earpiece dislodged in the commotion.

'He's dying anyway,' Mike shouted in Mandarin. Win Kyi grabbed Mike's lapels, pulling McKillop down with the weight of his body. His eyes were moist and bloodshot. Saliva dribbled down his chin. A shard of glass was lodged in his neck. Win Kyi could only whisper, but Mike couldn't make it out.

The police were closing in. The body twitched. Win Kyi coughed. Blood and saliva spewed out of his mouth. His head fell back, and the neck muscles slackened at the moment of death. The policeman pulled Mike away, but he resisted, at least to lower the body onto the concrete. McKillop stumbled as he got to his feet. He wiped his hands on his suit. He saw a kite, the picture of a bird with huge wings and a long, floating tail, drift across above the mausoleum of Mao Tse-tung. Guides, with flags held high above their heads, led tour groups from monument to monument. Police surrounded the body. One asked Mike for his identity. McKillop showed him his pass for the conference and that was enough. The Communist Party knew why Win Kyi had died. It had killed him. It knew Mike too. He was of no interest to them.

Chapter Four

Scott Carter watched live television coverage of the corruption conference from his secure work complex in the American Consulate in Hong Kong. He had been studying China long enough to know what he was looking for. He tapped instructions into his keyboard: the faces of the new generals, a flamboyant sweep of President Kang's arms, spectacles held between his thumb and forefinger, and swinging back and forth. In the intelligence business, detail was the key. It bored Scott Carter, but not enough to deter him from his ambition to rise high in his chosen profession.

It was ten years since China had taken back control of Hong Kong. For three, there hadn't been much of a change as the two societies wondered which was more powerful, the sheer Goliathian weight of the world's most entrenched one-party state, or the slick financial wizardry which stoked the economic engines of China and had given her the taste of international wealth. After that, the Communist Party cadres became more confident. They moved into the uncorrupted institutions bequeathed by British colonialism with the pride of the victor. But there was no sense of battle, of achievement, and no attempt to borrow the knowledge of how the British and their Chinese colonial subjects had made Hong Kong work so well. The courts, the newspapers, the civil service and the country parks were the booty of a modern unfought war.

This was Scott's third year in Hong Kong. He was due for a transfer within the next few months. Back to CIA headquarters at Langley for a stretch. After that he had been promised a front-line field post. He had earned a reputation as a talented operator in Hong Kong. At thirty-three, he had collected adequate samples of carpets and silk to give style to his less colourful life back in the States. He had found a girlfriend, too, whom he would probably have to leave behind. Yet, in times of uncertainty he had thought of asking Ling Chen to marry him and wondered mischievously how she would be received by his family. She had met his father, but here in Hong Kong, on neutral soil. Andrew Carter was charmed by Ling's description of her childhood in Communist China and, when they danced until the early hours, he remarked to Scott his surprise at her being so cosmopolitan and well-informed.

That was when Scott told him she was a Yale graduate. 'So, she's really one of us,' his father replied.

'Not in bed,' thought Scott.

The internal phone rang, jolting him out of his daydream. 'Get your butt up here.' The caller was Warren Hollingworth. Officially he was head of station in Hong Kong. But Scott had learned much about institutions and bureaucracies while with the CIA. Hollingworth, a crusty anti-intellectual, wielded a thuggish authority as the intelligence chief for the Asia-Pacific. Scott had watched Hollingworth move satellites and re-route warships, only to notify Washington afterwards.

'You think I'm some dinky little spy runner on the ass end of China,' he said when Scott had dared to show surprise at the cavalier manner in which Hollingworth handled Langley. 'It's who you know back home and who will cover your ass. That's power. Remember that, Scott.'

At fifty-eight, he was one of the few Vietnam veterans left in the agency. He wore his hair closely cropped as a badge of his service in the Marine Corps and enjoyed the intimidation it wrought among colleagues.

Scott took an upright chair. Hollingworth dropped himself into a black leather sofa: 'Tonight, you have to meet a Korean agent. A room has been booked on the executive floor of the Emperor Hotel. Just ask for the key at reception. You're already checked in, under your own name. Use your civilian passport. Those name cards we had done for you . . .'

'Vivatone Electronics.'

'That's right. So you're a visiting foreign businessman. The Korean flies in from Pyongyang at 20.30. The meeting is for 22.30. Be there in good time, in case he's early. His name is Kim Chol. He's a good man. I'll be downstairs in the ballroom at an American Chamber of Commerce dinner with the bloody Chinese army.'

Ling complained when Scott called to break the evening's arrangement. She would have dinner at a friend's house, she said. She gave him the number and he would call her to meet up afterwards. Hollingworth might disrupt his evening, but he would not intrude on his sex life.

Scott locked the computer and left the Consulate at nine thirty. He flashed his ID clearance to the Marine guard who let him through the two security doors into the balmy night on Cotton Tree Drive. It was one of the few roads in Central Hong Kong which had kept its name. Others like Des Voeux Road, Queen's Road, Pottinger Street, MacDonnell Road which once paid tribute to the officials of colonialism had been stripped of their title.

New signs had quickly gone up for the warriors of modern Chinese history, Chou En-lai, Zhu Rong-ji, Jiang Zemin, Qian Qi-chen. A whole sweep of reclaimed land, flyovers, electric rails and the international airport was devoted to Deng Xiao-ping. Mao Tse-tung was given the barracks and a compound of luxury apartments on the Peak where the colonial masters used to live. Smaller roads had been left unnamed because of squabbles among officials. Scott's apartment was on an unnamed road, but it was close to the city centre and, popular with joggers, it had become known in Chinese as 'city running track under trees'.

Scott took the lift to the executive floor at the top of the hotel. The night club and French restaurant had become tatty: they served too many Chinese officials who didn't pay their bills. The People's Liberation Army owned the hotel. The management company had cleverly maintained some exclusivity on the Executive Floor. It divided at the lift. To the right were rooms reserved for the Chinese officials. The wing was little more than a brothel, the costs written off as a bad debt. Then, through fire doors to the left, were rooms for the few international travellers who had stayed loyal. The inheritors of the city used everything as their right. They rarely paid, believing perhaps that something magical hovered among the skyscrapers to replenish the dowry while it dwindled.

Scott memorised the name badge of the security officer. It simply said David. He was a short, muscular Nepalese man, a former British army Ghorka, who had become a security guard. The big companies who hired them hoped that their first loyalty would be to their employers, not to the Communist Party.

Scott paced the room, sitting on the bed, on the chair, opening the curtains again to digest the glittering, but now too familiar skyline. He had to get this meeting right. To say the right things. You're only as good as your last operation and he was back at Langley soon enough for this to be the finale. He assumed Hollingworth had the room wired.

He watched television pictures flash on from the conference and poured himself a Coke from the mini-bar. He must be careful with the eavesdroppers at the consulate who would be monitoring the meeting. They would record everything. No flippancy. Just do it quickly. Don't speak if it's not necessary. Don't offer a drink. Don't befriend him.

Scott walked around the room, with a restlessness. He tried to calm himself by thinking of peeling off Ling's clothes so that she was standing naked in front of him.

The first time they had made love, Ling sat cross-legged on his silk Kashmir carpet. On either side were peanut trees in pots of pastel pink, hand-painted with geese in full flight. She had let Scott undress her. They should have been high enough up for there to be no need for curtains, and the window stretched from the carpet to the ceiling, giving them a stunning view of Hong Kong.

They watched sheets of rain blow across the tops of the buildings. He draped an Italian scarf around her shoulders. Her black hair fell on top of it, covering parts of her breasts. Ling stared straight at him. He knelt in front of her. She hadn't let him take any clothes off.

She leant forward and kissed him. 'You're thirty-three. Did you know you had to have ten women at once?'

Ling excited Scott by preaching to him the Taoist way of sex. She spoke softly in oriental-accented English, her pronunciation precise. 'The Yellow Emperor controlled twelve hundred women and ascended as an immortal. Ordinary people shorten their lives by having one woman.'

She smiled at him and pushed her hands through his hair. Ling elevated sex to an art. Scott followed willingly, his keen mind eager to absorb more. He read up on the Taoist Way, memorising long passages to recite to her next time.

Tantalisingly, she led him around her body, taking his hands and placing them, moving a fingertip and brushing it somewhere intimate. When, together, they had explored her face and her chest, she stood up. The scarf fell off her shoulders and she stepped back so Scott could see her completely. Ling showed Scott subtlety, with a finesse he had never found in America. Mockingly, she described how the ninth-century Taoist men wanted their women to appear and behave. Her voice is settled and her silken hair is black. She has delicate skin, slender limbs and is neither tall or short, large or small. The slit between her thighs is high. Her emission fluid is abundant.

Scott had planned each meticulous, tormenting move for the night as if it was her first seduction. She had promoted their relationship to an intense sexual level. It was the most important aspect. Deliberate, perhaps, because he was leaving. Her taunts about infidelity were an antidote to the loneliness which would follow.

Scott was her first Caucasian. It was happiness mingled with terror, she had said, when he touched her. In China, the Party forbade women from having relationships with foreigners. 'What would happen?' he had asked. She shrugged. Now she was in Hong Kong, it probably didn't matter. She was working for an American joint-venture. Everybody did business together. They might as well sleep together too.

For months he hadn't told her he was a diplomat. When he did, he regretted it. She retreated a bit and went quiet. 'The Party wouldn't like it, if they knew,' she had said.

'Do they?'

'I don't know,' she had replied. 'I may not know for twenty years and then they'll put me in a room and ask me about an affair I had with a young American called Scott Carter. You'll be gone. You'll have children and an American wife. We would have forgotten each other, except for happy memories of times like this which we hadn't told to our families.'

Tree branches knocking against the bedroom window. Typhoon winds. Jazz saxophone. He would spread the Italian scarf down by the window for them to sit on. She had a key. She would let herself in. Perhaps. Ling was unpredictable. She was intelligent, wild, individual, but her culture had tamed her at least in the art of physical love.

And all that shortly after midnight if everything went to plan, Scott thought as the telephone rang and David called on the internal phone telling him that a Mr Kim Chol was there to see him.

He put the empty glass on the top of the fridge. The coldness from the drink stung his throat.

Kim was thin like a toothpick. His ill-fitting suit was crumpled from the flight. He looked straight at Scott, both confident and uneasy. He smiled. But Scott had seen the smile of a Korean face before. Even more than the Chinese it was detached from the eyes, from any other part of the body. Kim Chol sat on the edge of the bed and settled his briefcase on his knees.

'We haven't met,' he said. 'Hollingworth said you were his best agent. I agreed to deal with you.' His English had traces of a Russian accent.

32

'Mr Hollingworth sends his apologies. He may be available soon.'

'That may not be possible. We don't have much time.'

'Did he tell you anything about Heshui?'

'Just to collect whatever you gave me.'

'Tell him this data is now two days old. Heshui is close to collapse.'

Fifty-seven floors below, Warren Hollingworth picked at triangular slices of brie and stilton and half a dozen grapes on his side plate. A glass of red, and a glass of white wine in front of him. Any moment the bottle of Extra Old Hennessy cognac would arrive and he would be given no choice but to drink it in honour of his hosts. Tiny American and Chinese paper flags decorated the centre of the table.

To his left was Stephen Cranley, whose official title of deputy trade commissioner was adequate cover for his real job as head of Britain's Secret Intelligence Service operation in Hong Kong and China. Across the table was Li Tuo, the head of the Ministry of State Security in Hong Kong. He grinned and raised his glass.

Hollingworth smiled and raised his glass in response, pushing the cheese around the plate with the blade of his butter knife.

'A bit keen, Warren,' whispered Cranley.

Hollingworth covered the brandy balloon in front of him with his hand. The waiter hovered, poised, and looked to General Li for advice.

'We drink to America and China, Hollingworth,' insisted the General.

The American patted his stomach and instead raised his glass of red wine, stood up and swallowed it in one. The general roared with laughter.

'When I want brandy instead of burgundy, I'll join the fucking Communist Party,' said Hollingworth quietly, sitting down, tilting his head and smiling broadly at General Li. A waiter refilled his glass of red.

'Out of bed the wrong side today, Warren?' said Cranley.

'Got something on. Don't feel right about it.'

The chairman of the American Chamber of Commerce, cradling his own brandy balloon, moved to the podium. Hollingworth settled in for an hour of speeches with English, Mandarin and Cantonese translations. It would give Hollingworth time to think. He hoped Kim Chol was giving him the documents exclusively and not passing them to the Japanese as well. Intelligence from Japan leaked up to Beijing like it did from West to East Germany during the Cold War. Anyway, Scott was good. He was cool. His training was first class. The eavesdroppers were at the Consulate.

'. . . that trade is power,' the chairman was saying. 'We – the United States and China – have an unbreakable bond. We have buried our ideological differences. You now understand that we are quirky about electing our leaders and then humiliating them on television (Laughter). We have accepted that your historical and cultural tradition has created a different style of government. But from both systems, ladies and gentlemen, have risen great and powerful nations who together can make the world a richer and a safer place.'

Hollingworth's pager vibrated against his waist. General Li turned and looked first with surprise and then offence as the intelligence officer weaved through the tables towards the door.

A thud had alerted the American eavesdroppers, followed by the tearing of wood as the lock to the hotel room broke. It had taken ten seconds for the page to reach Hollingworth. Within forty he was out of the ballroom and by the lift. One minute ten seconds later he was on the executive floor.

Scott had his back to the door as the two attackers burst in. Kim reacted first, throwing himself to the floor, crawling and coming up again in another part of the room. Scott reached for a gun, instinctively, before remembering he hadn't carried one.

The first man into the room lunged for Kim. The Korean ducked and spun round striking the man with a body kick and drawing a knife. He held his attacker by the collar, pulling his neck towards the blade. But the attacker grabbed Kim's hand, twisting the blade round and breaking Kim's wrist. It was over in seconds. Kim was on the ground, his head stomped by the attacker's foot.

Scott evaded first contact with his assailant by sidestepping the blow. But the room was too small and the man ducked under his retaliatory blow and came up behind him. He smashed his fist into Scott's windpipe, then grabbed his neck and pulled him to the ground. He pressed both knuckles into Scott's carotid arteries, blocking the blood flow to the head. The door was open. The television was on, its volume low. Scott lost consciousness, then the killer snapped his neck and Scott was dead.

He went through Scott's pockets. Scott had been thorough. No diplomatic identity. Only Vivatone name cards in his wallet. His

34

credit cards were personal. The assassin glanced at the picture of Ling, laughing to himself and put everything back. He lifted Scott's limp body onto his shoulders. The second attacker pulled Kim to his feet and held a silenced Browning 9mm handgun to his neck. He pushed the envelope Kim was to have given Scott into his jacket pocket, then ordered the Korean to go ahead of them across the corridor to the fire exit and up to the roof.

Hollingworth ran out of the lift and turned right. He saw the broken door before identifying the room number, and inside the turned-over armchair, the crumpled bed and the traces of the fight. The phone rang. It was the eavesdroppers. 'They've both gone,' said Hollingworth. 'Keep it within the station.'

As he spoke, Scott Carter's body fell from the hotel roof, landing just to the side of the driveway, far away enough to hide the horrific mess, close enough to cause a consternation and bring the death into the public domain. The eavesdroppers picked it up immediately. 'We have a body off the roof,' said the accurate and unemotional voice on the other end of the phone.

'Shit,' responded Hollingworth.

'Caucasian.'

'One body?' Hollingworth asked.

'Affirmative. One body, sir.'

Chapter Five

Like most nights, Mike McKillop dreamed of Sally. Or the kids. The family was always there. Sometimes real memories blurred between wake and sleep, like when Charlotte asked him if he really had been a policeman for the British Empire and Matthew had stood on a chair using his chopsticks as a pistol: 'Bang, bang, bang. All you Chinese dead. That's what you did, didn't you, Daddy?'

'It wasn't quite like that,' Mike had responded weakly. But it had been happening so often lately that he had lost his energy to fight it. Sally called the maid: 'Felly, can you get them ready for bed?' And when they had gone, Mike asked Sally: 'Why don't you tell them the truth?' But she just said: 'They're being taught the truth,' and she kept clearing the dinner plates without looking at him.

He would often dream of himself sleeping while Sally was making love to other men and tonight, after Clem and Beijing, she was in bed with Li Tuo, smoking with him and sharing a glass of brandy, and laughing at Mike trying to get in to stop them. Mike rattled the bedroom door. Charlotte and Matthew were there, door open, allowing him to watch, but with Heckler and Koch MP5K sub machine guns. The children's eyes were unyielding as Mike pleaded with them to recognise him as their father and let him in. Charlotte shook her head. Mike was on his knees. Then Charlotte's eyes hardened, like they do in a killer who is about to shoot. Mike saw the finger tighten over the trigger and a sickly smile appear on his daughter's face.

The explosion of machine gun bullets in his dream became a loud and piercing ringing sound in the real world. The hands of his clock shone through the darkness at five minutes before midnight. He woke in the familiar surroundings of his bedroom. Their bedroom. The sprawling colonial apartment on the Peak which had always come with the job. Some of Sally's clothes were still in the wardrobe. Things she hadn't needed stayed on the dressing table. Mike had thrown his own suitcase on the stool there, where his smell of grubbiness mixed with the scents and creams she had left behind. He saw a trail of clothes he had discarded along the floor from the sitting room. Billie Holiday was playing. He had put the CD on when he got back, trying to discipline his racing thoughts with her songs. He liked her sadness. Long ago Mike had played jazz piano. He used to serenade Sally and take over pianos at Asian seaside resorts, singing to the bar, soft, rueful and unassuming. And Sally loved it. He knew she was watching. She would dress up in a light tropical dress which fluttered around her in the breezes from the beach, confident and proud that she and Mike together had laid bare myths about how cross-cultural marriages couldn't work.

Instinctively, he reached for the telephone. Nothing. He put down the receiver and picked it up again. Dial tone. Quietness. An expectation, however brief, that it might be Sally. But no. Out of habit, every so often, he lifted the telephone receiver to check that the line was not out of order. It had become a routine symbol of his despair.

But this time it was the doorbell. Mike stumbled across the living room. Through the spyhole he saw his driver, smoking, outside. He opened the door. The man had red eyes. He had been woken, too.

A foreigner had been found dead, he said.

Mike arrived at the hotel fifteen minutes later, stepping out of the lift and straight into the room where Scott Carter had died. McKillop had been called because a foreigner was involved. He would never control the case. He knew that. Fine. He was used to it. He looked around the hotel room. All chances of a fingerprint, any forensic clue had vanished. There were half a dozen people in the room, hotel staff and Chinese soldiers. It was filled with smoke. The mini-bar was empty. He was hardly noticed. The twenty-four-hour golf channel on the television attracted more attention. It didn't anger him any more. He was part of the system.

McKillop walked up to the roof. People stood at the edge, looking down across the harbour. At least the view hadn't changed. It remained the most spectacular city in the world. The Party couldn't rid Hong Kong of its skyline. Nor would it want to. The harbour lights gave it the façade under which it could exercise its power.

A voice bounced across the humid August wind: 'Mike. Great. Which bar did they drag you out of?'

'I was at home,' McKillop replied bluntly.

Superintendent Tommy Lai clapped his shoulder. The brother of Jimmy Lai, murdered on a jungle river bank, shook his hand.

'Who was he?' asked McKillop.

'An American. Booked into the room. Businessman. Dead. What you been doing with your life?'

'Making your country look sweet, Tommy boy. Representing our esteemed police force at the Beijing corruption conference. And you're playing golf with the Commissioner, I hear.'

'Working for the greater glory of China.'

McKillop laughed. Tommy had been the fourth man with Clem and Jimmy. Jimmy was the chameleon who slipped undercover. Tommy was the linguist, the ham radio enthusiast who was at police headquarters, listening to conversations from Burma on the night his younger brother died.

Six months after Jimmy Lai was murdered, Mike tracked a trawler through the Gulf of Thailand to the South China Sea until it was in international waters fifty miles off the coast of Hong Kong. A rusted old Chinese tramp steamer waited at the rendezvous. This was Li Tuo's first exported cargo as the drug lord of Yunnan. And when the two vessels met up, Tommy and Mike were waiting. They blew the boats out of the water with high explosive cannon from their police launch. After that, Jimmy's murder didn't seem so bad.

They went out drinking. A celebration of the life of Jimmy Lai. Without him, the partnership with Tommy strengthened. They trained together with the Special Duties Unit. They learned to fly helicopters together. They busted more drug gangs. They got drunk, always toasting absent, murdered friends. Then in early 1999, Tommy Lai found his classified intelligence reports were stamped: 'Not for eyes of L/I Officers.' L/I or Linguistic Inability, meaning that Mike was being edged out of the loop. It was a euphemism for not being trusted by the new regime.

'Your Cantonese is excellent,' Lai had urged. 'A year and you could pass the exam.' The requirements were to speak Mandarin and Cantonese and write and read seven hundred Chinese characters. Some British civil servants had sat the test, and all had failed. Mike had not bothered. Although he was fluent in both, language wasn't the issue.

The wind strengthened and came up from the harbour, cooling the gathering on the roof: 'So we got ourselves a body?' answered McKillop.

'Mike, this job was professional,' said Tommy Lai. 'Two big multinationals fighting it out. Something like that. Let them do it. We'll do the post-mortem. In the morning, there'll be a statement. Suicide. End of story. Murder is bad for business.'

McKillop's next stop was the police morgue and as he swung open the doors he was relieved to see Joss McEwan in a blood-stained white coat, deep in professional concentration over Scott Carter's body. McEwan was also an L/I. Like McKillop, his name would be on the reports which would be forwarded to the American Consulate and quoted to any congressman or journalist who might show an unwelcome interest in the case.

McEwan looked up: 'Ah, Mike. You've been defossilised as well?'

McEwan was twelve years older than McKillop and had worn the pressures of the Party better. His avuncular features had been reddened by adequate colonial drinking over the past thirty years. McEwan brightened up the steel chill in the basement.

'I've been ordered to investigate, Joss,' said McKillop drily.

'Investigate. Strange word for this town,' retorted McEwan.

The corpse was laid fresh in death on top of the bench, uncovered, and apart from the legs which were horribly twisted.

'He hit the building at least once on the way down,' said the older man. 'Always the poor legs. Landed feet first, just on that piece of grass where it dips down across from the stretch limousines. You know the place?'

McKillop nodded.

'So we have the bruises and breakages consistent with a fall from a great height.' The doctor pointed to the legs and worked his hand joint by joint up the body. 'Lower half shattered, of course. Pelvis broken. Spine an unmitigated disaster. Right shoulderbone gone. Left survived, God knows how. But skull in remarkably good shape. Face contorted but fine.'

'Identification . . .'

'Let me finish, young man. I haven't discussed with you cause of death yet.'

'Don't we know?'

'We should if we still worked as professional policemen. This is just a preliminary poke around. On the surface we have a man pushed or fallen from a skyscraper. But look here.' He beckoned McKillop to come closer to the corpse. 'Look at the neck, the bruise on the right, the swelling and the larger bruise on the left. These are not consistent with falling from a high building.'

The pathologist stepped back, wiping his hands on the damp cloth, clearly enjoying a revival of professional satisfaction: 'Those marks are consistent with murder, my friend. Our corpse here was probably dead before he was dropped from the roof.'

McKillop looked at bruises, small and easy to overlook: 'What will you put in your report?' He asked.

'The truth, of course.' McEwan threw the towel into a sink. 'You free for lunch tomorrow? We could get in nine holes.'

'They'll block it.'

'Course they'll bloody well block it. But what comes out of my office will be accurate.'

'But the final official cause of death will have your name on it.'

'We'll keep our little mouths shut, won't we Mike. We've got no choice, lad.' McEwan pushed an American telephone calling card into McKillop's hand. 'Found this before they stripped him,' he said. 'His name's Scott Carter.'

As Mike looked at it, McEwan said: 'And this. It's a phone number and a Chinese girl's name.' The pathologist handed Mike a folded piece of paper, then walked over to the basin, turned the taps on full, squeezed the antiseptic liquid soap out of its dispenser and scrubbed his hands. 'Will you call it?' he asked, his back to Mike.

'I don't know,' replied Mike. 'I'll tell you at lunch.'

He dialled the number shortly before ten the next morning. An American girl answered. 'Is Ling there please?' He didn't know her last name.

'Ling Chen, you mean?'

'Yes,' ventured McKillop.

'No. She was here for supper last night. But she doesn't live here. And she left to see Scott – oh let me see – well before midnight.'

McKillop enjoyed the innocence in her voice: 'I was asked to call her. Someone must have got the numbers mixed up. Do you know where I can get hold of her?'

'She's just moved apartments last month and I guess she hasn't given me the number yet. You could try her at Scott's place . . .'

'Have you got the number?' McKillop gently intervened.

'Sure.' He heard the rustling of telephone pad and within seconds the girl reeled it off. 'And if that doesn't work, I guess you can try her at the office or Scott at the Consulate tomorrow.'

'Yes, of course.' McKillop suppressed his surprise. 'Thank you.'

He called the Consulate: 'Scott Carter, please.'

'One moment, sir.' Telephone music and the clicking of internal exchanges. Another voice: 'Political section.'

'Scott Carter, please.'

'He's not in today, sir. Can I take a message?'

'When's he due in?'

'Can't give you an answer on that, sir. If you leave your name and telephone number, I'll get him to call you right back when he's next here.'

Suddenly his victim had acquired a lifestyle. He had a girl-friend. He had a sex life. He had an apartment. She was round there a lot.

Scott Carter was an American diplomat. Murdered. But not a murmur from anyone. Nothing on the satellite channel news. Did he expect it? Was there anything about Win Kyi's death? About a shooting on the Third Ring Road last night? An Audi with a smashed tail light? Back in his office, he scrolled down the CNN and BBC wire services. The screen flickered in the corner of his cavernous office, and there it was.

Death of American businessman.

Mike opened up the file, but there was no Scott Carter, only a correction for a previous entry. The businessman who succumbed to a heart attack on an Air India flight from Singapore to Bombay was in fact Christopher Watson, it said. The aircraft diverted to Yangon in Myanmar in an attempt to save him.

Mike scrolled back a few hours to the first story.

The assassin was looking for Clem, Win Kyi had told him. *But he didn't board. The man who died was Christopher C. Watson. An innocent. A cock-up.*

And they hadn't written Christopher Watson the first time. The name appeared as Clem Watkins and McKillop felt a chill as he read it about an organisation which had authorised the publication of Clem's death announcement before he was even dead.

The words spun around as he took them in. His hand shook over the computer mouse.

Mike took the lift down from the tenth floor of Police Headquarters and walked across the courtyard with its array of luxury Mercedes and BMWs from Germany, Lexus from Japan, Proton limousines from Malaysia and Hyundai saloons from Korea. McKillop carried on along Wu Yi Road, heading for the hotel and exhibition complex owned by the Chinese Ministry of Foreign Trade and Economic Cooperation (MOFTEC). He made some attempt to check whether he was being followed. But if they wanted to put a tail on him they could call on every street vendor, garage mechanic and strip-club bouncer.

The policeman stepped into the hotel lobby. He knew there was a telephone outside the door of the Champagne Bar. But when he got there, it was out of order. Hong Kong was getting as bad as the Britain he remembered. He carried on to the left, through the entrance of Romanesque statues towards the Grand Ballroom. He picked up the telephone. As a waiter headed towards him, McKillop continued dialling and flashed his police card. The man cowered away. The telephone in Scott Carter's apartment rang four times before the answer machine intervened. 'Hi. I can't come to the phone right now. But don't ring off. Leave a voice message after the tone or send a fax.'

He immediately dialled again, this time to Police Headquarters. He spoke sharply in faultless Cantonese: 'I need an address on a telephone number.' He reeled off Tommy Lai's five-digit security code. There was a delay. He heard the tapping of computer keys. He was banking that the code hadn't been changed. His own hadn't, but it had become useless. As soon as he used it, the request would be flashed up in the security screens. McKillop and Tommy had exchanged codes ten years ago when the British policeman was trusted and the Chinese were under suspicion because the force was becoming infiltrated by mainland agents. Now, their roles had been reversed.

'The address you requested is apartment block 5E, but the street has not yet been allocated a name.'

McKillop swore under his breath: 'Officer comrade this a murder inquiry. Please identify the Colonial street name.'

'Your Party referee?'

'Comrade Li Tuo,' said McKillop. He hoped that the inefficiency of Chinese bureaucracy would have left the linked names of Tommy Lai and Li Tuo at the bottom of the long-forgotten data bank.

'Yes, comrade. The pre-reunification title was Bowen Road.'

A large hand clasped his shoulder as he moved away from the telephone stall. McKillop turned and found himself face to face with Tom Elton, the tall, blond, tanned, self-assured public relations consultant for the Hong Kong government. Elton had arrived eighteen months ago from New York charged with the job of instilling international confidence into Hong Kong, and he had quickly become the cosmopolitan media face of this Chinese city. At thirty-nine, he was the Asia-Pacific vice-president for a large American public relations firm. He wore impeccably styled suits, hand-tailored from the Mandarin Hotel's shopping arcade. He spoke in twelve-second soundbites and sold Hong Kong and its way of life as the society of the future.

The first time Mike came across Elton had been when two American congressmen were arrested during a pro-democracy demonstration outside the Legislative Council building. Elton took over the whole case, pushing on network news the argument for trade-led authoritarian government. He guided Mike through the court hearing, the conviction and the deportation, all within a twenty-four hour period. Barely a week went by when Elton was not watching over a case Mike was involved in. Sometimes he despised Elton even more than the Chinese government. But sometimes he wondered if Elton, too, had a secret for being here and doing a job for which few decent men would have the stomach.

Elton smiled at him, his right hand outstretched, while a jazz piano medley delivered a Communist Party song around the hotel lobby.

'Mike, how are you? How you been?' His voice carried clearly above the drones of conversations around them.

'Fine, Tom.'

'I didn't know you frequented such salubrious places.'

'Had to catch up with someone,' McKillop lied. He edged further out, away from the telephone. Elton let go of his shoulder. 'How was China?'

'It was OK. Kang made an interesting speech.'

'So I saw. So I saw.' Elton was leading him away, further up towards the ballroom where there were fewer people. 'Hoped to see you this morning. Couldn't find you in the office.'

'I was up all night with the Carter death,' interrupted Mike.

'That's it. That's our new problem. Businessman falling from the roof of a hotel. So difficult for everyone. We've decided on suicide. Cleanest way to wrap it up.' Elton leant forward and lowered his voice. 'If we start a police investigation, it will get very messy. The Comrades will get involved. The Gestapo. There could be questions on the Hill. Journalists nosing around. So just to say, Mike, make your report about what you saw.

'Keep it straight. If you get any calls, pass them on to me. That's what I'm paid for.' Elton smiled.

'Has anybody suggested it was anything but suicide?' asked McKillop.

'You called the American Consulate.' Elton's hand was on his elbow now, gripping it hard. 'Jesus, Mike, you know nothing is secret in this town. You shouldn't have done that. That's beginning an investigation. Let's keep this easy. Better for everyone.'

McKillop felt the grip loosen and Elton sprawled his hand across Mike's back. 'Great tip for the two thirty at Shanghai. Keep it quiet. Number four. Red Lantern. Rank outsider. Keep it quiet.' With that, Elton released McKillop. He hailed a figure on the other side of the room and was gone.

Chapter Six

Ling Chen decided not to go round to Scott's apartment after he didn't call her at the supper party. Instead, she went home. She lived on Lantau, the biggest island of the Special Administrative Region, just one hour's ferry ride from Hong Kong. It was quiet and she and Scott used it for weekend breaks.

The northern side of the island was developed with the Deng Xiao-ping airport. The south remained unspoiled. There were clusters of villages along the coast and a small settlement at the ferry terminal at Silvermine Bay, overlooked by two misty peaks and a fertile valley of rice fields and pig farms.

Ling caught the last ferry and walked in the clear, warm moonlight back home. She enjoyed Hong Kong and on nights like this she thought how lucky she had been to escape from the drudgery of Beijing to a well-paid job here. Sometimes, she couldn't even believe that she had once been a senior member of the Communist Youth League who, while at university in the States, had loyally reported back intelligence which she thought her government might find useful.

But that was more than six years ago and China had moved on. No one from the Party even bothered to contact her any more. It was ten years since she had been picked for military training and sent to an elite women's unit near Tianjin. After three years she had left for university in Beijing and a year later won a scholarship to Yale, taking with her her military certificates in handling small-arms and explosives, her parachute wings and a martial arts black belt for unarmed combat. She always laughed to herself when she wondered if her tutors had ever known who she really was.

These were elements of her life which she rarely talked about in Hong Kong and had never mentioned to Scott when he had tried to probe into her past. They had argued a lot about communism and democracy. He hated the Party and she knew she could never change him. She didn't bother to explain that the Party and China were as one, because without Mao and communism, China would never have been liberated from foreign powers. The slavery would have continued.

Scott had tried to convince her. If she ever had a problem which crossed the Party, no one in China could help you, he said. No one goes against the Party.

She had laughed, a nervous laugh. She didn't believe him. It started as a joke. Then she felt hurt because he had no right to be so arrogant with her.

'If it's the truth, I do have a right,' he had said.

'No, you're racist,' she shouted at him. 'You're frightened of us. We're too smart for you. We have five thousand years of civilisation. That's why you insult us. You're jealous.'

Then Scott calmed her down and got her to tell him about her father. She hadn't been allowed to see her father before he died. His mother suddenly said he was ill in hospital. Then six weeks later she said he was dead and he had already been cremated. It wasn't until later, when she went to the States and told the story, that she realised how wrong it was for a daughter not to be allowed to her father's funeral. Not to say goodbye.

'Was he a loyal communist, like you?' he nudged gently.

She told him how one day when she was fourteen, her father had found her reading foreign newspapers in his study. He touched her on the shoulder and she jumped. 'Is this story true? About Premier Li?' Ling blurted out. 'It says the Chinese people don't like him.'

'Ah, yes.' He looked at her daughter. 'It's true in the way they see it.'

'But isn't there only one truth,' Ling had persisted.

Her father removed his spectacles and placed them on Ling, hooking the ends around her ears. 'Here,' he said, 'look at that.

Suddenly, her vision was distorted. The black and white of the newspaper print were blurred together. The room was smaller. The shelves, crammed with files, were squashed closer to each other. Ling smiled and lifted the glasses so she could see clearly again. Then she dropped them down. The room disfigured again.

'Everyone sees things in different ways,' said her father. 'It's like having different types of glasses.'

'So who's right?' persisted Ling.

'Depends how you see it, doesn't it,' said her father, smiling.

Scott always talked about cultural differences. That day he had chuckled and leant over and kissed the edge of her shoulder. The sun streamed through the trees. It was hot and they threw off the bed covers. As Scott talked, Ling saw their bodies, young, different hues of flesh against the white sheets, the physiognomy of races, her anger against his confidence, her pride against his logic. That was the day he exposed her naïveté, her willingness to believe everything the Party told her.

The narrow concrete path to her apartment was well lit by the moon and Ling, lost in memories, jumped when she woke a dog chained to a wall. The barking set off a chorus of dogs through the valley, disturbing villagers who turned on lights and watched her through curtains.

She climbed the stairs to her flat as quietly as she could and when she got in she tried calling Scott, but just got the answer machine.

Ling woke early and showered. The typhoon warning had been raised, so she was keen to get an early ferry back in case the services were suspended because of the weather. By the time she got to her office on Hong Kong Island, the rain was heavy and unrelenting. She telephoned the American Consulate and was given the same answer as McKillop: Scott Carter wouldn't be in today.

Ling told her secretary she was going to a previously unscheduled meeting and hailed a cab. She found herself in the back of a taxi, leaning forward pleading with the driver to take her to 'the city running track under the trees'. She spoke to him in Mandarin. Her Cantonese was shaky, but he was a young man and would have learned enough of the official language to understand her. She had asked first for Bowen Road and received no response. Neither did he acknowledge the running track, but with directions from Ling they soon arrived, amid a downpour and gusts of typhoon wind. As she got out branches of the trees swirled around her.

Ling checked Scott's mail box. Just the *International Herald Tribune* from the day before. With the key Scott had given her, she let herself in through the outer grille door. Unlike many of his colleagues, Scott had opted to live in one of the older buildings. More character, he said. Uncharacteristically for an American diplomat, his block was unguarded. She walked down two flights of stairs to the lower basement. There was no natural light on the stairwell. Only naked bulbs and the whir of a ventilating fan, caked in grime. She pressed the doorbell to the apartment with the apprehension that he might have been in there with another woman. There

47

was no answer. With the typhoon signal up, the maid would not have come.

The living room was tidy, but cluttered. Scott's oriental fabrics were flung over State Department furniture. Carpets from India and Iran scattered on the polished parquet floor. Plants and cushions nestled in with each other by the window. The Italian scarf was folded up on the corner of his Kashmiri rug, together with a half-played game of computer chess and a book of short stories by Franz Kafka. The radio was on. Scott believed it was an adequate burglar deterrent. The news was ending with a wrap-up of the headlines. Local items about cleaning up the beaches; the successful opening of the anti-corruption conference; an international item about the hegemonous intentions of Japan.

She turned the radio off and called out: 'Scott? Scott, are you in?' She went into the bedroom. The bed hadn't been slept in. She moved quickly through the apartment she knew so well, in and out of every room, within seconds, looking for a note, a scrap of paper stuck with a plastic strawberry magnet to the fridge, perhaps. But it was instructions for the maid. There was washing in the machine. It was still on. The red light flashing that the cycle was over. Scott would have switched it off. The lightbulb in the second bathroom was still broken after yesterday, the sort of thing Scott would have fixed. She checked the answer machine. A lot of clicks. A lot of irritating tones and bleeps. Then a message from Scott: 'Hi Ling, if you get in before me, I should be finished by twelve. Make the music low and the sheets cool.'

Ling heard steps on the unlit stairwell and the scraping of metal on metal as the security door to the lower basement level was moved backwards. She froze, her hand on the door-handle. She was about to leave, but she looked through the eyehole and saw a tall, good-looking Chinese man with a furled, dripping umbrella. He paused at the bottom of the stairs, opened a briefcase and pulled out a pistol.

Without rushing, he screwed on a silencer. Then he rang the bell. In complete silence, Ling tiptoed away from the door. She wished she hadn't turned off the radio. Unlike most apartment blocks, Scott had no back entrance. It backed onto the side of a mountain. The front had a panoramic view across the cityscape to the harbour. The back went into a tiny patio of flagged red Italian tiles, a jungle of plants and two outhouses, which Scott used for playing late-night poker and storing carpets and books he picked up on his travels. There was a flat roof on top and because of the threat of intrusion from the road, Scott had put up coils of barbed wire on the wall surrounding it.

Ling had nowhere to go except backwards. She was in the maid's area with an ironing board and piles of Scott's dirty sheets and unpolished shoes. Next to the washing machine was a dying plant. Scott kept the key to the patio door in its pot, mixed up with the brittle, fallen leaves. Ling rummaged through, picking up clogged soil and the key. She slid it into the lock of the old door. At the same time, she heard the lock clicking back and forth on the front door. Ling was out in the patio.

The gunman let himself into the flat. He quickly went to each of the unfamiliar rooms. Ling turned the key to lock the patio door from the outside. The man with the gun moved slowly. He turned over pieces of paper. He examined drawers in Scott's study, slipping computer disks into his briefcase. He found an address book and took that. He played the answer machine. Ling heard Scott's cheerful voice. The cool sheets.

Rain dripped onto the tiles, its noise helping her. She imagined he was moving around as he listened. She was in Scott's outhouse poker room. She smelt the damp and locked the door behind her. One of its windows looked into the bedroom. Another, the one she could escape through, was inches from the steep slope. As she opened it, the assassin tested the handle of the patio door and found it locked. He turned and kicked the door, connecting with his heel, in a twisting movement which broke the lock and shattered the glass, leaving the door itself swinging listlessly on its hinges.

Silently, Ling squeezed through the window. There was no evidence that the gunman knew she was there. She heard footsteps across the rainwashed tiles. She hoisted herself up. Only someone as waif-like as she could have squeezed between the bars. Then she was out, dropping herself onto the leaves and debris cluttered on the hillside, the rain hiding her sound.

She slid away from the window and pressed herself hard against the wall. Her wet blouse clung to her. Tropical woodland was all around her. Spiderwebs on her skin. Mosquitoes circling her face.

There was a crack of wood splintering. This time the inadequate plywood door of the outhouse disintegrated. But the gunman spent less than a second in the room. It was empty. That was enough.

She watched him go back inside and stop. If he turned she could see him. He was unscrewing his silencer. She looked up. He looked up and as their eyes met she did everything to stifle a scream. She stayed absolutely still. For a full five seconds his eyes were on her and all the time he kept unscrewing his silencer, then putting it in the briefcase. He snapped it shut, turned round and left the room. Ling scrambled round away from all windows. She was in a gully of sloping rock, sliding on moist leaves. Just above her was Bowen Road. If she could get there before him then she could run. It didn't matter where. She heaved herself along. She listened. There was only the rain. Loud and unsubtle on the trees around her.

Ling stumbled onto the road and ran through the rain. She was screaming. But no sound came out. She looked back just once. She saw him again, but he made no attempt to follow her. She kept going down the main road, right out in the open, like a jogger, her hair all over the place, matted together and dripping. Only when she reached the crowded streets of Central did she stop. She walked round and round the pedestrian concourse to let her heart and her thoughts slow down.

It was his confidence which terrified her. Why didn't he shoot? Why didn't he care that she had seen him?

Joss McEwan didn't show up for lunch and that evening he wasn't at home, so McKillop called in at the mortuary. The room was empty apart from the night watchman, Kwai, who for more than twenty years had kept vigil on Hong Kong's murder victims. Mike went over to Kwai's desk and ran his finger down the few names in the log book: 'Has Superintendent McEwan been in tonight?' he asked.

'I heard he gone, sir.'

'When?'

'Don't know, sir. Only heard tonight from Mr Elton.'

'I thought he was involved with the Gweilo's body.'

Kwai shuffled to his feet. 'The Gweilo? He's been taken.'

'Any more in?' Mike pointed to another entry about a shooting.

'He came in, but gone already.'

'Where to?'

Kwai spat on the floor, then picked up the book. It was an antiquated system of keeping a record, a special dispensation to the watchman who had been unable to master a computer keyboard. During British rule, Kwai had been a low-level agent, and with thousands of others he had formed the backbone of China's intelligence-gathering operation. There were two entries for the day. At 10.38, Scott Carter's body had been claimed by a Warren Hollingworth from the American Consulate.

At 18.47, the body of an unidentified Asian male, shot through the heart, had been removed. It had only been in the morgue for twenty minutes. There was no signature next to the claimant. There was no need. The column bore the stamp of the Nim Kai, the secret police of the Party.

The Nim Ching Kung Chu was colloquially known as the Nim Kai or austerity shop. It had its own building, formerly the Murray Building, later renamed Zhou Nan House, after the great spymaster and diplomat who battled Britain in the last days of colonial rule. Nim Kai had its own surveillance equipment and prison cells. In English it was still known as the Independent Commission Against Corruption, an organisation set up by the British in the 1970s to wipe out one of Hong Kong's more destructive habits. It was successful because its powers were enormous. It worked alone and could arrest and imprison without charge. When China took over, the commissioner and his senior men were gradually retired, Party officials were installed in their place and the Nim Kai was taken under the wing of the Ministry of State Security. The Chinese kept the nickname Nim Kai. Europeans referred to it as the Gestapo, the man in charge was Li Tuo, the man who saw Ling in Scott Carter's apartment worked for him. When he reported that he had seen a woman there, his commanding officer automatically referred the matter up to the office of Li Tuo.

'Did she see you?' he was asked.

'Yes, comrade.'

'Why did you not take action?'

'That was not my orders.'

'Her name is Chen Ling,' said the commanding officer. 'If she saw you, she will know that Carter's death was not as we are reporting it. I suggest you make yourself useful, comrade, and do something about it.'

McKillop was at his desk reading through the report on Scott Carter's death when the telephone rang at the reception outside. He planned to get the report out of the way by lunchtime. He needed to get out into the fresh air, far away from the office. If the weather cleared, he could get in nine holes in the afternoon. Nim Kai had rewritten Joss McEwan's pathologist report, deleting the bruises on the carotid artery. Cause of death was from a broken neck, consistent with a fall from a high building. The police found there were no suspicious circumstances. Mike signed the document. The telephone was still ringing. Outside, there was not a secretary in sight, abandoning their desks precisely at 12.30 p.m. for lunch. The foreign affairs section of the Hong Kong Police headquarters was empty apart from McKillop.

'McKillop. Foreign,' he said impatiently, picking up the phone.

'I have a query to make about a missing person.' The voice was Chinese, but the English excellent with a slight American accent. It was hesitant, but at the same time assertive.

'A foreigner?' said McKillop.

'Yes. His name is Scott Carter. I think he might have been murdered.'

McKillop sat on the corner of the desk. He picked up a pen and notepad. 'Your name?'

'I'm Ling Chen. I'm his girlfriend.'

Tommy Lai walked into the office as McKillop took down Ling's phone number. 'The best person to talk to about this is Tom Elton. I think he's aware of this case.' He gave her Elton's number, then paused and added with hesitation: 'But if you need any more help, give me a call back.'

He put the phone down. Lai stood over his desk. 'What rules you breaking now, Mike?' he said in a tone which could either be joking or serious. McKillop didn't answer. Lai indicated that they should leave so they could talk more freely. The two men went out to the police car park.

They walked slowly between the cars. 'But something the hell is going on,' said Tommy. He lit up a cigarette nervously, forgetting to offer one to his colleague. 'Look Mike, I want to tell you . . . Last night, there was a homicide, right?'

'I thought it was suicide.'

'No another one. A guy shot in the heart on a speedboat. The Marine Police had made an arrest. Smugglers. No big deal. Catch them every day. But one of them pulled out a gun and shot one of the guys with him. The next thing he started putting the pistol to himself. Our guys stopped him. Took him off the boat. The dead guy turns out to be a fucking Korean diplomat. Flew in last night from Pyongyang. That's number one complication.'

Lai drew on his cigarette. His head moved from left to right, unable to stay still or feel safe. 'So, the gang were taken to Number One Prison in Central. I arrived this morning to question them. The guy who shot the Korean is dead. The other two have gone.'

'Escaped?'

'No. Gone. They've vanished. There's no record of them ever having been in the jail.'

'How did the other one die?'

'Strangled. He killed the Korean. Someone killed him. There's a lot of violence in this one.'

Lai threw his cigarette to the ground and trod on the butt: 'Mike, I'm getting out of this. You know who took the victim's body. Nim Kai. I'm out and you better stay out.'

'I'm not in.'

'Carter. Security alarms. Don't investigate, Mike. Joss is crazier than you. I beg you, leave this one alone. Go play golf.'

Tom Elton was alerted to the bleep within a second of it activating. He was watching the seventeenth hole of the Motherland Cup on Star Golf. He activated the remote to get McKillop's reprimand running across the screen just on top of the fluttering red flag in the green. 'Supt. L/I Mckillop. Access attempt diplomatic list. Search area: Warren Hollingworth. Access denied.'

Elton watched the putt, the ball curving beautifully along the line of the green and in: 'Where's McKillop now?' He spoke loudly towards the direction on the intercom on his desk.

'Gone from his office to the car park.'

'Alone?' responded Elton.

'With Superintendent Lai.'

'Shit. Trace him and track him.'

Elton ended the conversation in time for the tee-off on the eighteenth, the same number as the months he had left of his contract. Then he planned to go back to Manhattan and the real world with enough money in the bank for a beach house in the Hamptons and a helicopter out there on the busy weekends. He was on a three-year contract with a twenty-five per cent lump sum if he finished and illegal bonuses far above his annual salary from stock market and horse racing tips. Hong Kong was a long way from Brooklyn and from the squalor amid which he had been brought up. For Elton, luxury was like a drug. Once tasted he never wanted to be far away from it. Elton had had enough poverty in his childhood and now detested it more than anything else. He had come to Hong Kong for the money and once he had made enough he would leave. No one would stay any more. You couldn't breathe. The water was thick with grime. The nuclear power station across the border kept shutting down with faults. Soon it would explode and take the skyscrapers and secret bank accounts with it.

Until then, there was money, money and money. It was a system where a man who didn't interfere could become very rich. No one was really poor and not even America could boast that.

Elton swung his feet off the coffee table and muted the television sound. Then his external telephone rang: 'There's a Chinese-American lady to speak to you, a Miss Ling Chen,' said the switchboard operator. 'About a missing person.'

'So. What's it to do with me?'

'She said Superintendent McKillop referred her.'

He flicked the television into the quadruple split screen to receive Sky Television, Cable News Network, Bloomberg and the British Broadcasting Corporation. He set the internal surveillance camera onto the car park and listened to the frightened voice at the other end of the line.

'I was told you could help me,' said Ling. 'My boyfriend Scott Carter was meant to have . . . well, he's not around. He would have called me. Do you . . .'

'How long has he been missing, Ling?'

'Since last night. He would have called. Whatever he was doing he would have called. I know him.'

'Listen, Ling. Nothing has come across my desk on this. I will run a check and get back to you. Where do you live?' Ling told him. 'Why don't you go there. I'll call you in a couple of hours.'

Elton didn't replace the receiver. He dialled another number. 'Did you get that?' he said, confident as to who would answer the phone.

'We'll take this over,' said Warren Hollingworth.

Chapter Seven

The tiny apartment with its breezy roof terrace and corner balcony was within walking distance of the ferry, nestled in the pretty, undeveloped valley at the foot of the two peaks of Lantau Island. Ling couldn't rid herself of the sense of a hostile world closing in on her. As she travelled on the ferry, she found herself staying inside with the air-conditioning and sealed windows just in case the man she had seen appeared again. She never stayed close to one person for more than a few seconds. The ferry passengers dispersed into the buses and taxis waiting at the terminal. Tom Elton would ring within the next couple of hours, he said. She could stay at home. Wait until it was all over.

Ling walked towards her apartment. Even with her dark glasses she found herself squinting against the fierce sunlight. Soon she was off the main road, walking briskly along the single-lane concrete path with vegetable fields stretching out on both sides. It was just like any other day. The villagers had seen her before. She sang to herself. There was nothing different. She sang louder to herself so that she could hear her voice. She felt better when the dogs barked. She passed the first house and the woman laying out the washing smiled and said hello. They couldn't all be murderers. A smile meant a smile. Nothing else. And suddenly she found herself walking up the stairs to her little flat. It all seemed so normal. The door was double locked as she had left it. The television was on the cultural music channel, playing black-and-white revolutionary films. It was Scott's idea, his cheap anti-burglar device. It was stifling hot inside. She went straight across and opened the French windows onto the balcony. It was all right. It was fine. She drank some orange juice from the fridge. The fan cooled her down. She stood under it, noticing her deep breathing. For a moment, she was safe.

The few moments inside her own apartment allowed her to clear her thoughts. She undressed to have a shower. She liked

55

the apartment because she could walk naked with the windows flung open and no one could see unless they were far away on the slope of the peaks with a telescope. She tilted her head back in the shower and let the cold water splash all over her face, round her neck and shoulders which had become so sticky in the heat, the water coming with such a roar that it was two or three rings before she heard the telephone and stepped out, wrapping herself in a towel to stem the drips. Warren Hollingworth introduced himself as a diplomat in the political section, Scott's superior.

'I'm afraid Scott's dead,' he said gently.

Ling cried. She knew she would. She just needed to be told. She wiped her hair down with the towel. 'He fell off the roof of the Emperor Hotel,' continued Hollingworth. 'He always asked me to contact you if anything happened to him.'

'He was murdered.'

'No. We don't know why he killed himself. Perhaps it was some trouble he was having back home . . .'

'I'm telling you he was killed.'

'We think he may have taken his own life.'

'A man was in Scott's flat. With a gun. With a silencer. He kicked down doors. Help me. Please . . .'

She breathed heavily. She was crying a lot. The last words she heard him say were: 'Ling, stay where you are. We're bringing you in.'

She asked him to repeat it. Hollingworth said he would bring her to safety. All she had to do was wait. Ling dried and dressed; long cotton trousers, long-sleeve shirt to keep away the mosquitoes. She threw more clothes into the holdall and put her laundry into a plastic bag, then stuffed it in, too.

Bringing you in. Wait for the call. What did it all mean? Why couldn't they do things normally? In a human way.

Mao Tse-tung was on the Cultural Channel. He was smiling. He waved. Behind him was a steelworks, with a computerised control room. As if he was alive. Everyone knew it was superimposed. What did they think there in the depths of secretive China? On the farms? In the far-flung deserts? Did they know it wasn't true? Ling lay on the sofa. She listened to her own heavy, irregular breathing.

Ling was jolted again by the telephone. 'Ling, this is Andrew Carter. I'm calling you from Washington. It's one thirty in the morning, here. Are you all right?'

The voice was firm. Carter was in control. 'No. No, I don't think I am,' she said.

'Do you know about Scott?'

'I think he's dead.'

'Yes.' There was a pause. 'Yes, I believe he may have been murdered.'

The confirmation from Scott's father gripped Ling again with terror: 'I saw the man who killed him.'

'Where?'

Ling told him. 'I'm so very afraid,' she said, holding back tears.

'All right,' said Carter gently. 'Do you want to come over here? To the States?'

'Yes,' said Ling quickly. 'Yes,' she repeated at the offer to take her to safety.

'All right. I'll get you out. Do you have a visa?'

'Multi-re-entry business visa,' she said.

'I'll book you onto the United Airlines to Los Angeles. Warren Hollingworth at the American consulate will make sure you get safely to the airport. You'll have your ticket and everything you need. Do you understand?'

'Yes.'

'Good. Just wait there. You'll be safe soon.'

Ling held the receiver for a few seconds after the call had ended before putting it back. She got up and collected a photograph of herself and Scott from the bedroom, a calculator, a bundle of pens, a diary, a notepad from the desk, a book on Tao massage which she would have given to Scott. It was panic packing. There was no way she could take everything. Someone else would clear it out. She unhooked a line of blouses from the wardrobe and dropped them on their hangers into the case.

Ling squatted down, dropping the things into a pile on the floor. She moved and swayed. She covered her face with her hands as if sensing that something terrible was around her and she didn't hear the first thud, as a bullet hit the armchair behind her. Then she saw the mirror on the back of the open bathroom door shatter, her eyes so transfixed when it happened that she only heard the sound later after the glass was on the floor. Immediately, another sound, softer, just above her. Air swished past her ears. Plaster sprayed out from the wall as bullets smashed up everything around her.

The bathroom window shattered. Cloth tore off the sofa. A bullet smashed into the wall. Ling listened to her own breathing. Sweat from her body dripped and ran onto the floor. She covered her head with her hands, more to block the sound of the destruction around her than for protection. Ling's training with the Chinese army had taught her that nothing in the room – no furniture, no door, no inner wall – would protect her from a high-velocity bullet.

She crawled into the kitchen and lay on the tiles. A washing machine was next to her. A smell of stale vegetables hung around the rubbish bin nearby. She listened to sounds of water running through the pipes in the block, and in the frightening quiet she looked at the gas pipes from the two-ringed stove on which she cooked and the pans piled up below amongst them. The kitchen was cooler without the sun. There was even a chill on the tiles. A cockroach ran across the floor inches from her face.

From a mirror next to the fridge she could see the hills and perhaps a glint of light reflected on a telescopic rifle lens. She moved closer to the back door out of the line of sight of the gun and reached up to draw back the bolt. But she remembered she had wedged in a piece of metal to jam the lock as a safety precaution. The gun was silent. The shower dripped. She remembered that the wet towel was lying on the floor. She looked back. The French window onto the tiny balcony was ajar. A dog barked below. An owner shouted and hit it with a stick. She recognised the voice. Outside there was calm. Normal village life went on while the crack, crack, crack of the rifle penetrated her unprotected, isolated home. She eased herself up to get more strength to open the door.

As she pushed the lock back, it gave way suddenly and she lost her balance again, falling clumsily against the pile of pans. The shelf shook above her head. She rolled back and two piles of crockery disintegrated around the tiny space. He fired again and again. He knew where she was. Could he see her? Was his telescopic sight that powerful? She tried to scream but couldn't, as if he was so close by that the sound would give away her position. But he wasn't. Fear and survival were taking over. She looked at the door and wondered how long it would take her to get up, open it and run. And whether a man could get closer and kill her as she escaped. She inched forward and a pain shot through her hand as it was cut on the sharp edges of a piece of the broken china which now covered the kitchen floor. The sun was going down, bringing with it a sub-tropical dusk, a clear but low, weeping light over the whole island.

*   *   *

When Mike McKillop knocked, Tom Elton, Hong Kong's international image-maker, was hunched over the papers on the table with a yellow marker, so absorbed in his task that he waved Mike in without looking up.

Elton's office was a sprawling, colourful corner room, sheets of glass clipped in at angles, a floor-to-ceiling view of angry skies, water dripping down, drops breaking off in the wind and making their own way through seventy-five storeys to the streets or wherever the monsoon winds took them. Elton had split the television screen into StarGolf, StarRacing and StarJazz which provided the background music. His jacket was slung onto his desk chair, looking as if it was hanging out to dry over the harbour. He wasn't wearing a tie and he'd moved his work from his desk to the coffee table, laying out sheets from the newspapers, printouts from the news channels, documents sent to him during the day, and on the large monitor on the back wall he had projected a map of the South China Sea. A purple line marked the area claimed by China. Red denoted the Asian Friendship Zone.

'Coffee? Brandy?' he invited. He ringed a paragraph on a sheet of paper. 'Good flight? Bit bumpy, I expect,' he continued making no mention of their meeting in the hotel because he knew Nim Kai might have the offices bugged. Elton pushed the paper aside and got to his feet. 'Sorry about calling you in at such short notice, Mike. This conference on regional security and everyone wants us to explain the territorial disputes, you know Spratly's, Paracels and all that. Every country in Asia's meant to be going to war over them but no one's got around to it yet. There'll be demonstrations. Arrests. Bad for the old image, so I need your help.'

Elton stood up and shook McKillop's hand, a firm, confident grip, the eyes right on him, unflinching. Elton released him, ushered him to sit down, while he went to the wall of windows, observing the room through its reflection. Everything that happened inside was forced into perspective by the spectacular potency of the elements outside and man's attempt to live amongst them. Elton stood in a triangle of high-technology architecture, far above the ground, the weather sweeping across the skyscrapers, the rain smashing against the glass an inch from his head.

'And a few things going on up north which are puzzling the comrades,' Elton continued still looking through the glass. Mike could see the reflection of his eyes, distorted in the lights thrown out by the city. 'We thought you could help us sort things out a bit.'

He turned round and used his remote to change the projection on the back wall from the map to a video. It took McKillop a few seconds to recognise it. This wasn't the face in the mirror, the crows' feet and grief lines that he saw every morning. This was a face of action, angry and defiant. Mike had seen dozens like it. The task of a covert police cameraman was to produce evidence. Shakiness, soft focus, hazy lighting were irrelevant. Here there was enough for Mike to see himself, shouting across Tiananmen Square, the dying man in his arms, the scene made more dramatic because there was no sound; mouth open, forehead creased, fury in the eyes as he screamed at the policemen to hold their fire. The screen was mute and black and white like a movie from seventy years ago.

'Shouldn't bother us really. But they just wanted to know if he said anything to you.' Elton froze frame.

Mike moved closer to the screen, as if he would get a better view, but he created a shadow across it. 'He said he was a Burmese general. That's just about all I know. He said he had been on one of my training courses here. That's about it.'

'You find him or he find you?'

'He was next to me at breakfast. I didn't choose the seating.'

Elton turned off the projector. 'Nor you did, old sport. Nor you did.' He sat down at his desk, swinging in his chair as if he was testing it in a furniture showroom. 'I'm E-mailing you his file. He was some kind of dissident. Plotting terrorism among the comrades. Explosives. Assassination. That sort of thing.'

Elton pressed a button on his keyboard. 'There you are. Gone. You'll get it when you log in. He was about to knock off half the Chinese politburo or something.'

'Half the politburo wasn't there.'

Elton stood up, jerked his head violently to one side. 'Bloody neck's killing me.' He massaged his shoulder with his right hand. 'Christ, Mike, I neither know nor care where the politburo were. That's the official line, and if you say he didn't say anything, that's your official line and that's even better.'

The projector came on again with a whir. 'We've got more of a mess here to sort out.'

A flicker and the face of an attractive Chinese woman appeared: 'Miss Ling Chen, a rising star with the Sino-American property conglomerate, Prime Coasts.' Elton turned and smiled at McKillop. 'And still the police detective says so what? But not for long, Mike, old sport. Because both you and I have spoken to that woman. Missing persons, remember?'

Mike recognised the next picture instantly: the body of Scott Carter laid out on Joss's slab in the mortuary.

'Scott Carter, American diplomat, committed suicide by jumping from the Emperor Hotel. You're on the case. Fine.' Elton snapped off the picture and walked over towards Mike. 'Trouble is, he was screwing her.'

The screen quivered. The picture was clearer. The colour better defined. A peanut tree, blurred window frames, her hair on bare shoulders. The two of them naked on Scott's Kashmir carpet.

'See,' Tom Elton continued, quickly flicking through them. 'He was an American spy and she's the product of Beijing People's University, the spiritual soul of the Chinese Communist Party. It's against the laws of harmony.'

'Everybody sleeps with everybody in this town.' Mike shifted in his chair, wondering what compromising path Elton was leading him down.

'Everyone except you, Mike,' Elton retorted. 'Your file says that apart from a few Suzy Wong goodtime girls, you behave impeccably.' Elton flung himself into an easy chair. 'But you're right. Everyone sleeps with everyone and everybody watches everybody.' His huge hands cupped around the edges on the back as if he was on a gym machine: 'And for a reason about which I am completely unclear, the comrades are very nervous about this one.'

A gust of wind threw rain against the window like water from a bucket. Elton leant forward to pick up documents spread out on the coffee table. 'They want you to find out where she's coming from, old sport.'

Mike looked back at Elton: 'Me?' he asked failing to hide his surprise.

'Has to be,' said Elton, shuffling papers together. 'You're the investigating officer. See, she thinks her lover was murdered. Scott Carter was a foreigner, so it's only natural. Has to be you.'

Elton dropped the folders onto his desk and took a squash ball out of the top drawer. He threw it against the wall, caught it, threw it again and kept on as he spoke. 'In a few days, old sport. Right now the Special Administrative Region of Hong Kong in all its benevolence is sending you to Bali to play golf.' He spun round, ball enveloped in his hand, with a grin spread across his face. 'Elton tours. Need to clear our heads. Get out a bit. Focus the mind.'

The squash ball hit a light switch and went askew landing on Elton's desk and bouncing onto the floor: 'See, I think they've got something in mind about your family. I'm working on it.' Elton bent down, picked up the ball, tipped it back into the drawer and closed it.

Chapter Eight

Ling Chen saw only blurs and shapes, encircling and moving in the crowds around her. She ran along the path in the village. She knocked into people in her rush. She stumbled over discarded drink cans on the path, through tiredness, in panic. The clatter made noises which frightened her more. Her memory lasted only seconds. Her mind raced, driven by fear, an inability to absorb, a necessity to escape. Her thoughts were instinctive. The mirror shattering. The sofa torn apart. The split-second transfer from normality to death.

Things, people, dogs came up in front of her like obstacles. She thought she might have screamed. Was it the same killer as in Scott's apartment? Were there more shots? On the path perhaps? Any unusual sounds at all? The dogs barked. But they always did.

She ran out from the narrow concrete path onto the main road and kept going down, following the curving, descending road into Silvermine Bay. She saw the police at a small village reporting centre, a hut by the bus stop, surrounded by stalls of beach games, sun hats and cold drinks. She recognised them at first as a sanctuary. Then, jumbled up with her terror, there was Scott, dead, his flat broken into, a killer confident enough to look her straight in the eyes. Her apartment shot up and abandoned. A voice saying: 'We'll take you in.' Her trust. And Scott's voice, more distinct than any of the sounds around her. 'If you come unstuck with the Party, my silken yellow flower,' he had said, touching her lips, then kissing them, holding both her shoulders, and staring at her with those huge, blue American eyes. 'Jump over the wall to the Consulate. We'll look after you.'

So she ran past the police post. On the ferry she sat inside, with a family. She helped the mother, holding the bottle while she unstrapped the baby from her shoulder harness and lowered him onto her lap. They talked. Ling was getting married soon, she

63

lied. Yes, of course, she wanted a boy. The mother was lucky, she had two sons. She involved herself with the family for the whole journey. Behind them hikers played cards. In front, she watched a man, by himself with an umbrella and a briefcase. He drank three cups of coffee. Their eyes met once. Ling looked away.

She carried a bag for the family off the boat. When they were gone, she felt danger surround her again. She moved quickly onto a walkway. There were people clustered around black-marketeers with contraband on the floor: teddy bears which walked and clapped; watches with television screens; fake designer T-shirts. She paused, then felt cornered as other people pressed against her. She pulled herself away, back into the moving crowd. She tried to tell if she was being followed. A woman in a yellow anorak and jeans stayed behind her right until she turned into Wan Li Road, Central. Then she was gone. A European, Mediterranean, perhaps a Portuguese from Macau, with a blazer and pink shirt stopped when she stopped, passed her, lingered at a shop window. Then he was gone. A policeman crossed an intersection with her. He smiled at her. She peeled away to the left, straight into the lobby of the Mandarin Hotel.

She sat there in a leather chair in the foyer. It was too smart. She was in the world she'd first heard about in the travel orientation class. They wouldn't kill her here.

The tag hung from Mike's golf bag. The passport lay in a pile on the check-in counter. McKillop had never seen his air ticket. He hadn't paid. Elton docked his monthly leisure allowance and messaged him on the desktop. They gave him a *Holiday Happiness* pack at the terminal: cap, three golf balls, towel with club logo, tees shaped like a woman, breasts, hips, flowing plastic hair in pink, yellow and blue. A CD ROM of the thirty-six holes, another for golf tips, a club T-shirt made to measure from his own security file and a photograph of McKillop in full swing printed on the back.

Elton, the collaborator, Elton the mercenary beckoned him, the huge hand splayed open waving him forward to the check-in counter. 'Bring your luggage, Mike,' he shouted. 'We'll get you through first.'

McKillop lifted his clubs onto the conveyor belt.

'At least they can't bug the airport,' said Elton. 'Sorry about putting on this junket, old sport.' The hand landed splayed open on the small of McKillop's back. 'The comrades wanted you out for a couple of days. Nothing serious. The Carter murder getting a bit sensitive.'

The clerk clipped tags onto the luggage. Mike didn't say anything.

'Did you get that horse I told you about?' Elton began to go, his boarding pass protruding from behind the silk handkerchief in his top jacket pocket. 'Take the money and run, Mike. That's my advice.'

'Smoking or non smoking?' asked the airline clerk.

'Smoking,' said McKillop.

'There you go Mike. Happiness tours,' grinned Elton. 'You couldn't smoke on flights before China ruled the world.'

Bali was a *Propaganda Free Area*, one of the few places in the Asian Friendship Zone which operated solely on commercial lines. The roads were well-surfaced. The power and telephones worked. The posters advertised consumer products and resort hotels. There were no political slogans.

The last time Mike had been here was with Sally and it came back to him vividly. The hotel stretched like a Hindu temple back from the beach, its pathways and gardens decorated with the terracotta statues of gods; and before he got there he remembered the bar under the roof of bamboo and reeds with the piano which he played to her as the wind and waves went wild outside. The bellboy showed him in and Mike felt a rush of adrenalin.

It was the same room. He remembered the number now. A bottle of Cuvée Dom Perignon 1988 Champagne was in an ice bucket with two glasses on a silver tray. The bellboy opened the fridge to show him fresh strawberries and cream. Just as he had ordered for her. And there was the bathroom with the tub where he had soaped her, sunk into the ground against a window facing the ocean.

When the phone rang, Mike was testing the shower temperature. He jumped and water splashed on his wrist and sleeves as he turned the tap off. His mind automatically tuned into Sally's voice: *I'm dropping by for a drink*, she would say. *Then come and see the kids before they go to bed.*

'Not the knock at midnight, my old friend.' The voice of Joss McEwan came over loudly on a long-distance call. 'But as good as. I ring to fare thee well and toast you with a Laphroaig from Islay and the winds of the Western Isles.' There was a laughing bitterness in the voice. Mike heard Joss drinking. 'Ahhhh. I warm with the sensations of peat sinking down my throat.'

'Joss, I might be getting a call from Sally,' McKillop said firmly.

'I know that. I know that,' retorted Joss. 'The same call that hasn't come for the past year.'

'I'm in Bali.'

'Of course. I called you here. They've put you on Happiness Tours because you've got something big coming up. We've all been there.' Joss coughed. Mike heard the drag on a cigarette. 'Just listen, OK? No need to speak. If Sally does call you can be sure they'll put her through.'

Mike sat on the edge of an armchair.

'So this is what happens. Two days ago, the morning after the Carter murder, Tom Elton appears at my flat. "Joss, I'm afraid they're letting you go," he says, standing in my doorway. "Straight away, Joss. We'll send on your stuff."

'"Who says?" I ask. But, that's it, Mike. I make a token query, like the paw of a fox reaching out as he's about to be disembowelled by the hounds. So Elton answers. He points his finger at the air, at the lightbulb in the hall. Meaning Nim Kai, the Gestapo, the gods. He gives uncle Joss an American smile, the one which bears no relation to the catastrophes going on around us.

'"You'll get full pension plus another hundred and fifty thousand dollars a year if you keep your mouth shut. American dollars, of course. My advice, Joss. Take the money and get the hell out of here. They won't touch you now. But mess with them and they'll kill you. It'll happen to me sooner or later, Joss. It's a club we'll never get to join."

'Then he takes off his jacket. Makes sure I see the Armani label on the inside pocket, designer, not Emporio, he told me once. He loosens his tie. The guy's sweating.

'"Leave your shipping address," he says.

'"Will you send my boat over, too?" I ask him. But he doesn't see anything funny.

There was the sound of rain on the balcony and Mike stayed quiet.

'Anyway, Elton says: "Take only what you need for the next two or three weeks. Your ticket will be at the airport. Any flight tomorrow. Your choice. We'll put the first hundred and fifty thousand US in your account in the morning. A year today there'll be another hundred and fifty plus inflation. It'll keep coming until the empire falls."

'And with that, he's gone. Walks off with a wave, jacket slung over his shoulder and your dear old friend and colleague, Dr Joss McEwan, Her Majesty's pathologist eminence, is in Scotland. It's beautiful, Mike. Fucking beautiful. Don't know why we stayed so long in that mess!

'Get in the *Islay Malt*,' Joss offered. 'Sail her over to me.' His voice went softer, more emotional: 'She's yours, Mike. I suppose that's why I'm calling to give you my boat. Take her out, escape in her if you can.'

Joss rang off. Mike closed the door. His eye caught the umbrella in a stand provided by the hotel, and, suddenly, it reminded him of Charlotte. Always there was something.

'Father, get me my umbrella,' she commanded.

'Say please and I'll think about it,' replied McKillop lightly.

'You didn't say please when you stole our land.' Her eyes were bright, staring at him, not angry so much – worse than that, Charlotte looked at him from a position of unemotional power, something which swept the love between father and daughter away into nothing. She pushed past him, took the umbrella out of its stand.

'And besides, adults must also obey children.'

She walked out of the door, leaving it open. McKillop closed it. He wanted to call her back. He wanted to cry. He turned round. Sally had watched everything from the kitchen door.

Sally didn't come but Tom Elton knocked on the door before dinner, a grin, hand outstretched to clasp as if they hadn't met for months: 'Mike, my friend,' he said. 'You're causing me heartache. They say you're talking to strange people on the telephone.'

Lights from the lagoon glistened through the glass. Mike had his own whisky going. He resented the intrusion and didn't offer a drink to Elton: 'I'll talk to whomever I want on the phone,' he retorted. He waved his hand at the champagne bucket: 'And what's all this shit. What are you trying to prove?'

'You're lonely. I know,' said Elton. 'Families mean a lot to me, too.'

'Me too,' said Mike, sarcastically. 'But if you've come for business, let's stick to it.'

'I'm your friend. I can protect you from these animals. Your ice is water, baby. You could sink anytime.' Elton flung himself into an armchair, hooking his leg over one of its arms. 'Don't lose me, Mike. I'm trying, Mike. I'm trying. Don't you think I feel for you?'

McKillop walked over and opened the balcony door. A breeze blew through the curtains and he took a deep breath: 'What the fuck is all that meant to mean?'

'This McEwan. Stay away from him, Mike. He's gone home. He's not in our lives any more. You let him speak, Mike. You knew that was wrong. You're on probation for a reunion. They're watching real close.' Elton picked up the room service menu to fan himself as if it was too warm. 'But if you slip away, I flip away,' continued Elton.

'If I slip, you flip,' repeated McKillop. 'You're more full of crap than the comrades.'

'Just a phrase,' Elton laughed. 'I'm a marketing man, Mike. I don't know why they sent me here. I make good things happen. It's my job. That's what makes me happy.' He let his voice drop to a whisper. 'Nim Kai put me in touch with Sally. Sally wants to see you. The kids adore you.'

Elton got up and walked over towards him. 'These bastards play around with us. Don't let them get to you, Mike. Your family loves you. I talked to them.'

McKillop stiffened: 'You what?'

'I told them.' Elton spoke in an exaggerated whisper. 'The Chinese. I told them that if I was to get you to toe the line, I had to talk to Sally and the kids. Long chat with Sally. She's a great woman. She really wants to see you, to sort everything out.'

McKillop sat down and drank his whisky: 'If you're pissing me around, I'll kill you, Elton, and I fucking mean it.'

Elton was on his feet: 'I'm not pissing anyone around.' He put his hand round Mike's shoulder and steered him out onto the balcony. He looked up as a signal to say they were out there so their conversation wouldn't be recorded. Night squalls blew into their faces. 'I need you, Mike, to help me do my job. I really do. Fine, I can handle all the trade stuff, even a lot of this shit over democracy. But I need a guy like you with me from the police. We're white men in an Asian game. We have to work together.'

'Joss called me,' Mike said bluntly, angry at Elton's manipulation. 'I didn't call him.'

'Don't let it get to you, old sport.' The huge hand squeezed his shoulder then unwrapped itself from him. 'If there is a moral line in this swamp, we crossed it a long time ago. You and me. I just want to go back to New York with dollar signs dripping from every pore in my body. And you, you Mike, why are you doing it all? Because you want to see Sally and the kids again. Don't lose that focus, Mike. You can help me survive this fucking pit. I can get you Sally through the comrades. Don't throw this deal away, Mike. Right now, it's the only one you've got.'

'Your deal. Your terms,' said Mike.

'It's their terms. You know that.' Elton turned to go back into the room. 'Getting to Sally was really hard. The comrades are edgy. You know. You've got to look at it from their point of view. They don't know why you're calling these people. The American Consulate, for Christ's sake. It's not just McEwan.'

'Do you know where Sally . . .' McKillop said but he didn't finish before Elton interrupted. 'Help me help you,' he said. Elton walked across to open the door.

The curtains were swept back by a gust of wind which came with the sudden equatorial darkness. 'We let McEwan know he shouldn't go calling people in Asia any more. That was the deal. He's had his golden dragon handshake. Great opportunity for him. Nothing to make him stay. No family, anything like that.'

When Elton was gone, the television filled the vacuum, a newsreader saying that China was reaffirming its claim to territory in the South China Sea. How many times had he heard the same announcement? Mike turned it off.

Chapter Nine

Ling Chen's clothes were wet and clung to her body. The blasts of air-conditioning in the lift chilled her. Smoke from earlier passengers hung there. Ling shivered. She saw herself in the mirrors. She ran her fingers through her hair and flattened it. She adjusted the sodden sports shirt and straightened her trousers. She had waited out until she was too scared and too tired to stand it any more. Her colleagues should have left by now. The lift slowed. She pressed a button which changed the mirrored door panels to a video monitor. She could see the dark wood reception desk. Empty. To the left, the sofa, two chairs, a coffee table. No one. A voice announced the lift's arrival. The door opened and there was the same scene in colour, in reality. The red and yellow Prime Coasts logo on the facing wall. A mirror reflected her dishevelled shape. The security door to the left shut. Music, but not piped. From a radio. The lift began to close. Ling stopped it with her foot. She wasn't sure. To the right, the fish tank. Lights on. Bubbles pumped through. Fish swimming in circles. Tranquillity. Then she caught sight of a light blue beret, further to the right, a blue shirt, epaulettes, a brown Nepali arm and finally, by the time she had stepped out, reassured, suddenly feeling safe, Leonard was there, armed, courteous and unflustered, evidence that whatever horrors had happened and were chasing her they had not yet reached this office. It was Scott who had told her about the Ghorkas. In the ten years of Chinese control, there had not been one case of a Ghorka guard betraying his company to the authorities.

'You're a bit windswept, Miss Chen.'

'Raining out there, Leonard,' she replied in English. 'Many people in?'

'Mostly gone home. Why you working so hard?' Leonard was writing Ling's arrival in his log.

'Everyone works hard around here.'

Leonard pressed open the lock which let her into the tiny security chamber. She closed the door behind her and only after it was locked again did she punch in the combination and her password to get through the second door. Once there, she sat heavily on a brown leather sofa. A powerful feeling of exhaustion came over her. She closed her eyes. The day played itself before her. The gunman. The shattered mirror. The dogs. The running. The cold, wet night in the undergrowth. And the silence there. The absolute terror. The telephone calls. 'We will bring you in.' The American. Who was he? The British policeman who wouldn't talk to her. Her disorganised thoughts ran through and then lingered. She couldn't relax. Ling pushed herself onto her feet. She walked unsteadily to her office. In the cupboard was a change of clothes, a bathrobe and a towel. Ling undressed, wrapped the robe around her and walked into the corridor and to the office shower.

The water warmed her. When she turned it off she stayed in the steam, in the cocoon of the shower cubicle, reaching for the towel, bringing it in and wrapping it round her. The screen above the door lit up, showing her direct line was ringing. She stepped outside, dripping across the floor, picked up the extension in the bathroom, dialled in her security code and waited for the caller to speak:

An American voice: 'This is Andrew Carter looking for Ling Chen.' Ling didn't reply. She was too frightened. But she kept the receiver close to her mouth. The safety of her office was shattered. Between her and danger was only a telephone line, a sheet of glass, twenty-seven storeys, darkness outside, flashing harbour lights in filthy air in a place where she could never go out again without fear of death.

'Are you there, Ling? Are you all right?'

Ling heard herself answer, automatic but cautious. 'No,' she whispered. She fiddled with the towel, tightening and tucking it in so it didn't slip down.

'Tell me what happened?'

'Someone tried to shoot me.' She sat on a wicker stool next to the telephone. 'After you called.' Her hair was wet and turning cold from the air-conditioning.

He was the father of Scott, thought Ling. Scott, who had told her about the Party. He had come to Hong Kong once and they all went out to dinner. They talked about jumping over Embassy walls, good steaks and American values. The restaurant had been high up like her office. Outside it had been a clear night, filled with the harbour lights, like now.

Afterwards, Andrew Carter had taken her onto the dance floor just like a father-in-law.

'I'm frightened, Mr Carter. I'm really afraid,' she blurted out. Her eyes were wet but she couldn't tell if it was tears or shower water. Ling shivered and pulled the towel closer around her.

'Is there anyone else in the office?' continued Carter.

'Only Leonard.'

'Who?'

'The Ghorka.'

'You'll leave in a few hours,' Carter went on gently. 'Stay where you are. Two men will arrive. They will be absolutely reliable.' Ling cried uncontrollably, heaving as she released her tension. 'That's what you told me last time,' she said.

Warren Hollingworth had given up trying to reach Clem Watkins. The E-mails stayed unanswered. At the business centre in the China World Hotel in Beijing, Watkins had paid cash. Somehow he had checked into the Air India flight to Bombay, but never boarded. Yet a businessman called Watson, on the same flight to Bombay, was dead.

Clem had vanished. Hollingworth had trained him too well. The past midnight hours were gone. Soon it would be dawn, and a lost man with secrets was dangerous. Hollingworth got up and stretched. It had been a long night. He'd let Pat, his wife, sleep, understanding as always the demands on his time. No point in waking her up for nothing. Better to see the night through. He paced the room, relaxing with the muscle movement.

It was twelve hours at least since Donald Zuckerman, the President of the United States, had called on his secure line, the voice, smooth, over-familiar. 'Warren, it's the President here.'

Zuckerman had made the call himself, no switchboard, no holding on to make sure Warren was there. 'A very close friend of mine, Andrew Carter, will be calling you. His son has been killed on your patch. Give him everything, will you Warren?'

Hollingworth never gave everything. At the weekly heads of department meeting, he kept quiet. In routine intelligence briefings to visiting officials, he told nothing that could not have been read from back-copies of the Far Eastern Economic Review, the regional weekly magazine based in the Philippines.

'Of course, sir,' he replied automatically.

'You're doing a great job out there, Warren. We appreciate your service very much.'

With the click on a decision originated from the White House, the conversation was over. How many calls did he make like that a day? A massage. A threat. The twist of an arm. Each less than a minute of his time.

With instinct and a lifetime of discipline, he called up the CIA database from his desk-top. He ran through the files on Andrew Carter, a high-profile newspaper tycoon, and jogged his own memory of their brief acquaintance more than a decade ago.

When Andrew Carter set up the meeting, the big names of missile technology were there, academics from the conservative think tanks, Republican senators. No eloquent speeches were needed. The argument was simple, the participants were in agreement. Russia and the Ukraine, both nuclear powers, were unstable. Even Western Europe with its multi-ethnicity was unreliable. To halt military research now would run down the arms industry and make it impossible to rebuild.

A coffee break. Summer. New York was hot and the conference room opened onto the hotel gardens where the men walked, breaking away in twos and threes to different parts of the lawn. That day covert American investment began at Heshui in the form of a joint venture signed between Evans Engineering, a manufacturer of hi-tech firefighting equipment and the Jilin Fire Department. Hollingworth brokered the deal. Evans set up a research centre in Heshui. No threat. No broken laws. The umbrella company, Multitechnologies, was listed on the Hong Kong and New York stock exchanges, a legitimate player in the Pacific Rim economy, yet owned by the Chinese military.

President Clinton who had dodged the draft was wrecking the defence of the greatest nation in the world. Where was stability? Who was the ally? Where was the next super-power? Hollingworth even wrote the official CIA memorandum on the deal: 'American peacetime technology, manufactured at low-labour rates in China, marketed throughout the world, is part of the economic global village in which we now live. The agency believes such arrangements are beneficial to the national interest and to world peace by supplying and monitoring that supply to the developing world at affordable prices.'

Heshui lay high in the mountains of Jilin province, isolated, secret, stark and cold. It wasn't a town any more, just a complex of square, low-rise concrete buildings. Snow covered the roofs, grey snow coloured by the soot and sulphur from the air. The

73

civilians had gone long ago, moved out in trucks in the bitter winter of November 1950. Heshui was a legacy from the Korean War, when conflict was close and America was the enemy. It became a community of China's most brilliant scientists, their aim to develop missile delivery technology which would match that of the United States.

30 June 1997. Hollingworth was a new kid on the block. So was Li Tuo. The Chinese had got it right about Hong Kong. They wanted it for money and for their blue water navy. Hollingworth went out with Li Tuo on the night the British left. Each man pretended to be drunk. Each was sober, so the secrets were hunted down through personal vulnerabilities and as dawn broke, with the smells of nicotine and spilt beer on their clothes. Hollingworth probed. He needled Li Tuo. He prised open the Chinese inferiority, the patriotism.

'We don't need to build any more bloody weapons, until yours shoot straight,' said Hollingworth. They leant on the bar, buying each other brandy. When Hollingworth went for a piss he gulped in twenty mouthfuls of water and took caffeine tablets. His mind stayed clear. 'What's the point,' he deliberately slurred. 'We're there. We're number one. Four hundred years of civilisation and we did it. Not five bloody thousand.'

That night Li and Hollingworth sensed the other knew about Heshui, the illegal, covert, Chinese American operation which researched thermal-imaging guidance systems long after Nato had slowed it down. The American President was becoming at ease with power. As he inspired the poor, he moved billions from defence to social services. There was no enemy as technologically advanced as America. As long as it stayed that way, the world was safe, like when America and only America had the bomb. Until the Soviets got it from British and American traitors and the Cold War began.

Now there was a different President. Like Americans had picked John Kennedy, a Catholic, for the highest post, they had now elected their first Jewish president in Donald Zuckerman. He was decorated for bravery as a tank commander in the Gulf War and in 1992 joined the Republican Party and went into politics. At thirty-seven he was a comparative late-comer, but he worked his way from Congress to the Senate, fighting off racial prejudice and suspicions. Privately, Hollingworth did not approve of a non-Christian leading his country, but his personal respect for Zuckerman as his head of state remained undiminished.

Carter spotted Zuckerman as a Washington rising star shortly after he was elected to Congress and the two men became genuine friends. Carter, ten years his senior, guided the younger man through the pitfalls of political life and gave him free introductions at his weekly breakfast meetings which cost most guests twenty thousand dollars a head. Half went to party funds, half to a think-tank foundation.

With his reputation as an opinion-maker, Carter ensured Zuckerman stayed out of trouble until he was experienced enough to steer himself towards the White House.

Hollingworth kept scrolling down the information pack. Carter's eldest son, Geoffrey, was being groomed to take over the business. There was a daughter, Madelaine, who was just finishing a post-graduate degree in journalism at Columbia University. And there had been Scott, the second son who less than a week ago was a young high-flyer in the State Department, but was now dead. Carter had married young, at twenty-four, in the fall of 1969. The marriage was strong with no blemish in its thirty-eight years.

'It's tragic, Mr Carter. I'll do anything I can,' he said, when Carter called.

'I gather the Hong Kong government is saying that Scott killed himself.'

'I don't believe that is official yet.'

There was impatience in Carter's voice. Anger, grief, authority and helplessness, Hollingworth thought. He had often seen such conflicting emotions tear powerful men apart. 'My son was a young American with everything going for him. He would not take his own life.'

Hollingworth fingered the edges of a single sheet of paper typewritten with the letterhead of the People's Hong Kong Police Force. He understood the reference codes on the top left-hand side, which would have been meaningless to Carter. The report had gone to the Nim Kai before being released. It was signed by the police pathologist Joss McEwan and the chief investigating officer Mike McKillop. The four-figure number indicated that it had also been authorised by the New China News Agency, the inappropriately named organisation which took its orders from Beijing and advised on Party policy.

The report simply said that Scott Carter had committed suicide.

75

His body was now ready for collection by the family or American consular officials.

Hollingworth paused. Complete silence. He didn't want to appear hesitant. Just thoughtful. 'I understand that, Mr Carter,' he said.

'Go on,' said the other man.

'Your son was murdered, sir. He was on an operation. The enemy must have been tipped off.'

'Who is the enemy?'

'I don't know, sir. But the evidence points towards the People's Republic and . . .'

Carter interrupted: 'Are you saying the Chinese government murdered an American diplomat?'

'That might be the case.' Hollingworth checked his watch. Two in the morning in Hong Kong was early afternoon in Washington. Carter might not have slept the previous night. He was distraught. He'd lost a son.

'I want everything and don't fuck with me. I want it all,' Carter said.

Hollingworth took him accurately through the arrangements of the meeting with Kim, the dinner in the ballroom, the eavesdroppers, his pager and the rush to the executive floor.

'What was in the room?' asked Carter.

'A mess. Nothing else.'

'What was Scott collecting?'

'When we know that, sir, we'll know why your son died.'

Carter hadn't mentioned the meeting years ago. He had made no reference to Heshui. Maybe in his role as deal-maker and ideologist he had never even known the name and forgotten he was involved. Maybe it was cleaner that way.

As Tony Zhang, private secretary to the Chinese President, walked through the entrance of Zhongnanhai in Beijing, the guards saluted him. This was one of the most impenetrable compounds in the world, ringed by high walls and secured by the most loyal and rugged regiment of bodyguards in China. The men on the gate came from the Special Guards Unit, which used to be known as Unit 8341, handpicked for being uneducated, mostly illiterate, highly trained and utterly loyal. They prided themselves in never losing a Chinese leader to violence and right now, Tony Zhang, aged twenty-eight, was part of that special group of people.

They had been expecting him. They knew his face and style and only took a casual look at his identity. They were used to him arriving in blue denims, an open-neck shirt and Nike trainers.

A soldier showed him to the stairs. He climbed them alone to the second floor. Red cloth draped cream banisters. Paint had dripped onto the steps. There was a chill inside the foyer, made more acute because of the warm sunshine outside. The ceilings were twelve, maybe fifteen feet high. Above his head, a bare lightbulb shone with a dim yellow glow. Further along there was a crystal chandelier, but many of the pieces of glass were missing. At the top of the stairs the paint was fresh and glossy, but only where visitors could see. In the dimmer light, the walls were faded. Kang's picture hung with those of Mao Tse-tung: Mao inspecting the harvest; Kang at the Shanghai stock exchange; Mao standing on the top of a dam; Kang lecturing at Harvard University. And so on. No one else was revered. That had been Tony's idea. Deng Xiao-ping's capitalism was going out of fashion and Tony wanted to give the public a clear picture of whom the President had succeeded and where he was taking China. Mao may have caused famine and slaughter, but his reputation as the Great Helmsman had survived and only he was considered the true father of the modern Chinese nation.

Tony had taken weeks to focus Kang's different, intellectual mind on the problems of corruption and then to persuade him to tackle the problem head on. But the President saw Tony as a surrogate son which meant Tony could answer back without fear of retribution. And Kang was his mentor. Only a highly intelligent leader listens, plays with ideas and sometimes throws pragmatism to the wind. Logical thought was for civil servants. It had no place in a presidential think-tank, and right now Kang and Tony were using their powerful minds to take China that extra step to be a modern society.

The idea for an across-the-board pay rise for civil servants had been his, discussed for hours with Kang and his economists, who agreed that it was a hard choice but one of the first steps towards reaching the final destination of a modern China. Tony Zhang walked quickly down the long, dank and sunless corridor, his sneakers bouncing silently on the torn, maroon carpet. Life was good inside the walls of Zhongnanhei, the place people called the new Forbidden City.

Zhang had escaped the rigours of being a Chinese citizen. His hands were soft. His body had never strained like the men and women heaving cement on construction sites. The Party gave him

77

a good flat east of Tiananmen Square and he rattled around the rooms, his CD player on at high volume, one day European opera, another Chinese classical.

Most of his university friends had gone into business. The best and the brightest of the young China had either become tax-dodging millionaires or been hired on high wage packets with six-figure bonuses by Western multinationals.

Kang had asked Tony to stay with the Party, and he had come to understand the divisions between the men who led the country. He read what Western newspapers had to say about the disintegration of central rule, about power being wrenched away from the Party, about wealthy provincial rulers, about a return to warlordism. But Tony knew this was a massive miscalculation. The Party would remain as the dominant force. The military would remain loyal and follow orders from Beijing. Wayward provincial leaders would always be an irritant. The challenges to power in Communist China came not from the outside but from within the walls of Zhongnanhei.

As soon as he entered the room, Tony wished he hadn't worn his trainers. The double doors at each end were closed. The table in the middle stretched out like an inhospitable northern plain, rugged, chipped, polished, dominant. President Kang had asked Tony to an informal brainstorming session, but this was a meeting of some of the most powerful men in the country, with Tony dressed like a yuppie in an American shopping arcade.

A petroleum geologist from Shanghai University, Song Wang-yi, was answering a question from Li Tuo when Tony arrived. Sitting next to him was Tang Heng-gao, the head of the Navy; then Ding Zhenyi who controlled the Second Artillery Regiment, the unit responsible for China's missile programme; Liu Zhenxiang the brilliant aerospace engineer who had given the airforce in-flight refuelling capabilities; Xu Lingyun, widely regarded as Li Tuo's hatchet man who was in charge of special projects – except Tony had never known what they were.

This was a military meeting, with no foreign, finance or trade representation.

'Anything is possible,' said Song, agreeing with Li Tuo's request. Tony noticed he was hesitant, more a reluctant acceptance of whatever Li was asking for.

'But the American oil exploration company has its own report which would contradict our findings,' intervened President Kang.

'The Americans are always disagreeing with us,' snapped back

Li Tuo. He slapped his hand on the table: 'And I don't accept that Comrade Zhang has any business at this meeting.' He looked at Kang. 'He should leave immediately.'

Tony noticed the guard reaching for the doorhandle, anticipating the order to show him out.

'He is my private secretary,' said Kang, quietly. 'He must stay.' The tone followed by Li's response of silence convinced Tony they would be in for a rough ride long after the meeting had ended.

Kang leant forward and lifted the lid off the top of his teacup. Steam drifted up. Tony began to take notes, but the conversation was too confrontational for any minutes to be published. He doodled, then, realising that one of the generals would disapprove, quickly turned over the page.

'We can also hire American consultants, Comrade President,' said Admiral Tang Heng-gao. 'And they would agree with our new findings.'

'What sort of findings?' said Kang.

Li Tuo sat upright, expanding his presence in the room. 'Those which would be in the national interest,' he said slowly.

'But for what purpose?' responded Kang. 'Are we not moving towards a modern China? He paused to blow on the tea to cool it and drank. Then went on, looking directly at Li across the top of the cup. 'Away from the need to lie.'

'Comrade President, have you forgotten your history?' Li persisted. Tony watched Li while he was speaking. Li was technically just the Ministry of State Security chief in Hong Kong, certainly not a senior post compared to the generals, but they were following his line, as if he had been put up by them to persuade Kang, as if . . . maybe, Li was their stalking horse.

'What happened to a modern Soviet Union when it dispensed with the national interest? What I am proposing is for the good of China. It is no more and no less,' said Li.

'Is not China trying to become more international . . .' But Li interrupted the President of China and turned back to the geologist. 'Professor, what scientific assistance would you need to come up with a credible document?'

Song Wang-yi paused, but his eyes did not waver from Li. To have shifted them, to have been seen to consult the President at this stage could have meant being posted to examine rock formations in Tibet. 'I will have to look at the validity of the American preliminary findings,' he said slowly. 'If the comrade general needs a document that will withstand international scrutiny,

I will have to rewrite the arguments, possibly introducing an acceptance of the theory of abiogenic methane . . .'

'How long will it take?'

'A month,' replied Song.

'Do it then.'

Tony caught the eye of the President, who was concentrating on his tea. There was an air of intellectual confidence about Kang. He looked as if he had been mugged by idiotic thugs, yet he would emerge with slight bruising but able to continue with his journey of reform unchanged.

Tom Elton phoned Mike on the thirteenth hole as he was at the zenith of his upswing. He carried on, the head of the seven iron hitting the ball square and lifting it in a high arc, clear of the water, pushed in by the wind and coming down with a bounce on the fringe and rolling uphill to finish three feet from the hole. Almost certainly a birdie. Applause from the younger men. Mike took off his glove, wiped a towel across his forehead and pressed the answer button:

'I'm back in Hong Kong and so will you be soon, old sport,' said Elton. 'Some new flap over Ling Chen.'

'Where is she?' A hot breeze blew across the course.

'Don't know. That's the problem. You're on the afternoon flight. First class. Smoking.'

Chapter Ten

'We're into heavy politics here, Mike,' Tom Elton began as soon as Mike arrived in his office. 'They have gone mad. They are round the fucking twist. They haven't got enough feet to shoot themselves in.'

It was still raining, as if Hong Kong had been washed down with monsoon for weeks, and Mike was still in his golfing clothes, now damp and cold in the air-conditioning. McKillop sat deep in a leather chair and accepted the glass of whisky which Elton put in his hands. Elton paced the office, slapping the palm of his hand with his fist. Then he leant against the window, his head resting on his forearm.

'Is there anything specific, Tom?' Mike asked gently. The whisky calmed him. 'You mentioned Ling Chen.'

But Elton ignored the prompting: 'They want this place to look good, and every time we gloss it up, they come round flicking ink all over the fucking place. I tell you, Mike, they're beginning to piss me off, real bad. It wasn't my idea to put the ice bucket and all that in your room. I thought it was sick.' He stopped and pushed his hand around his chin. 'And I swear, Mike, you help me on this one and I'll get you to see Sally and the kids. You have my word.'

Mike had been here before. He answered softly: 'OK, so what do we do?'

'You signed Scott Carter's death certificate. His father's going crazy in Washington, saying it's a cover-up. Even suggesting the comrades were involved.'

Mike sipped the whisky, drawing in the tastes and smells of peat from the Scottish moors. Elton paced.

'Why don't you fix it yourself?' asked Mike. 'You have my signature on file. Change it to accident.'

Elton shook his head. 'More complicated, old sport.' He pulled open the door of a fridge underneath his drinks cabinet and took

81

out a Sprite. 'Scott Carter was screwing Ling Chen. He dies and she says someone's trying to kill her. The police have been round to her flat and it's all shot up, and right now she's hiding out in her office and has been talking to Carter's father.'

Elton snapped open the can and drank thirstily. He put it on a ledge above the fridge and sat down next to Mike. He leant over, dropping his voice, as if not to be overheard in a crowded restaurant. 'So I mentioned that you've got to talk to her. They're really keen now. First thing tomorrow. Like in the old days as if it were a murder investigation.'

'Find out what she knows,' suggested Mike, turning in his chair to catch Elton's softer voice.

'You're the man to do it, old sport. And if you get it right, they show you your family. They've agreed. Sick. But that's the deal.'

'So you've said.'

'The comrades reckon she was leaving him. He was distraught and that's why he jumped. She's one of them, you see. Went to the best ideological universities. One of her old boyfriends is now private secretary to the President. Believes in the Motherland and all that.' Elton pushed himself up restlessly: 'So we've got to find that out and let Carter know so he'll realise the truth.'

A sheet of lightning shot through the sky. The American smiled. 'But before that I need a hand with the cockroaches. You and I, old sport, have to give a joint-press conference in two hours' time. Nine in the evening here. Morning shows in the States. Lunchtime in Europe. Whole works. Just tell them about Joss's autopsy. It'll be fine.'

Across the Pacific Ocean, a rough-shaven man in a red and black checked shirt and jeans drove a battered Chrysler saloon down a cluster of side streets in Santa Monica. The clothes had been bought an hour earlier. The hair had been dyed in beach changing room. The road tax had two months to run. The dealer offered no receipt, nor did the buyer want one. He paid cash and drove off.

Jet lag and tiredness came over him in waves, like a man walking on snow who kept getting caught in drifts. But the sluggishness evaporated, all instincts alert, when Clem Watkins turned into the road which had become so familiar to him. Year after year, assignment after assignment, he had come back to this place.

The guards at the gate had become used to his foibles, to the smile spread right across his face which said it was worth visiting all those shit-holes if he could come back home like this. In between debriefings and briefings he would get to know his colleagues again: the quiet and clever John White, who told him the staff had been suspended on full pay, and the sensitive family man, Martin Hewlitt, who was killed at the same time as Clem was ordered out of Heshui.

Always, he had made a point of walking the last few hundred yards, sometimes taking off his shoes to feel the warm, soft Californian grass on the soles of his feet and breathing deeply the dry air of America's West Coast. But this time he drove close to the gate. He expected what he saw but had to look at it himself.

The guards had been changed. The brass plate announcing the offices of Geotech International Inc had been replaced by a board warning that guard dogs patrolled the premises. The decorative iron fence, which was usually entwined with flowers, had been reinforced with rolls of razor wire. There were figures moving around the grounds. Clem caught glimpses of movement inside the building as well, and as his slow speed began to attract the attention of a security officer, Clem noted the logo of the firm on his uniform, then moved away and headed back towards Los Angeles.

The Party scuttled away leaving it to the white men of Western democratic values to satiate their own. The Chinese press received a separate briefing, a meeting of consensus, tea, biscuits and understanding. There were no live broadcasts; no statements; only a gentle unsigned, unquestioned account from which the world emerged in an enviable clarity.

McKillop lay back in a chair. A make-up artist brushed his cheeks. Someone asked about lighting. Did he mind it high, hot? Better for the satellite pictures to retain quality. CNN asked for a three-minute delay on opening statements. They had live pictures coming in of new fighting in Albania. The BBC and StarSky had no objections. Elton dressed down, no pocket handkerchief, the striped shirt changed for light green. More broadcast-friendly, he said.

Mike's uniform hung in polythene wrap, ready for him, freshly pressed, dry-cleaned, and the valet tag sticking out from the coat hanger. They had gone into his apartment and taken it. There was a new driver, too and a bigger car, a Norinco stretch, but no explanation. Elton said he looked great. He and McKillop were in charge. No one else was around. No briefing papers.

'Nothing,' said Elton. 'No facts. No authorisations. We don't even know what the truth is meant to be. Just wing it, Mike. You're a pro.'

'Of course, it's impossible to know what was going through Scott Carter's mind when he died,' said Mike. The lights glared, giving him a furrow on his forehead as he tried not to squint. He couldn't see faces in the audiences, just a blackness whose sounds of shuffling and impatience were fed back to him on the public address system.

'So why are you convinced he committed suicide?' The questioner was out there somewhere, American, confrontational.

'Can you identify yourself and your media organisation?' interrupted Elton. 'Superintendent McKillop wants to know who he's talking to.'

'Jake Weinberg, *New York Times*. Are you convinced, Superintendent, that he committed suicide?'

'In my profession, nothing is ever one hundred per cent. Andrew Carter, Scott's father, has also asked me for confirmation. The findings were taken from the pathologist's report, the structure on the roof of the hotel, which rules out an accident.' Here Mike paused deliberately. Sweat was building up inside his collar. 'And we are looking into some possible unfortunate circumstances in Scott's personal affairs which might have motivated him to take his own life.'

'What circumstances?' Weinberg shot back.

'As I say, we're still looking into it. It would be premature . . .'

'Danielle Rice, *USA Today*.' A coarse voice from the back of the auditorium. 'But he could have been murdered?'

McKillop ran his hand around the back of his neck. 'Andrew Carter has asked us to reconsider all angles. And that's what I'm doing. The key question is that Scott was a strong and very able young man. There would have been a fight to get him up to the roof and there are no signs of any struggle at all.'

The audience shifted in their seats. 'Great stuff, Mike,' whispered Elton. His hand wavered, forefinger out, to grant a question to someone else. 'Sophie, yes, your turn.' McKillop couldn't see her. But the question was for Elton.

'Tom, if we could move off the Carter murder just for a moment . . .'

'Death, Sophie, not murder.'

'Well, if we could move away because there've been some statements from Beijing about China's territorial claims . . .'

'This is only reaffirmation, Sophie. Nothing new.'

Elton leant over to McKillop as she talked: 'Have to watch her. Real cute. She'll start a kitten and end a tiger.'

'Even so,' Sophie persisted. 'For those of us whose foreign policy comprehension is worse than a six-year-old's can you explain what the issues are? It does seem a little unfair. I mean some of these islands are closer to the Philippines or Malaysia than to China. So if there is oil there, surely it should go to those countries?'

'A very good question, Sophie.' Elton was on his feet. A chart up. Elton on the remote, drawing boundaries, activating lights.

'You have to remember, Sophie, that the claims on the Lansha, or Spratly Islands as you call them, were only lodged during the Colonial times by the occupying powers, Britain, The Netherlands, Spain. The Motherland never recognised the unequal treaties by which the powers took over the country. And let's face it, in the twenty-first century, the invasions of sovereign territory which took place would be ruled as violent and illegal acts.

'China's own right to command the South China Sea goes back thousands of years, as you know. The government feels that regional stability and prosperity is far better served if we base territory on claims made before colonisation.'

'But that's because China wants all the oil or minerals or whatever's there,' Sophie interrupted.

'Absolutely not, Sophie. Your viewers can be assured that there's never been any question of China taking all the reserves – if indeed there are any. China has always said it would develop jointly . . .'

Sophie Lange had heard it all before. But she let Elton talk as the minute hand of her watch crept to the bottom of the hour. Through her earpiece, she listened to the time-check, the headlines, her own cue in. Then the television crew threw a spotlight onto her face.

McKillop saw her for the first time, blonde gelled swept-back hair, a hard face, on her feet, clipboard balanced on the seat in front of her, all heads turned towards her: 'Excuse me for interrupting, Tom, but GlobeNet Asia has late breaking news, and we need a comment from Superintendent McKillop.'

Sophie didn't pause. Elton trailed off. 'Mr McKillop we have reports coming in of a body washed up on Cheung Chau Island. Preliminary identification has named the victim only as David, a Ghorka security guard at the hotel where Scott Carter died.'

The light on her went out. McKillop felt the glare on his face. He squinted trying to find Sophie, but she was in darkness.

'I know nothing about it,' he muttered. Blackness, glare and heat. McKillop stalled, his instincts confused.

McKillop's eyes flickered. He took them off the spotlights, moving them to refer to Elton, eradicating their authority. Eyes are everything to a camera. Elton was poised, motionless, suspended until he was on air again. His chart lingered. Both expressionless as if off-air was on ice. McKillop looked back again, so bright, so uncertain, that he stared downwards.

'Is it that you don't know, or that you're not telling us, Superintendent.'

'I can only say . . .

'We're running out of time,' interrupted Sophie. 'The latest news is that it's been confirmed now that David was murdered. He was forty-three years old. His wife and two children live in Pokhara, Nepal.'

'That's pure speculation . . .' attempted Mike.

'Now back to New York,' broke in the correspondent. The light on her faded and Mike saw her talking into her earpiece, smiling and sitting down as her producers congratulated her on her performance.

'You were great, Mike. But you never want to answer a bitch like that.' Elton tore off his tie and unbuttoned the neck of his shirt. He threw his jacket over a chair in his office. McKillop stayed by the door, oppressed by the weight of his police uniform set against the colours of Elton's designer labels.

'So. Was she right?' he said.

'You bet. If the networks put it on air, live like that. Access. Accuracy. Speed. Shock.' Elton had his sleeves rolled up and a can of Coke from the fridge. He threw one to McKillop. 'Fucking corruption. Some cheap cop tipped her off.' He snapped open the can. 'I don't know a damn thing about it. And don't you start going investigating, Mike.'

McKillop sat down. He put the drink unopened on the coffee table. 'Now what?'

Elton moved to his desk and reactivated his computer. McKillop watched him, the stormy, modern backdrop outside the window suited Elton's expansive mood. He called up his message file, read it and spoke simultaneously. 'Tomorrow night, I got a dinner party. Taking the staff and colleagues out.'

Elton pressed the print command. The printer whirred. 'Would invite you, Mike, except I have a feeling your performance might have earned a little something from the comrades.' Both men were silent for the few seconds it took before Elton tore off the paper.

'Technically, I shouldn't be giving you this yet because you've still got to go see Ling Chen.' He handed Mike the printout. 'But you've done well. One more job and I'd say you're there.' Mike began reading, but Elton's hand was curled around his shoulders propelling him out of the room. 'Read it in the lift. There'll be more back in your office when you get back from seeing Ling Chen. The uniform looks great, Mike.'

Mike stood in the corridor and Elton locked his office door behind him. He stared at the message, reading it over and over, as the lift arrived, the doors opened, the bell rang, then they closed again with Mike absorbed and uninterested in anything else except the paper in his hand.

'Your behaviour since the separation from your wife has been exemplary and you have observed the rulings of the court. Your former wife has agreed to meet you with your children at a time in the near future. An official from the Hong Kong People's Civil Court will call at your home to arrange the meeting.'

Chapter Eleven

Ling found a change of clothes in her office wardrobe, face creams and a hair dryer. Leonard was comfortingly there outside at the reception desk. She watched him on the monitor as she put the hairbrush on her desk. She shook her hair to let it settle and sat down, feeling secure, less frightened, an Asian executive in a multinational, for the moment not terrified, for the moment not running. Carter would call again and men would arrive to take her to a safe place.

'You leave on United Airlines UA38,' Andrew Carter had told Ling gently. 'The men who come to your office will be absolutely reliable.'

'Yes,' said Ling.

'Do you feel OK?'

'I'm fine,' she answered.

'Good. When they get there go with them. You needn't know their names. They will see you onto the plane. Once there you are, in effect, on American territory and perfectly safe.'

'But do they have the power?'

'Yes. They are from MOFTEC. No one will touch them.'

MOFTEC, The Ministry for Foreign Affairs, Trade and Cooperation. They were the reformists. Everyone in Hong Kong knew it was once a powerful institution, whose urbane, international officials coaxed in enough foreign investment to make China powerful. If MOFTEC wanted something, it was done. But that was before nationalism, before Nim Kai, before Hong Kong had decayed into a playground for corruption.

Leonard, still relaxed, watching a Nepali movie, then turned his head, tensing, getting ready according to his training, when the light came on that people were downstairs in the lift lobby. Ling followed it all in the monitor. They pushed the button and rode up in silence. They were both Chinese. The older one had a receding hairline and wore a suit and open-neck shirt. The other was in dark slacks and a sports shirt. Ling couldn't make out the colours on the black and white screen. They stepped out into the foyer of Prime Coasts. It all seemed fine. She'd told Leonard they were coming. They showed him their cards. He shuffled through the fridge, fixing refreshments, glancing up at the clock as it got close to the end of his shift. They sat in the corner, opposite the aquarium. Leonard handed them drinks. Ling leant against the edge of her desk, about to leave, but not ready yet, not sure. She turned up the voice monitor.

'. . . the Natuna gas fields,' she heard the older one say.

'When was that?

'This morning. I think we're looking for as much support as possible against Vietnam in the Lansha Islands.'

'But the Natuna are worth billions.'

They didn't look like killers. They were relaxed, involved in straightforward foreign trade. No black-market. No security links. Just getting China rich and making sure the world liked her. Andrew Carter had asked them to come. The father of Scott, who had been killed, who was in a dangerous job. A shiver. The inhospitable gusts outside, where she had to go to escape. Ling disciplined her careening mind.

'Could be the biggest marine gas fields the world,' said the older man. He sipped his drink gently. 'But we've been quite clever. Indonesia – Pertamina, and Exxon, the American company, signed a deal on them back in 1994. Thirty-five billion dollars' worth, way before the Asian Friendship Zone was created. Nothing happened because it was disputed territory. Now we say, help us with the Lansha and Vietnam, and we'll give you Natuna. Indonesia will say fine. We'll get a cut of the profits.'

'Not the gas?' The younger man took a long drink and wiped his brow.

'We'll get so much money we can buy all the gas we need. And it's oil we want. You can't fly aircraft on natural gas.'

'Does the Lansha have oil?'

'That, my friend, is the billion dollar question.' He paused and looked at his watch. 'Do you think she's coming out?'

Mike hung back. It began to rain again in puffy squalls which freshened his face, then evaporated into the wind. There was an alleyway at the side of Ling's office building with garbage bags at the entrance, smelling of vegetables and paint. People were sleeping in clumps on the ground, warming each other against the rain. Mike had to step over them to a gap in the fence of a construction site which had fallen silent months ago. It had been an office block, bought and pulled down by a Shanghai company which had run out of money. Drawings at the site were sullied with the erratic changes of weather. The vision of multi-layered swimming pools, gymnasiums, intelligent car parks and security lifts were no more than a futuristic sketch of an ideal which would never happen. Wet weather and sea spray had left a layer of rust on the pile driver. Filthy water splashed back and forth in the craters in the ground. Brown stains streaked down the earth-moving equipment, once bright yellow, now obsolete and abandoned. Mike found his way into the site. He could see through the broken fence to the entrance of Prime Coasts' building and beyond to the traffic flow of a rush hour which was just beginning.

He hung back because the men from MOFTEC had arrived first, Mike had seen them go in and their driver take the car away. He rang Elton on his mobile and told him they were there: 'What's the deal now? If I don't get her, does the Sally offer disappear again?

'Your call,' said Elton. 'You've got to give us Ling's role in all this. What did she do to cause Carter's death? That's the bottom line.'

'If I try to override MOFTEC's game, it'll be all over town.'

'This isn't MOFTEC's town any more,' said Elton. 'Remember who's making the deal with you. Remember with the comrades always focus on what you want to achieve. Nothing else.'

Elton cut the phone. Mike leant up against the fence. Elton sounded irritated. Tired. Bored with the affair so perhaps he had let slip the real reason for Mike to take in Ling. To silence her. To threaten her. Then to throw her out as the cause of Carter's death so the file could be closed.

Mike's weight dislodged a cache of water which slopped down around him. He always loved the monsoon season, when for days and days it would rain so the waterfalls in the hills overflowed and cascaded down. He loved the coolness it brought to the stifling city and the memories of the wet weather of the Scottish autumn, the hot baths, the whisky, the contrast between the weather in the hills and the warmth of the home. Today would be like that. His sleeve was soaked. The wind buffeted the construction site so it rattled like a yachting marina.

The car came back and pulled up outside the building, engine running, air-conditioning on, the driver on the phone looking skywards. The younger man held up a bright red and blue Prime Coasts umbrella, ducking with Ling and guiding her by the elbow into the limousine. The older man followed with just a raincoat, his head hunched into his collar. Mike checked his watch. They had only been up there for twenty minutes. Thirty minutes to the airport, possibly more with the rush hour beginning. That meant ninety minutes before the flight departure. So Ling was checking in just like everyone else.

She concentrated on the window wipers going back and forth. The filthy, monsoonal tropical morning stretched all over the South China Sea. The rain, black with pollution, splashed on the car window. Outside, people, heads lowered against the weather, moved along the waterlogged pavements, stepping to one side to avoid broken paving stones, puddles and overflowing gutters. It tried to get light. But black clouds stayed overhead. Dawn broke. A darkness remained over Hong Kong. She counted the wiper strokes. Her escorts sat on either side. She didn't know their names. They hadn't introduced themselves. The older one said only that Andrew Carter had invited her to a Pacific trade conference in Seattle. At the bottom of the windscreen, just above the bonnet, black grit gathered on both sides. From time to time, the driver blasted it away with a jet of water. A model of Mao Tse-tung hung from his mirror, swinging back and forth as the car slid forward through the traffic. They sat in silence listening to the morning news on Radio Television Hong Kong.

'The statesmanlike generosity of the fourth generation of leadership has solved the pressing question of the Natuna region of the South China Sea . . .'

The whole airport building was glass, rising from the ground, bending at angles to itself until it covered her completely, shimmering, reflecting, deep blue and a swirl of monsoon morning sky. She felt as if she was in a greenhouse. Plants crept around everywhere. At the check-in they hung from the ceiling. On the walkway, splayed across the wall. In the waiting area, more gentle in silver and glass pots. She was in a cocoon. Where there wasn't glass, mirrors or plants there were huge screens with calm authoritative voices: 'The Hong Kong Deng Xiao-ping International Airport was opened on June 30th 1998 to mark the successful and peaceful return of Hong Kong to the Motherland.'

A virtual reality superimposition of Deng Xiao-ping walked down aircraft steps, hand waving, frail but alive.

'The airport was the vision of our paramount second generation leader, Comrade Deng Xiao-ping. In the spirit of reconciliation he insisted that the creation of his concept be shared with the outgoing colonial power. Many Western companies were allowed, under close supervision by our engineers, to partake in the glory of the construction work.'

The younger man brought her a coffee. The older one flicked through the *South China Morning Post*, ignoring most of the news pages and concentrating on the business section, the only part which had remained reliable. 'Indonesian gas shares haven't moved,' he remarked.

'Then it's not going to happen,' replied his younger colleague.

'Strange, though. You would have thought someone would want to make a killing.'

'Too hot to handle.'

'No, it's fine,' said Ling taking a sip of coffee.

The younger man chuckled. 'Sorry, I was talking about a business deal.'

Ling smiled, embarrassed. They both looked at the screen. 'Huge amounts of earth, rock and mud were moved, the equivalent to the volume of 367 Empire State Buildings.' Dumper trucks crossed the sandy wastes of a construction site. Dredging barges spewed water in the background. 'You will have crossed the spectacular one point three mile-long Tsing Ma Bridge, linking the islands of Ma Wan and Tsing Yi. The main span is 4,518 feet. That's 318 feet longer than San Francisco's Golden Gate Bridge.'

'Do people really believe such garbage?' said the younger man idly.

'I used to,' said Ling.

'I think we all did.'

'What irritates me,' said his older companion, 'is the way the Party compares our achievements to American ones. As if it matters.'

'If you're in the superpower game, rubbish your opponents.'

'If only we could have remained the factory of the world.'

The video moved onto graphics, shooting back and forth. It showed how a fishing village of a thousand people had been transformed into a shimmering metallic airport city of two hundred thousand. As the statistics came and went in reds, greens and blue, Ling's flight was called, a drab tickertape of a message, trailing along the bottom of the screen, saying it was thirty minutes before the boarding gate closed.

Higher and shinier buildings blocked the China Traders' Hotel from the waterfront. It was a shabby and discreet place with a worn façade of which the owners were unashamed. The hotel was full and several of its twenty-six floors were permanently rented out to mainland Chinese corporations. The guests who thronged around the vulgar lobby were not the high-flyers of the Asian jet set. They were the foot soldiers of the obsessive quest for wealth, flying in from Thailand, Indonesia and Burma on cheap package deals to pay their respects to the business machine of the Chinese Communist party. As they packed themselves into the lobby that morning, exchanging name cards and cigarettes, Warren Hollingworth wished Li Tuo had chosen a more refined place for them to meet.

He eased his way through and when he reached the lifts more people poured out, with plastic carrier bags, weighed down by gifts for the Party and briefcases bulging with documents of contracts they hoped to be awarded. Wafts of cigarette smoke followed them. Hollingworth held the lift until it cleared then quickly pushed the Door Close button so he was able to travel up alone.

When he stepped out on the fourteenth floor, two men in shabby, green fatigues were in the corridor to meet him. They carried machine pistols and didn't speak. Li Tuo was already in the room, smoking, documents on the desk and a map of Southeast Asia pinned onto the doors of the wardrobe. Bodyguards hung around him. A brandy bottle stood on a coffee table. Weapons lay on chairs. A satellite station ran Cantonese pop videos.

Li Tuo got to his feet and embraced Hollingworth. Then he offered him a drink, but the American refused, instead taking a seat by the window so that the Chinese would have to look straight into the light. Li Tuo spread his hands across the top of the desk. 'Warren, I wanted you to know straight from me, face to face, that we had nothing to do with the Carter killing.'

Hollingworth stayed silent, looking through the gaps between buildings towards the smoggy harbour.

'The Koreans did it,' Li Tuo was saying. 'They're still in a mess after unification. It wasn't us, Warren.' Li Tuo held up his hands and smiled: 'Really.'

Hollingworth shifted himself, but remained leaning back against the window. He would make Li wait for the answer. He didn't speak for some time. Nor did the Chinese security chief. The other men shuffled in their seats. The sound of two foghorns in quick succession broke through from the harbour.

'Whether I believe you or not,' said Hollingworth eventually, 'what was in the documents they were giving to Scott?'

'What did the Koreans tell you?'

'Don't piss with me,' snapped Hollingworth. 'The President's involved. That means this whole fucking baby is getting way out of control.'

Li Tuo had an ability to hold a smile longer than anyone Hollingworth knew. It was an Asian smile, which was a completely different form of expression. In Asia, people laughed at car accidents. They smiled when confronting enemies. It was a nervous, uncertain declaration, but now Li Tuo took away his smile and spoke to Hollingworth like a European would: 'A Korean agent found out what Heshui was really about. He gained access to the wards.'

Li looked towards the guards as a sign that he would not be going into any more detail: 'Korea is still a mess. It's barely a year since the collapse of the North. The northern generals resent troops from the South moving up and taking over their turf. Some of them are crazy enough to dream that we'll send our army in again to win it back for them.'

'You won't?' asked Hollingworth wryly.

Li Tuo laughed: 'Frankly, Warren, we're not happy that such a close American ally has set up military positions just across our border there. And don't give me that crap that American troops aren't there as well. Because we know they are.'

Hollingworth didn't respond. A voice broke into the television music to announce the price rise in a new share issue: 'Anyway,' Li Tuo continued, 'the Koreans believed the Heshui information was so sensitive that it should be delivered straight to the CIA at a place outside of Korea. Not to Seoul. Definitely not anywhere in Pyongyang. A section of the Korean military loyal to the old Northern regime found out about the Hong Kong meeting and sent men in to stop it.'

'Why didn't they just tell you?' said Hollingworth.

'I suspect they wanted to score points with us by doing us a favour. Which they were. Also they resent the slavish contact and reliance the South has on America,' said Li Tuo. 'So if you want to get more play out of finding Scott Carter's killer, I suggest you look for members of the former North Korean 22nd Battle Group of the Reconnaissance Bureau . . .'

'Their special forces,' said Hollingworth.

'Correct.'

'Which brings me back to my first question,' said Li Tuo. 'What are the Koreans saying?'

'Nothing,' said Hollingworth. 'They've closed up completely.'

Another foghorn burst out through the harbour and black rainclouds came down over the Kowloon hills, the first of the morning. A Chinese helicopter flew in from the west towards the military headquarters on the harbour front.

'I understand you have had trouble with Clem Watkins?'

Hollingworth nodded: 'The day you told me, I ordered him out. But he sensed something was wrong. Maybe he's found out the same as the Korean agent. He's missing.'

'We spotted him in Beijing that evening,' said Li Tuo without looking at Hollingworth. 'He escaped.'

Hollingworth didn't ask because he knew that would have been an attempt on Clem's life. He loathed the contradictions of China where trade competed so starkly with ideology. The clashing beacons of human rights and money cared nothing for the details. Historians would look back on the late twentieth century as a grave march of folly. After two world wars with Germany and the Cold War with the Soviet Union, another monster was being coaxed into the ring, but this time with the active help of the Free World, with the help of men like him, who years ago had been drawn across a line and had no way back. Hollingworth hankered for the moral clarity of his beloved Cold War.

'We're moving the central operation out of Heshui,' said Li Tuo. 'It's too exposed there. Too many people are getting to know about it.'

'Makes sense,' said Hollingworth.

'I'm telling you so you can explain the military activities away on your satellite photographs.'

Hollingworth remembered Li's last words to him on Liberation night. They were in the street. The flags were changed. The taxi drivers tied red streamers to their aerials. The five stars rising hung from the tenements. Democracy activists burnt candles on the balcony of the Legislative Council building then went home with no stomach for a real fight. Li and Hollingworth had walked to the waterfront, ignoring the smell of the harbour, concentrating instead on the reflection of the lights in the water, lights which didn't bother to show up the filth and gave the city the glitter it needed.

'I am the most powerful man here now.' Li had stared at him. Eyes straight, quite clear, no smile. No joke. No body language. Nothing. It wasn't a boast. It was a message.

Chapter Twelve

'Carter's murder is creating a mess which could interfere with everything,' said Li Tuo.

'Like I said, the President's involved,' said Hollingworth quietly.

'I know, and Carter's father is crying for blood.'

'And President Kang is due in Washington this month,' added Hollingworth.

Li Tuo looked up at the television and called a bodyguard over to fill up his glass with more brandy: 'But I think we have a way out. Ling Chen is on her way to the airport. Carter has got her a ticket to the States. The British policeman McKillop has been sent down to intercept her and bring her in for questioning over Scott's death.'

'To achieve what?' said Hollingworth.

'Who is this girl, Warren?' said Li Tuo avoiding a direct answer. 'Who is she working for? You? Us? Herself?' Li Tuo opened a drawer in his desk, took out a transparent plastic folder and gave it to a guard who handed it on to Hollingworth.

'Keep it,' continued Li Tuo. 'It's a précis of her background.' He took his own copy out of the drawer, flicked through the sheets of paper and stabbed his finger as he spoke, highlighting the main points: 'Comes from a prominent Party family. Her mother's alive and lives with her older brother and his wife. The file says her father's died from cancer. But in the Nineties he got involved with an intellectual group wanting grass roots reform and ended up in a labour camp. He was a middle ranking official in the Ministry of Agriculture who got too close to disgruntled farmers. The family have been told to keep quiet. Ling doesn't know about it.

'After school she did three years of military training. She was a star, handling small arms, unarmed combat, even parachuting. She was asked to join one of the elite infantry units, but went to Beijing People's University instead. Did well in economics and international politics. Slept around a bit, but nothing abnormal.

One of her lovers was Tony Zhang who's now a personal adviser to the President. No record of them keeping in touch. She went on to get an MBA scholarship to Yale, came back to Beijing, messed around with a couple of joint-ventures and ended up with Prime Coasts.'

'What's that?'

'Looks like a regular property development company. Golf courses and resorts in Southern China. Looks like a concern which wouldn't interest a woman like Ling Chen unless it was into something else.'

'But pays well?' said Hollingworth.

Li Tuo nodded, dropped the papers onto the desk and pushed his chair back. 'So where does she fit in, Warren?'

'Maybe she's just a career girl whose boyfriend's been murdered.'

'Before moving she did the Travel Orientation Course,' Li Tuo went on. 'A lot of people don't any more, and we don't force them. Too many lied in the debriefings and the information was useless. But she did it, which means that every time she goes back to Beijing she has to report in.' He held up another folder. 'She's done a lot. All accurate stuff. Nothing to kill for, if you'll excuse me, but good solid information.'

Li Tuo stopped talking. Hollingworth waited, watching a man and a woman on television, singing through mobile phones to each other, one on a motorcycle and one in a Mercedes coupé convertible.

'She's not one of yours is she, Warren?' asked the Chinese security chief softly.

Hollingworth shook his head. 'And I didn't order Scott Carter to seduce her.'

'Or the British?'

'Ask Cranley, but I expect he would be more agitated if she was.'

Li Tuo stood up nodding. He walked over to Hollingworth and rested his arm on the American's shoulder. 'We can use Ling Chen either way. The girlfriend who left Scott Carter and drove him to suicide through love. Or the Chinese agent who seduced an American diplomat and drove him to suicide through guilt. Or if that fails we can pin a murder charge on her.'

Li brushed away cigarette ash which had fallen onto his lapel:. 'McKillop will carry out the interrogation to give it credibility. The American people will trust a white face.'

'What does McKillop know?'

'Absolutely nothing. He's got instructions to carry out a straight-forward murder inquiry. We've promised him a meeting with his family if he handles this one well. The man's desperate. Miserable, lonely. Drinks. He will not be a problem.'

'Desperate men are always problems,' muttered Hollingworth.

'You and a couple of others should be there for the questioning to cover us. I've asked Cranley to send one of his men along.'

'That way we're covered,' said Hollingworth sarcastically.

Li nodded: 'And Tommy Lai will be in the listening room.'

'And Carter?'

'He wants to know why his son died. Let's give him a reason he'll be able to live with.'

Li Tuo's eyes shifted quickly from the harbour to Hollingworth, never settling or looking straight at him. They were brown, dark and unfathomable just like in the photographs and films Hollingworth had studied so often and for so long.

'The whole Carter thing could be settled by tonight and we can concentrate on what we really set out to achieve.'

'Go on,' said Hollingworth, resting on the window sill.

Li moved over to the map. 'You probably heard that we have come to an agreement with the Indonesians over the Natuna gas fields.'

'On the news this morning.'

'Greater China is expanding, Warren. Natuna means that Indonesia now accepts us and if we have Indonesia we have control of the sea lanes to the Pacific without a shot being fired.' He looked up at one of his guards who held out an ashtray for him to stub out his cigarette. 'What will America do?'

'We advocate trade being the cornerstone of foreign policy. A commercial agreement has been signed, that is all,' said Hollingworth.

Li Tuo laughed. 'That's why I like you, Warren. You are a pragmatist.'

'The alternative to the pro-China movement in Indonesia is Muslim fundamentalism, parading under a banner of nationalism,' Hollingworth continued, knowing that even in this sordid and secret hotel room he was delivering an official message from the American government to one of the most powerful men in China. 'Your record in dealing with Islamic movements in Central Asia reassures us that Indonesia will not become yet another Islamic rogue state we might have to handle.'

The guard lit another cigarette for Li, who took a long drag, inhaling deeply, and then blew out the smoke through his mouth and nostrils. 'Your Congress is still pushing us on human rights.'

Hollingworth shrugged, bored with a discussion which was repeated around China every day. Li was speaking in English and Hollingworth wondered how much of this the guards understood. His fingertips played restlessly along the sill. He felt tired, the familiar fatigue which enveloped him in a situation of insoluble choices.

Li Tuo edged over to him. Aftershave, tobacco, brandy, sweat dried into the uniform. He placed his hand on the window sill, less than an inch from Hollingworth's. 'We've got a big contract to sell our new medium-range missile to Indonesia. It's part of the Natuna deal.'

Li moved away a bit, smoothed down the lapels of his jacket and stubbed his cigarette underneath his foot. The room was clogged with cigarette smoke. Hollingworth and Li Tuo were standing. The rest sat, even the guard by the door, his leg hooked over the arm of a chair, watching the television.

'The missile was created at Heshui.'

'If you're talking about the East Wind 33,' queried Hollingworth, 'I've seen nothing which we could even think of as being a break-through. Our own American advances have outpaced anything at Heshui.'

'You think we would tell your government?' Li signalled to a soldier, who pulled himself to his feet and carried over an ashtray for the security chief's cigarette. Li drew deeply, stubbed out the cigarette, then exhaled, not bothering to avoid Hollingworth. The smoke mixed with foul breath wrapped around Hollingworth's face and dispersed.

Li handed him another transparent plastic folder. Inside were scanned copies which Hollingworth recognised as Clem Watkins's reports from Heshui. Watkins' name was there together with Chinese scientists'. Hollingworth leafed backwards. A report on the first of every month. For the past four years, Clem Watkins and Martin Hewlitt had chronicled the discovery, the development, the testing of submarine-launched missile delivery systems. The last test had been carried out from the headquarters of the Northern Fleet at Tsing Dao on 22 December, four months earlier, on the birthday of Mao Tse-tung.

Li looked towards Hollingworth. 'They're false,' said the Chinese bluntly.

Hollingworth shook his head. 'The test results?'

'No. Everything. It's what we gave Watkins, Hewlitt and whoever was before them. It's what's believed in America.'

'And Beijing?'

Li pulled up a chair by the desk and sat down. 'Beijing is not such a unified institution as Washington. We differ over our vision of the Chinese dream.'

'President Kang is unaware?'

Li Tuo ignored the question. 'When the missile deal is announced, there will be a flutter of an international crisis. The Indonesian high command will make a statement about the superior quality of our missiles. Your personal shareholding will rise rapidly and could end up worth seven hundred and fifty million US dollars. You will sell on the Chengdu and Shanghai stock exchanges a week after the news is released. It will be untraceable. Buyers will be plentiful.' Li put his elbows on the desk and rested his chin on them. 'Then, Warren, you and I will be very rich men.'

McKillop ran his fingers through his hair and flattened it to tidy himself up. He had forgotten a comb. The rain had left smudges down the front of his uniform. The bottoms of his trouserlegs were damp after a hotel limousine had driven too fast outside the airport terminal and splashed him. He had taken a chair at the back of the immigration office. Work went on around him. They ignored his presence, yet respected his high security clearance. He watched Ling on monitors, then as she approached the immigration counter he saw her clearly for the first time through a two-way mirror.

She couldn't conceal her nervousness, although she moved confidently under the protection of her MOFTEC escorts. Her eyes scouted out her surroundings as much in curiosity, it seemed, as in fear of danger. There was nothing about her which suggested cruelty or deception. She hailed from the cosmopolitan world of high commerce, had been raised on the values of the one-party state and had now inadvertently tiptoed back into the underbelly of her society.

But all Mike saw was an innocent and he wondered what Joss McEwan would have done. Whether he would have crossed this line as Mike was about to. Ling Chen was inches from the free world and Mike McKillop was about to drag her back just so he could see his wife again. Sick, said Elton. Yes it was.

The younger man from MOFTEC pushed his pass onto the counter on top of Ling's passport. Mike turned up the audio channel and heard the official explain, as planned, about a security alert. The special pass was invalidated.

'You could probably get in in about half an hour's time,' offered the immigration official. 'That's how long these things usually take.'

'The flight will be gone by then,' said the young MOFTEC man.

'We should have gone through earlier,' said Ling.

The immigration official shrugged. 'You never know when these things will happen.' He handed back the MOFTEC card. 'There's been a spate of illegal immigrants stowing away in the cargo holds of planes. Some racket they want to break.' He smiled, gave the card back and flipped open Ling's passport.

A queue was forming at the counter. A family of Thais, too impatient to wait, bundled themselves over to another line. The immigration official ran Ling's passport through the scanner. 'Will you still be going through, Miss Chen?'

Ling hesitated and looked around for an answer. Her young MOFTEC escort asked to see the senior official, but the older one stepped forward and touched him on the elbow. 'I think she'll be all right,' he said softly. He looked at Ling who shifted her shoulder bag so she could slip her passport back into the side pocket. The schedule screen in front of her showed the United Airways flight was boarding. Images of Deng Xiao-ping were shown underneath the orange data. Above that a hologram of the dead Chinese leader curved through the glass roof which changed colours as rainclouds blocked and unblocked the fierce spring sunlight.

'If you're confident it's OK, I'll go through,' said Ling.

Mike tracked her on the monitors through the hand baggage security check. A pen and a silver lucky charm set off the metal detector alarm. A security official swept a hand detector around her body while she stood, legs astride, arms stretched out like a bored international traveller. It was that look which reminded him of Sally, when the whole face appeared resentful of what was going on around. Sally adopted it in situations she didn't like or didn't know how to handle.

Two patrolling police commandos, in dark blue short-sleeved uniforms and chewing gum, walked in between Ling and the Duty Free Shoppers' emporium.

Mike arrived through a security door at the end of the concourse. He stayed right at the back of the boarding hall, positioning himself so that he had a line of sight into the airbridge and the cabin of the aircraft. He saw Tommy Lai just inside the plane. He was in a dark suit, hardly distinguishable from the steward who glanced at boarding passes and guided passengers to their seats.

Ling stopped just before the gate to rearrange her bag, pushing the magazines down inside. She knelt to re-tie the laces of her sports shoes. Thoughts of escape raced through Mike's mind. That she would make a run for it. He looked for ways out for her, hoping she would get out before he took over. But she couldn't. There was nowhere to go. And the Party would make sure she would be picked up with the minimum of fuss because airports were dangerous places: too public and too international to fall completely under anyone's control.

Ling walked past the queue of economy class passengers and showed her business class boarding pass.

The hostess asked for her passport and Ling had it out straight away, opening it to the back page for them to cross-reference her identity. The flight supervisor came and looked at the documents. He flicked through the pages of the passport and Ling showed him the multiple re-entry American visa which she had kept going since Yale. Tommy Lai came out from the plane and walked to the bottom of the escalator which came down to the boarding hall.

The supervisor smiled: 'We've had a message from our check-in desk about you, Miss Chen,' he said.

'What about?' asked Ling. She still didn't show any agitation.

The supervisor laughed: 'They haven't said yet. But whenever this happens my guess is that they've overbooked in business and are getting clearance to upgrade you to first. I know there are a couple of seats still available up there.'

Through the terminal window, Mike looked at the fuselage and tail of the airliner. The markings represented the developed world, a symbol of safety and freedom, suddenly appearing so close for Ling. Smells came down from the fuselage of new seats, scented air-conditioning and food being prepared for microwave. There was innocuous music and all around the bustle of travellers, disorganised with too many bags and too little space, and the repeated double click of the machine which took in their boarding passes, cut them in two and threw out one half, which was their signal to board.

'If you could stand just over there, Miss Chen,' the supervisor was saying, his hand gently on her waist guiding her away from the airbridge.

103

It was then Mike saw her panic. Adrenalin rushed through him; that within seconds he would be drawn into the plan to frame her. He walked from the back of the hall, through straggling passengers. Ling saw him and turned away, looking only through the window towards the aircraft. He wanted to say: *It's OK, get on. I'll make sure no one stops you.* But instead, he felt her tremble as he approached her and tapped her on the shoulder from behind.

'I'm Superintendent Mike McKillop. We spoke briefly a few days ago after Scott was killed,' said Mike softly. 'And I suggested you talk to Tom Elton.'

Ling nodded. 'Has this got to do with my not getting on the flight?' she said, looking at him with eyes which both accused and pleaded.

'We got a message about twenty minutes ago from Andrew Carter,' Mike lied. 'He is very keen to find exactly why and how Scott died. There has been an attempt on your life and you may have seen the killer in Scott's apartment. Mr Carter asked us to talk to you before you joined him in the States.'

As he spoke, Mike took out a name card, embossed with the emblem of the Hong Kong Police Force and handed it to Ling. 'It'll only take a few hours, I expect, and then we'll put you on the next flight out. Your escorts from MOFTEC are now fully informed and we're in touch with Mr Carter.'

They drove back the way she had come. The radio was tuned to a programme on economic growth among the minority tribes in Yunnan province. She was in the back with McKillop. The windows were darkened and she saw the driver's eyes watching her in his mirror.

'Sorry about this,' said Mike. 'Something's cropped up and we want to get to the bottom of what happened.'

Ling gazed out of the window, her right hand resting near the handle lock, fiddling nervously with it.

'He wouldn't kill himself,' she said softly.

The car came out of the Western harbour tunnel on auto-toll so it didn't have to stop and they turned right away from Central, following the coast around, past old houses on the cliff sides bought or built with refugee money from China half a century ago; then winding down into Liu Huaqing Bay and the new money with its arrogant, bright apartment blocks and views across the brilliant blue waters and green, barren hillocks which reminded

Mike so much of Scotland. The weather was clearing and the driver turned off the wipers.

'Someone tried to kill me, too. In my apartment.'

'I know, I know,' said Mike sympathetically. 'That's why we need to talk to you.'

They turned right onto the Shek O peninsula. Two long white pleasure yachts were anchored off the coast. In the respite between storms, a water-skier took advantage of the flat sea.

The houses were Mediterranean in style, with sprawling roof terraces and high wrought iron gates. Dogs barked behind them and Filipina servants with buckets cleaned cars. They turned into a compound and Ling saw the barrel of a sub machine gun carried by the guard who opened the gate. The cars inside had both Hong Kong and Chinese number plates. Two BMWs were prefixed by WJ, the initials of the People's Armed Police, the keepers of Party policy everywhere in Greater China.

Mike took Ling up to the roof with views of two beaches and a dry warm wind blowing across the peninsula. He poured her some orange juice and let her drink it pensively, then showed her down to the second-floor room, where French windows were thrown open letting in the noises of music and people from the street below. He left her there, saying he would be back in a minute and as he was stepping out towards the listening room at the back of the house, his phone went off, vibrating without sound so no one else need know.

It was Clem. But Mike couldn't speak. He rang off.

Chapter Thirteen

After picking up the Chrysler and passing by the Santa Monica complex, Clem headed for Martin Hewlitt's house. He'd been there before, a neighbourhood of quiet streets, children on bicycles and skateboards, well-kept gardens and lawns stretching back to homes more than houses. Clem made that distinction because this particular strand of American life-style had always eluded him, yet it so efficiently encapsulated all he was fighting to protect. He had remembered Martin's house as brilliant white with huge front windows on each side of the door and hanging baskets filled with trailing honeysuckle outside. The curtains fell in crumpled waves over the windows. This was Joyce's creation: intelligent, level-headed, loyal and beautiful. The furniture in the living room was covered with family photographs of Martin, Joyce and his two daughters, Samantha and Nancy, and their grandparents.

When Clem first went round, Joyce had asked him to stay to dinner. But he felt uneasy, in such an ordered household. Instead, she had brought them coffee, and he talked with Martin in the back yard near the basketball net, telling the girls to stay away and play out the front.

Martin had hated Heshui. But he would have stuck it out for the full term, because he needed the money to pay off his loans. It was when they started blocking his E-mails to Joyce he had asked to leave.

'No one knows what our role is there,' he told Clem. 'Are we meant to be spying on them? Helping them? Are they an ally? Or an enemy? You go ask anyone in Washington in our business, Clem, for an official line and they won't tell you.'

Hewlitt had been right on that. He was more politically in tune with the CIA than Clem would ever be. 'Most of them don't even know Heshui exists. Have you seen the circulation restrictions on it? The smallest I've ever come across.'

Clem admired Martin for his decision to go home. Yet he had

left that afternoon excited to be off to China. Those who protected the American dream were not necessarily those in tune with it. If Clem had been ill at ease with the environment Martin and Joyce had created, then a place like Heshui would suit him.

Now, a year later, Clem turned right into the Hewlitts' road.

Suddenly, he had to brake, throwing himself forward so that his seatbelt locked. A white tape cordon was strung between two trees across the road. The flashing orange lights of police cars and fire engines were up ahead. A cluster of local people stood on the left sidewalk. A sheriff's deputy walked over to Clem, gesticulating with his hands that he should turn round.

'You visiting someone in the street?' he said. He glanced at the number plate but didn't reach for any pad to note it down.

'Only taking a short cut,' said Clem. 'I'll back right on up and get out of your way.' Sirens screamed behind him and two ambulances turned into the street blocking his exit. Four paramedics jumped out. The deputy shouted for them to run up ahead.

'You'd better wait until they're through,' said the deputy. 'Or we'll get one hell of a traffic mess here.'

'What you got, a fire?' said Clem. He sounded more polite than interested.

'Deliberate, by the looks of it.'

'Nasty,' said Clem.

'Seems like a woman went crazy and burnt down her own house.'

'What was she so pissed about?'

'Life's been a bitch to her,' said the deputy shielding his eyes from the sun. 'Her husband killed in a car accident a few days back. Worked for the government. She must be real distraught.'

The figure being brought down to the ambulances was struggling wildly. Paramedics controlled her as best they could, holding her firmly by the shoulders. Clem knew it was Joyce. She was angry, but not deranged and when she saw the group of onlookers on the pavement, then Clem's car, she quietened realising that the public were watching. She recognised one of the women there and shouted out: 'Carol, can you call Michael Strutt, our lawyer, and tell him what's happening? Remember you met him at dinner at our place about six months ago?' They were moving her along as she spoke. She was crying, too. 'Sam and Nancy are next door with Margaret, so they're fine.' She was at the ambulance and they let her get in herself, her hands handcuffed behind her, her clothes smudged with black ash.

107

The ambulance backed up. The deputy held up two cars which were coming down the road at the junction, then he banged gently on the roof of the Chrysler and leaned down: 'All clear to go, sir.'

'Was she going to hospital or a police station?' said Clem as he put the car into reverse.

The deputy shrugged: 'What pisses me about this is that the FBI have taken it over. The guy being in government and everything. They've ruled it out of our jurisdiction.'

Clem gave it three hours, then went back approaching from the other end of the street so, if challenged, he could say he was taking the same short cut back. The tape had been removed and only the wreck of the house itself was cordoned off. The fire had destroyed everything, leaving only a charred shell. Books, toys, pictures and cutlery were strewn about the garden. Clem drove slowly, and it wasn't until he was nearly beyond the house that he saw there were dog handlers in the garden in uniforms with the same logo as the guards now outside of Geotech. No one else was there. The house of Martin and Joyce Hewlitt had been burned to the ground and sealed off.

He found a motel along the coast and had to pay an extra twenty dollars to get a room with a direct line. The girl at the check-in counter could have been no more than eighteen. She had her feet up on the desk with the room prices written on the soles of her shoes, facing straight at the door, in bright red felt-tipped pen. The right shoe was with air-conditioning. The left shoe was without. Clem Watkins had to laugh.

'Is that just the price of the rooms?' He quipped taking out his wallet.

The girl chewed gum and leant over to turn up the radio.

'Write your name in the book,' she said. Clem was using Matt Simons and he planned to get rid of the car in the morning and buy another one, probably fifty or so miles further on, just south of San Francisco.

'Are you going to do it, or can't you write?' said the girl. She flicked back strands of blond hair which had fallen over her face. Clem noticed dark brown or black at the roots. Soon she would have to get it dyed again. It had been a long, bad day for both of them, perhaps. He was running. Probably she was too. Clem pressed a hundred-dollar bill into her hand and closed her fingers around it.

He let himself into the room and called Mike. But Mike hung up.

McKillop committed Clem's number to memory, then went down to the listening room at the back of the house. It was a tiny space, designed only for a washing machine which had been removed and a sink which had a single dripping cold water tap. Tommy Lai had set up screens and keyboards on tables as best he could, and rigged up monitors above them for the five cameras in the interview room. A bench was pushed against the other wall. There was no air-conditioning, so the door was ajar.

'Welcome to our humble command HQ,' Tommy Lai said with a grin. 'We did Henry Druk here, remember, Mike?' McKillop nodded. 'You'd have thought we might have spent a bit more on it by now,' Tommy continued.

'You must have inherited stinginess from the British,' quipped Mike, wiping his face free of sweat which had gathered as soon as he stepped into the room.

'We're recommending you for charmer of the year, the way you got her out of the airport,' said Tommy.

A young man with a receding hairline sprang up from the bench: 'Jeremy Haskins from the British Consulate. Only sent to listen, not interfere,' he said quickly, shaking Mike's hand.

'Can you take notes?' said Mike. Jeremy nodded enthusiastically. 'This stuff takes so long to unravel,' Mike continued. 'Do it like minutes, so I can digest it straight afterward.'

Tommy Lai held out an A4-sized brown envelope. 'A letter came hand-delivered,' he said.

Mike could make out Tom Elton's erratic handwriting on the envelope, which was stiff with reinforcing cardboard.

'Just a couple of things our foot soldiers have picked up,' continued Tommy. 'Apparently she was overheard at the party saying she was off to see her boyfriend at the Emperor. And a neighbour on Lantau saw her coming home around two thirty in the morning.'

'So you're saying . . .'

'Nothing, Mike,' said Tommy. 'Just passing it on. I'll get the written notes if they come in on time.'

The back door opened and Warren Hollingworth came in. Mike made out two, possibly three other white faces behind him. Hollingworth shut the door on them.

'Superintendent McKillop,' said Hollingworth, introducing himself. 'You are aware that this is happening on the specific request of President Zuckerman.'

'What does the President want to achieve?' said Mike softly.

'What you want to achieve, Superintendent,' snapped back Hollingworth, 'is either to get a watertight alibi or a confession.'

'If it's murder she's our only suspect,' contributed Tommy Lai, his hands on the keyboards running through the software systems. 'According to our records, she has been through a rigid Communist Party education. Her parents belonged to the highest echelons of the Party. Her schoolmates are now working in the inner circle of government.'

'Are you saying . . .' began Mike.

But Hollingworth was ready for the question: 'Apart from myself and the Korean diplomat now dead, she was the only person who might have known Scott would be in that hotel room. We have to establish if Ling Chen had any motive whatsoever to kill Scott Carter.'

'I'm getting some fresh air,' said McKillop, making his dislike for Hollingworth plain. 'I need to clear my head before things start.'

'When did you last do one, Superintendent?' said Hollingworth.

'Mike and I broke some of the finest gangsters in Asia in this house,' said Tommy Lai.

Mike walked into the compound. The Americans were standing near the railings, but hidden from the road. Chinese guards hung around. Mike found a space behind a white Lexus. As soon as he opened the envelope from Elton and saw the photograph, he was thrown back into the past when he lived with his family around him. Here was Elton's reminder as to why he had brought Ling in, a reminder not to waver from his task.

The picture had been enlarged. Matthew and Charlotte were much younger at Waterworld during a hot summer long ago. They were all smiling. Mike and Sally held hands and she was stunning in a one-piece pink floral swimsuit. The short hair which had been the subject of so many little arguments looked fantastic, accentuating her long, beautiful neck. Mike looked good, too. Even then well over thirty, no flab, flat stomach and shoulders, arms, stature all evidence of a man both fit and filled with confidence. Charlotte, in her tiny, dripping bathing suit, clung to her father's back, a huge grin on her face. Matthew bounced a beach ball.

Elton had signed it expansively on the back: 'Good luck.'

*　　*　　*

'They found Ling Chen and she was safe,' Carter began without any preamble.

President Donald Zuckerman stood behind him, a hand on his friend's shoulder.'She was Scott's girlfriend, right?'

Carter nodded. Zuckerman walked over to the drinks cabinet and poured a brandy for Carter and a mineral water for himself. Among the photographs around the room was one of Carter and Zuckerman after a golf game at Camp David, five years earlier in the first hundred days of his presidency. 'Have to get us a new one, Andrew,' said Zuckerman, indicating towards the picture. Both men were younger, both now showing the strain of power.

'At least we'll make it a different golf course,' said Carter, managing a smile. He swirled the brandy in the glass but didn't drink it.

Andrew Carter had arrived at the White House without an appointment and waited only fifteen minutes to see the President. Visitors to the famous presidential office often found the room smaller than they had imagined and out of proportion with the awe it commanded. But Carter was far from being a first-time guest. He had been with Zuckerman when they stepped inside after the first election victory and this time, as soon as he was shown in, the President called through to his secretary to hold all further appointments.

'A pathologist from the Consulate is doing another post-mortem, then they're releasing the body,' said Carter. He drew his hands down his face, ignoring the protocol of a presidential audience. 'We're planning a small funeral early next week,' he added.

Zuckerman sat down across from the coffee table. 'Would Jane and I be welcome?'

'Of course,' said Carter, making no effort to hide his grief. He put the brandy glass on the table and slapped the arm of the chair. 'I'm sorry, Donald, barging in like this.'

Zuckerman waved his hand dismissively: 'Don't mention. You and Susan have been good friends for far more years than we've both been rich and famous. Scott's death is a tragedy.'

'I appreciate your thoughts, Donald,' said Carter. He paused, then continued: 'But I'm not just here for the sympathy. The pathologist in Hong Kong who did Scott's autopsy called my head office switchboard this morning, out of the blue, looking for me. Eventually he was put through to my secretary. The upshot is that the Hong Kong authorities changed his original report.'

Carter took two sheets of folded paper out of his top pocket and gave them to Zuckerman: 'After the call he faxed these over. He found bruises to the carotid arteries, indicating that Scott had been killed before being dropped from the hotel roof.'

Zuckerman scanned the faxes: 'Why's he talking?'

'It could be justice. Could be professional pride.' Carter now brought a small tape recorder out of his jacket pocket and put it on the table. 'Listen to this.' He turned on the tape.

'Tell Mr Carter that the Communist Party killed his son,' Joss McEwan was saying on the long-distance call. 'If he finds out who controls the system, he has the murderer.' Carter switched it off.

'Who in the hell is he?' said Zuckerman.

'His name's Joss McEwan. My secretary checked that he's listed in the Hong Kong Government directory. Except, she then rang the number for him and was told he no longer worked in Hong Kong. Apparently, he was calling from Scotland.'

'And your conclusion?'

Carter leant forward in the chair to pick up his brandy glass. But his hand was shaking with tension and anger. So he left it on the table. 'Hollingworth believes Scott was killed by his own girlfriend? He made a point of telling me that she had been to all the Party training institutions. They wanted to pull her off the plane before she got over here to me.'

'But why . . .'

'Don, I don't know and I wish I did.' Carter gripped the arm of the chair with his right hand to control his fury. 'I want whoever killed my son brought to justice. I'd be happy to shoot them myself. But there's more at stake than Scott's death. I'm here as a warning bell, Don, that you've got big problems with the Chinese government, yet you've got the Chinese president coming over any day now.'

The intercom sounded on the President's desk and his secretary's voice came through it clearly: 'The National Security Adviser is requesting an urgent meeting,' she said, with a confidence which made no apology for the interruption and which anticipated an acceptance.

'Send him through,' shouted Zuckerman across the room.

The door opened and Peter Mackland came in hurriedly. He was an awkward but highly intelligent man, with few social graces, overweight and wearing an expensive but ill-fitting suit. His blue shirt was crumpled and untucked and as he walked across towards Zuckerman he held a sheaf of papers in his left hand and tried to tidy himself with his right. It was more a ritual of respect for the presidential office than an action in which anything would be achieved. 'I'm sorry to disturb you, Mr President,' he began, and then stopped when he noticed Andrew Carter on the sofa.

'It's OK, Peter. If it won't take long. I'll ask Andrew to wait outside.'

Following Zuckerman's lead, Mackland sat down in the comfortable suite around the coffee table. 'There's been an announcement of a gas drilling and exploration deal between China and Indonesia on the Natuna fields,' he began. 'Until a few hours ago, it was disputed territory, what we called a flashpoint. Now it means Indonesia has finally accepted China's role as the Asian superpower. That's step one. Step two is that in the next hour or so, both governments are to announce the sale of China's new long-range ballistic East Wind 33 missile to Indonesia. There are two versions: land-launched and the more dangerous submarine-launched. Indonesia is buying both.'

Zuckerman stayed silent so Mackland carried on: 'Unconfirmed intelligence reports coming in through our station in Hong Kong say that the missile guidance system is better than anything we have. Apparently the Chinese have designed it for themselves.'

'Or bought it from the Russians,' suggested Zuckerman.

'The Russians don't have anything that good either. We don't know how accurate this information is, but the fact that Hong Kong ranks it enough to report back is significant. I'm passing it to you because you need to be alerted of China's new military dimension in the Pacific – albeit a subtle one.' Mackland looked down to his papers, shuffling through them to find the appropriate one. 'Especially, given the . . .'

'. . . upcoming visit of Kang Guo-feng,' finished Zuckerman. The President got up and walked over to his favourite spot just between his desk and the window, where he could see glimpses of the society whose values he had sworn to protect. Traffic and people moved in the distance like a faraway stage play, while the President was the cramped, uncomfortable spectator in a seat with the view restricted, hardly able to hear yet desperately trying to anticipate the plot.

'How good's this new missile?' Zuckerman asked bluntly.

'It hasn't been tested much. Their navy is still twenty or thirty years behind ours. Their submarine capability is dismal. It's not a direct military threat, but it does pose the problem of technology catching up which has to put us on our guard.'

'And what's the political danger?'

'China has succeeded in wresting away Indonesia as one of our main allies in the Pacific. Indonesia used to look to us for support in neutralising first Communism then Islamic fundamentalism, nationalism and all that. But we're refusing to sell them weapons because of human rights abuses so China's done a deal to get them into its camp.'

'Indonesia has a fairly nasty government, Peter.'

'I don't judge those things, Mr President. My job is to balance power.'

Zuckerman moved away from the window, read the document briefly then dropped it onto the coffee table. He sat down heavily: 'The television networks might not think a gas deal's sexy enough, but a new super Chinese missile . . .

'Do you mind if I get some instant public mood advice on this?' said the President.

Mackland nodded: 'The announcement's imminent anyway.'

Zuckerman called Carter back in. 'Andrew, the CIA is telling me China has a new missile which threatens America and that it's stealing one of our most powerful allies in the Pacific.'

'We think it's a new thermal-imaging device,' Mackland added looking at Carter. 'So if they wanted to send their missile through that pane of glass,' he pointed to a section of the Oval Office window, 'technically they could.'

'You got that, Andrew? What will America want me to do?'

Anger and fatigue swept through Carter. Flashes of hindsight came to him, contradictory questions of how his government, how the President, how he himself could ever have dealt so closely with such a blatantly non-democratic, one-party state. Yet he knew it should be no surprise because it happened all the time, except usually the consequences were not so personal. Carter put his glass on the table, clasped his hands. He shook his head. His bottom lip was quivering. He needed sleep. He wanted to get back to Susan. He wanted her with him at the airport when Scott's body arrived. He needed the family. He would arrange a funeral befitting both the mourning and the celebration of Scott's short life. He wanted to show China that it could not murder his son and get away with it.

'Americans do not want to be blown up by Chinese missiles, Mr President,' he said. 'I think that is your bottom line. Everything else is detail.'

Chapter Fourteen

'I know you've been through it once before,' said Mike softly. 'But let's just run over it again.'

Mike was standing and leaning down to talk to Ling. 'We have to know about your relationship with Scott. We can't just let it go.'

Like Scott, McKillop was from an arrogant race. When she answered him, he remained expressionless. When she became frightened, close to tears, he withdrew from the room, and the others followed. They left her alone. She stood by the French windows looking out over the small lawn to the walled garden and the trees in it. They had brought her to a nice place where she could hear the sea in the distance. Not a cell. No naked lightbulb. No bars. No good-cop-bad-cop routine. They let her hold back her tears. Retain her pride. Then they came back in and started again.

'The night Scott was killed you were at a buffet supper with a friend?'

Ling nodded.

'Who was she?'

'Alice. Alice Ventura.'

'From Sacramento, right?'

Ling nodded.

'You say Scott did talk to you before his meeting?'

'Yes,' she said.

'Yet you tell us you didn't know where he was and had no idea what he was doing.'

'I told you. He just said he would be late . . .'

'He cancelled a dinner date so you went to the supper instead.'

'I've told you already.'

'OK, but you say Scott's usually reliable. So didn't he make an arrangement to meet you somewhere?'

'Back at his flat.'

'Time?'

'It was loose.'

'I'm sorry to put this to you, Ling,' McKillop said, 'but one of the guests at Alice's party heard you saying you were going to meet your boyfriend in the lobby of the Emperor Hotel just after midnight.'

Ling stiffened. She had never said that. She had never named the hotel.

'That's a lie,' she answered.

'That he had a ten o'clock meeting . . .'

'It's not true,' she shouted. 'You're trying to . . .'

'Which ferry did you catch?'

'What?'

'What time was the ferry you took to Lantau.'

'Midnight.'

'You have a ticket to prove it?'

'No. I have a season ticket.'

'And to get from the jetty to your apartment takes how long?'

'Ten, fifteen minutes.'

'Then why did the villagers not hear you coming back until well after two in the morning? Are you sure it wasn't the one o'clock ferry?'

Ling looked straight at McKillop, but he wouldn't meet her eyes. 'It was the midnight ferry,' she said firmly.

'Fine,' said Mike. 'We'll check that up further. Witnesses can be so unreliable at times.'

She ate lunch alone in the room from take-away boxes brought in from a restaurant in the village. Then they came back. Mike poured her an orange juice. 'Tell us about your links with the Communist Party,' he began.

'Why? I don't see what that's got to do with Scott's death.'

'He was employed by the American State Department. You are a member of the Chinese Communist Party.'

Ling was finding it difficult to control her hostility to McKillop's questions. 'You're implying . . .'

'If you answer my questions factually, Miss Chen,' snapped Mike, 'no one will be implying anything. Now, tell us about your links with the Party.'

'I joined when I was in the army. Everyone in the unit had to.'

'Did you believe in it?'

'What does that mean?' she asked angrily. She felt stronger after the food.

'Do you believe . . .'

'You joined the police,' she interrupted. 'Do you believe in the police?' She thought she saw McKillop hesitate when she said that. She smiled at him. He acknowledged she had scored a point and smiled back. Briefly, his role had changed from questioner to something altogether more vulnerable.

'All right,' said McKillop. 'But your father was a Party member, wasn't he?'

'He died of cancer,' she said quickly. But he didn't ask that and she had reacted too abruptly.

'I'm sorry.' It seemed he was, the way he looked at her and gave her time before the next question.

'I understand he was very loyal to the Party?'

'I was young. I don't know what my father thought.'

'So you joined the Party because of your military unit, but then you chose to go to the Travel Orientation Course before your visit to the States.'

'We had to.'

'But you were one of the star pupils, Ling. You believed in it.'

Ling didn't answer.

'You were obliged to make a report on your activities while outside of China?'

Ling nodded.

'To the Party.'

'Yes.'

He was making her remember the classroom at the Beijing People's University, the ideological heartland for Party policy. Windows stretched along one side of the room. The snow had freshly fallen overnight. It was below freezing and the branches of the trees hung with icicles. Students, wrapped in shawls and heavy overcoats, trod carefully across the campus so as not to slip on the ice.

'What was the room like, the room where you had the lectures?' pressed Mike.

'Above the blackboard was a portrait of Chairman Mao,' she said.

The photograph of Mao shook in its frame and became a television screen of a montage of young Chinese people. They were engineers in the American desert, students in a British library,

118

dance teachers in Paris and automobile designers in Milan. Chinese expatriates were on every continent and while the class watched they were told that, as Chinese in these societies, they must never lose sight of their purpose.

Ling stopped speaking and for a moment no one moved, made a sound or did anything.

Then Mike said softly: 'What thoughts did you come away with, Ling? Loyalty or fear?'

Ling thought for a moment: 'More than that, a great love for Chairman Mao and my country.'

'Mao?' prodded Mike. 'Wasn't he a monster? So many people dead . . .'

'He saved our country from Western imperialism. He allowed the Chinese to stand on their own feet and never be slaves again.'

'But so much chaos,' Mike used the Chinese word *luan*, adopted by the Communist Party to describe tumult, violence and political upheaval.

'The chaos was there before,' argued Ling. 'The feeling we have towards Mao is like a Chinese child has towards her parents. Something you might not understand because it's different in the West. There's not so much respect.'

'My children are half-Chinese.'

McKillop stopped suddenly and looked straight at her, revealing through his hesitation that what he said wasn't part of the interrogation. It was something altogether more human, as if he understood the horrible cultural line she had to tread in her relationship with Scott.

'You were upset when Scott cancelled your dinner?' Mike whispered, barely audible, but she heard him clearly enough and the question made her swallow hard.

'He had his work to do.'

'You loved him?'

She nodded. 'I suppose so,' she said.

'That's all right,' said Mike. 'It's sometimes difficult to know.' He walked across to the other side of the room and his voice approached her from a different direction. 'Whether Scott was murdered or killed himself, we have to establish motive. We need to know if your relationship with him was a factor, or indeed if your membership of the Communist Party was . . .'

'Neither,' said Ling.

'All right. But bear with us. Did you tell the Party, your line managers in Beijing, about your relationship with Scott?'

119

'I don't even know to whom I should be reporting any more, Superintendent. You're trying to pin something on me that stopped seven or eight years ago. The world has moved on. I work for Prime Coasts on international property development, if you hadn't remembered.'

Mike persisted: 'Did you report your relationship . . . ?'

'No.'

'Why not?'

'I just told you.'

'But the Party would condemn the relationship, wouldn't it?

'Probably.'

'Unless, of course, you had been assigned to seduce an American government official.'

Ling shook her head.

'You say you loved him. Yet you thought he was a racist.'

'It's complicated.'

'Did you believe in Scott's views about individual freedom?'

'Not completely. But I was interested. His ideas were new to me.'

'In what way?'

'He wasn't right,' said Ling quickly. The wind had dropped and the afternoon sun was streaming in from the west, warm in the airless room and hot on her face. 'Not completely right.'

'Why not?'

'He didn't understand us. He was American.'

'Was he trying to turn you against your country?' Mike's voice was getting louder.

'I don't know,' said Ling. She tried to conceal her emotions. But she was getting tired. Tears were welling up in her eyes. 'He was persuasive. Very persuasive about what he believed in.'

'Were you going to marry him?'

Ling shook her head.

'And live in America as an American citizen? Although you are a Party member?'

Ling kept shaking her head. She pulled a tissue out of the box, but didn't want to use it, to show her weakness to these men.

'How does that work, Ling? How does it work that you share your bed with an American agent?'

'It doesn't,' she said. 'Not long-term. It wouldn't have worked.'

'So it was a casual affair.'

Ling didn't answer.

'You had other men?'

'Watch your lip, Superintendent.'

'It was complicated, wasn't it.'

'Yes it was.'

'So, did you kill him because of it?'

'No.'

'Did you break off the relationship?'

'No.'

'Were you ordered to kill him?'

'No,' she screamed and screwed the tissue into a ball. She gripped it tightly, both fists clenched, her head down, knuckles against her forehead, eyes on the floor.

From behind her, Hollingworth intervened: 'OK, calm down, Ling. It's been a long day. We're nearly finished. We're tired. A little longer.'

He let her absorb that. Mike seemed to pull back. She looked up and saw Hollingworth's eyes on Mike for just a second. Hollingworth pulled up a stool so he was facing her, leaning forward, his arms resting casually on his knees.

'Scott told me about you refusing to take a Western name,' Hollingworth said conversationally.

He appeared gentle, a friend, the man Andrew Carter had said would see her safely through the airport.

'He told you about us?' she asked weakly.

Hollingworth didn't answer directly. 'Apparently, you compromised by putting your given name first, so you became Ling Chen instead of Chen Ling.'

She nodded: 'I was Chen Ling.'

'I like it,' said Hollingworth. 'Scott told me how you took him around the Forbidden City when you first met,'

'Told you,' she repeated. She had learned to control tiredness in the army. To control aggression in combat. But she had never been taught anything like this.

'As a State Department employee he is obliged to report back on his contacts with foreigners,' he said.

Ling looked at him blankly. His face was craggy and his eyes weren't friendly any more. They moved back and forth between irritation and mockery and offered no lasting comfort. 'He said he persuaded you to show him your heritage. Didn't he say he wanted to see China through your eyes?'

He drew sheets of folded paper from his back pocket. They were stapled together. He opened them and flattened them out with the palm of his hand.

'This is how he reported it, Ling. Tell me if he was right. You went in through the northern gate. You bought the tickets and you began telling him about the Forbidden City, just as you were taught at school. You said it had five hundred and sixty years of history covering 720,000 square metres, contained nine thousand rooms . . . all that sort of stuff.

'The stone carving was 16.57 metres long, 3.07 metres wide and 1.07 metres thick. But Scott was getting playful. He ran his finger up and down your spine in front of the tourists there. He talked about sex and embarrassed you.

'Then he got distracted when he saw the American Express sponsorship for the Palace of Heavenly Purity.'

Until then Hollingworth had been solely addressing Ling. Now he turned away and spoke to the whole room. 'Sounds fucking crazy the way Scott tells it. A tinny loudspeaker is hidden in the trees saying . . .' and Hollingworth turned the page to another sheet, running his finger down to find the line: 'Our great helmsman Mao Tse-tung dismantled the Imperial throne and opened up the palaces here to the masses.'

'Not true, Scott tells Miss Ling Chen. The Forbidden City ended in 1911 when Sun Yat-sen overthrew the Ching dynasty. Ling Chen asked Scott why he was insulting China. 'Is truth an insult?' responded our Scott. 'Why is your greatest cultural monument kept under repair with sponsorship from the American Express card? Where's your national pride?' He pointed to the stagnant streams which oozed between the buildings and said America would never let its great museums fall into such decay.

'You argued with him, didn't you? But he played with you. He tossed your ideas into the air like bubbles, let them drift and then blew them into nothing.'

Ling tensed as she realised that Scott had given their whole relationship to the American government. He had betrayed her. They were bullying her race. The failure of her country. Her features. Black hair, slight cheeks, small breasts, narrow eyes, olive skin.

Hollingworth continued, but she wasn't listening: 'He led you through towards Tiananmen Gate, didn't he, and he bought you a T-shirt with a picture of Mao on it? He turned you towards him and held you by both hands and kissed you American-style, French-style, call it what you like but it wasn't Communist Party style. He kissed you with real passion, that's what he told me, and ran his hands over your whole body. That's what he . . .'

The tears and violence came at once. A huge racking sob and uncontrollable rage. When she started to get up, Hollingworth leant forward and held both her wrists. But she had been trained for that. She kicked him on the shin and in the midriff, then broke free running. The orange juice spilled on the carpet. Hollingworth staggered back and she kicked him again in the small of the back. She ran out the open French window into the garden. Jeremy Haskins was on his feet, but she heard McKillop say calmly: 'Leave her be.'

Hollingworth swore: 'Fucking bitch.'

But Mike said again: 'Leave her be.'

She stopped in the tiny garden, close to the wall near the sea, but with enough distance to fight, yearning for the clarity of unarmed combat to calm her. But there was no enemy. They held back and her breathing and emotion took over again into huge gasping breaths that she couldn't control. She lashed out into the air with tears streaming down her face, kicking, punching and yelling, her hair in her eyes, hitting at nothing, until she fell on her knees, crying aloud, not caring who heard her, then letting it settle into quiet, private sobs, her head buried on her knees, so when she opened her eyes all she saw was the intimate darkness of her own body.

Mike came out into the garden. He closed the door, so the others couldn't hear. He kept his distance. 'He had to do it,' he said gently.

Ling looked up at him and got to her feet: 'I didn't report back on him,' she said.

'Scott was CIA. He had to tell them.' Mike walked closer to her. She tensed. 'Scott didn't betray you. Hollingworth betrayed Scott by telling you.'

She brushed damp earth off her hands. 'I didn't kill him. I . . .'

'I know,' said Mike. 'They can't hear us out here. We're not recording. And I'm telling you, I know you didn't kill him.'

Chapter Fifteen

Mike left Ling in the garden with Jeremy Haskins watching her and went to the roof. As soon as he stepped through the tiny, low door which led up there, his mobile phone rang. He glanced down, expecting it to be Clem, somewhere in the States, hiding out, waiting to hear from Mike. But it wasn't. Instead Tom Elton was on the line: 'Jesus, Mike. You guys are going a bit hard,' he said. 'What did you do that for?'

'Ask Hollingworth,' said Mike angrily.

'The comrades reckon she's as guilty as hell. What with witnesses both at the party and in her village.' McKillop imagined Tom with his feet up, throwing his squash ball and looking across the clear, rainless vistas from his office to the Kowloon hills.

'Is she?'

'What do I know, Mike? I'm an image man which is why I'm calling. The press have got hold of the fact that we've taken her in. The line is that we're holding her overnight. But if anyone asks refer them to me. Or Tommy Lai. He's handling the Chinese press.'

Wind blew across the roof, knocking down a set of barbecue forks which were leaning against the wall. 'She's expecting to get on a plane . . .' began Mike, but Elton broke in: 'You got the photos of Sally and the kids? I got Nim Kai to give them to me. The kids look great. Really great. The reason I rushed them to you is that the meeting with Sally should be tonight, old sport.'

Mike couldn't respond, except for a knot of excitement in his stomach. After framing Ling for murder, the prize was a meeting with his wife.

'But I'm doing this,' said Mike, weakly.

'They reckon you've done such a good job. The press conference. Ling. Just you and Sally tonight, then if it works out, you can both take the kids out in a few days' time. They're both here in Hong Kong and they're all getting ready for it.'

Mike looked down into the garden where Ling was kneeling on a bench, both arms resting on its back and her wrists hanging loose. She stared out ahead, where there was just a whitewashed wall with razor wire and broken glass on the top. But beyond was the sea and she could hear it.

Her face showed how much she understood what the Party was trying to do to her.

'But no more stuff about your own feelings,' Elton was saying. 'Not necessary, this stuff about you having half-Chinese children.'

Mike moved back so that Ling wouldn't be able to hear Elton's booming voice through the phone set. 'A couple of other things. Just tipping you off that the Comrades know. And we don't want to blow anything.'

'Like what?' said Mike.

'The call from the States. You didn't call back. That's great. They've tracked it to a motel on the West Coast. Does the name Matt Simons mean anything?' Elton kept talking, not letting Mike answer. He had said it. The Party was listening on the line. Elton was protecting Mike from his own unpredictable reactions. 'Didn't expect so. Good, so best leave it be, OK?'

'OK,' said Mike, pushing away images of Clem Watkins hunted down to a shabby Californian motel room.

'And McEwan called Andrew Carter's office. His secretary rang here to check his name on the government list. Jesus, Mike, I wouldn't take a life insurance policy out on that man right now.'

'I know. I know,' said Mike impatiently. In a few hours, maybe he could see Sally. He could touch her. He could confront her. He could look at her. Maybe, they'd let him take her out, so they could talk, just the two of them.

Maybe he could play some piano. He thought of booking a table at the Verandah restaurant in Liu Huaquing Bay. Sally was his wife. He cherished that word with all the possession, intimacy, security and freedom it encompassed. Anticipation rushed through him just like any other time he was going into action when to lose would hurt unbearably for the rest of your life.

He didn't want to win against Sally. He didn't want to hurt her, teach her, control her. He wanted to be married to her again. He wanted her to love him and bring back the children. He craved for her to re-create their home. A wife or child was far more dangerous than the enemies in the jungle. If Sally rejected

125

him, she would inflict the ultimate pain on him. Yet he could do nothing except plead. Helplessly.

'The meeting should be about eight at your place,' Elton was saying. 'Tommy's going to tell you to knock off now. I've got the press statement. Good luck, old sport. Really mean it. Talk to you tomorrow.'

McKillop was walking the last mile, letting the mountain wind and cold drizzle clear his mind. There was plenty of time. Mike looked at the photograph again. Sally was vibrant in it. There was a glint of flirtation in her eyes, glancing across at him and smiling.

The fog on the Peak came and went through the headlights. There were two police cars, three motorcycles, then four policemen, right on the junction, with the beams of yellow and red lights beams splayed out by the fog. A bus approached just as the road narrowed where a bridge went across it. Mike pressed himself against the wall underneath to let it pass. He crossed the road, so he could get a clearer view.

He could only see a hundred yards, but a light was on in his apartment. And the maid never left the lights on. The French window onto the balcony was open and latched back, rocking with the weather. McKillop edged himself into the undergrowth.

He kept to the shadows. On his left was a raised pathway. On his right, shrubs which scratched his face as he pressed in close to them and a few feet beyond that a telephone box. Police lights flashed against the wall ten feet away from him. He moved back into the dark undergrowth.

The drizzle was more persistent now. The wind was loud. The policemen blocked off the road with fluorescent cones, the lights on the roofs of their cars turning round and round from orange to red to orange again.

A forceful hand gripped McKillop's shoulder, driving him back down hard, pushing him over so Mike lost his balance and fell onto the wet ground. He smelt cigar smoke and whisky on the breath. 'Mike, for Christ's sake. It's Tom. Shut the fuck up and listen.'

Elton pulled up McKillop by his forearm and led him down the path away from the shopping arcade. They walked in silence for two hundred yards, then cut their way back into the bushes. They crouched uncomfortably. 'Nim Kai ordered your arrest. Don't tell me how I heard, but I did.'

McKillop stared uncomprehendingly. Elton handed Mike a

plastic bag. 'I cleared your desk. There's money. IDs. I got you two passports. One's your own. The other's fake. But I got your picture put in it. It's registered in our computers so you can use it. Probably one shot.'

McKillop tucked the documents underneath his shirt and into his waistband.

'Fucking game's over. I'm on a plane to New York in the morning. They'd kill you. Tommy didn't like it, He was nervous. Chain smoking. Ling's finished.'

'Stop,' said Mike quietly. 'Stop and tell me . . .'

'I'm telling you. They're going to get rid of her in the morning. Tommy's cleared out the fucking listening gear. It's over.'

There were voices from the road above them. Elton dropped to a whisper: 'What's going on now is evil. Worse than anything.'

'How do you know?' whispered McKillop.

Elton stood up, swaying. Mike said nothing. Elton was backing away. His huge frame was pushed against damp undergrowth. Water droplets soaked into his jacket.

'Hide, old sport. Something's happened so they don't care any more, see.'

'For Christ's sake, Elton. What the fuck are you talking about?'

The American brushed down his jacket. 'Stay where you are. I'll stroll out. I've got the party over the road. Staff party, changed the venue when I heard you were in real bad trouble. Just to save your ass.' He grinned. The hand on the shoulder again. The squeeze.

'You said you saw Sally . . .'

'I talked . . . I talked to someone who said she was Sally. Who knows who she was?'

'So it's not happening?' But he knew the answer. As Elton stared at him, a wild man in panic in a pinstripe suit, Mike was swept through with anger and his own stupidity. He grabbed Elton by the lapels: 'Then where the fuck is she?'

'Don't ask,' said Elton, beginning to push Mike's hands away.

'I'm asking.'

'I heard she was somewhere up north. Something's going on up there, Mike, which is scaring the shit out of the comrades. Something no one wants to know about. Not you. Not me. No one.'

McKillop let Elton go. Both men were breathing heavily.

'Do you know where?'

Elton shook his head. 'No. I'm here to save your life.' He smiled. 'So don't give me a hard time.'

Mike looked at the rain running down the big man's face as Elton smoothed down his crumpled collar and tie.

'Thanks,' said McKillop softly.

'Give it five minutes, then make your way wherever,' said Elton. 'I don't want to know.'

Elton took out a cigar and played with it, unlit. Across the road were the blue lights from the police motorcycles. Along the path was Elton's restaurant. The perfect cover. Drink on his breath. Fresh air to clear the head. He could hear the laughter from the terrace, as Elton's staff challenged each other to drinking competitions.

Elton came out of the undergrowth onto the pavement. It was half lit, confusingly with streetlights and headlights. A thicker fog rolled off the Peak. Buildings and cars became images. A pair of lights. A shape through the mist. With the coolness came a wind which blew the trees and created a background noise, a rustling, which mixed in with the other sounds, the laughter from the restaurant, Elton's footsteps, the police radio outside the apartment.

McKillop didn't hear the crack.

He only saw Elton crumple up, his huge body jerked back, then collapsed. His head hit the kerb. His hand smashed onto the ground, throwing out the cigar which rolled into the gutter. There was a second shot. McKillop matched the source of the sound with the target and pinpointed the position.

An ambulance was parked in a row of garages on the road. Its lights came on straight away. The police cars moved off, a hundred yards each way to cordon off the upward lane of the road. The ambulance backed out and turned. Its headlights picked up Elton's body, lighting it up, while officials came down from the apartment. McKillop heard people arguing in Mandarin, loud and unsubtle.

They had hit the wrong man. But he was white and the weather was dark and misty. An easy mistake. With a rifle fired from McKillop's own apartment.

Tony Zhang walked through the swing doors of the Lost Oasis bar in Beijing. He planned to stay maybe an hour and have something new when the President next asked him about the aspirations of the young cosmopolitan China. The customers were a mix of Russian engineers, American bankers, late twenty-something Chinese professionals, a handful of diplomats, journalists and clumps of scruffy European travellers. The bar staff were Chinese and European. The music was American, with enduring songs of a generation earlier and audible from the narrow and potholed road which led down to the bar.

For the first time since winter, it was warm enough to drink in the road and escape from the crowds and the noise.

But Tony pushed his way through. The bar was monopolised by half a dozen Russians, leaning heavily, smoking, a mess of ash and beer on the bar itself, their cuffs and sleeves grubby and damp with it, but the conversation so loud and animated that they didn't care. While edging past them, Tony slipped on a pool of spilt beer and had to clutch the shoulder of a Shanghainese prostitute to stop himself falling. She glared at him and complained loudly. He slipped her a 100 yuan note and moved on.

The band was Filipino, but with a special guest Chinese singer who had openly declared his homosexuality and then had a sex change. Patricia had to be declared partially insane before it was allowed. But in China madness and a painful sex change was more socially acceptable than homosexuality, and now she was a respected and revered entertainer. Tony cited Patricia's case when discussing whether legislation or evolution was the best method of social change for China.

Patricia was ending her song. The applause was starting and Tony spotted Lucy Yu whose voice cut across the room to him from the dartboard in a corner. She flung her arms around him, kissed him on both cheeks and the lips, then abruptly moved away to mark up the score of the latest player. She was half an inch under six feet tall, had hair falling to her waist and earned part of a living, with half a dozen languages and fast arithmetic, scoring darts in the Lost Oasis.

She was also on Tony's payroll. Lucy had spurned offers from the business and the diplomatic worlds and was delighted to take a small, but steady cash income from Tony in exchange for snatches of information. Lucy was a night owl and one of Tony's feeders. He had maybe a dozen around China, who reported directly to him, and he to the President.

Tony had known Lucy since university. She was infuriatingly intelligent, wildly gregarious and completely promiscuous. Lucy had broken his virginity after a spring picnic in the Western Hills. She had led him away from the party and into the pine forests, where she quickly and skilfully seduced him. He was both ashamed at his dismal performance and filled with a misplaced pride that fate had secured him such a beautiful woman to be his wife. The next day when he broached the subject, Lucy threw back her head with natural and sympathetic laughter. In the afternoon, she introduced Tony to Ling Chen, who was equally beautiful but less unpredictable. Since Tony had learned the rudimentary procedure from Lucy, Ling allowed herself to be seduced, albeit clumsily. He managed enough finesse for them to begin a relationship which lasted the summer and ended without acrimony when Ling went off to Yale and Tony found himself heading towards the President's office.

Stretching on tiptoes, Lucy drew a glum expression above the left-hand score, even adding teardrops to emphasise the defeat of the losing team. The players from a Japanese tour group shook her hand one by one as they filed away into the crowd.

Lucy turned round and wrapped her arms around Tony again so that her mouth was nestling against his ear: 'The Russians at the bar have been here for hours,' she said. Tony listened without looking round at them. 'They've come in from somewhere in the north-east. The one on the far left in the blue shirt keeps talking about it getting too dangerous. Then the others, mostly the one in the middle, tell him to shut up.'

She untangled herself, but kept her hand resting on Tony's arm. 'Johnny's got one of their names in full because he handed over his credit card to guarantee the tab.'

'Anything else?' said Tony.

'The police came in to check on Patricia. The Ministry of Culture says she can perform, but can't sing, in case the words are political.'

'But her performance is singing,' said Tony, looking over towards Patricia who was doing her lipstick in the mirror at the back of the stage.

Lucy shrugged and wiped the scores off the blackboard. 'Nothing happened anyway. They hung around, then left. And she sang.'

Tony took Lucy's hand and moved her towards the bar: 'I'll buy you a drink and we'll listen to the Russians.'

The Russian tab was running into hundreds of dollars. Their accents were rough and not from Moscow or St Petersburg – more Vladivostock, Tony judged. They had probably been working on the UN trade zone project and found the temptations of Beijing preferable and safer than the lawless streets of the Russian Far East. Lucy ordered her own drink, an Extra Old Hine Brandy with a cappuccino and pulled up a stool right next to the man in the blue shirt. Tony stood alone several feet away, his back to the bar, listening with admiration as Lucy drew the man into conversation.

Tony was getting bored and Lucy said she would call him in the morning. He pushed his way out into the street, emerging with one leg soaked by beer and a cigarette burn on his shirt collar. It was late, but the bars were even fuller. Taxis heading in both directions and the drivers refusing to give way to one another blocked the way. Hands thudded on car roofs to try to get movement. Tony turned right and walked purposefully through the mayhem and soon he was in quietness, his surroundings much darker. He planned to walk home now that the Party had given him a flat just at the back of the Jianguo Hotel in Jiang Guo Men Wei, so much closer to the heart of Beijing. He was taking a short cut and turned right again into an alleyway which was lit only by the households still awake in the government apartment blocks on either side. In the abrupt quietness, he heard footsteps fall in behind him. He turned round, thinking it was Lucy, and saw a figure disappearing into the shadows.

Tony took out his identification pass which was the highest grade of entry into Zhongnanhai. Any sensible Chinese mugger who saw it would flee. Even a visual identification from a man of Tony's rank could send him to the execution site. Tony moved slowly back the way he had come, hearing nothing except the low thud of music from the bars and the irritating horns from the taxis. In the distance at the end of the alley a platoon of guards for the diplomatic compounds marched past in a change of shift. Spotlights shot up into the sky from the Workers' Stadium where China was playing Ukraine in a friendly football match. Tony stopped when he heard the scrape of a shoe, a cough and then someone stepped out from a compound gateway. Tony moved back quickly, ready to fight, but then relaxed when he saw who it was: 'Gurjit, are you following me or what?'

Gurjit laughed. He was an intelligence agent at the Indian Embassy and belonged to the same international set as Tony. They had met while Gurjit was on a university fellowship in Beijing.

'I've been waiting for you to come out of that bloody bar for an hour now,' said the Indian. 'Then I took a leak, missed you leaving and saw this Tony-like figure scuttling away down here.'

131

He put his hand on Tony's shoulder and steered them both to keep walking in the direction they had been going. 'Some lousy spy I make,' he added.

They had reached a spot midway between the two ends of the alley and Gurjit stopped. 'Tony, my friend, something very strange is going on in your country. There was a murder on one of our planes. It put down in Burma and the body, an American businessman, is being held there.'

'Not the sort of thing which would cross my desk,' said Tony.

'Have you heard about the troop movements in the north-east?' Gurjit followed up. Tony shook his head. 'The expulsion of foreigners from an area up there? Koreans, Japanese, Russians, all told to get out?'

'I'm not with you at all, Gurjit,' said Tony with genuine impatience.

'OK. The bottom line is that our government thinks there's a coup d'état or something going on in China. Or a warlord's got out of control. And if you – or the President – don't know about it, you bloody well should.'

Tony Zhang took out a cigarette, cupped his hand and lit it. The flame illuminated Gurjit's face. Figures came towards them from both sides in the alley. Tony offered Gurjit a cigarette and when the Indian took it Tony saw his hand was shaking. His jacket collar was pulled up, yet beads of sweat gathered on his forehead. Gurjit looked as if he had a fever. The Indian smiled: 'I tell you, Tony, I'm not bullshitting.'

Tony walked back towards the bars. Gurjit fell in beside him. A couple coming the other way separated to make way for the two men and Tony stopped as the alleyway became wider and opened up onto the road, which was more crowded and an easier place to talk.

'Are you trying to wreck our relationship with Pakistan again?' suggested Tony softly.

Gurjit shook his head vigorously. He stammered a bit before beginning: 'The Pakistanis have taken order of twenty-six East Wind missiles. Solid fuel rockets. Range 12,000 kilometres. Fired from mobile launchers. Satellite photographs show them being transported by train to Tsing Tao. Two Pakistani-registered freighters, the *Lahore* and the *Rawalpindi*, are there, not at the commercial port, but at the naval base. They're due to sail for Karachi tomorrow night.'

'We've sold them missiles?'

'Sold. Given. Doesn't bloody well matter. But not you, Tony. Not you. Not the President. It's the military. They're doing something that will alter the balance of power on the sub-continent, if not the world.'

A bellow of laughter broke out a few feet away as five Westerners walking abreast and taking up the whole path brushed past them. Tony caught the smells of their cigar smoke and, over their heads, he saw Lucy come out of the Lost Oasis. She was holding a drink. Her hair got caught in the wind and she brushed it from her face so she could look back into the bar. Gurjit tugged at Tony's sleeve: 'Pay attention, for God's sake man. I'm telling you . . .'

'The President doesn't know about this,' said Tony, looking back at his friend.

'You tell me he doesn't, Tony. Please tell me he doesn't and that he has the power to reverse the sale of these things.' Gurjit drew hard on his cigarette, threw it to the ground and pulled his scarf more fully around his neck.

'Why would we be doing it?' pressed Tony.

'They, Tony. They,' said Gurjit quickly. 'Not you. If they have Pakistan on side, they will have a secure line to the Islamic oil-producing governments of the Middle East. Then they can guarantee their energy supplies if something happens with America and the West.'

'But the President's going to Washington. Nothing's going to happen.'

'We have wacky people in India,' said Gurjit. 'But we know who they are. Here . . .' Suddenly he and Gurjit were caught in the headlights of a turning taxi. Tony pulled Gurjit away, back down the alley again. 'Look at Mao,' Gurjit was saying. 'Here, you have no bloody idea who the madmen are until it's too late, until they've wrecked the whole damn country.'

Chapter Sixteen

Mike scrambled down the hillside, not caring about the noise as he dislodged rocks and broke through dank, sodden foliage. They would put up road blocks on the way down and cordon off the walking track around the Peak and up Plantation Road. They would bring out helicopters, maybe dogs, except the waterfalls and streams would make it easy to lose them. They would say they were catching illegal immigrants and, when they found him, they would kill him straight away just like they did the illegal immigrants.

He heard the shouting. Headlights and searchlights cut through the undergrowth. The ambulance with flashing lights drove down the hill with the siren wailing. Kwai would be waiting to take the body into the mortuary.

Mike was perfectly still. His breathing was silent. Not a branch around him moved. Not a drop of water fell from the foliage because of him. He was back at Maekok. His training took over. Men spread out. He could hear them, taking up positions for the search. He smeared earth over his face to help conceal him from their wavering torchlights. Soon they were among the foliage, their sounds enough to cover his own, so Mike edged down foothold by foothold going further than they thought was safe. He used the foliage as a mountaineer would use a rope, testing each plant, each root, then giving it his whole weight as he lowered himself. The hillside was a sheer drop at times. The unforgiving granite was concealed by the undergrowth. But Mike knew this terrain and his pursuers didn't. They were conscripts from the mainland, dressed in the uniform of the Hong Kong police. They would have been in the territory for no more than three months because any longer and they would become embittered by the wealth. Mike knew the walking tracks around the Peak, built by British civil servants for the British to enjoy. He became more certain and moved faster until he reached one, gently easing himself onto it, a place where he had jogged so many times before. They were above him, far enough away for him to escape, and Mike just ran. He sprinted the first two hundred yards, then slowed, making sure he could pace himself, and he brought his breathing back under control.

He ran on tiptoe to keep the sound down. Soon he was round above the harbour and he stopped where he had to cross a road to hear if they were watching, if they had blocked the path which would take him down from the Peak. Nothing. The sounds of the night. That was all. It used to be called Chatham Path, but it had not been given a new name and the Chinese had little use for the eccentricities of the British. Mike breathed deeply and slowly. The road in front of him was empty. Two of the street lights were broken. One flickered erratically, making it more difficult to see, giving him an advantage. He broke out, keeping close in on his side, crossing a stone bridge, then dashing straight across back into the safety of the foliage.

The air was thick with smells of tropical forest, wild flowers and rotting vegetation. Even at night, his eyes now accustomed, he could see butterflies of brilliant yellows and reds cutting back and forth across him as he pounded down the track. On both sides, there was the sound of cascading water and as he ran on it became louder than anything else around. A searchlight bounced off the tops of the trees. The first helicopter was out. But they would never see him in here. Mike stopped at a stream, pulled out his handkerchief, soaked it in water and washed the earth off his face. He splashed water onto his torso.

'Fuck them,' he thought. 'Just fuck them.' He plunged his whole head into a little rock pool, letting the fresh water clear his thoughts, while mantra-like he kept repeating *Fuck them, just fuck them. Fuck them, just fuck them.* First it was a prominent thought, then a whisper, then, as the helicopter came down lower, the sound of the rotor blades loud and distinct, and the cicadas started up like a vacuum cleaner around the whole forest and the water crashed down from the rocks above, he shouted it out, not caring if anyone heard, wishing the enemy would appear so he could fight them.

There was no Sally. His children had gone. His days of shame were over. There was no Sally. She didn't exist.

Mike shook his head, wiped the damp handkerchief down his face and began running again. He turned a corner into the brilliant night view of the harbour and noticed the sounds of the frenzy down there, even at night, of the jackhammers and cranes, and the thud of city discotheques and dealing rooms. The first big house loomed on his left with two covered golf carts outside to take on the narrow, steep path instead of cars. The lights were off. Not even the dogs barked as he went by. Another helicopter was up there, its searchlight following the descent of Magazine Gap Road. Maybe there were more over the South Side. Shek O, Liu Huaqing Bay.

It was less than half an hour since Elton had died. He'd been on the path no more than fifteen minutes and was nearly down. He was still free. He slowed to walking pace, watching traffic along May Road which twisted a third of the way up the Peak like an English country lane. Nothing unusual. The road blocks must have been higher around Barker Road and Coombe Road.

A policeman pulled up his motorcycle opposite a block of flats, checked his watch, took out the police reporting book and recorded his visit. He appeared to be on usual visiting rounds. Two pedestrians lingered irritatingly on a bridge. They leant on it, looking at the view, then turned to kiss. A taxi, its meter on, people in the back, passed by. A deep blue Mercedes E-Class saloon turned into the car park of the same block. A minibus stopped just across the bridge and let off two passengers. The driver of the Mercedes wound down his window to speak to the policeman and apart from that the activity was suddenly gone, no vehicles, no people, just a quiet Hong Kong road with the distant sound of a helicopter high overhead but somewhere else on the island. The Mercedes went into the car park. Mike moved forward. The policeman bent down to turn up the radio on the back of the bike and that was when Mike hit him on the neck. The policeman collapsed. Mike secured his hands behind his back with the policeman's own cuffs and stuffed his handkerchief, damp from the waterfall, into his mouth. He lifted the man a hundred yards back up the path and pulled him just enough into the undergrowth to hide him. He took his police identity card and his .38 pistol, together with two magazines of ammunition. He looked around. There were no witnesses.

The helicopter was louder now and the startled lovers, several yards away, were caught in its spotlight.

Mike loaded the pistol, put on the helmet and pulled down the visor to hide his white face. He gunned the engine, turned the bike round, took it down Magazine Gap Road, into Garden Road, through Wanchai and up onto the Expressway where he opened up so the needle hovered around 120 kilometres an hour.

They're going to get rid of her in the morning, Elton had said. With a clear road he could be back at the Shek O house in twenty minutes.

'You've murdered an American citizen.' Hollingworth spoke in clipped, angry tones from his apartment in Garden Road. Pat was in the bedroom getting ready for the opening ceremony of Hong Kong's first casino at an old military barracks. Hollingworth stood by his desk in the study, his mouth close to the telephone, his voice low and angry.

'Never call this number,' said Li Tuo.

'Don't hang up on me,' Hollingworth swore. 'Or I'll pull you and your whole pissing operation apart.'

'And reveal the great Hollingworth to be a corrupt little traitor.'

Hollingworth heard Li spit, then laughed back into the receiver: 'And you, General Li. And you.'

'So, Warren, why don't you first tell me what has happened to make you so upset? I've already told you we had nothing to do with Carter's death.'

'Elton,' said Hollingworth. 'Tom Elton was shot dead outside McKillop's apartment by the Nim Kai.'

'So I've just heard. But McKillop killed him, Warren. In a fit of rage. It was something to do with seeing his family again.'

'McKillop wasn't armed.'

'Apparently, he drew weapons from the armoury after leaving the Shek O house.' Li coughed. Hollingworth heard the click of a cigarette lighter and the Chinese general draw on a cigarette. 'He assaulted a police officer in May Road and stole his patrol-bike. Right now he is heading down the Shek O peninsula.'

Mike let the machine do the work while he tried to think. Light came in from across the sea. To his left there was the blackness of the hills of the peninsula and, for stretches where the street lights had broken completely, there was a bleak and fathomless wall of darkness.

He saw a yellow flashing light as he rode over the top of the hill on his way down to the village. Two police cars were parked on the left with red cones closing off half the road. Four police officers, the helmets still on, their visors down, in motorcycle boots, pistols in their holsters, waved down cars with illuminated batons. Mike slowed, and with little other traffic around, they caught his headlight immediately and even from a distance called him in for checking. Mike turned up the police radio. Messages about an illegal immigration operation were mixed in with everything else of that evening. But there was nothing about Shek O itself. Mike took the .38 from his pocket and held it in his right hand while working the throttle. He turned on the blue flashing light at the back, gunned the bike, its power pushing him hard back in the seat. The distance was closing fast. The figures were blurred, keeping their positions, but recognising him as one of their own, and a hand waving him through.

There was crackle on the radio, then a message for him specifically. Or the man he had knocked unconscious. Did he require assistance? Mike didn't answer, braking and changing down as he reached the village, turning off the siren and the light, and skidding round to turn up towards the headland.

Then over the radio again: 'Patrol officer is authorised and does not need assistance.' He thought he recognised the voice. For a moment a chill shot through him. That they knew. Another game. They had just let him do it. Suddenly a shriek to his right. The front wheel hit a pothole. The bike skewed, the wheel slipping from one side to another. Mike put his right foot on the ground so he didn't lose his balance, stopping the bike and steadying himself. Another shriek. The noise came from a group of Americans who were around a pavement table at a bar, getting drunk. But not even looking at him. Watching a darts match. And he was nearly there. The road widened. The village behind him.

The top of the house rose from the high walled compound. Fairy lights were strung around the roof. Smoke curled up from a barbecue. Sparks of red ash flew off in a sudden breeze. Shapes and silhouettes were up there, and Mike made out at least two people, probably more, but not moving around so much. There were lights in the garden as well and music around the house. The white metal gate to the compound and the side door were shut.

Mike came up fast, light flashing but no siren, stopping outside the compound and screaming up for them to open the gate. As they pulled it back, Mike took off his helmet, so they would recognise him. The interrogator. He parked the bike across the back of a BMW saloon and the two guards returned to their card game. They knew him but didn't seem to care about him and, with their concentration elsewhere, Mike took off the petrol cap and shook the bike around, letting fuel run out. He left the bike with the back wheel protruding so the gate wouldn't close again.

The guards had been sitting at the back of the car park. They had set up a bench as a table for cards. A radio hung from a wire strapped between two nails in the wall. There was tea in the flask, but Mike also smelt brandy. One had taken up his weapon, an automatic machine pistol. The second pistol was on the ground under the bench. Mike's eyes flickered back and forth.

'I'm here for only one minute,' he commanded.

He walked straight through the front door. Ling would be in the bedroom on the second floor. That was where they had always kept the visitors to this house. The guards would be radioing back for instructions right now. He heard the crackle.

The door was ajar and not a sound from the room. Mike opened it slowly with his left hand, the revolver in his right. The covers of the single bed were crumpled. A can of Coke was on the bedside table, together with a glass which was a third full. The air-conditioning was on. Lace curtains were drawn across the window. The overhead light was off. The room was illuminated by a desk light on the table underneath the window. A notepad was on the desk, two ballpoint pens on top, one of them rolling slowly down on the incline. The chair was pushed back.

Mike opened the door further. But from behind, there was a tap on his shoulder and he felt the cold metal of a pistol against the base of his neck.

Through the crack in the door he saw Ling. She was barefoot, hiding in the room itself. Men were coming down from the roof. He heard shouting below. And the gun held against him now was evidence of their orders to take him. Mike spun round, the metal moving on his neck. He brought up his right arm, deliberately not thinking, letting experience and training take over as if there hadn't been fallow years. He squeezed the trigger of his .38 just once, far enough away to see the astonishment on the Chinese soldier's face and the surprise just before the bullet crashed through his skull; close enough to feel the warm blood on his hand, but he had felt that before and he let the body fall, twitching, just like Win Kyi on the steps of the Great Hall of the People.

He moved back into Ling's room. The guard was slumped on the steps outside. Ling recognised him immediately. But she was inert.

'You've got to trust me,' he said quickly. She didn't speak. She didn't ask whose side he was on. Why he was killing her guards. She put on her shoes, picked up her bag and slung it over her shoulder. Mike looked back at her. Her face was expressionless. Across the tiny hallway were the stairs leading up to the top floor and the roof terrace. It was half open and he could see the fairy lights and smell the barbecue.

'How many?' whispered Mike.

But Ling didn't have time to answer. The roof door opened. Perhaps they hadn't heard the shot. Perhaps they were stupid. Or badly trained. Or had never been under fire. They both appeared at once, coming down two steps. When they saw the body of their friend, they stopped one behind the other and that was when Mike fired, two shots, one, then another quickly following, this time balancing his trigger arm with his left, so that each one was hit in the head. The .38 was not powerful enough to do anything else except go for a kill.

'That's all,' said Ling calmly.

'They were going to kill you,' said Mike.

Ling took her jacket off the back of the chair and slipped the notebook into her bag: 'Or maybe you will,' she said. Mike twisted round to look her straight in the eyes. There was no fear, no vulnerability like before.

'Right,' said Mike, more to himself than her. He pulled out the chamber of the .38, ejected the three used cartridges and inserted fresh ammunition. He edged out from the cover of the room. The door opened inward which put Mike at a disadvantage. He paused long enough for Ling to notice his hesitation: 'I'm going out,' she said, and before Mike could answer Ling shouted in Chinese: 'Help. Help, shooting, shooting.'

She pulled open the door and was frozen in the glare of spotlight. But the lamp was in her eyes not Mike's, making the man who held it a target. Mike fired, yelling and pushing Ling down at the same time. His bullet grazed the Chinese soldier's skull on the left, throwing the man backwards, and from behind, further away, near where they had been playing cards, came a line of automatic fire from a machine pistol which splintered the wood above them, stopped and began again lower, less than six inches from Mike's head. Mike flattened himself, his body covering Ling. He fired two shots. The first hit the attacker in the shoulder, the second in his chest. The man collapsed and there was quiet, just the radio and two dogs barking from outside because of the gunfire.

The gate was still open. The bike blocked the exit of one BMW.

But the exit for another was clear. A smell of cordite mixed with the smell of spilt petrol and barbecue smoke from the roof. The wounded soldier with the automatic pistol cried. His scream was like a child's. The ignition keys were in both cars. He told Ling to get in through the driver's side door and crawl over. He opened the door for her, then went round and opened the boot. He tore the felt cover away from where the CD player was kept and on the other side where the back windscreen washer tank was and the first aid kit. Again his memory and instincts were working together, taking him back to when the Chinese were the enemy and he had known where they kept their weapons. He took out three more machine pistols, boxes of ammunition, spare magazines and threw them into the back seat.

Mike started the engine and backed the car straight out, deliberately catching the handlebars of the motorcycle so it fell down with petrol gushing out of the tank. That was when Ling screamed for him to watch out, but Mike didn't stop what he was doing. He wound down her electronic window and fired his last three shots at the tank of the motorcycle so the petrol caught immediately, the first tongues of flames leaping the full three storeys of the buildings.

'Watch the roof,' yelled Ling for the second time. As the flames receded, leaving black charred stains on the white walls, Mike saw a single figure standing there firing at him with a pistol. He reversed to get a clear exit, changed gear and accelerated out as the bullets cut up the asphalt on the road ahead of him, then hit the bonnet and up into the windscreen with a searing pain to his left shoulder as two more rounds tore into the back seat before Mike took the car round the corner and down from the headland into the village.

Then an atmosphere of normality returned. The glow of the fire in the back mirror blended with the street lights. The Americans were still playing darts, drinking on the pavement, ignoring the Chinese military car with the driver slumped at the wheel. It was only minutes since he had passed them on the bike. Just over an hour since Tom Elton was murdered.

'You've been hit?' said Ling.

Mike nodded. His right arm manoeuvered the car through the narrow road out. The seafood restaurant on the corner was still full, and past there, Mike was getting onto the empty road of the peninsula. The road block was five hundred yards ahead. Mike struggled to keep his concentration. His right hand was

141

sticky with the blood of the first soldier he'd killed. His own blood was seeping into his shirt and trickling down his chest. Waves of nausea swept through him. The number plate of his car bore the red prefixed letters of WJ, the Wu Jing or People's Armed Police. Like Nim Kai it was another wing of the Chinese security which operated in Hong Kong with impunity. The Hong Kong police couldn't touch them. Or so Mike hoped as he saw the lights of the road block and the officer with the torch baton waving him in to the roadside.

Chapter Seventeen

Mike's left arm hung useless. He swallowed hard to stop himself vomiting. His head pounded. He slowed on the approach to the road block. He remembered last time. Ten minutes ago. After he had gone through. Crackling through the radio. *Patrol officer is authorised . . .*' Heavy static. Outside noise. He grappled to place the voice. They let him get to the house. But they didn't expect him to go in shooting. Mike enjoyed that. Killing them. The lights ahead blurred into each other. The police baton floated up and down telling him to slow down. The cones curved right into his path. He felt Ling's hand on the wheel steadying him. The torch shone right through into his eyes.

Mike squinted, shaking his head, clearing his vision enough to see that the police were in the standard position to intercept a suspect car. Not like before when he first went through and they were more relaxed. He felt Ling leaning over to support him, her hand on the wheel but riding with his, just in case he lost consciousness. He pushed the accelerator to the floor, with the gearbox automatically changing down to get the speed and he winged each cone like ninepins one after the other. He swerved in further so as not to hit the officer with the baton, then he hauled the wheel over more, and that was where Ling helped him, not questioning, just giving him more strength. The right side of the BMW smashed first into the front of the stationary police van, then Mike teased the car round to catch the handlebars of the motorcycle parked just ahead. He pulled back again and, in the rearview mirror, he saw the van was off the road, its front wheels in the ditch. But the motorcycle had disappeared. Out of sight. He kept going, letting the car take the corners and climbed up far out of the village, fast when he could, knowing that the enemy behind would soon be the enemy in front. Blurs came and went. The nausea was easing. But blood seeped from his shoulder. His throat was parched, crying out with thirst.

'Switch on the radio,' he ordered Ling.

Two shots. One hit a road sign warning of a sharp curve ahead. The second shattered Ling's wing mirror. Mike took the corner, losing the attacker, gaining ground on the straight road ahead. But soon the motorcycle was with them again, a lone police officer riding with one hand, shooting his standard issue .38 with the other.

Over the radio: 'Do not intercept.' That same voice. That same static interference, so Mike couldn't quite place it. 'Repeat, do not intercept suspect.' They were on the peninsula with the sullen, dark hillsides on the right and the cliffs down to the sea on his left. Mike coughed and a shrivelling pain from the wound burst through his shoulder.

The motorcyclist dropped back and the road was completely clear. Nothing at all. No helicopter. No taxis. No late-night motorcyclists. Something was happening.

'They don't want the police to handle this,' said Mike in the sudden calm which surrounded them. He spoke like he had in the garden, when he said she hadn't killed Scott. He was wounded and had killed to get her out.

'How badly are you hurt?' Ling turned, looking around the car and saw a bottle in a pocket on the back seat. She undid the top and tilted it up to Mike's mouth. He drank clumsily, water splashing all over him.

'If the normal police catch us, the secret will be out. See what's happening? They're frightened already.'

Mike stared straight ahead. The water was an injection of strength. Ling found a torch in the glove box and shone it over Mike's shoulder. His shirt was torn. The blood was maroon and congealing. Without cleaning it she couldn't tell the extent of the injury. 'Try to use your arm as little as possible,' she said gently. 'To stop the bleeding.'

It was lighter than before. The moon, intermittent and brooding, was out from behind the clouds and the lights from the apartment blocks streaked across the cove. Mike stopped and wound down his window.

'They've cleared the roads so they can follow our headlights,' he said. 'So simple. Cordons up at the junctions with the road to Big Wave Bay, South Bay and Chaiwan.'

He turned off the headlights and waited for the moon to fade again. He eased the car forward to a darker section of the road on the brow of a hill, where the streetlamps were broken, and trees and undergrowth dimmed other light around.

'This is it,' said Mike. He opened his door and got out, having to stop his legs buckling from weakness. He leant against the side of the car, catching his breath.

'Remember, they're frightened,' he repeated, more to himself than to Ling. She was out of the car as well, being practical, finding a bag from the back seat, putting in the weapons, the ammunition and the water. She was doing it automatically. No questions. No suggestions.

'Aren't you interested where we're going?' said Mike.

'Something very dangerous is happening,' she said briskly, leaning in and switching off the inside light. 'If I try to escape,' she continued, 'I'll be picked up and taken in again. If I stick with you, at least I know you'll kill the people who are trying to kill us.' She smiled and looked up at him. 'Which means I'll help you, wherever you're going.'

She found the first aid kit, took out some gauze and poured drops of iodine on it. 'This will hurt. It's inadequate, but it'll help stop the bleeding,' she said. She dressed Mike's shoulder and he stifled a cry from the pain which pulsated through his whole body when the ointment touched the wound.

'It still hurts like hell,' said McKillop wincing.

'Then, I'll carry this,' said Ling, slinging the heavy bag of weapons over her shoulder.

For the second time that night Mike was scrambling down a cliff side relying on the undergrowth to lower him safely. Except now he was weak and Ling guided him. There were no walking tracks, only concrete catchments of fast-running water, layered one on top of the other like rice fields, and between them shrubs and sharp bushes through which he eased himself by holding onto one and sliding down until he find a foothold. Below the last catchment ditch was the coastline: no beach, just inhospitable rocks, the unforgiving waves and their currents.

She's yours, my friend. In all her glory, Joss had said, offering his boat. *'Take her where you want.'* Damn right I will,' said Mike to himself. His breathing was heavy, his lack of exercise slowing him again. He knew how to get to the marina from here, where they could come off the cliff onto the rocks and a few yards away there was a gap to get straight onto the walkways which ran between the boats. At low tide, it was a clear slippery surface. When the water was up, it was a precarious rock pool. He could hear the wind on the mast stays. The helicopter was coming lower and the sound of the rotor blades was more distinct. It was a police Blackhawk, not a Hong Kong Auxiliary Airforce Sikorsky which had no thermal imaging equipment on board. The Blackhawk might, so it would cut through the dark and the mist and pick out the hot engine of the BMW like a bonfire burning along the road. On the boat, too, there would be temperature differences between the hull, the mast, the fibreglass of the cabin and the deck, the water and the wake. The crew would get a black-and-white image sharp enough to blow Ling and Mike out of the water.

He ignored the helicopter and concentrated on the new sound of the water lapping against the boats. A single red lamp shone on top of the gate to the marina, and water was washing back and forth across the rocks. Out to sea, there were other boats, but no police launches and the helicopter crew was concentrating on a land search. Drops of water fell, slowly at first, so Mike didn't realise it was rain. Then it picked up into a steady downpour which cooled him, refreshed him and gave them the cover they needed to get the boat out. Solemn, dark clouds moved across the sky, cutting any light from the moon.

Mike pointed out their destination to Ling. 'It'll be slippery,' he shouted above the noise of the rain.

They were down on the rocks, the cold seawater splashing around their ankles. Sometimes a stronger wave would crash against them, soaking them, and they edged along, holding onto crevices and foliage to protect themselves from being swept out. The currents of the bay and the sea came together there and swirled around as if they were unsure of where to pull. The water twisted and frothed in little whirlpools. In places it repeatedly broke itself against the shoreline like mad people smashing their heads against a wall. The rain pounded around them and far away lightning streaked through the sky filling up the sea like a wartime flare.

The storm had brought in a higher tide and the rock pool they had to cross to get to the marina was covered with a mass of surging water. The rain made the sea more wild. The algae and seaweed on the surface was treacherous. It wasn't far, maybe twenty feet, but the rain was so hard now that it was pouring down their faces and into their eyes. The wind chilled them. Mike shivered. His wound, the loss of blood, his exhaustion cut through him. Ling was tiring, too. The bag of weapons hung heavily from her shoulder. She was slipping more, holding Mike's arm to steady herself. They couldn't speak. The gale tore their words away. So Mike went first. Balancing on his own, he lowered himself into the water. As the waves came and went, the current pulled his legs towards a tiny channel out to sea. The water came up to his thighs and he eased himself round the side, not straight across, to be sure of keeping the shallow depth. Then he was there, heaving himself up with his good arm and sitting, breathless, panting on the wooden walkway of the marina.

When he turned, Ling was already in the water, the bag on her left shoulder, her right hand clutching the higher rock. She had gashed her hand. With each surge of water, her balance weakened and she had to stop to steady the bag and check her foothold. She was lit up by another streak of lightning, closer this time, with the thunder coming straight away. Out at sea, the boats had slowed. Three junks close to the shore rolled heavily in the swell, with plastic sheeting drawn down, and their dinghies bobbing wildly behind them. A yacht with only the small jib up was being tossed around, using only the engine and heading round the coast to her mooring. With the thunder came a massive gush of water, which pushed Ling hard against the rocks.

She was kicking to find new footholds, but when water came she only had her hands and as it pulled her away the bag dragged against her shoulder like an extra force of destruction and her hand tore against the jagged rock with such pain that she felt she could hold it no longer.

'Let go,' yelled Mike. And she heard it on a gust of wind buffeting right against her. She managed to get her head round and Mike was gesticulating that she should let the water take her. Then everything was flashing in front of her. The storm. The gunfire. The dead guards. The gunman in Scott's flat. The bullets shattering her apartment; the calm voice of Andrew Carter who would take her to safety; the airport, Mike, now screaming at her, and his interrogation which had made her cry again and again. And whether she was right to trust a man who had just killed four men.

Spray covered her face. Her sodden hair hung over her eyes.

'Drop the bloody bag!' Mike shouted.

She let it slide off her shoulder. The bag sank quickly. She felt the strength of the water pull her and twist her around. Water splashed into her face. Mike was leaning over, his good arm outstretched. She swam two strokes towards him and he grabbed her. She found footholds and a crevice for her hand and then she was over the rocks and with Mike on the marina walkway.

The rain blurred the lights on the marina, but Mike could make out Joss's twenty-four-footer *Islay Malt*, her outdated wooden foredecks distinct against the gleaming white fibreglass of the pleasure boats around her. Ling was limping. Blood streamed down from the cut on her hand. A cold and relentless wind tore through them. But the ground was solid and quickly they were on board and in the cockpit. The key was taped, as usual, just under the locker. In your honour, Joss, thought Mike.

He took her out slowly past a fishing village, where the junks were anchored with smells of stale fish and washing flapping in the air. They ran through an oil slick and clusters of rubbish on the surface. Then, as she left the protection of the cove and marina, she began rolling with the swell, so Mike gave her more power to steady her in the rougher water. She pitched on the confluence of the currents at the headland, but conditions were better, the lightning further away, out in the South China Sea towards the Philippines, and the thunder barely audible. Mike knew the night lights of Hong Kong and a place not too far away where he would be safe.

Mike found the oilskins and even a change of clothes downstairs for both of them. There were thick T-shirts, sweaters and baggy cotton trousers which covered Ling completely, so when she emerged Mike could only see her eyes amid the heavy nautical clothing. Joss must have been on the boat only a few days earlier. Ice packs kept the freezer bag chilled. There were six cold cans of beer and packet of cheese and ham sandwiches wrapped in cellophane. Ling bandaged her gashed hand from the first aid kit and, once they had settled, she looked at Mike's shoulder more closely.

'The bullet missed the scapula,' she said. 'It may have gone straight through the muscle.' She took off the dressing. 'How do you feel?'

'Like shit,' said Mike. He eased the tiller towards him to bring the boat into the swell. Ling touched the wound and Mike flinched. 'The bleeding's stopped. The salt water was good for it.' Ling got out a fresh bandage and redressed it. 'It should be done properly when we find some sterilised water,' she said. She folded a triangular bandage and put it round his neck to act as a sling.

Mike didn't turn the lights on. The rain thinned, except for sudden squalls which soaked them, rattled the empty stays and then blew on. Clouds moved fast overhead. But they always replenished themselves and hid the moon completely. The helicopter crew would be having a rough time if they were still up there. He could make out the lights of the Shek O peninsula.

Ling slumped down beside him: 'Where are we going?' she said.

'To see a gangster,' said Mike.

'A friend?'

'I got him out of jail once,' said Mike. 'So he owes me a favour.'

'And why can he look after us?' she asked with a mix of curiosity and exhaustion.

'He's neutral. So nobody dares touch him. Nim Kai, the police, the PLA all use him to launder their money.'

Pain throbbed through Mike's shoulder and he asked Ling to take the helm. She steered them in among the freighters, stretched out from the crowded Western Harbour. Mike switched on the topmast light. A boat, visible but unlit, would attract attention. He touched Ling's hand to move them away from the closest freighter.

'So did you kill Carter?' he said.

'Why,' asked Ling. 'Do you think so?'

'I don't know it matters. What I suppose I mean is did you sleep with Scott on orders from the Party and then were you ordered to have him killed?'

Ling shook her head and wiped her hair out of her face. 'I slept with Scott because I liked him.'

The boat rolled heavily as the wake of a jetfoil spread across the water towards them. 'And what about you?' she said. 'You were my interrogator and now they want to kill you.'

'Bring her round,' said Mike, his hand gently with her on the tiller again: 'Keep on course towards those lights.' Mike leant forward and pulled a lifejacket out of the cockpit locker to use as a cushion to take the pressure off his back. 'This boat belongs to Joss McEwan. He did Scott's autopsy and found that he'd been murdered, strangled probably.'

Ling didn't answer and Mike went on: 'The first American you spoke to on the phone, Tom Elton, was shot dead earlier this evening.'

'He was a policeman?'

'No,' continued Mike. 'He was a media man, a public relations consultant. He was employed to make sure no one found out about the murky side of the Party and the Hong Kong government.'

'So where do you fit in?'

'They meant to kill me instead of Elton.'

Ling looked straight ahead, easing the helm and using the lights of Lantau Island as a point of concentration to separate her thoughts from the chill of their conversation. Mike's telephone rang. It was still clipped to his belt and he looked down to check the number of the caller, recognised the Californian prefix and pressed the answer button. He estimated thirty seconds before an intercept tracked his location.

Chapter Eighteen

'Kidnapped?'

'So I gather,' answered Stephen Cranley. The unexcitable tone of the head of Britain's Secret Intelligence Service in Hong Kong contrasted with that of his American counterpart.

'How?'

'This particularly wild policeman, McKillop, went back, shot his way into the house where you were questioning her, killed the guards and dragged her away.' Cranley rolled his cocktail glass back and forth in his hand. 'All rather Hollywood, don't you think?'

Stephen Cranley had found Warren Hollingworth in between conversations at the opening of the Chinese army's leisure and casino complex on what used to be called the Stanley, now the Chek Tsu, or Naked Pillar, Peninsula. The Colonial military barracks with its landscaped lawns, parade ground and sweeping clifftop views was opening as a casino, night club and hotel. Chinese troops in ceremonial uniform kept guard at the entrance like model soldiers reminiscent of those outside Buckingham Palace.

Stephen Cranley smiled at everyone who recognised him, while taking Hollingworth's elbow discreetly to steer him through the room to the terrace where sudden rain squalls were keeping most guests inside.

'How much is McKillop one of yours?' said Hollingworth.

'Technically, he is a British citizen,' said the diplomat. 'He's a Scot. Been here for twenty years or more. Married to a Chinese who left him.'

'Is it only you, Haskins and I who know about the session today?' asked Hollingworth.

'And whoever is on the Chinese side,' replied Cranley. 'I suggest we wait and establish what happened before we pass anything at all to our capitals.'

'I tell you, Stephen, even if it was straight political killing, the Carter murder is getting very messy for no reason I can understand.'

The two men stood at the corner of the terrace. Cranley wiped his brow with a handkerchief. 'I do think this is all rather quaint,' he continued as a non sequitur. 'What purges would Mao create if he knew his peasant boys were being used to coax the tourist dollar to a gambling and sex den? All very twenty-first century Asian chic, don't you think?'

Hollingworth leant heavily on the balustrade. His eyes were pale and tired. He let the sweat run down his face. His collar was wet with it. 'I thought you Brits had a deal with them not to turn these barracks into a casino?'

He finished eating a cocktail sausage and let the stick fall onto the floor.

'Many years ago, Warren,' said Cranley. 'An agreement with the Chinese generally has a shelf-life of six months to a year, with decay setting in at its inception.' Cranley twisted his own cocktail stick in his fingers, his eyes shifting without inhibition around the party in search of a waiter with whom to deposit it.

'How many billions of dollars' worth of contracts is Zuckerman signing when Kang visits?' continued Cranley.

'I don't eavesdrop on the White House,' responded Hollingworth, refusing to rise to Cranley's attempt at point scoring. Instead he fixed Cranley with a stare which told the Englishman to back off. 'McKillop killed Tom Elton earlier this evening,' he said. 'After that he kidnapped Ling Chen, our main suspect in the Carter murder.'

'Suspect?' Cranley dropped the cocktail stick onto a passing waiter's silver tray and plucked off a biscuit draped with smoked salmon.

'She works for the Party. McKillop was a damn good interviewer and was beginning to break her. Then he goes crazy. So, if you have anything at all on McKillop, I'd be grateful for it.'

Cranley dabbed his lips with a napkin. As Hollingworth relayed more of the crisis, Cranley seemed to deliberately become more unalarmed. 'Pity America,' he said patronisingly. 'We fought our ideological tiff with the Chinese in the Nineties over this place.' He smiled and put his hand on Hollingworth's forearm. 'Our policies were, I assure you, the most ridiculous. We lost trade and failed to save Hong Kong. But history views our withdrawal as honourable. The last Governor, a fighting national hero. The British government acquitted.'

Cranley turned to look over the peninsula. 'But it was all puff,' he finished. 'We just handed the mantle over to you, Warren. Good luck.'

Hollingworth was distracted by parts of a conversation about Elton's murder.

'Catch you later,' he said, leaving Cranley alone on the terrace and edging through the room, handshake by handshake. The source of the murder speculation was an Australian designer, who supplied new-look uniforms to the PLA. She was telling how she had been stopped by police while driving down from the Peak, shown a photograph of Mike McKillop and asked if she had seen him. Hollingworth moved on, becoming briefly trapped in between the Thai trade commissioner and a Thai businessman who were more concerned with a land auction on the border. Bidding reached thirty per cent more than the asking price, the ambitious investment of a French-Cambodian consortium. Next, the Bosnian Consul General hauled him into a discussion with his Korean counterpart on the skills of national unification.

It was then that Hollingworth spotted Li Tuo and made his way towards him. By the time there was a hush for the Hong Kong Chief Executive to speak, Hollingworth and Li Tuo were next to each other. Guests raised their glasses.

Cranley stayed by the door of the terrace from where he had a better view of the room. He listened to the refrain of 'stability, prosperity and democracy,' and as the Chief Executive announced the toast, a giant roulette wheel was lowered down from the ceiling. Instead of red and black, the roulette slots were gold and stainless steel to represent both ancient and modern China. The wheel itself was bright red with clusters of five stars to honour the symbols of the Communist Party. The Chief Executive took a magnum of Tsing Tao champagne which, like the launching of the ship, he smashed against the wheel, spraying the closest cheering spectators. An orchestra struck up from behind the podium. Waiters entered through double doors at both sides of the room, carrying portable gaming tables of Black Jack, Twenty-One, Dice and other games.

Stephen Cranley broke another cocktail stick between his fingers and watched Li Tuo and Warren Hollingworth, ignoring the activity around them, in angry and animated conversation.

*   *   *

'Let's leave the missile issue to one side,' said Donald Zuckerman. 'Give me a rundown of Kang's schedule and what we hope to achieve.'

Zuckerman had chosen the cabinet room for the meeting, although with only a few of them the large rectangular table and its high-backed chairs were hardly filled. The President paced around his chair at the top, while he prepared to absorb information and make quick decisions. His National Security Adviser, Peter Mackland, had papers strewn in front of him and Zuckerman noticed without comment a stain of spilt coffee on the front of his shirt. Samantha Lo, his overseas Chinese Trade Secretary, had only a blank pad of paper for taking notes. The rest of the information would be in her formidable memory which he expected her to use with ruthless precision if the room became divided. Unlike the others, Mike Clarke, his urbane Secretary of State, had not taken off the jacket of his charcoal grey pinstripe suit. Zuckerman had given up trying to force Clarke into the informality enjoyed in the White House. Clarke was leaning forward pulling out the sheet of paper which had Kang's itinerary on it.

'I'll run through it,' said Charles Murphy, the White House Chief of Staff, who was stepping in to protect his presidential territory. For Murphy, who had clawed his way to Washington from a violent upbringing in New York's Bronx, Kang was coming to see the President, and no one else but he would be in charge of the visit.

'The Defense Secretary and the CIA director are both overseas, Mr President, and send their apologies,' he added.

Zuckerman nodded. Murphy continued. 'Kang will fly straight to Washington, not LA as the Chinese first suggested. You will have two sessions of formal talks with him. There's an hour-long slot for just the two of you with no agenda before the state banquet. Interpreters will be available, but Kang's English is fluent and I suggest . . .'

'Is his wife coming?' interrupted Zuckerman.

'Yes, but apart from the banquet she's on a completely different programme,' answered Murphy.

'I'll see Kang alone,' said Zuckerman.

Murphy picked up the thread. 'From Washington, he'll go to Detroit to tour the General Motors factory. That will be the main official visit to American industry. General Motors are setting up a new factory in Chengdu which Samantha can brief you on.'

Murphy pulled out the next sheet from his file. 'Now, here's a strange one. Most of this itinerary is being done through the Chinese Embassy here. Microsoft in Seattle have been in touch to say that Kang's private office in Beijing has made direct contact with them. Apparently, he's the personal friend of several Microsoft executives and wants to see them very privately and very confidentially. They've fixed up a night in the company's log cabin resort.'

'But they haven't informed us officially yet?' asked Mike Clarke.

'No. There's time that day for him to visit the Boeing factory in Seattle so he will be in the right place to slip away.'

'There could also be protests by people being put out of work because Boeing is manufacturing in China,' added Samantha Lo. 'Chinese leaders don't like that sort of thing.'

'He's been warned about that,' said Murphy. 'And the Chinese still want it as an option.'

'He's the boss,' said Zuckerman.

'Then finally to San Francisco where he's meeting the overseas Chinese community,' finished Murphy.

'The banquet guests,' said Zuckerman. 'Vet them and vet them. I don't want to pick up any crap about sleaze money and China buying our foreign policy.'

Murphy made a note. 'Sam,' said Zuckerman, turning to his trade secretary, 'while we're on the topic of money, how much trade is all this going to generate?'

'You'll be signing fifteen billion dollars' worth of contracts. Of those we would only expect about half to come to fruition smoothly over the next five years,' said Samantha Lo. 'The General Motors deal will be the focus and we know it will happen because the factory is already built. When Kang leaves the United States, we want trade to be the linchpin of our relationship with China, meaning that human rights, weapons sales and all the tougher issues can be quietly negotiated in private. And that's how the Chinese like it.'

Peter Mackland was erratically moving papers around on his desk, waiting to intervene: 'Mr President, apologies for interrupting, but I must stress that in the light of the recent intelligence reports from China, the linchpin of trade, if we go down that path, will unbalance the balance of power, as it were.'

Once speaking, Mackland pushed his files away from him and took off his glasses. 'And it's my job to stop that happening. What the Trade Secretary is envisaging, I think, is to create a rather dull relationship with China like we have with Brazil or India, or even Singapore or Malaysia. But my assessment is that China is pulling us into an intractable abyss of blackmail. We are moving towards a situation where the blue chip companies of the New York stock exchange are beholden to the Communist Party of China for their profits. Examined in geopolitical terms, the irony of it is terrifying.'

Zuckerman had taken his seat while Mackland was speaking: 'Sam,' he said. 'Respond.'

Samantha Lo thought for a few moments before she spoke: 'China's economy needs us far more than we need it, right now, Mr President. But Peter is right in warning that the balance of that equation is changing. There are more and more American communities that are reliant on trade with China. Jobs and families are tied up in it so the knock-on effects, be they beneficial or adverse, will mean change in voting patterns.'

'Paint me a picture,' said Zuckerman.

'In California, exports to China keep 416,000 people employed. In Seattle, 112,000, many of them with Boeing. In Arizona, 16,000; New York, 100,000. Clearly, any disruption to our trade with China will have an effect, which would be reflected by the electorate in the next elections. And to give you an idea, California has fifty-two Congressional seats going in the next election; Washington has nine; Arizona, six; New York, thirty-one. Florida, with 32,000 jobs at stake, has twenty-three seats. Throughout America there are 469 seats whose representatives will take China trade to their election platform.'

'And is it getting worse?' interjected the Chief of Staff.

'Worse, Charlie?' queried the President. 'Don't take sides.'

'Well it's sounding like Peter's right. They're getting us into a vice and we don't even know about it.'

'Mike,' said Zuckerman, turning to his secretary of state. 'Give us a diplomat's view.'

'The policy of constructive engagement, Mr President, is doing precisely what both Samantha and Peter have outlined,' said Mike Clarke. 'Their disagreement is over the level of risk. Will China, with a more cosmopolitan population and higher standards of living, evolve naturally towards the democratic process? Or will it exploit our technology and our investment to build a monstrous dictatorship and evolve towards being America's natural enemy? There is little dispute about what is happening. Only about China's intentions.'

Zuckerman nodded: 'And you're saying that with a closed society and no mole inside their citadels we don't know their intentions?'

'Correct, sir,' said Clarke. 'The ultimate question we have to ask ourselves is: how close can we get to a government who sends senior non-violent religious leaders to forced labour camps?'

'But we're getting results,' interjected Samantha Lo. 'There have been a number of significant releases . . .'

'Crap,' said Clarke angrily. 'They keep human beings like equity stocks, which they sell off to us every time they want something. After the presidential visit in 1997, they released the prize dissident Wei Jingsheng, not into his community, but into exile. And people like you, Sam, hail it as a victory. Then they turn round and arrest a dozen more whom we don't know about. They encourage the Western press to write about them as heroes, fattening them up as bargaining chips when they want something else. This, Mr President, is no way to run a mature relationship with an aspirant superpower.'

'What releases are we asking for as a pay-off for this summit?' said Zuckerman more calmly.

'Bishop Chu,' said Mackland. 'But they said it was non-negotiable.'

'Chu?' asked Charles Murphy.

'Paul Chu, the Catholic Bishop of Hebei province near Beijing,' said Clarke. 'Hasn't been seen for nearly ten years. We don't know where he's being held. Even if he's still alive.'

'Sorry,' pressed Murphy. 'But why's he so special?'

'Most dissidents are only known by educated intellectuals within China and human rights campaigners outside,' explained Clarke. 'While in China, they're silenced. In exile, their glamour wanes and they quickly disappear into the academic and immigrant community. Paul Chu is different. The last time he held Mass, a quarter of a million people turned up, after which he was arrested. His appeal cannot be overestimated, Mr President. He is to the Catholic Church in China what the Dalai Lama is to the Buddhists or what Nelson Mandela represents to the black African.'

'I'm hearing you,' said Zuckerman.

The meeting fell silent while the President noted down details of the conversation. 'I'll ask Kang to let him go,' he said, underscoring Chu's name on his notepad.

'I'll get the file,' said Murphy.

157

Zuckerman leant back in his chair, tilting it to stretch his back. 'And talking about aspiring superpowers, let's talk about these damn missiles. They appear to be all over the place: Pakistan, Indonesia and God knows where else.'

'Our intelligence from Hong Kong says that the Chinese have successfully tested a new long-range missile which can hit its target for a change,' said Peter Mackland. There was a brief burst of spontaneous laughter.

'Peter, can you explain what you think is going on?' asked Zuckerman bringing his chair back again so that all four legs were on the carpet. 'The Indians are talking about a Chinese deal to sell long-range missiles to Pakistan.'

'If I may talk in general terms at first, Mr President,' Mackland began. 'There is a view that with the restructuring of the military and purchasing of new weapons, it was inevitable that sooner or later the People's Liberation Army would do something both to justify its role and pay for it.

'Missiles, Mr President, are what China's military is all about and with missiles they have a record of breaking international agreements. In 1988, they violated the Missile Technology Control Regime (MTRC) accord which they had signed a year earlier. It bans the sale of missiles or technology for missiles that can carry a payload of more than 500 kilograms a distance of more than 300 kilometres. A year later, China sold thirty-six intermediate-range CSS-2 missiles to Saudi Arabia, which paid more than $3 billion for them. It did a deal to sell its newly developed M-9 missiles to Syria. It's been involved with Iran, Iraq, Pakistan, Syria, Saudi Arabia, Egypt, and a few others.'

'But not only Islamic countries, Peter,' interrupted the Secretary of State. 'Aren't you veering a bit?'

'Let me finish, please, Mr President.'

Zuckerman waved his hand from the top of the table to indicate that Mackland should go on.

'We first put pressure on China in 1987 when it sold Silkworm missiles to Iran. Then it got worse. In 1989 and 1991 Chinese and Iranian companies struck what in public looked like a commercial deal. But the product was nuclear – an electromagnetic separator for producing isotopes and a mini-type reactor. The Chinese said it was being used for medical diagnosis and nuclear physics research.

'Atom bombs can be made using a concentrated uranium isotope. That particular deal was dropped, we think because the

Russians came up with a better one. But let us assume that Iran is about where Iraq was in the early nineties. It's exploring the nuclear path, but isn't there yet. The next thing we know is that China's sent over what we call *calutron* equipment, which is needed to enrich uranium. Our intelligence also finds evidence of China supplying Iran with chemical weapons material, thiodiglycol and thionyl chloride, both of which are very nasty substances. The upshot is an aspiring nuclear enemy, possibly with an additional arsenal of mass-destruction chemical weapons.'

'We are talking about events of almost two decades ago,' argued Samantha Lo.

'That's why I'm telling you. We've uncovered more since then which shows a three-tiered foreign and defence policy. The first is to encourage trade. The second is to forge alliances with governments potentially hostile to the United States. The third is to develop a high-technology missile and naval force. The latest evidence we've been given – which is since I last spoke to you, Mr President – is Indian satellite photographs of a rail shipment of twenty-six missiles being taken to the northern naval base at Tsing Tao. As we speak, they are probably being loaded onto Pakistani freighters destined for Karachi.'

'Pakistan is our ally,' said Zuckerman.

'It is also Iran's ally, Mr President,' replied Mackland. 'The Indians say they are the latest East Wind 33 missiles with a new guidance system. That is unconfirmed, though.'

'And Iran might have them in its arsenal?' said Zuckerman.

'Not these. But the East Wind 32. Same missile, but not so accurate. Its payload can be a 700-kilogram nuclear warhead. If fired from Chinese soil, Mr President, the East Wind 32 could get to Alaska or Western Europe. We also believe they're working on a new submarine-launched ICBM. If they got one of those into the Pacific, they could attack Washington and New York.'

Peter Mackland gathered his papers in a pile and pulled them towards him, an indication to everyone in the room that he had finished speaking. Donald Zuckerman pushed back his chair and began pacing again at the end of the room. 'Are you saying, Peter, that President Kang's friendship summit here is a smokescreen of a long-term plan to . . . to . . . to what? I don't know. To become the enemy of another Cold War?'

'Don't know, Mr President. Don't know.'

'We're getting different signals from the reformist faction,' said the Secretary of State. 'And the military, which can be a law unto itself.'

'And what about the Indonesian arms sale?' said Zuckerman.

'The assessment of Warren Hollingworth, station chief in Hong Kong, is that it's a purely commercial transaction and we would be wrong to make anything of it,' answered Secretary of State Mike Clarke. 'There's no reason why China should not make a buck out of the arms trade, just as we do.'

'Have we got anything on the guidance systems?'

'Nothing more than at our last meeting, Mr President,' said Mackland.

Zuckerman sat down and drank from the glass of the water on the table in front of him. 'We need a much better handle on all of this. Sam, get me a complete national break-down on the trading and economic impact if our relationship with China runs into difficulties. I need the immediate and the long term, going twenty, thirty years on from now. Mike, get reports in from every embassy in Asia – both CIA and State – on China's capability and its intention. And Pete, we've got secret missiles, diplomats being murdered and a presidential visit which is turning into one hell of a mess. Get Hollingworth over here. I need to hear things from the horse's mouth.'

Chapter Nineteen

C lem Watkins paid cash for two more nights, pulled the car out of the motel parking lot and accelerated north up the highway with the Pacific Ocean crashing in below on his left. Twenty miles along he called the motel, checked for messages and told them to put the phone in his room on divert to his mobile. Fifty miles further on, he drew up at a roadside diner.

Clem had let his hair run wild and dirty. He wore his clothes filthy and crumpled and hadn't taken a shower since he had landed in the States. The people in the diner were his type, quiet, suspicious, dirty and poor. Or at least they looked it, like Clem. They sat alone, eyes on their food, their coffee and their vehicles.

Clem chose a table by the window looking out both sides, onto the Chrysler and the petrol station. He ordered a black coffee and a cheeseburger. He had tried McKillop during the day but Mike had cut the line, which meant it was too dangerous to talk. Clem sipped his coffee and thought. There had been two people whom he trusted absolutely because he had known them for so long. He would have counted Hollingworth until four days ago. He thought of calling a friend in the FBI about Joyce Hewlitt, but that would blow his cover. His number would show up and they would track him. There were two men outside of America whom he could talk to safely. Satish Krishnan, the office administrator in Bombay, wouldn't have an incoming number identification on his phone and Win Kyi, who should be back in Yangon by now. The waitress set a steaming cup of coffee down on the table and told him the burger would be another five minutes. Clem asked where the washroom was. He followed the directions and went outside. When he finished, he crossed the parking lot to the payphone at the petrol station.

He used his AT & T access number from the Heshui account and found it hadn't been cancelled. Satish Krishnan was surprised

161

to hear Clem who began flippantly: 'Hi Satish, did you think I was dead?'

'I've got the message about your assignment here,' said Satish. 'It got fouled up and delayed in the system.'

Satish sounded normal, his urbanity covering the irritation of being disturbed during his evening meal. Clem heard him pause and swallow, then scold a child who appeared to be tugging at his shoelace. 'Do you have a flight number for me now?' Satish Krishnan was saying.

'Should have tomorrow,' said Clem brightly. 'Hong Kong want a China debrief, but I just needed to check with you that I was actually expected.'

'How is it up there?' said Khrishnan. It was a strange tone, the sort onlookers might adopt as they gather outside a besieged city.

'In what way?' said Clem cautiously. He cupped his hand around the mouthpiece to ensure that no loud American voices betrayed that he was not in China.

'There's rumblings in the defence ministry about instability in the Chinese government.'

'Haven't heard anything,' said Clem.

'At least in India we know when the country's falling apart.' Clem heard a smack which must have been Khrishnan disciplining his child. A driver started his truck in the parking lot and revved the engine, spewing out black smoke from the back which caught in the wind, enveloping the phone booth.

'Where in the hell are you, Clem? On the highway?'

'China's always been a mystery,' said Clem, signing off the call. 'Glad to be assigned from one ancient civilisation to another.'

Khishnan laughed. 'Let me know when you're coming in.'

Khrishnan's air of normality lifted the tension from Clem. He was even tempted to call Hollingworth. Maybe the layers upon layers of the Chinese system had blurred his judgment. Maybe the great Clem Watkins was losing it. Maybe he had just been the target of a drive-by shooting in Beijing. What if it had happened in Los Angeles? Would it have meant that the American government was falling apart? Maybe he was really meant to be relocated to India. A senior Chinese official visits Heshui, so it's reasonable that they want the American spy out. And what about Joyce Hewlitt? Maybe she did go crazy and burn down her home. Martin was in the trade so no wonder they didn't want the local sheriff's office to handle it. And Mike? The way Mike drank his whisky and spoke about his family was the character of a broken man. God knows what blackmail the man was suffering. God knows why Clem thought Mike was the same man he had worked with thirteen years earlier.

Clem stepped out of the phone booth and walked around the parking lot. It was warmer, and the traffic on the road was getting heavy in the early morning. The waitress caught his eye through the window and he put up his hand indicating he would be there in a few minutes. Had Clem been in China a little too long? Perhaps the vicious argument he had with the security guys at Heshui over his swipe card not working had been reported back to Hong Kong and the experienced Hollingworth decided it was time to give Watkins a break. Maybe Clem needed to get back to head office, to get back into the system again, cool down a bit.

Clem headed back for the phone booth and picked up the receiver to dial the home number of Win Kyi in Burma. The phone rang three times before someone answered and Clem began a conversation which he had rehearsed with Win Kyi years earlier.

'This is Michael Bentley, a friend of Brigadier General Win Kyi,' he began affably in English. 'Is the general in?'

There was pause. 'Which company?' said a young man's voice.

'It's a personal call. I'm with Voss International. The general knows it. We deal with security and . . .'

'Wait a moment,' said the man. He must have pressed the hold button because Clem heard Mozart's horn concerto come down the line, then a click and a different, older voice.

'Mr Bentley, I'm afraid you have called at an inconvenient time. General Win Kyi died in a car accident in China two days ago.'

'Died?' said Clem with incredulity.

'His funeral is later today. If you could . . .'

Clem hung up and tried Mike once more. This time McKillop answered, but sounding hurried, and like Clem, a hunted man unsure where his enemies were.

'Mike. You OK?' said Clem.

'No,' said Mike. 'The Chinese have tried to kill me. I'm on the run.'

'Are you hurt?'

'Winged.'

'Shit.'

'They shot Win Kyi on the steps of the Great Hall.'

'Car crash,' said Clem more to himself than to Mike. 'They said it was a car crash.'

'You were right.'

'Sweet fuck, I was, Mike.'

'But it's not safe now,' Mike was closing the call, afraid of intercepts. 'Let's speak in a few hours, if either of us is still around.' McKillop cut the line. Clem stepped out of the booth. The waitress saw him and pulled the cheeseburger from under the warming grill.

Mike checked his watch. Twenty seconds. They would never locate the call in that time. Clem was alive. In the States and, like him a fugitive. The sea lanes were less crowded. The lights of Peng Chau island were to their left. Passengers were boarding a ferry docked there after their seafood dinners near the jetty. Mike took back the helm and pulled the *Islay Malt* round away from the lights, still heading towards Lantau, but to the darker side of the island. At midnight, they listened to the news. The lead story was on President Kang's visit to Washington, followed by a massive search for a wave of illegal immigrants to explain the helicopters and police road blocks on the south side of the island.

The third item reported the killing of Tom Elton and named Mike McKillop as the suspect. The presenter read out a police statement and then a message from Sally to give himself up: 'The suspect's wife, Wong Wai-lok, a leading fertility specialist at the Hong Kong Number One Hospital, has appealed to Superintendent McKillop to hand himself over to the authorities.

'In a statement issued to the media Dr Wong said: "Mike, you are ill. My heart goes out to you in this time of torment. But you must give yourself up and return to your family who love you. We will support you and stand by you in this time of great trouble."

'Superintendent McKillop is a highly decorated police officer,' continued the presenter. 'He has two children, Charlotte aged thirteen and Matthew who's nine. The Wong-McKillops live in government quarters on the Peak. Superintendent McKillop had represented the Olympic Hong Kong shooting team and he was a qualified police marksman, but had recently been undergoing treatment for severe alcoholism.

'In Berlin, the German Chancellor . . .'

Mike switched off the radio. The wind had died almost completely and the harbour lights glistened behind them. Away from the disturbance of the boats, the water was steady and predictable.

'How long have you been married?' said Ling.

Mike turned off the mast light, so the boat was once again in darkness. He didn't answer for a while. 'Sally's my estranged wife,' he said without emotion. 'She didn't want to be married to a foreigner any more so she took the children and disappeared.' They were closer to the coast of Lantau, its shoreline rising quickly up towards the ridges which loomed over them.

'Recently?'

'A year ago,' answered McKillop. 'They promised me a meeting with Sally if I got you to confess to Scott's murder. I owe you an apology,'

Ling looked at him, the wind blowing back her hair: 'But I didn't confess.'

'That's not the point. They never meant to honour the deal. They tried to kill me and shot Tom instead. Then they were going to kill you.'

'So you have nothing to apologise about.' She brushed her hair out of her eyes. 'You saved my life when you could have made a clean getaway.'

'If I hadn't have pulled you off that plane, you would be safe in the States by now.'

'Someone else would have pulled me off.' She looked down at the water, thoughtful for a moment. 'You stopped me from running away,' she said. 'Scott's been murdered. Someone's tried to kill me, so I'm involved. The grief and responsibility don't evaporate just by getting on a plane.'

'Andrew Carter . . .'

Ling didn't let him finish: 'He doesn't matter. I've had one dinner with him. It was his son whose bed I shared, not his. Who knows whether I would even be safe in America?' she asked, her tone softening. 'And what do I do there? Become another Chinese exile wheeled out as an exhibit at Washington dinner parties to give them an atmosphere of something oriental?'

Mike laughed: 'It's got to be better than being on this boat with me.'

'No way,' Ling retorted. 'I get sick of people who think if they live in America everything will be all right. I'd take this boat anytime. Because we're doing something. We're not running away.'

He brought the boat round, taking it into a cove where the wind dropped: 'Anyway, accept my apologies for whatever. I'll feel better for it.'

'Until we find out who was trying to kill you and who was

165

trying to kill me, neither of us is safe. Whatever you have done in the past twelve hours hasn't changed that.'

'Fine,' said Mike. He turned the boat into the wind and put the engine into neutral. The current wasn't strong and she bobbed on the ebb and flow of water coming out from the coast.

'And what about you?' asked Ling. 'Are you really serious about seeing Sally again?'

'Oh yes,' said Mike, looking straight at her. 'A man can do an awful lot of bad things if he loves his wife too much.'

'It seems right now you're stopping bad things happening.'

He lashed down the tiller: 'We have to get to the dinghy on the foredeck,' he said moving forward. He held out his hand to help her out of the cockpit and they climbed round, supporting themselves on the stays. 'Would you and Scott really have married?'

They edged along the deck and she could have let the question go. But as he was unfastening the dinghy, she replied: 'I doubt I'm the marrying type. And all that stuff I said about the arrogance of his race, I wasn't making up.'

McKillop looked up: 'Did you love him?'

'Yes in your Western sense of the word. But in my culture, love takes longer to settle. That's what worried me most about marrying him, turning up back home with his China doll on his arm. Sorry. Not me.' She wiped the sea spray off her face and squeezed her eyes. 'Anyway, he's dead.'

'Yes, he is,' muttered Mike as they lowered the dinghy into the water. Ling brought it round to the stern and tied the painter to the safety rail. Mike knelt on the deck of the cockpit, opened the lifejacket locker and felt underneath where a .38 revolver was taped up. Next to it was a box of ammunition, just like Joss had told him there would be. He stuffed the weapon and the sandwiches into his pockets. Mike took the engine out of neutral and turned the *Islay Malt*, so her bow pointed away from Lantau. Ling clambered into the dinghy. Mike followed and, just before he left the boat, he moved her up to full throttle. He freed the painter. Ling was in the centre with both oars and they watched the empty boat head off towards the South China Sea.

Ling brought the dinghy into a cove which was littered with plastic bags, driftwood and rusting tins embedded in the sand. The small boats of local fishermen were there, their anchors stretching across the beach. Ling and Mike pulled up the dinghy, leaving it among the others. They had reached villages which had little regard for the ideology of the Party and the writ of the government had little authority here. The dinghy from the *Islay Malt* would be noticed by the villagers, but they would probably do nothing except paint it over and use it as their own.

Not much had changed on this part of the island. The airport, the monuments to China's control over Hong Kong and the base for China's southern attack aircraft fleet, were on the other side. McKillop led the way and found the path which wound round the coast underneath the golf course. They followed it to another longer beach. He found the track going up towards the hills. He was sweating hard. His shoulder regressed to a dull throb and then suddenly erupted into shooting pains which made him stop and rest. His calves ached and his breath was rasping as the climb cleared his under-used lungs. The moon was covered. His eyes became more accustomed to the dark, picking out the paths as they split here and there without signs, heading towards the lowland between the two peaks of the island and a place where they might be safe.

The last time he did this walk, it had taken four hours. But he was younger then, not hungry, not shot-up and exhausted. Slowly, resting at times, they made their way up. Ling helped when the wound became too much, then she pressed on ahead, sure-footed on the slippery track. Mike enjoyed her touch and the closeness of a woman. There was a sense of companionship; that he was no longer so completely alone. But also something in his policeman's mind gnawed at the logic of her being there, at her own motivation, at the ease of their escape when a helicopter machine gunner could easily have blown them out of the water. He had seen enough trust, betrayal and death to know that the beautiful woman now climbing the hill in front of him might turn out to be the enemy they were both meant to be running from. And with that thought, fatigue swept over him. He stumbled. She looked back. He caught his balance and pressed on.

Towards the top, the mist was thick and wet, moving in clumps through the blackness, sometimes glowing from the little moonlight and brightening up the path. For half an hour on a last stretch to the first summit, they were in woodland, then they broke out just as they crossed a stream, to the barren mountainside. Mike could make out patches which had been burnt away by bush fire and the sparse moorland where they were heading. The path forked above him. The left route headed across and down towards the smuggling town of Tai O.

'How much further?' said Ling. She caught her breath. The humidity of the clouds around the mountain top was mixed with her sweat.

'Somewhere ahead is safe territory,' said Mike. He leant against a rock and pulled out of his pocket the packages Elton had given him. 'At least I think so. We have just got to go in and see who meets us,' he said.

First he checked his money. The notes were damp and stuck together. Two thousand Hong Kong dollars and some change. As good as nothing. Credit cards. Yes. The Barclaycard still registered to his account in Jersey which would bypass the system. He flipped open his fake passport, where the plastic bag and laminated cover had protected it from much of the water. He was Michael Kentwell, a teacher, aged thirty-nine. Elton had been generous.

He felt mentally drained as well as physically exhausted. The radio bulletin with Sally's bogus appeal had brought home his absolute helplessness. He had no plan except to get over the summit to territory he knew was out of the Party's control. Next to Ling, he felt old and useless and all the time he looked at her now he saw something of Sally: the confidence, the curiosity, the intelligence. Oh yes, and not forgetting the treachery, a Chinese single-mindedness to achieve a goal.

'Why did Elton help you so much?' asked Ling, looking at his new passport.

'I don't know,' he said, wearily. 'I don't know who Elton was even. Whose side he was on. I don't know who Hollingworth is or Scott Carter. Or whose side any of us are on, or even who you are.'

'You know who I am. You interrogated me all day,' said Ling quickly.

'Twelve hours ago my brief was to get you to confess to causing a death. Twelve hours ago you were telling me how you reported back to the Communist Party how you had been sent out to spy for them. You told me how you resented Scott Carter's arrogance and the way he laughed at the failures of the Chinese Communist Party. Then I leave you to go and see Sally, my wife, for the first time in a year. You and she were interlinked. Your confession was my meeting. That was how the Party sold it to me. Except she didn't exist. There was only a sniper who killed Elton. So I escape and they've got helicopters and men scouring the undergrowth for me. Then Elton says your life is in danger and I get you out and you come without a murmur. I'm killing everything around us. But you still come. And suddenly, there's no one hunting us. We've got the whole fucking world to ourselves . . .'

'You think . . .'

Mike pushed himself up. 'I don't think anything, Miss Ling Chen. We get a pissy little boat across here with no one even coming in to catch us. So maybe I'm just as much in jail now as if I had been caught. Or maybe I'm just tired and pissed because I've been shot and my shoulder hurts like hell.'

Ling's head was turning from side to side, then she squatted down burying her face in her hand. 'What are you saying? That I'm spying on you? That it's a set-up?'

Mike put the rest of Elton's packets back in his pocket. 'I'm sorry. I'm saying that I don't care what you're doing. I've been dead ever since they killed Elton and they started all this fresh bullshit about Sally.'

'I saw how you killed those guys at Shek O,' she said softly. 'You're angry, man.'

'You only saw half of it,' said McKillop curtly. He turned away so she couldn't see him. Suddenly, on this empty mountainside, a lump came to his throat and his eyes swelled with tears. Humiliation and remorse swept over him and for a moment he couldn't control it. His breathing was loud and rasping: 'Let's get on,' he said.

'I'm not your enemy,' said Ling.

'I hope to hell you're not,' said McKillop, moving off and scanning the hills around them. He saw the pattern of the stream running down. He picked out the single-strand yellow spiderwebs woven between trees. In gaps in the undergrowth and when the mist cleared, he could see the skyline of Hong Kong, disdainful, haughty and unforgiving. The primary neon colours flashed at him, taunting him, telling him that they had broken yet another man but they didn't care. Mike was drained. He tripped on rocks. An aeroplane's lights were high above. He heard water, just six feet from the path and stepped off the path towards it. He crouched down and felt it with his hand, splashing it onto his face. He cupped his hand and lowered his head close enough to catch it and drink. He heard a sound behind him and thought it would be Ling. The rush of water was everywhere. Perhaps a shadow. His night training was so long ago. He turned, but too slowly. The blow caught him on the back of the head. He was conscious and tumbling. His elbow was wet. He remembered that, but nothing else. Then another blow.

Chapter Twenty

Mike was woken by a gentle shaking, which sent pain shooting through his body. A maid brought in steaming coffee, a bottle of single malt and a glass on a tray and set it down on a chair next to McKillop's bed. Clothes were laid out on a chair, a blue-collared shirt, pressed and folded, and beige cotton slacks on a hanger. His mobile phone and the .38 were lying on a table. His whole body ached. Someone had wrapped him in a sarong. His wound had been redressed. His arm was in a new sling. He reached over for the pistol, opened the chamber and saw it was empty.

He got out of bed. The room covered the whole first-floor corner of the building. The black and white marble tiles of the bedroom were cool on his bare feet. A living area stretched back behind him, but with a pine floor, covered with carpets from Shiraz, Kashgar and Kashmir. The room purred with air-conditioning. Mike stepped onto the balcony and beneath him was a swimming pool with a drinks bar half submerged in the water, everything smuggled in to this palace by the criminal underworld of China.

There was a shout from below: 'Michael McKillop, I salute you.'

Henry Druk took a glass of champagne off a silver tray carried by a maid. Sweat covered his face and fell in droplets around the folds of skin, nestling in a pool in crevices on his neck. A grubby singlet stretched over his enormous stomach. 'The Americans, the British and the Chinese Communist Party are hunting you like a dog and you choose to seek sanctuary with me.' Druk raised the glass to Mike. 'You have given me more face than any man.'

He roared with laughter.

Shouts and bangs bounced around the village with the boats back from their runs to the mainland and the money and gold being counted out before lunch. That night, they had delivered five cars, hand-stolen by his men from the car parks of Hong

170

Kong. There was no violence. Everyone was richer and happy, especially Druk.

Druk arrived in Mike's room, embracing him as an old friend and telling his staff to leave them alone. He poured Mike a glass of champagne, then lowered his huge frame into the armchair. 'I never thought I would see the formidable McKillop again,' he said. 'It's a genuine pleasure. Tell me, did you choose to come to me or . . .'

Mike nodded. He sipped the champagne. 'I got into a spot of bother last night,' he said. 'I had to rescue a girl who was about to be killed and got shot.' He lifted his left arm, showing off the sling. This was how he had always talked to Drunk, flippant, laid back, unflustered.

'So I heard. So I heard,' said Druk. He passed Mike the morning papers and let him read them undisturbed, while he stood on the balcony and watched his men through binoculars. They worked in teams of ten or fifteen, bundling boxes of video recorders from the back of a truck into a long, sleek powerboat, its stern low in the water, weighed down by four outboard motors.

Mike's picture ran on most front pages, with Sally's appeal for him to give himself up strapped across some headlines. Stories underneath said she had been forced to take the children away because of his drunkenness. There was a new picture with the children in white shirts with red ties. Matthew wore blue short trousers, and with his posture showing just a bit of his walking difficulties.

Charlotte was in a pretty red dress and they were in Beijing gathered under the picture of Mao Tse-tung above the gate of Heavenly Peace at the entrance to the Forbidden City. Their heads were looking up. They were with two Party officials, each with a hand on their shoulders. McKillop couldn't see Sally. He searched the picture for her, amid the tiny images of people around Tiananmen Square. But she wasn't there. It was the first proof he had had that they were even alive, but they were austere and disciplined, so like the children he had seen in his dreams.

'I must apologise on behalf of my men for hitting you so hard,' said Druk from the balcony. 'It was absolutely necessary, I assure you.'

'I think I've hit you before,' said Mike.

'Ling Chen put up a great fight as well. Knocked one of my guys out.' Druk walked back in. 'She's sleeping in another villa.'

'The Chinese have always been good gangsters,' said Mike.

171

'But we're lousy at governing ourselves,' replied Druk, sitting down. 'We can't imagine that the people who rule us are less devious and less ambitious than we are. So we try to cheat them and we call it revolution.'

McKillop laughed cynically. The sun warmed him. The drink eased the pain in his head.

'That's why I never bought you off all those years ago. If I'd killed you, the British would have sent someone else after me. That was the system. It was that bloody communist, Li Tuo, who framed me on the heroin racketeering precisely because I refused to let drugs into my territory. And it was you, the British, who got the charges lifted. I respect that in a system.' He waved his hand out towards the work below: 'Look at this mess. I pay more for weapons than I ever did in taxes and bribes.'

'But you're the emperor,' coaxed McKillop.

'Like hell. To get out of this place, I have to go by a stinking fishing trawler to Macau, trussed up like a grandmother, then sneak onto a flight on a fake passport and had to even buy an airline to make sure I could get a seat. Bloody mess, Mike. Bloody mess.'

'And I'm a fugitive,' said Mike.

'I know what happened,' said Druk. 'Or I know enough. And I know you didn't kill the American. That's what I liked about you Mike. Very steady and no moral crap. You British blew half of China apart trying to ship drugs here. Then you jail me for smuggling television sets and cars.' The gangster pushed himself to his feet. He wiped his face with a towel he kept tucked into his belt. 'Fugitive. Yes, you are.'

McKillop stayed sitting down. He found himself looking straight up at Druk.

'Mike, I can protect you a bit. But the communists can bomb me out tomorrow if they want. I pay them off. Fine for as long as they like it. But I don't mess with their politics and I have a feeling you're a lot more important to the Party than any of us know.'

'So?' said Mike, sipping his drink. 'What do we do?'

'I tell you Mike, if the Nim Kai want you, I can't protect you. There would be fighting and we don't do it over things like this. Only money.'

He thought Druk might laugh, like he usually did when he was up against it. But the gangster looked up at him and he was serious, sad almost, that his homeland had sunk into such decay. 'You, the British, knew how it would turn out,' said Druk. 'But you didn't seem to care.'

'Yes,' said Mike, drily. 'You're right.'

'You can stay for a bit, but your hourglass timer is running.'

Ling turned erratically, so tired that her fear and dreams mixed together. She was being tossed in the sea, the bodies of her dead guards around her, the water streaked with their blood. She was at her father's funeral, but he was there too, squeezing his hand.

She was in a bed, draped in fabric and when she woke, she pulled it away. The room was full of bright sunlight, streaming through from windows on two sides. Outside, there were trees. She remembered fighting people, then strong arms restraining her.

She sat up. The sun was too bright for her, but she shielded her eyes and swung her legs out over the bed. It was a large room and at the other end, sitting upright on a chair, with a gun resting on his knees was a young man. She walked over towards him, expecting him to move, but only his eyes followed her. She walked past him. He didn't stop her. The sun shone through the nightdress and lit up her body. She felt the warmth and he watched her. She had no recollection of undressing or putting on a nightdress. Her hand was on the handle of the French windows. In front was a balcony.

'May I?' she asked. He nodded and she went outside. The weather was cool and fresh and her view to the hillsides which she recognised, like the view from her flat. Two boys played basketball below.

When she turned around, the man with the gun was gone. She went back inside. The door to the room was open. It led into a corridor with white doors coming off it. The gun lay on the chair. The floor chilled her feet, but she enjoyed the sensation. Ling was rested and excited. She wasn't sure why, but she felt safe. The doors along the corridor were closed. Through them there were sounds familiar to her: noises from her childhood of the mahjong tiles sliding around the tabletop; voices in the dialects of China; sounds of cooking and the smell of incense.

She walked downstairs, the steps curved, with marble pillars, to a hallway decorated again in white marble. At the bottom of the stairs, she heard a radio broadcast, not paying attention, the crispness of the morning weather catching her, together with the warmth of the sun and the coldness of the marble.

'So you slept well?' A voice from behind took her by surprise.

173

She turned round to see a woman, about her age, in faded jeans with a red shirt and a cardigan. 'Don't worry, you are still on Lantau. Do you know that?'

Ling nodded. 'Where are my things?'

'The men would have them. They said you were shivering and that you only came with what you had on.'

The woman held out her hand: 'My name is Zhou Xiao-mei. Call me either Xiao-mei or Helen. I'm the niece of Henry Druk.'

'I don't know him,' said Ling.

'Yes, but Superintendent McKillop does and that's why you're here.' Helen smiled. 'Don't worry. We're on your side.'

She opened a door off to the right. 'Get changed then come and have lunch,' she said. A round table was set on the balcony, laid for two, with a pot of tea and a bowl of roasted peanuts in the middle.

Staff came out with steaming dishes of prawns, crabs, lobsters, duck, pigeon and vegetables. 'You gave one of our men a nasty black eye,' said Helen, pouring the tea.

'I'm sorry,' said Ling. 'I thought . . .'

'No it's fine. But where did you learn to fight like that?'

'I was in the army,' said Ling. Helen plucked food up in her chopsticks and put it on Ling's plate. 'Where's Mike?' she added softly.

'He's fine. He's with Druk.'

Helen's easy manner relaxed Ling and, as they made small-talk, her attention wandered with muddled thoughts, panic, fatigue and guilt that so many people were dead. Then suddenly she would remember something trivial, that she hadn't renewed her US dollar fixed deposit or she hadn't picked up her dry cleaning from the Valet Shop in the Landmark. She didn't even know where the cleaning ticket was.

Helen put her hand on Ling's elbow. 'Have you been to Shanghai?' she asked.

'On business, quite a bit,' said Ling.

'I was brought up there. The Party wanted to make it the New York of the Pacific.' Helen threw her hands in the air, turned to face Ling and laughed. She reminded Ling of the French or Italians. Full of expression.

'It was dangerous for my father. The Party wanted to show that Hong Kong was inferior and create Shanghai.' She shook her head. 'But the corruption. The purges. No one heard about them. One day you were deputy mayor, the next you were gone. And Shanghai. Oh dear Shanghai. What will it become?'

'The Wall Street of Hell?' suggested Ling.

'A twenty million-people garbage heap,' added Helen. She put down her chopsticks and sipped her tea. Suddenly a seriousness came over her face: 'My father was in charge of the 2015 vision. You know, make Shanghai a modern city by then. Airport, freeways, hotels, banks.' She poured more tea for both of them. 'They broke him, you know.'

'Broke him?' repeated Ling.

'They charged him with corruption. He lost his job. There was a public trial on television and in the newspapers. They took our house away. I was criticised at school and made to denounce my own father. His only crime was to have been appointed by Jiang Zemin, the president then.

'He went mad. They took him to a hospital for the insane. We weren't allowed to see him. Then one day my mother got a letter saying he was dead. With the letter was a bill for the cremation.' Helen's eyes were wide open and clear. She looked confidently at Ling, not with sadness, but anger.

'That's like my father. I wasn't allowed to see my father before he died.'

'You see,' said Helen, 'I don't even think my father's dead.'

McKillop worked out in the gym with the air-conditioning off. Druk gave him fresh clothes and he went gently at first, trying a programme on the Stairmaster, reminding him how his legs gave him so much pain on the climb up the Lantau. He kept the video on StarSex, the soft porn channel with rhythmic Cantonese pop music favoured by Druk's men. The couples on the screen, multi-racial, multi-positioned, reminded him of sex with Sally, one element of their marriage which had never become stale or embittered. Then when Ling came in, unannounced, he changed the channel. But one of Druk's men switched it back and Ling told him it was fine and to leave it as it was. She was much fitter than him and she coached him through, putting him on the rowing machine to help the injured muscle beneath his shoulder.

When he felt comfortable, his heart beat down, breathing regular, he moved to the running mat. Stainless steel mirrors lined the room. His face was distorted and magnified as if he was jogging towards a series of shaving mirrors. The digital gauge told him the metres, then the kilometres he had run.

175

He let the sweat gather in pools at the bottom of his neck and drip off him, imagining how each drop could be an exorcism of the past year. A large dark patch formed around his stomach on his T-shirt. He felt the cotton at the back clinging to him. He didn't stop to wipe it away. He let it gather and go cold and wet.

He had enjoyed talking to Druk again. Druk was proud. He regarded his success with simplistic self-congratulation. 'I'm a pioneer for the new decentralised China,' he had said. With his homespun philosophy he applied the success of the smuggler as a contributing factor to the fragmentation of world's most populous country.

There were dozens of pocket empires like his torn away from the central government, allowed to survive because of the money they created. Up in the north, on the Central Asian, Russian and Korean borders and right along the coast from Hainan to Dalian. Everywhere with trade to be done, there were men like Druk. They compared prices on the Internet. A television set via Druk was a third of the price of the same model sent across the land border to Kazakhstan. Only slightly cheaper than taking one into Korea from Tumen.

Druk came in as Ling was doing aerobics in a bright red leotard and McKillop was on the Stairmaster. Druk was in a singlet caked with the grime of his trade. He fanned himself with a newspaper, then sent the breeze towards McKillop.

'Don't know why you torture yourself in this heat,' laughed Druk. 'I'm a rich man, you know. I have air-conditioning.'

'A Presbyterian obligation,' panted McKillop.

Druk unfolded the newspaper. 'You're still making news,' he quipped. 'They believe you're hiding out with a renegade gangster.'

'It's tautology,' said McKillop, his calf muscles screaming for a rest. 'A gangster is a renegade.'

'A gangster in the Chinese environment is more often the most honest man around,' Druk laughed. 'I'm a traditional oriental warlord.' He sat on a stool near the weights. 'They haven't named me,' he said becoming serious. 'When they do, you know you'll have to go.'

'How long do you think we've got?' said McKillop.

'Forty-eight, maybe seventy-two hours. They've moved men into the hills in front of our positions, only a few yards from where we picked you up.'

Mike stopped, plucked a towel off the bars and wiped it around the back of his neck: 'Have you pulled back?' he said.

'Not yet.' Druk leant his heavy frame against the weights machine. 'This is different to what it's ever been. You know. If someone up there is willing to order all this killing, it means that China is turning in on itself again.

'Kang isn't a madman,' said Ling. She took a paper cup from the cold water dispenser and filled it up.

'You're right,' said Druk. 'He's a thinker. But there are others up there who just want to make money. Arms, drugs and rigging the financial markets. The last madman who destroyed my country was Mao.'

'And you think Li Tuo's the next one?'

Druk shook his head. 'Not the same calibre, but that makes him even more dangerous.'

Chapter Twenty-One

McKillop was the first to identify the rotor blades. It was the Blackhawk again. He moved straight to the doorway to look up and saw the dark underbelly pass loudly overhead at no more than a hundred feet.

The helicopter climbed clear of the jetty and turned in one sharp manoeuvre to come back. Tops of the trees blew backwards and forwards, as if there was a typhoon, and Mike saw the barrel of a heavy machine gun mounted on the side and the door locked open.

It swept overhead, its shadow moving fast beneath it over the little town and its harbour. Then suddenly over the water the pilot dipped the nose slightly, took the helicopter up and round again so it was over the fields and the gunner opened fire. Sending lines of 7.62mm bullets into the ground.

As soon as the sound of the helicopter was fading, the telephone call came. It was for Mike.

'You've got to give yourself up, Mike,' said the voice and now he recognised it because there was the same static, the same tone that he had heard on the way into Shek O and on the night that Jimmy Lai died in Maekok.

'Who says?' asked Mike. Druk was listening on another phone.

'OK, Jimmy's gone. We know that. You've got to put it behind you. Sally's gone too. You've got to forget about her. Find a new girl. Not that difficult,' said Tommy Lai. 'Come on in and they'll give you what they gave Joss. A safe ticket out. Money in the bank. You'll never have to work again in your life. Don't worry about Ling Chen. She's a decoy. She works for them. She's very big in the Party. She'll go straight up to Beijing for a debriefing. This is even bigger than Nim Kai. The whole thing about Scott Carter went wildly out of control.'

'And what about Win Kyi?' said McKillop, trying to keep him talking, trying to find things out, trying to think.

'Different, Mike. So different. He was carrying explosives. He was going to blow himself up in Tiananmen Square. A suicide bomber. He'd been trained by the Muslims. He'd been to Kazakhstan and on the West Bank. Any security force anywhere in the world would have done what they did.'

'Bullshit,' retorted Mike.

'You've got to believe me. He was part of group determined to destroy the Party. He was a terrorist.'

'Crap.'

'Then who got the weapon to Clem Watkins?' snapped Tommy. 'Win Kyi came to the conference under diplomatic protection, Mike. You saw it. We know you saw Clem. You know I'm telling the truth.'

'You tried to kill Clem?'

'Not me. Like I said, things are getting out of control.'

'And Elton?' returned Mike.

'Elton was from the same group. He was about to assassinate you, Mike. We don't know exactly why. But we had been tracking him for a week.'

'Sally?'

'That was all Elton. You never got anything from us, did you? It was all through Elton's office. I don't know where Sally is. I don't think anyone does. It was his scam. We've never lied to you.'

Then Druk cut in across the line: 'Then tell me, Superintendent Lai, what in the hell you are trying to achieve by buzzing me with a Blackhawk. Why didn't you just call like you are now?'

'It was the pilot,' said Tommy Lai. 'He wasn't meant to be there. He's a friend of one of the guys Mike killed. He was out for revenge. It wasn't us.'

'Us?' said McKillop. 'Who are you associating yourself with?'

'Mike, stop clinging to the past. I work for the Hong Kong police. My family live here,' said Tommy Lai. 'We're giving you a ticket out. Take it.'

Then Druk was back on the line, speaking clearly and looking straight at Mike: 'Tell General Li, Superintendent, that I accept the explanation about your rogue pilot. The other matters don't concern me. If he can guarantee a return to the status quo. McKillop and Ling Chen will be sent back to you within twenty-four hours. You must guarantee their safe passage.'

They were in Kang's private office in the Zhongnanhei Communist Party complex. It was just past eight in the evening and the

179

President had returned from a banquet with the visiting United Nations Secretary General, a former Prime Minister of Japan. Tony had used an official car to take him through the sweeping brick red entrance with the sign in large Chinese characters telling the government *To Serve the People*. Along the wall on the west side of the gate a slogan read: *Long live the great Chinese Communist Party*. On the east wall another paid tribute: *Long live the unbeatable thoughts of Chairman Mao*. Tony had always been awed by Zhongnanhai. The impenetrable citadel, one of his Harvard friends had called it. The roads were broad and uncluttered. The tranquillity was conveyed by drooping willows in the summer and frozen snow-covered lakes in the winter. Its cluster of reception rooms, villas, surveillance cameras, microwave dishes, and radio transmitters were no less mysterious, no less prohibited than the Forbidden City had been in Imperial times.

Tony was waved through without a fuss. Kang put on his spectacles to read the memo his young protégé had for him. Tony Zhang sat opposite, turning an unlit cigarette back and forth in his fingers, irritated that Kang did not allow smoking in his office. In earlier days, he had joked that Mao held a burning cigarette in the picture above Kang's desk, so China's present ruler should either follow suit or remove the portrait. But Mao was one subject on which Kang was intractable. Tony disagreed violently with Kang about Mao's role in modern China and years ago, when he was at university, Tony had compared Mao to Hitler and argued that until his legacy was exposed, China would fail to modernise.

Only Kang's intervention had stopped Tony being sent down, but the enemies he created then dogged him on every step of his career. Tony fiddled nervously with his pager. He filed away a string of needless messages. The markets in London were rising. Hong Kong was steady. The flashed news was the sharp rise in Chengdu and Shanghai of the China Second Fire-fighting Equipment Company. Tony knew it was a military-run company; it wasn't until he checked later that he discovered it was the direct commercial arm for missile sales of the Second Artillery Regiment, the unit which built China's missiles.

'I'm not sure what this amounts to, Tony,' said Kang placing the document neatly in front of him. 'There are too many disparate strands.'

But Kang never did like absolutes, preferring through his legal and academic training to always have a differing view. Tony stood up, moved round to the side of the desk where Kang was sitting and leant over his shoulder to run down the bullet points on the memo. 'I don't have a summation,' he said bluntly. 'But Gurjit is highly reliable. He would not have come to me unless he really thought something was going on. The Russians . . .' Tony shrugged. 'They could be meaningless, except they're also talking about the north-east. And . . .' he stopped speaking, causing Kang to look up at him.

'And what, Tony?' he prompted.

'The death of Scott Carter is causing a furore in political circles in Washington and this could make your visit more difficult.'

'No,' said Kang smiling. 'You were going to say something else.

'I didn't like the tone of the meeting the other day,' said Tony abruptly. 'Li Tuo was being blatantly insubordinate, telling that professor to falsify geological reports.'

Kang shrugged and gave the memo back to Tony: 'Just politics. Believe me no one in China will risk all our successes and drag us backwards. The path which was begun by Deng Xiao-ping in 1979 is irreversible.'

Kang told Tony to sit in the more comfortable chairs: 'If you must, you can smoke. But turn that damn pager off. The younger generation have the concentration level of gnats. Who knows? One day you may be in my position with one of my great-grandsons advising you on how to run China.'

Tony sat down in a black leather armchair, lit a cigarette and used the spittoon as an ashtray. Kang took a chair across from him. He removed his spectacles and clasped his hands in front of his chest. 'The next few weeks are crucial to the development of our world,' he began. 'The billions of dollars of trade deals with the United States will herald generations of friendship and justify the American policy of constructive engagement and our policy of accepting it. In Washington, I will suggest to Zuckerman that our two countries also forge a strategic alliance, such as we have with Russia and as the United States has with Japan. If he agrees we will sign it when he visits Beijing next year before the Presidential election. In security terms that will put us on an equal footing with Japan and create an unbreakable global security umbrella in the Asia Pacific region. The three most powerful countries in the world, America, China and Russia, will be interlocked by defence treaties which will make an outbreak of hostilities unthinkable.'

'There is no such thing as an end to war,' said Tony.

'Don't be so cynical so young. If we don't strive for these things,

181

they will never happen,' said Kang. 'After the Washington summit, I will propose a similar summit in Japan. Within a year we will have a real New World Order, with the dominating beacons of trade and economic development, secured with a global military balance agreed by treaty.'

'Are you sure your own position is secure?' Tony said after a pause. He flicked ash into the spittoon and leant forward in the chair, his hands on his knees.

Kang laughed gently. 'You have been seeing too many war films,' he said. 'You have to understand what we are trying to achieve. I wanted the ink to be dry on the Natuna deal before Washington so that when I'm with Zuckerman, Southeast Asia and China will have formed a united diplomatic front against Japan. Once Tokyo realises it cannot assume an American-style security mantle in this region, power will be balanced and we can concentrate on modernising and democratising China. I let the military take the lead to take their minds off the anti-corruption campaign. Of course there are elements of unpopularity, but, Tony, this is the march of history. These might be greedy men. But they are not stupid and our squabbles are irrelevant to the big picture.'

Tony Zhang shook his head, but kept his doubt to himself. He had no suggestions: he had only come to warn. 'When I'm back from Japan,' Kang was saying, 'I'll announce a Motherland Day and we'll have huge celebrations in Tiananmen Square. Bigger than the return of Hong Kong.'

Wind blew in from the sea, sweeping Ling's hair into her face. She pushed it away. 'When will they come back?' she asked.

Druk shrugged. He was unusually pensive for his ebullient character. 'If they do it will be for the kill. If you two don't leave, they'll return maybe today. Maybe tonight. But the die has been cast. My town and my people will not be safe until Li Tuo is beaten.'

'I'll second that,' said Mike softly. They were on the balcony watching his men set up armed positions.

Druk shook his head: 'This isn't how modern China was meant to be.'

'You mean the gangster's lair is threatened?' said McKillop lightly.

'I don't think that's what he meant,' intervened Ling. 'I've been in the army. The nationalism, the racism, the bitterness about

China's weaknesses, the hatred against the West is enough to drag our country back into feudalism. It is about power, not modernisation.'

'High ideal apart,' said Mike. 'Like you said, Ling, we don't have anywhere to run except into exile. So if, we don't win this, it's likely we'll all end up dead.'

'You have a suggestion?' asked Druk.

McKillop laughed and lit a cigarette. 'I've always had a complete inability to plan,' he said. 'But I'm convinced from what Clem said that the key to all this is whatever is going on in Heshui. Even Elton said something up north was scaring the shit out of the comrades.'

'Like what?' pressed Druk.

'Don't know. He even said Sally might be involved.'

'Which is why you want to go there?' Ling began.

'It seems we can lay a lot of ghosts to rest with this one,' answered Mike.

A maid appeared on the balcony with coffee and they were quiet while she poured each of them a cup.

'You remember I told Hollingworth and you about how I switched my first and last names around?' said Ling to McKillop. 'The student who wanted me to get a Western name?'

'By putting the Ling in front of Chen and not taking a Western name,' remembered Mike.

'What I didn't tell you is that it was a pact with my boyfriend at the time. He kept saying China would never modernise if foreigners could never get our names right. Anyway, that guy is now a personal adviser to President Kang.'

Druk sipped his coffee and put the cup down on the table: 'Are you in touch with him?'

'I could be.'

'Would he tell you anything?'

'If it's as terrible as it seems, and he knows anything at all, he'll tell me, I'm sure.'

'It's too dangerous,' said McKillop.

Ling threw back her head and laughed: 'Why? You went back to get me out of Shek O and have lived to tell the story.'

'If they . . .'

'If they come back here tonight, we could be dead by tomorrow, Mike, like you said. If we can find out what's going on at least we can plan how to stop it.'

'How would you get in?' asked Druk calmly.

'If you can get me out of here . . .'

'Do you have documents?' interrupted Druk.

'Not reliable ones,' answered Mike for her.

'I can run you up a new passport or China travel card,' continued Druk. 'We can get you to Macau, which thankfully is less in control of the Party than Hong Kong. I'll get you on an Air Macau flight to another Asian capital – Bangkok, Phnom Penh, Kuala Lumpur – and you catch a connecting flight from there to Beijing. I own most of the airline,' he smiled. 'So you should be treated very well indeed.'

'How will you contact Tony?' asked McKillop.

'I have a girlfriend I can call. She'll get through to him.'

'Mike,' said Druk, 'Why don't you go to Shanghai and wait for Ling there? I can protect you south of the Yangtse River. Anything north of there is in the Party's hands. If you cross that line, you're as good as dead.'

'What about her?' said McKillop.

'In the territory of the Party,' said Druk, looking at Ling. 'I have no one to help you in Beijing.'

'Don't worry about me,' answered Ling, smiling. 'I'm a Beijing girl. I'm one of them.'

A navy business suit with large white buttons. Power dressing, Helen said. Two cotton blouses, one pink, one white; tights, panties, bra; two scarves, one plain, one Paisley; accessories, two pairs of shoes, one black leather with slightly raised heels to be packed, the other casual, soft, for travelling. She showed Ling the Saatchi hand carry case, like the ones air hostesses used. Feminine, but practical. Inside were a tracksuit, T-shirt, toiletry bag, socks, a laser disc player with CDs and two of the latest films.

Ling would only take hand luggage. She would leave the airport by a side-entrance, avoiding immigration, and the boat would be waiting on the jetty off the tarmac. Helen showed her the passport. The picture looked like her.

The picture's of my cousin, said Helen. Two years older than you. You are Melanie Nelson, a Canadian citizen, divorced from John Nelson of Calgary. If you use this there will be no record of you leaving the country. Your enemies will believe you're still here. They won't chase you. If things go wrong we'll try and get you back. Like what? Helen touched Ling's elbow with her hand.

There was a second passport. Canadian again. Similar cover, except there's no divorced husband. Your name is Carol Li and you are already in China. It has an entry stamp. If you're discovered as Melanie Nelson, become Carol Li.

Keep the wallet messy. An expired permit for Yoho National Park in the Rocky Mountains. A used ticket stub for the jetfoil from Hong Kong to Macau. An out-of-date Mark Six lottery ticket. The more disorganised it is the easier it will be for you to appear absent-minded, shambolic. Your life is arranged by secretaries and travel agents. Detail bores you. You are rich. You are successful. You know powerful people.

The name cards were gold-embossed with her company's name, Hok Twang Investments. In Macau and Hong Kong, they know this is a Henry Druk operation. Henry named an apartment block on the south side of Hong Kong Island after one of his racehorses. You're in property. You run overseas Chinese investment in Vancouver, Toronto, Seattle, San Francisco, Los Angeles and in Lisbon and the Algarve in Portugal. You deal in investment immigration. These are the rules for Canada and Portugal. Read them now. Don't take them with you. Memorise them.

Helen smiled sympathetically. The clothes, the money, the wallet, were laid out in rows. 'This is all for the plane journey. Druk is really proud of keeping people safe and once we leave here . . .' she looked out the window. It was dark now, but a blue tint hung high in the sky, the sun reluctant to relinquish totally its influence to the night.

'It's dangerous, right?'

'Yes,' said Helen. 'Stay here. There's a bathroom off to the right.' She embraced Ling but Ling was unused to such a show of feeling among Chinese.

'Thank you,' she whispered. Then Helen was gone and Ling was left alone, staring at her new belongings.

She had asked Mike how to tell if she was being followed. There wasn't time to teach her, he said. Druk wanted them out straight away. 'Do everything differently, if you can,' he said. 'Walking, sitting, looking in your handbag. There are people out there who have studied your movements, looked at the films. They know how you do things, your physical and mental character.'

Helen took Ling in the early morning before dawn to Macau on a speedboat which came up right alongside the runway. Helen said Druk owned Air Macau so it would be all right. She kissed her on both cheeks. They had arranged for Helen to get a message to Tony through Lucy that Ling was coming up. Mike would go later at dusk when it was really dark, on board a fishing junk. He wanted to be taken right up to Guangzhou where a white face would melt away among the thousands of tourists. But Druk would only take him to Zhuhai a few miles away on the south China coast. He would have to take a taxi, as if he was a businessman and fight his way through. Then Druk would blow up the junk and tell Tommy Lai that Mike and Ling tried to escape.

There was an explosion and everyone was killed, Druk would say. The bodies may be down with the wreckage.

Chapter Twenty-Two

Outside the terrain was brown. The monotony of the North Asian plains was broken up by lines of trees, stark and recovering from a cruel winter and by rivers, green and yellow, with chunks of ice which refused to melt with the first onset of spring. As the aircraft banked to the left, Ling watched a herd of sheep and their shepherds slipping on cold wet ground and struggling along a river side as if they had come from another age. Hard mud flats, pockmarked with the prints of animals and birds, stretched back from the water to the bank which was firm, dry sand with broken and gnarled bushes, like the edges of a desert. Then a golf course was beneath her, the fairways cut up from the cold weather and beyond that a racetrack with a huge digital screen in the middle and, a hundred yards further on, a rider in black hat and red coat practised dressage in a paddock.

The Boeing 757 straightened out over the six-lane highway into Beijing and Ling saw the red-patterned eaves of the toll gate and the roof of the Movenpick Hotel before the runway lights rushed in under her, the plane jolted, then ran smoothly. As it slowed to a crawl, turning towards the terminal building, people rose as if on command, steadying themselves on the backs of other people's seats and reaching to the overhead lockers to haul down their luggage. They started making phone calls.

She wrapped her scarf around her face as much for the pollution as for disguise and she shuffled forward, head down, in the line for the special airport taxis. She spoke English to the driver and told him she came from Canada. He wanted to practise his language, so they talked about the overseas Chinese. He had taken hundreds of fares just like Ling who were coming back to experience the Motherland. Did she have relatives here? No, she lied. They were in Vancouver.

Ling got the taxi to drop her on the west side of Tiananmen

Square just beyond the Great Hall of the People. She was determined to take in the full horror of the system which had killed her lover and was trying to kill her.

The last time she had been here was with Scott when he was teasing her about Chinese culture. She had hated him then and the resentment lingered. She thought she had understood her country, but Scott exposed it and now, angered by her own innocence, she walked around the Mausoleum of Mao Tse-tung and past the Monument to the Martyrs of the People, which Mao had inscribed with his own handwriting *Eternal Glory to the People's Heroes*. Ling's final view was north towards Tiananmen Gate, where Mao proclaimed Communist Party victory in 1949 and where his enduring portrait still hung.

'Clem Watkins. CIA. In from Hong Kong. You should be expecting me.' Clem chose three in the morning to pull up in a new car hired at Los Angeles airport in his name and run up the steps to the county police station where Joyce Hewlitt was being held. The officer at the desk was listening to Jazz FM radio, sipping black coffee and about to take a bite from a Big Mac he had had delivered ten minutes earlier. Through the back room, Clem saw another officer leaning back in an armchair, feet up on another with his cap pulled across his eyes to keep out the fluorescent light. Beyond that, two steps led down a corridor which seemed to run towards the cells. Clem saw no sign of human activity apart from the two men, which worried him that Joyce would already have been moved. Or he had got the wrong police station. He had never seen one so empty. Even at night.

Clem was clean-shaven with closely cropped hair, almost Marine style, and wore a dark grey pinstripe suit he had bought off the peg from the Giordano store in Malibu. He carried a Samsonite briefcase and Armani spectacles which he took off as he announced himself and showed the officer his identity card.

'Are the FBI here?' Clem said quickly as the officer put down his coffee cup. He leaned forward and Clem noted the name on his uniform, Torrance. 'What's your first name, Torrance?' Clem kept talking. He put his briefcase on the front counter, spun the combination lock, opened the lid and drew out documents in a transparent folder. After he had run them off at a print shop, he had covered them in red ink stationery shop stamps of *confidential, secret, eyes only*.

'Name's Chris,' Torrance replied. 'I wasn't told you were coming and the FBI checked into their motel many hours ago.' And with that he took a bite of his hamburger, wiping the excess sauce from his mouth with a paper napkin.

'Call me Clem,' said Watkins who was taking sheaves of paper out of the folder and shuffling them around just enough for Torrance to see the letterheads and stamps. 'This is it,' Clem continued. 'Joyce Hewlitt, aged forty-one, suspected arson attack on her own home.

'The FBI are here because her husband Martin used to be a spook, like me. CIA. That's confidential, but you look like an intelligent guy. It's the middle of the night and I wouldn't be here if it wasn't to do with national security.' Clem kept talking as he was reading: 'Mr Hewlitt got killed. His car smashed into a truck. Or the other way round. Anyway she went crazy and torched the family home. At least that's what it says here. So I've got to have a word with her.'

Torrance turned in his chair: 'Mickey, wake the fuck up. The CIA is here.' Mickey kicked away the chair his legs were resting across and jumped up, rubbing his eyes which were caught in the glare of the overhead lights.

'Thought it was the FBI,' he said, walking through to the counter where, without asking, he drank the coffee from Torrance's cup.

'Just flown in from Hong Kong, Mickey,' said Clem. He shook the policeman's hand. 'The plane was late. I have to talk to Mrs Hewlitt, then head off to Washington,' Clem paused to look at his watch. 'Shit, it's getting real tight.'

Mickey was the station sergeant. Early forties. Overweight. Probably mortgaged up to the hilt, thought Clem. 'We better check this out,' said Mickey to Torrance.

'I know those FBI guys were out drinking,' said Torrance.

'Ring 'em anyway,' said Mickey. 'We've got no note that he's coming.'

Clem snapped shut his briefcase, leaving the folder on the top. 'The notification should have come straight from Langley or Hong Kong.' He dropped his voice. 'You know how it is between agencies.' He began writing down two numbers: General staff inquiries at CIA headquarters and the duty officer at the American Consulate-General in Hong Kong. Neither was confidential, but a call to each could buy Clem the time he needed.

'I wonder if you'd do me a favour, Mickey. You've seen my ID. If they've screwed up getting a message down here, call these numbers. They should have confirmation. Then let me in to see

Hewlitt. That'll let me catch my plane and if I don't add up you can lock me up with her.'

Joyce Hewlitt wasn't asleep. Friends had brought in fresh clothes and she was wearing a beige jumper and jeans, sitting, back to the wall, her knees up, her deep brown hair falling over her face and her intelligent eyes staring out through her spectacles, unmoving at the wall ahead. Her meal was untouched, her Coke and coffee undrunk. She held a paper cup of water in her left hand and leant forward to put it on the ledge by the bed when Mickey opened the door. When he said it was Clem Watkins, she concealed any recognition. Mickey asked if she wanted a lawyer present, she shook her head, and Mickey left them alone.

'We only buried him two days ago.' Joyce didn't look up. 'Do you know how Sam and Nancy are?' she said.

'I've just got in from China.'

Joyce brushed back her hair and looked at him. 'From Heshui?'

Clem nodded: 'The Communist Party killed Martin, Joyce. And they're framing you now.'

'No,' she said. She unwrapped her hands from around her knees, sat up straight and put her feet on the floor. 'Martin murdered. Yes. Me framed. Yes. But the Chinese. Impossible. Not here in America.'

'Then who?'

Joyce shook her head: 'How are you involved?' she said.

'I need to know what Martin told you about Heshui. Anything at all.'

'He didn't leave Heshui because he missed the family.' Joyce finished the water, crushed the cup in her hand and threw the litter towards the bars of the cell. 'There's a labour camp up there, Clem,' she said angrily. 'Martin wanted to get a look at the nuclear waste site, because he's interested in that subject. He said the security was really appalling sometimes and he got in. But around the bunkers where the low-level waste is meant to be stored he got no reading at all. Zero. Then beyond that he saw a high wire fence and prisoners out for morning exercise.'

Tears were running from behind her glasses and down her cheeks. Joyce wiped them with the cuff of her blouse. 'Martin told Hollingworth. Is that who you reported to?'

Clem nodded.

'Hollingworth said he knew about the camp and that it had been there long before the project started. He went into a lot of stuff about the difficult moral choices in bringing round a country like China, that the camp wasn't part of the Sino-American Heshui project as such, but it was no different to any other labour camp in China. At the end of the conversation he reminded Martin about the security level of the Heshui project. In other words, don't tell anyone else you've seen it.'

'And that's when he left?' Clem could hear Mickey down the corridor on the phone to Langley, shouting with impatience.

'Martin gave it a decent interval,' Joyce continued. She stood up with her back to the cell door, angry, but fit and in control of herself. 'But he was a bit of a do-gooder and it ate away at him. A week or so ago, he got back into the computer, right deep into the Heshui file. It took him hours Clem, but he did it. He kept changing terminals, going from one coffee shop to another on the West Coast. First it was all the usual stuff that you've both seen. Then he got through to another layer and that was when alarms must have gone off. It flashed the words *unauthorised access two*. Martin probably stayed on too long, but he kept going and found out there had been another hacker from Seoul, Korea, just two days earlier.'

'Did Martin get anything?'

'Martin reckoned he must have. It went onto disconnect.' Joyce shook her head. 'Then he was killed. Two days later.'

Mickey's voice carried in echoes down the corridor. 'And you say you're the only guy on duty in Hong Kong?' He rammed his hand down onto the telephone to cut the call.

Clem heard the opening of doors. Keys rattled. Mickey shouted for Torrance to come with him. Clem picked up his briefcase, got to his feet and smoothed down his suit.

'Thank you Mrs Hewlitt. That's all been a great help,' he said, holding out his hand and she took it, hers being cold and clammy with sweat.

'You don't check out, Hong Kong boy,' shouted Mickey down the corridor. 'No one knows who the fuck you are.'

Mickey was at the door, his eyes deranged with the type of hatred Clem had forgotten flowed like cankers through American police forces: a loathing of lawyers, politicians, social workers and any wealth which didn't pour into their own pockets.

The door was open: 'Until you check out, you're not going nowhere.' Mickey moved forward, shifted weight to attack Clem. Clem protected Joyce, pushing her behind him and back into the cell. Mickey's head came down, ready to head-butt straight onto Clem's skull. Clem's right arm came up protectively, but at the

191

same time he stepped aside with the finesse of a ballet dancer. Torrance was in the corridor, his holster flap unbuttoned, drawing his weapon. And as Joyce screamed, Torrance shouted again but with more venom. The bell rang on the front desk. Someone was there, like Clem a few minutes earlier finding a police station strangely undermanned.

Joyce's legs were jammed against the toilet. Clem deflected Mickey's huge weight and the policeman's head crashed into the prison wall. Clem brought his knee up into the stomach and his right fist in between the eyes which were smearing with blood from the head wound. Mickey fell double onto the bunk, then he stumbled, trying to get to his feet, but Clem wasn't interested. He hurled himself forwards towards the door of the cell and caught Torrance in a rugby tackle, wrapping his arms around the policeman's legs just above the knees. Torrance's head whiplashed back, striking the concrete hard. Clem freed himself and brought his hand down on Torrance's wrist. The weapon dropped noisily.

'Behind you!' yelled Joyce. And as Clem turned, he was thrown back against Torrance by Mickey. Clem felt the wind knocked out of him.

'Anybody there?' It was a visitor. Pressing the bell again in sharp bursts of impatience, loud and penetrating enough to distract Mickey. With reserves of air, Clem picked up the revolver and brought it against the side of Mickey's face. Mickey's neck cracked and in the same movement Clem brought the pistol down against Torrance who cried out as the metal of the butt ripped the skin off his cheek and tore into his bone.

'Coming,' shouted Clem to the visitor.

He stumbled back, his left hand outstretched to bring Joyce out of the cell. Mickey and Torrance were stunned but not unconscious. Torrance had already taken off the safety catch. Clem put a bullet in the breech, pointed the weapon at Mickey's head and pulled him by his uniform into the cell and closed the door.

'Move and I'll kill you,' he said, his breath back, in a chillingly controlled manner. With Mickey's crumpled and bloodied form in the corner of his eye, he concentrated on Torrance, first by hitting him in the face, then pushing him onto his front, face pressed against the cold floor, arms behind him, wrists in his own cuffs. Torrance groaned. Clem said: 'Shut the fuck up.'

He looked up at Joyce: 'Handle the front desk and play night shift,' he ordered. Joyce ran her fingers down her hair, took off her glasses so she carried them and walked purposefully towards the front counter.

Clem pushed the barrel of the pistol into the back of Torrance's thigh. His mouth was up against the policeman's ear: 'Who do you work for?' Even before Torrance answered, Clem shoved the barrel harder: 'You've got five seconds before I put you in a wheel-chair.' It had never failed. A bullet in the leg and the agony which followed always made people talk. Unless they had training. Mickey and Torrance wouldn't have that.

'And you say it's parked where?' he heard Joyce from another world a few yards away.

'It's been there, must be twelve hours now. Two flats and smashed windows.'

'And your address, sir?'

Clem waited until Joyce had got rid of him, then he fired once, right on the edge, missing the main arteries and careful of ricochet. Torrance screamed and writhed, but Clem held his head down hard, his cheek flat against the concrete.

'Who?' whispered Clem again. As Joyce came down the corridor, Clem asked her to find the first aid kit. 'Who the fuck is paying you?' he repeated.

Clem eased his grip. Torrance was crying. 'Don't know. Don't know,' he said.

'The order to clear the station? Leave only you two.'

'The Captain.'

'Name?'

'Fordham. Henry Fordham.'

'Where does he live?'

Torrance hesitated. Clem pressed his finger against the flesh where the bullet had gone in less than a minute earlier. The policeman cried out and told him.

Chapter Twenty-Three

The driver didn't speak. Nor did Mike. They travelled in silence after they had agreed the fare. And fast, Mike in the back seat, his bag next to him, not in the boot, and the radio turned up loud because by the time Druk's men landed him night-time racing at Happy Valley had begun. The driver used one hand to steer and the other to threaten: for the horn to squeeze to the edge of the coastal highway lumbering, belching trucks and bullock and horse carts; and to flash his lights at traffic coming at him and refusing to give way. He swore to himself either because of another's crazy driving or at a horse which failed to win. Mike looked out the side at clusters of lights spread back across the dark and waterlogged fields. The roadside was a trail of half-built towns, of hotels, bars, businesses, makeshift buildings of shipping containers and Portakabins, shops piled with televisions, video players, cameras, computers and cigarettes. No drains. No running water. No permission to create a city. Modern China's south was America's nineteenth-century west – and the guns were here as well, thought Mike.

'Remember, Mike McKillop is dead,' said Druk. 'Don't use my men unless you have to. You're on your own. Go to Shanghai. Wait there.'

Mike had bearded stubble and he had dyed his hair a red-brown. Ling had said it made him ten years younger. He wore clip-on shades to a pair of glasses, a pair of Levi's, trainers and open-neck blue shirt. He had a change in his bag and his travel documents in his back pocket. 'I'll be two days at least. Out of touch,' Ling had said. The car swerved sharply throwing Mike against the door. The horn cut through all the other noise. The driver swung back, swearing, the vehicles swaying and through the back window Mike saw a man in rags, his ribs protruding, one arm already a severed stump, trussed up with filthy bandages. The driver's eyes were in the mirror, on Mike.

'Did I hit him?' he asked bluntly in Cantonese. The driver turned the radio down. The beggar crawled back to the kerbside. Two motorbikes split up to go either side of him. Then he was lost in a swirl of dust as three trucks passed in quick succession. Mike's driver didn't slow and when the dust cleared, the beggar was leaning against a wall, ignored by everyone around him.

'Don't know,' said Mike, mistakenly falling into Cantonese.

'Always try to get themselves hit to claim compensation,' said the driver. 'Never happened before,' he said reaching over to the glove box. He took out a miniature portrait of Mao Tse-tung and showed it to Mike. Then he began a harangue against President Kang and the modern Communist Party.

Flags above the hotel flew strongly. Construction site cranes were lit up across the Beijing dusk. Grit and pollution blew through the city. The doorman wore a black fur cape, and a red greatcoat, which he buttoned up to the neck as the sun went down and the evening temperature dropped sharply. In the foyer, a full orchestra with a children's chorus performed Beethoven's Ninth Symphony. Clusters of white and Chinese faces sat together, taking their first drinks of the evening, their conversation confidential even from most listening devices because of the orchestra. Which is how the hotel liked it. The China World had been Ling's choice. There were fewer Party spies here. Not like others which had a line directly to the listening rooms of the Ministry of State Security behind.

When she walked into the bar it was empty apart from a waitress who polished brass on the bar. Piped music mixed with the more distant sounds of the orchestra. Ling ordered a Coke, picked a table right in the corner so she couldn't be seen from the door and read the *Economist* just like it had been arranged with Lucy.

Tony was ten minutes early and stood for a few seconds in the door, locked the keypad to his mobile phone and checked his watch before spotting Ling. They were gawky together at first because the last time was as inexperienced lovers. Tony kissed Ling on both cheeks, Western-style, and, like before, it was Ling who cut through any embarrassment, her eyes fixed unblinkingly on him, throwing out both a request and challenge.

'Someone in your government is trying to kill me, Tony, and I need your help. Unless you're one of them, in which case I'm dead.'

'Are you talking about Scott Carter?'

'That and more. Much much more.' And they sat for more than

an hour, Tony smoking a lot as Ling ran through everything. What she knew and what Mike had told her; Clem Watkins, Scott, Tom Elton, Win Kyi and finally Heshui.

'I've never heard of this project,' said Tony.

'So would the President know?'

Tony shook his head. 'He might not,' he said. 'If it's a military project they almost certainly wouldn't tell him.'

Ling's glass was empty, with just a sodden lemon resting on the bottom. 'Heshui is at the heart of everything that's going wrong,' she said.

'I'm not sure where I come in,' said Tony. He hadn't told her about the tension at President Kang's meeting with Li Tuo.

Ling played with her cocktail stick. 'You work in Zhongnanhai, Tony. If things are falling apart you can find out . . .'

'That's treachery . . .'

Ling snapped the cocktail stick and stared at him: 'Don't talk to me about treachery,' she said angrily. 'Our dream since university has been to create a fair, just and strong China. Deng Xiao-ping started it. Jiang Zemin continued it and Kang is really trying to modernise. But the military could swat him out like a fly, Tony, you know that. And this country will be dragged back thirty years just like in the Cultural Revolution. The men who make that happen are the traitors. Not you and me.'

Tony nervously lit a cigarette. Ling herself was shaking with emotion: 'If you had been through what I've been through in the past few days you would be determined to stop it as well. Nothing is safe, Tony. Nothing.'

As soon as the junk was blown up, Druk contacted Tommy Lai. An aide got a message to Li Tuo who was in the Grand Hyatt Hotel ballroom at Namibian National Day celebrations. Li moved over to take Hollingworth away from a conversation with the Singaporean Consul-General.

'Druk says they're dead,' said Li Tuo. 'He blew them out of the water as they tried to escape.'

'So we have now reverted to the status quo,' said Hollingworth.

'Not quite. Tommy checked along the south China coast. Business-men don't appear out of nowhere around there. They have people with them. A taxi driver in Zhuhai reports seeing a man who could be McKillop. The car in front of him in the rank is taking him to Guangzhou as we speak.'

'So . . .'

'We find McKillop and explain to Henry Druk that he has been insubordinate to the needs of the community and his country.'

'All yours, General,' said Hollingworth. 'I'm going to Washington.'

'I hope your loyalty will remain undiminished,' said the Chinese security chief.

Joyce read the street map and they found Henry Fordham's house in an expensive suburb, seven miles away.

'A straight police captain wouldn't be able to afford this,' said Joyce.

It was a quiet neighbourhood. Clem had wanted to check Joyce into a hotel, but she insisted on coming. 'If I'm alone, I'm scared,' she had said.

'It'll be dangerous,' said Clem.

'My husband's dead and my house has been torched,' she retorted, bringing the seatbelt round and clipping it in. 'You don't get much more dangerous than that.'

Henry Fordham's lawn sloped up to the verandah and the building was a new, sprawling, two-storey weatherboard and brick structure, which looked to Clem as if it might have been built by the policeman himself. Clem drove past once. The lights were on, both upstairs and in what would have been the lounge or dining room. Two cars were in the driveway. Black garbage sacks were resting on the garden lamp post as they were all down the street. A sign on the gate told visitors that the street was patrolled by a security company, although at almost four in the morning no one was around at all. Clem was driving past a second time before pulling up when he saw a streak of light coming across the lawn from the front door which was open. In a light breeze, it had swung on its hinges.

Clem stopped the car, turned off the lights and told Joyce to stay inside. He checked the chamber of Torrance's revolver, ensured it was on safety and pushed it into his waistband. Keeping in the shadows, he ran up the driveway, reaching the garage where he waited in the darkness for sounds and movements from the house. Three mountain bikes leant against each other on the wall between the garage and the house. Crouching to stay below the windows, Clem ran forward to the front door, onto the steps, pausing only for a second, before pushing it with his elbow to avoid fingerprints, and letting it swing backwards.

No one. The hallway floor was black and white marble tiles and they stretched back to a wide staircase of stripped pine wood. On the wall to his left was a large mirror, framed in patterned black and white. A white gloss shelf ran underneath with junk mail left unopened on it, together with a set of car keys, coloured golf tees and a scorecard from a local course. Three tennis rackets leant against the wall underneath. Clem slipped inside the house behind the door to hide his silhouette from the street.

He heard a click from the lounge. He tensed himself and pulled out the revolver. He rested against the white silk wallpaper which ran up the stairs and into other rooms in the house. Through the crack in the open door he saw Joyce, still in the passenger seat, bathed in the hazy light of the streetlamps, exposed and vulnerable. Another quieter click, but for sure this time, not a weapon. Music started. Louis Armstrong singing with Billie Holliday. Clem recognised it immediately because Mike used to play it to him all the time when they drank together. But nothing in the house moved. Door open. Lights on. Four in the morning. A CD player on automatic? Clem let the first track run through, then he brought the revolver up, steady with both hands and spun from his cover into the doorway of the lounge. He covered the left and the right, then straight forward again. It was a big long room with windows in the corner. The spotlights were dimmed, but on. The curtains were drawn across. One desk light near Clem showed photographs of Fordham's family and Henry himself at a police department reception. He was a fit, broad-shouldered man, with waves of thick blond hair and penetrating blue eyes. Both his son and daughter had captured their father's good looks.

At the far end of the room in an alcove near the corner window, the recessed spotlights were off and a single light shone over a dark wooden desk.

Henry Fordham was slumped over the desk with half his head blown off. On the floor was a shotgun. Blood seeped out from beneath his skull and dripped onto the carpet. Clem lowered his revolver. He tested the drawers, which were all locked. He ran out of the lounge, the revolver back and ready, into the kitchen, the rumpus room, the cloakroom, upstairs to the bathroom, then bedroom by bedroom, each one confirming his belief that the house was empty. The kids were away. Mrs Fordham was away. He stopped in a small attic room with a sloping ceiling built into the eaves, a workstation against the wall, a computer and piles of disks. The monitor was on screensaver, a picture of the Fordham family, with Henry's initials etched into the top right-hand corner.

Clem activated it. Fordham had been on the Internet until just after three when Clem arrived at the police station. The connection had been automatically cut at 3.07 because of inactivity. Just after that he would have died. Clem took Fordham's viewing back one by one, through web page after web page; a copulating naked couple called *Swedish Love Connection*; holidays in Mexico; the new Mercedes sports SLK sports coupé; The *Washington Post* personal finance page. A lot more. Too detailed. Too unknown for Clem to linger. A car's headlights swept across the garden. A new track from Louis Armstrong floated up the stairs. Clem thought he heard other sounds down there: a door opening, steps on the marble and the pine stairs. The car drove on, its tail lights blurry in the early morning chill. Then he was onto the E-mail, when Fordham had first logged on. Just one incoming, but a circular, tightly restricted, which said simply: 'HF blown.'

HF blown. Henry Fordham? Return to screensaver. Clem moved to the door, where he could see down the stairwell. No shadows sliding through the lights. No sounds any more. Maybe he was tired. Maybe he deserved to be. Back in the room, he looked out the window and Joyce hadn't moved. Perfectly still. Nerves of steel. The dead man's face beamed out at him, his arm around his wife, his two children radiant and backlit behind him. HF digitally etched into the picture. Henry Fordham? HF? And then Clem had it. Happy Family. Heshui. Operation Happy Family, slipping in an unused formatted disk, downloading the E-mail, pushing all the disks off the worktop into a large brown envelope. Down to the first floor, into the master bedroom, opening the window, his hand still wrapped in the handkerchief, and out onto the sloping roof, jumping in one movement onto the garage and then down a soft landing on the lawn and running. Joyce started the engine. Did he hear the crack of a pistol? Clem got behind the wheel, throwing the envelope onto Joyce's lap, and drove away, gently so as not to wake the neighbours, lights off to conceal the number plate, everything quiet. Was there a flash of gunfire behind them? Joyce and Clem didn't speak until they were on the freeway and safe.

'Happy Family,' he said, his arms straight robotically steering the car. 'It's here in California. All over America. The world.'

'What are you talking about, Clem?' said Joyce. She was more composed than him.

'We thought Operation Happy Family was confined to Heshui and China.'

'And it's not?'

'Not if it's what killed Henry Fordham. If that was his real name.'

'Murdered,' said Joyce.

'Don't know,' said Clem pensively, his eyes locked on the meshing lights ahead of him. 'Just don't know.'

The suite of offices used by the Chinese President was in the heart of Zhongnanhei overlooking a man-made lake lined with trees and crossed by two bridges. When he had won the presidency, Kang had built the complex so that he could concentrate his personal authority under one roof. He created a layer of power separate from the politburo and the central committee, where he pushed his feelers into China through loyal staff like Tony Zhang. Kang himself worked from a mostly windowless room decorated with pictures of China. The only natural light came from a narrow bullet-proof window looking out onto the lake. One door to the left ran into a private bedroom and sitting room, where Tony had been waiting for him two nights earlier. To the right, the door led to open-plan offices of his administrative staff and beyond that was a circular foyer, off which there were five other offices. Each represented one of Kang's special projects. Tony, who was the youngest, covered social aspirations. Wendy Zhou covered trade; Jeremy Tang did poverty; John Jiang monitored the economy; Alan Zhu handled security and the military, and they all used Western first names because of their contacts with think-tanks in America and Europe.

After leaving Ling, Tony went straight back into his office. He lit a cigarette, tuned the television to CNN rolling news, opened a can of Coke and booted up his desktop computer. He put his feet on his work table and left the door open so anyone there late like him could see what he was doing.

Tony waited, restlessly, his stomach churning with nerves. He was an intellectual. Not a spy. He was loyal to the President. Yes. But Kang didn't even know the danger he was in. That China was in. Tony watched the clock. Fiddled with his pager. Checked and re-checked messages. He flicked between CNN, CCTV and BBC World, then onto the satellite downlink channels which brought in the American morning news shows. Peter Mackland, National Security Adviser, sweat glistening through his make-up, on ABC. Not worried about China's new missiles, he was saying.

'America retains the most sophisticated arsenal of any country

and would not hesitate to use it to its fullest potential if threatened.'

'So you see China as . . .'

'Not at all,' interrupted Mackland. 'China is a regional ally
and that will be seen shortly when President Kang comes to
Washington for a state visit.'

Alan Zhu stepped in to say goodnight. One by one, his colleagues went home, leaving him alone with the sound of a vacuum
cleaner down a distant corridor. He knew Fu Mei, the cleaning
lady, well. He had given her envelopes generously stuffed with
hundred-renminbi notes for her family at Chinese New Year and
six weeks ago had been to her three-room apartment on the
Western fringes of the city as a special guest. He let her get
down into the foyer, close to the offices, and then swung his feet
of his desk and asked if she would let him into Alan's room. He
mumbled that he needed some papers from there and, without
question, she fumbled with a tangle of keys and swipe cards
hanging from her belt. He left the door ajar. Only a very few
were ever allowed into this inner sanctum of the President, itself
inside the world's most impenetrable citadel. Alan, convinced of
its security, had left his desktop on, booted up and the password
in. He was in the middle of a memo about the downsizing of the
military by half a million men.

The desktop was linked to the network of military and police
databases throughout China, just as Tony had a line into the
universities and think-tanks which dealt with social problems.
A screentop appeared from Alan's girlfriend asking why he was
late. Tony just left it there and pulled up the search programme
common to all five advisers.

He began with Heshui. If Alan had a record in his own office,
the reference would register immediately. And with Heshui a
closed border province area, streams of options appeared in both
Chinese characters and English. The location of military camps
in Jilin province; the names of the commanders, units and how
long they had been there; the capacity of airfields; organised-crime
smuggling routes into Russia and Korea; dissident groups at
universities in Yanji, Shenyang and other cities. He stopped the
cursor on the headline of satellite observation, with the options of
American, Chinese, Indian and Japanese. Tony split the screen and
called up viewing of all four. The American and Japanese were the
clearest and even Tony, untrained in satellite reconnaissance, could
make out the buildings of a village, lines of huts, huge hangars, a

simple network of roads surrounded by mountains. He pressed print and watched the high-speed machine run off image after image, pages numbered and with colour on some.

Fu Mei called out to him from his own office, her voice echoing around the building to be picked up by anyone else who was there. She shouted that she was leaving and appeared at the doorway of Alan's room with the tube of the vacuum cleaner banging clumsily against the doorframe. Sheet after sheet of paper fell, spewing from the printer. Tony tipped a handful of cigarettes out of his packet and dropped them into Fu Mei's hand. Her irritable husband could now smoke foreign-made cigarettes at the tea house and gain enormous face. Fu Mei left the door open and Tony looked back and forth between the printer and the clock. He lit a cigarette himself, drawing the smoke deep into his lungs to calm himself. He wasn't trained to spy, to be caught in a situation where there was no explanation except an admission of guilt. He heard Fu Mei shuffling down the corridor. He leant around the door to wave. The President's offices were empty apart from him.

He collated more than fifty sheets, resupplied paper to the printer from his own office, pulled back the search programme, added Happy Family to Heshui and pressed go. Tony watched the network of databases speaking to each other. The screen went to white and bold clear letters flashed on saying: User not allowed access to this site. Refer Lance Picton.' Tony cleared it and searched for Win Kyi. The same message. He punched in Clem Watkins. The same. Warren Hollingworth. The same. McKillop. The same. He closed the search programme and brought it back again just in case the searches weren't being registered and froze on Lance Picton. He punched them back in again. The same message appeared. Picton. Picton. Picton.

And Tony took it right back, frantically, page by page until the screen was where Alan had left it. Down the corridor, he could hear a guard was on the phone. The door to the villa was closed. Tony left quickly, turning his own desktop off, but keeping the television on, sound turned up and a lamp shining on his desk.

Outside, Tony's driver leant against the bonnet, smoking. As they drove off, three cars of the Special Guards Unit sped past them. Tony didn't recognise the guards. New men had been assigned. They checked his pass at the gate and asked for a matching ID. He got the driver to drop him at the Beijing Grand Hotel on the other side of Tiananmen Square. He was meeting friends for a drink, he said. And that was when the driver said there was a new security system because the government thought there were spies in Zhongnanhai. He shook his head as if such a thing had never happened before, not since the Revolution. It would never have happened when Mao was alive. As Tony got out, the driver said anyone who betrayed the Motherland should be disgraced and shot.

Tony agreed, slammed the door and walked towards the hotel. From the first floor he heard the orchestra playing Chopin's *Nocturnes*. An American tourist was telling the doorman how wonderful they were finding China. 'I just feel so perfectly safe on your streets,' she said.

Tony used the coin phone box to call Lucy.

Clem was scruffy again. The suit and the briefcase were gone. His jeans were torn at the knee, his shirt ripped under the arms and his face carried the stubble of a journey from the West Coast.

Pigeons flew out of the trees as he made his way towards the river front. Earth and stones were pressed hard and neatly into the path. Pine trees rose up on each side, making it darker. The first sunlight came from the east through the reeds and rushes, exposed in the low tide, and over the fields and marshes where a single gull flew through a murky morning sky.

It lit up the church, too, which looked so isolated and cold as if on its own island. Cobwebs brushed Clem's face, telling him that he was the first person down here this morning. Metal mooring stakes protruded from the mud flats. Anchor chains ran to dinghies, grounded by the low water. The river bank was lined with old trees, some dead with hollowed-out trunks. The land rose up sharply from the mud and a bull stalked around a field above the river.

A gate with bright green paint and oiled hinges carried a sign which said *Private*. Puddles from the overnight rain lingered on the path beyond. Concrete boulders were built against the slope to stop river bank erosion. Three small sailboats on trailers were lashed to them, with colourful covers, and further up there was a catamaran and four windsurfers. Further along, towards the church, Clem heard shouts from the shoreline and the barking of dogs.

He climbed the bank, ducked under fence wire and took cover in a wood at the end of the field. From there he had a view of the road down which Scott Carter's hearse would travel and of the church. Earlier he had scanned the newspapers and nothing appeared about the funeral. The news about China was being written from Washington and concentrated on Kang's visit; whether it was appeasement or confrontation which would lead to world peace. From Washington, Clem had tried calling Mike again and again, but, after a series of diverted calls, no contact and different answering services, he stopped.

Clem waited in a burrow, wet leaves and moss around him, a cold dankness seeping through his clothes. Shortly after 8 a.m. two helicopters flew overhead. Then three cars and two vans of the Secret Service drew up at the small gate which led through the cemetery to the church. Dogs and handlers jumped out of the van first. Marksmen took up positions on the perimeter of the churchyard, along the road and up in the belfry, where Clem reckoned they would have both infra-red and thermal-imaging equipment.

He hadn't factored any of this into his plan. That Zuckerman would be invited. Clem just wanted to get to Carter and tell him about Heshui. To have found Carter in Washington was too dangerous. Too many receptionists. Too many explanations. Too many people. Too many phone calls and each one would get them closer to him. Whoever they were. The terrible organisation represented by Mickey, Torrance and Henry Fordham.

But this was Carter's turf. The family had been buried at the church for generations, almost since the arrival of the Founding Fathers in the seventeenth century. Carter, the father, would be motivated to listen. And he had power to help. Clem watched as the mourners drove up, their invitation cards checked, mirror under the cars for bombs, dogs straining on their leashes sniffing for explosives. Everyone was happy to comply. Everyone felt safer with the Secret Service at a funeral for a man murdered by forces unknown. Jane and Donald Zuckerman were among the last, choosing, despite the drizzle, to walk with other mourners through the cemetery to the church. Scott's grave had been dug on sloping ground just down from the bell tower. Freshly turned earth was piled on one side.

Scott's colleagues in the CIA acted as pall bearers. The coffin was draped in the American flag and the family walked behind, Scott's brother, Geoffrey, and his sister, Madelaine, followed by Andrew and Susan Carter, her hair held in place by a plain, black silk scarf. They would not show their grief in public. The family moved forward united and dignified. The Carters had buried too many of their sons and daughters in too many foreign lands to break down now.

The marksman on the church roof didn't relax even when Zuckerman was inside. Clem heard the organ music. The drivers sat, three or four to a car, doors open to keep their cigarette smoke outside. Once he moved, however concealed, however fast, the Secret Service could spot him. So he had one chance to get there and say it. He would run up with his hands high when Zuckerman was in the church or in the car. Not in so much danger. So they wouldn't fire. Their obsession was Zuckerman. No one else. The music, the tributes and the prayers reached Clem and he watched as they came out, umbrellas up, for the brief burial ceremony.

Clem edged forward as the mourners clustered around the grave. He watched the men in the bell tower. No movement. No recognition. Forward again. Nothing. Forward again and now inches from the path, a hundred yards from the churchyard. The mourners dispersing. Zuckerman shaking hands with Carter. Susan and Jane embracing. Geoffrey and Madelaine looking on. And Zuckerman the first to go. The car up the church driveway this time. Because of the rain? Dark, solemn, low clouds hanging over the river, unbroken but spitting rain. And just then, Clem saw the activity around the church. He looked up and a marksman on the bell tower was bringing his rifle around. The other was on the radio. More men took up positions around the President's Cadillac. So Clem stood up, hands high, sprinting forward, slipping on the dampness, stabilising himself, only a few yards, but they were coming at him, the marksman following, steady with the rifle. He had to get through the first line of men. He had to get to Carter. Or he would be gone, sucked back. Happy Family would take over, get to him. Carter would be told he was a madman from the village and Clem would be gone.

The first was right in the path with a revolver straight at him. But he wouldn't shoot. Even if Clem didn't stop. The second went for his legs, just like Clem had done to Torrance, but Clem sidestepped. Then he heard, at just the second, over a radio: 'Take him out?' A question.

And a hesitation in the reply. Zuckerman's car was driving off. But Clem wasn't after the President. His hands, still revealed. No weapon. His breathing controlled for what he had to say. He had been there before, on the other end of the rifle. He understood the instincts. There was no order. He was close now, near enough to shout, but a gust of wind, a sudden squall and his words would be lost. So he raised his hands higher, this time holding his CIA card. He shouted for them not to shoot, which gave him the time to get to Carter. He stopped a few feet away, not attacking and they were on him, pinning his arms behind his back, trying to get him down, then seeing the ID card and easing off. 'Andrew Carter, my name is Clem Watkins, CIA,' he said calmly. 'I know who killed your son.'

'Clem.' A voice from the mourners. A pushing aside of people. 'Clem, what in hell are you playing at?'

Andrew Carter was just looking at him. Not speaking. Susan, too. He was a lunatic at the funeral of their son. The earth damp, fresh on the grave. The vicar, his Bible still open, holding it under his surplice so it didn't get wet. Rain on mourners' faces like tears. All within a cordon of guns and men with radios and dogs.

'I know this man,' Warren Hollingworth was saying, taking charge. And no one questioned him. Hollingworth nodded towards the head of the security operation.

'I know why Scott died,' Clem shouted, as they handcuffed him. From the back of the Secret Service car, an armed guard on each side, and Warren Hollingworth in the front, Clem looked out the window and watched Andrew Carter thank the mourners as if nothing at all had happened.

Chapter Twenty-Four

Mike went to Shanghai just like Druk had told him to. The walls of the Casablanca Bar at the Rainbow Hotel were covered in black and white photographs of Humphrey Bogart and Ingrid Bergman. A hostess in a long, bright red cheongsam held the lift door as Mike showed his room key and stepped out into the dim light. He had showered for the first time in two days, shaved off his stubble and left a moustache. This was his second night waiting for Ling. He ordered a Glenfiddich, no water, no ice.

The waitress' T-shirt was printed with more scenes from the movie. Outside the night skyline of Shanghai shimmered below him. They had filmed the end of *Casablanca* twice, Mike remembered, one with Ingrid Bergman getting on the plane and the other of her staying with Humphrey Bogart at the airport. The whisky burnt the back of his throat. It reminded him of Joss McEwan, whose boat had saved his life and who had chosen to defy the system before Mike had. He took a beer mat and started writing out two endings of his own. One was with him shot dead, Ling dead, Clem, Joss, all the others killed and Li Tuo the president of China. The second was with him shooting Li Tuo dead, or killing him somehow. Maybe pushing him out of a helicopter, starving him to death, forcing him to overdose on heroin, fighting him in the water and keeping his head down until his body went limp, strangling him with wire, or just killing him, a single shot in the head, like he had done to Jimmy Lai at Maekok.

He enjoyed the bar, the waitress bringing more drink every time his glass was empty and the criss-crossing view of freeways, skyscrapers and in the distance the boats on the Huangpu River, where Britain had built the greatest Colonial waterfront in the world. Shanghai had a more complex soul than Hong Kong, a more violent history and a more embittered past.

A jazz singer would come up soon and Mike would stay for the first set, like he had last night. They had started playing Billie

Holliday before to warm up the audience and when he heard the first song, Mike swung round to the window so no one would see him and he cried. It was good really, because he drank fast with it, and he thought of Sally and how maybe she was dead or whatever, but he would never see her again, just as Elton had told him as he lay dying.

Tonight they played Billie Holliday again and Mike kept his tears to himself. Instead he dreamt up his second ending after he had killed Li Tuo. In Scotland, with Matthew and Charlotte back, and Sally, rugged up in a cape and gum boots against a Hebridean gale, all of them together as if the past year had never happened. He closed his eyes with the music and the taste of the peat from the Glenfiddich. They were gathered at the stone circle of Callanish on the Island of Lewis. Somehow the music matched. It was a summer's evening, with the weather changing from squalls to sunshine and back again in a matter of minutes, just as his memory moved from the men he'd killed a few days ago to the days he'd spent with Sally around Asia when they were younger. He leant back in his seat, eyes closed, glass resting in his hands against his stomach, listening to the song, pushing away horror after horror.

Mike had let himself drift, unguarded and he jolted when the waitress pulled the chair out next to him and took a box of matches from her trouser pocket to relight the candle.

'Sir, your friend has arrived.' She touched him on the shoulder to make sure he was awake:

'One bill or two?' she added.

It should have been Ling, the light was wrong and he smiled at the figure approaching, not recognising that it wasn't Ling at all.

'Make it one,' said Tommy Lai, taking a seat next to him.

When the unsteady candle flame lit up Tommy's face, Mike's reaction was mechanical. Tiredness and drink fogged his instincts and memory. He smiled to welcome a friend.

Mike turned in his seat so he was facing the bar and Tommy: 'What are you doing here?'

Tommy Lai waved the waitress away when she asked to take his order and leant across, his chin cupped in his hands, his elbows on the table: 'I'm here to save your life, Mike.' He took a small folder from his jacket pocket and pushed it over to him: 'Virgin Pacific leaves Shanghai at 10.45 tomorrow for London. You're booked on it.'

Tommy Lai's voice was just above a whisper. His head only

inches from Mike. His eyes seemed to be pleading with him: 'No one wants you in this. Just go and leave it for the Chinese to sort out themselves.'

'And if I don't?' Mike suggested.

Tommy shook his head. He took out two cigarettes, lit both and handed one to Mike. 'Do what Joss did and you'll be fine. No one will touch you.' He unfolded a piece of paper he had in his hand. 'This is a photocopy of the monthly bank transfer. You can live like a king in your Scottish croft on that.'

Mike took the paper and held it against the candlelight. 'Thirty thousand pounds a month is way above my salary.'

'There'll also be a hundred and fifty thousand-pound gratuity every year inflation-linked, just like Joss. For Christ's sake, Mike, don't mess with them.' He paused. 'Clem Watkins has been killed. They got him.'

'Who's they?'

'The same people who killed Scott Carter. Who will kill you if you hang around.'

'How did Clem die?'

'Don't know.' Tommy smoked his cigarette in short, nervous puffs. 'Something about him being shot as he broke into a policeman's house. But I really don't know.'

'He's dead?' Mike asked again. The saxophonist let off a blast. There was a drum roll. Billie Holliday was turned off. Tommy nodded.

'The same people who killed Jimmy?'

'Probably,' said Tommy.

'And you're part of them?'

'Don't,' said Tommy raising his hand, palm open, to stop Mike going any further.

But Mike kept going: '. . . and you were tracking me from Hong Kong. All the way. Working for them.'

'I've been working for them since July 1st 1997,' said Tommy raising his voice. 'And so have you. But you won't accept it.' He stabbed his finger on the air ticket in the middle of the table. 'And you can get on a plane any time you want, Mike. Any time. But I can't because your fucking government wouldn't give me a passport. So don't give me any shit about working for them. It's my country. I work for it. And I'm here to save your life.' He stubbed his cigarette out in the ashtray. 'And mine, Mike. And mine.'

Mike looked across at his friend. 'I'm sorry,' he said. Tommy Lai was quivering with anger, his outburst unexpected by both of them.

Tommy shrugged. He lit another cigarette and asked the waitress for a glass of iced water. 'They wanted to kill you on Chatham Path. I told them to follow you instead. They wanted you on the way to Shek O . . .'

'I thought it was you on the radio,' said Mike softly so his voice was hardly audible over the band. 'Those words "Repeat, do not intercept suspect" have echoed around.'

'I've saved your life half a dozen times in the past week,' said Tommy. 'But this time Li Tuo sent me up here. He said if I couldn't persuade you to go, I would have to have you killed.'

'Thanks,' said Mike sarcastically.

'In the national interest.'

'He's a drug peddler.'

'I know.'

'He killed your brother in cold blood.'

'I know that, too,' said Tommy.

'And you . . .'

'I have no choice. You went to see Agnes when Jimmy died. Remember?'

'Of course.'

'I don't want anyone going to see Wendy and the kids because I've been blown away.'

'And after seeing me off, they'll want you to do something else, and something else and something else,' said Mike. 'I've been down that road trying to find Sally. And they always want more. Each time more despicable. More sick.'

'Right now, my job's to get you on the plane or kill you.'

'You would?'

Tommy's eyes were concentrated. His face serious, speaking with an authority as if it was absolute. Mike had seen the look before when they worked together, about to go into action, braced, tense and deadly. Then suddenly Tommy was pushing his chair back, about to get up and glancing towards the door, where the hostess was bringing someone over. As if the whole thing had been prearranged. Tommy knew she was coming. The hostess was expecting her.

'Ling's here,' said Tommy softly.

Ling looked at Tommy first and the light was bad again so Mike couldn't make out her expression. She was carrying a briefcase. When she sat down at their table she moved the candle out of the way, put the briefcase by the table and ordered a lime soda. The jazz band was loud, so no one spoke, but all the time, she never looked directly at Mike. There were more men at the entrance, too, talking to the hostess and pointing over towards the table.

'I've asked Ling to convince you to take the air ticket and go.'

McKillop looked towards her. Her head was lowered, then she lifted it to meet his eyes. 'If you stay, they will kill you,' she said flatly and looked away again.

'And you . . . ?'

Tommy laughed quietly. 'Mike, you don't get it do you? She's highly respected in Beijing. She is exactly the sort of young person modern China needs.'

'What don't I get?' said Mike impatiently.

Ling answered: 'What he's saying Mike is that you should leave the Chinese to sort out Chinese problems. It would be better for everyone if you left.'

'Is that what you think?' He noticed that neither she nor Tommy had mentioned anything about Druk, Tony Zhang or her trip to Beijing.

'Neither Superintendent Lai or myself want you dead,' she replied.

'Where did they find you . . . ?' he began.

'Don't,' she said sharply.

Tommy Lai leaned forward, picked up the air ticket and put it into the side pocket of Mike's jacket. 'No one likes what's going on, but let us handle it ourselves,' he said, getting up. 'Come down in the lift with us, book your airport car with the concierge, then go get a good night's sleep. Let me know where you end up. I'll send your things on from Hong Kong.'

Four of them were in the lift. Mike, Ling, Tommy and Yip, one of Tommy's men, who had Ling's briefcase. The music from the Casablanca Bar was piped through. Yip had tipped the hostess to switch the lift over so it was dedicated to them. Tommy pressed Lobby and then B2, the health club, the swimming pool, the car park and the underground exit up onto the airport freeway. Then he looked at a poster advertising a new singer for the jazz band, starting in June. Yip smoked. Ling looked straight at Mike. Different eyes from a few minutes ago.

Tommy said: 'You never understood race, Mike.'

'What's this got to do with race?' said Mike angrily.

'That's why you got into a mess with Sally and with us . . .'

'Your brother was killed by a Chinese.'

'Like I said, you don't understand the racial family.'

The lift jerked, slowing itself down. There was a blaze of lights

211

and noise of people from the foyer when the door opened. Loud music from a rock'n'roll band in the bar filled the area.

Yip asked Tommy if he should drive Mike to the airport in the morning. Tommy was answering and Ling let her hand deliberately brush McKillop's elbow. Her eyes flashed towards him and back again, but by then Tommy's attention was back and Mike was almost out of the lift. 'You've helped us all, old friend,' said Tommy, waving, and Yip pressed the Door Close button.

Mike was left standing on a grubby red carpet stretching out from the lift saying *Welcome to the Rainbow Hotel*. A Taiwanese tour group, each member in a bright red baseball cap, pushed past him. McKillop elbowed his way through them. The image of Ling was what he had wanted to see. That she hadn't betrayed him. Neither of them wanted him dead, she had said. Her flashing eyes were a plea for help.

Mike ran across the foyer to the concierge's desk. 'Where do the vehicles exit from the basement?' he asked quickly in Mandarin. The bellboy pointed to the forecourt which was crowded with onlookers.

He ran out of the main door and approached the first Mercedes limousine in the row. The engine was running, the air-conditioning on. Mike pulled open the driver's door and hauled the man out onto the concrete. He got in, put on the central locking, and moved the car forward. He was about to block the exit when a BMW shot up from the underground car park, not stopping, straight onto the slip road to the freeway, Yip at the wheel and Tommy twisting round in the front seat, looking out the back. And Ling? He couldn't see Ling in there at all.

A Korean tourist coach slowed to pull into the hotel driveway just as Mike was accelerating out. Tommy was on the slip road and would soon be on the freeway. Mike had his lights on high beam. His hand blared the horn. He slid the automatic gear lever into second, for immediate acceleration, taking the Mercedes between the bus and the hotel fence, scraping the side of the bus, tearing off his wing mirror, but getting out, going faster. Tommy was up ahead, forced to slow for two tankers, then filtering into the first lane.

The road ran high over Shanghai, a sleek motorway which took Mike above the crumbling, twisting streets of the old concession area, and through the jammed night-time traffic at the smart hotels, office blocks and shopping malls. Mike was back on five-gear automatic, the rev counter down to thirty, the speed creeping up past 140 kilometres an hour. Yip wasn't going so fast. He was braking a lot, looking at signs, squinting, unused to night driving and Shanghai traffic. Mike came up behind, not even certain if Tommy could identify his car, and there was Ling in the back next to Tommy, crouching forward, her hands over her head, like Tommy would have told her to do.

Druk had said the Party had drawn the Yangtse Line and controlled everything north of there. But Shanghai was south of the Yangtse, thought Mike. That's what Druk was saying. He had them covered. Except for Ling who was to be abandoned.

His headlights lit up the BMW, showing him what he needed to see, ending the doubt which gnawed at him, convincing him that for once he was doing the right thing. Tommy Lai held the pistol at Ling's head. He was shouting at her, then looking up and yelling at Yip. Ling was no agent for the Party, or at least not any more.

Soon they were coming to the end of the freeway, passing the Shanghai Centre and the JCL Mandarin Hotel. Driving with one hand, McKillop felt down in the space between his seat and the door, hoping that the Rainbow Hotel was in step with Shanghai's five star hotels and let its drivers keep a weapon under the seat. He touched the metal of a .38 which slid out easily as it was designed to. The chamber was full. Mike kept the safety catch on.

He stayed right behind the BMW as Yip edged it down off the freeway to the Nanjing Road. Suddenly they were at ground level, constricted by traffic, slow moving, the shops open late, crushed with people and the street ablaze with lights.

Three girls in red and yellow sequin dresses stepped into the road from the Pacific Hotel, elbows linked, oblivious of him. Mike braked hard and the girls scattered, giggling. The lights had just gone green and the road ahead was clear. Yip was going straight, maybe to the Bund, probably through the tunnel under the Huangpu River to Pudong, where the military and the police were in undisputed control.

The Communist Party was losing the old concession areas west of the river again. The great trading houses of Jardine Matheson, Swires and the Hongkong and Shanghai Bank had bought their old buildings and moved in like before, using China and making money from her. But in Pudong, the Party's writ still ran under the umbrella of a tax concession trading zone.

Within minutes Mike's cover would be gone. If he waited they would be in the underpass and come out in Pudong where Mike would have no way of escape. They would kill him.

Mike pushed the hotel guard's revolver into his jacket pocket. Tommy Lai turned round in his back seat. Maybe he saw him: it wasn't clear. But Mike wanted the initiative. They were a few hundred yards from the Peace Hotel on the corner of the Bund. The bizarre pink Oriental Pearl television tower rose up from the other side of the river. People spilled from the narrow pavements onto the road. Each lamp post had a flashing neon sign telling people to *Love China and Love Shanghai.*

Yip turned right down Sichuan Zhonglu which would take him to the tunnel. The road was darker, emptier.

Mike came straight up from behind, smashing the BMW bumper to bumper. Both cars crashed together and bounced off each other.

Tommy, clinging to his headrest in the back seat, turned to face Mike. He had the gun and he was shouting in Cantonese, lip synching, so Mike would make it out: 'I'll kill her. I'll kill her.' His face contorted, he gesticulated with the weapon. But Mike knew Tommy wouldn't. He didn't murder.

Mike was alongside. Yip wasn't up to this. His eyes flickered wildly. His head spun from side to side, his forehead bleeding as if he had taken a knock on the windscreen with Mike's first attack. His hands were clenched around the wheel. Tommy was leaning over into the front seat, getting something, getting another gun.

Mike swung in hard, but Tommy was there too, the back window down, with an automatic machine pistol, its barrel inches from Mike's face. Bullets tore through Mike's windscreen and embedded themselves in the leather seats around him. Then Ling grabbed the neck of Tommy's shirt and pulled him back. The bullets went high, exploding into neon signs.

Yip lost it. He mounted the pavement and Mike smashed into his back lights, crashing the BMW into the wall of a building. Yip was hurled across into the passenger seat, while Tommy's head cracked on the edge of the door above the open window. Mike fought to keep control of the Mercedes, first thrown against his tightening seat belt, then bringing it to a halt and getting straight out of the car, his revolver drawn. But Tommy was out of the BMW, too. He had the briefcase and the machine pistol. He fired off at Mike, but as a deterrent, nothing else, then ran down a narrow, dark road towards the Bund.

Yip was alive, but unconscious. Ling stumbled out. 'I'm OK,' she shouted. Mike pointed and they raced after Tommy, now almost through the alley and illuminated by the glare of the waterfront.

'Who the hell's side are you on?' yelled Mike as they ran.

'They would have killed you,' she screamed back. 'They picked me up in the foyer.'

They found a pace, jogging together: 'Tommy pleaded with me to persuade you to go,' Ling continued. 'They're threatening him and his family.'

'Jesus,' swore Mike, panting. Ling was as fast as him, but not out of breath.

'But Tommy has the briefcase,' she said. 'Tony is finished if he reads those documents.'

'Do you have the passport Helen gave you?'

'Yes.'

'What name?'

'I'm Carol Li now.'

'You've got money?'

'Yes.'

'Go to the Portman Gloria Plaza. Book in for a week. You need a fax line, Internet link with scanner, mobile phone and photocopier in the room. Wait for me there.'

'And you . . . ?' They ran until they came to the Bund, next to a Kentucky Fried Chicken store in the old British Club building.

'If I'm not there by the morning, go to the British Consulate – it's in the same complex – and ask for Stephen Cranley.'

Ling broke off and Mike sprinted after Tommy who was heading north, missing the first underpass to the river front, maybe planning to take the other one up by the Peace Hotel. He was jogging, steady, with the weapon hanging loose, not as frenetic as the street itself, not drawing attention to himself.

Mike swerved around pedestrians coming towards him. He leapt over the electric saws and timber of workmen renovating an old bank building. He saw Tommy going into the underpass towards the river front.

Mike jumped over the railings of the main riverfront road itself. Spotlights soared skywards onto the façades of the Colonial buildings. Headlights snaked towards him in all directions; a policeman blew a whistle to stop him. Mike dashed through the traffic, hands waving, banging bonnets of cars which had to pull up, over the central island barricades, and across the other side. Two steps at a time, Mike ran up onto the walkway, knocking over a skateboarder, but keeping going, barging through families with helium balloons, cameras and baby strollers.

He cupped his hand to conceal the .38. Mike held back just before the exit at the underpass. It was only seconds, but it seemed much more. A grimy family showing off two monkeys asked for money. Foghorns and noises from the river distracted him. Then Tommy came out, walking fast but not running, protected by people around him.

Tommy Lai. Mr Cool. The best there was once, apart from Mike and Jimmy.

'Lung Pui,' shouted Mike, using Tommy's Chinese name. There were twenty yards between them and a dozen innocent heads which could be blown off if either man fired. Tommy recognised the voice. Blood was on his suit. He clutched the briefcase and slung his jacket over the other arm hiding the weapon.

'Go back to Wendy,' Mike shouted again, this time in English.

Tommy kept walking fast, Mike running, edging along to keep up with him, pushing through until he was almost within reach.

Pain jolted through Mike's shoulder with every step, but his head was clear. Tommy was fitter than Mike, a couple of years younger. Jimmy had been the older brother and Mike had been closer to him. Jimmy had liked field work. Tommy was more thoughtful, more of a planner. He would be thinking now. In the briefcase he had Tony Zhang's documents, if the Party didn't have them already.

Tommy began to slow: they were reaching the end of the Bund. People were thinning because this was a dead end. Tommy didn't plead – never had – but if he didn't kill Mike, he had nowhere to go. No Wendy. No kids. No home. They'd do to him what they had done to Mike, except it would be worse.

Mike came up behind: 'Go back to Wendy,' he yelled, panting, the words faltering. 'Tell them I'm dead.'

'I can't,' Tommy yelled. 'I need proof. You know that.'

Tommy sidestepped and speeded up. He let the jacket fall to the ground and raised his right hand with the weapon, his finger already squeezing the trigger. Mike dropped, breaking his fall on the concrete, and rolled towards the river wall. Concrete chips spewed up around Mike, but Tommy's aim was off, too slow, following the target and not anticipating it. Mike threw himself forwards, the revolver in his right hand, hitting Tommy in the midriff and knocking him back.

Both men were on the ground, Tommy's machine pistol knocked out of reach, the briefcase even further away. Tommy's hands gripped McKillop's wrists and twisted to turn the pistol onto Mike. Their faces were inches apart, their eyes locked onto each other. Mike rolled back and forth, getting up momentum to throw Tommy off him. Suddenly, his shoulder wound erupted through his arms and he screamed out with his own pain. The strength in Mike's arm drained out. The barrel of the pistol turned to kill him.

Then, with all his reserves, he smashed his forehead against Tommy's face. Flashes of blindness detonated through his own skull. He knocked Tommy off balance, enough to scramble out, get to his feet and kick Tommy hard on the cheek, first with the toe and then before he was down with his heel.

Mike grabbed the machine pistol and the briefcase, before Tommy was up. 'Go,' he pleaded, gasping for breath. 'For Christ's sake, go.'

Blood streamed down Tommy's face. He stumbled back, shaking his head. His right eye was closed. His hair damp and pressed down over his forehead. 'You get on that plane,' whispered Tommy. 'Then I'll go.'

'And kill me at the airport. Like they tried with Clem.'

Tommy weaved towards Mike. 'You . . . we . . . we can't do anything to change it.'

'Go. For Jimmy's sake, go,' shouted Mike, stepping back. Tommy hurled himself forward, and Mike fired. His target cried out as he crashed down. Tommy stumbled, then collapsed, weakened and wounded, not even looking up.

Tommy was finished, on his knees, his head down, his body folded, his head limp. He was breathing hard and quickly. Mike came close to him, touching his shoulder. Tommy fell on his side. He was conscious, looking straight up, his eyes confused with the pain and the situation: 'What the hell happened?' he whispered.

'It's a flesh wound on your left arm,' said Mike. He knelt down: 'I'll fix it.'

Tommy shook his head. 'It'll be fine,' he said softly. Mike had a clean handkerchief out and pressed it against the wound. Tommy winced. He brought his hand up to hold it there.

'Do you know what's in the briefcase?' said Tommy.

'Whatever it is,' said Mike, 'we shouldn't be . . .'

Tommy laughed: 'Fucking right.' He coughed. 'Crazy isn't it, killing each other for something like that?' He pointed shakingly towards the machine pistol. 'Are you taking that?'

Mike nodded. Tommy tried to sit up and Mike helped him. 'Then leave me the revolver. It's a dangerous world you've got us into.'

They heard a police whistle. For a moment they had forgotten where they were, but now people were running towards them. A siren blared on the road below and Mike was on his feet: he was the fugitive, not Tommy. He picked up the briefcase and the weapon, but left the revolver where it was, close enough for Tommy to get once he was out of range.

He ran off, lurching unsteadily on his feet, his breathing in gasps and irregular. There were steps ahead to get him down to the road again. If he could make it there and they weren't waiting for him, he would be all right. He knew the alleys around the Bund: he had worked them years ago with Tommy, Jimmy and Clem.

It was a muffled shot and he wasn't sure he was right. He had to turn, slowing, stumbling as he kept going, running backwards. The police were clearing the walkway. They had spread out right across it. Mike knew what he had heard, but had to see for himself. A single shot from a .38. He was right. And Tommy, a distant, dark, skewed figure, his arms splayed out, had killed himself because he had nowhere else to go.

Chapter Twenty-Five

The President said he would call after the funeral and Andrew Carter's phone rang at home shortly after seven that evening. Susan was downstairs, fixing coffee with Geoffrey and Madelaine. Photographs of Scott lay in albums open on the coffee table.

'They've taken Clem Watkins to Langley,' said Donald Zuckerman. 'Hollingworth is handling it himself.'

'I need your help on this,' said Carter.

'Anything and I'll try,' said the President.

'Clem Watkins is a genuine CIA agent who has long experience in the Far East. Currently, he's attached to the Consulate-General in Hong Kong,' said Carter. 'Our security writer has checked his credentials. So, if he does know why Scott was killed and who did it, and if he's not some nutcase, why did he bother to creep up on the funeral like that?'

'What does Hollingworth say?'

'I talked to him once early this afternoon. He said it'll be a long process to establish Watkins' credibility. But if he is genuine, then he knows there's something rotten in our system which he had to bypass to get to me.'

'You want to see him?'

'Donald, someone – not Hollingworth – needs to talk to this man alone. In a place where he knows he can speak freely. Where the tapes aren't running.'

There were just the two of them. Warren Hollingworth, in a chequered lumber jacket, paced around the steel chair to which Clem was strapped. Clem had been stripped to a T-shirt and undershorts. The air-conditioning was turned to high cool and the chill in the room cut through him. He was barefoot. The concrete floor was almost too cold to touch. Spotlights shone on Clem's face, so bright that he couldn't see. He could only hear Hollingworth and his footsteps echo around the empty room.

'According to this report, you broke into a police station, shot one police officer, locked two up, broke out Joyce Hewlitt who was being investigated by the FBI for arson and other offences. You then went to the house of police captain Henry Fordham and shot him dead in cold blood. Joyce is now missing and we don't know whether you've killed her as well. So far we haven't notified her children that they might have lost a mother too. Then you turn up at a funeral being attended by the President of the United States saying that you know who killed Scott Carter.'

Hollingworth circled him, the voice coming from a different, fluctuating direction. 'In mitigation, and I am your mitigator, you have been in an asshole in China for too long and have gone crazy. To substantiate that, we have evidence that I was pulling you out and sending you to India for a rest, and we just didn't catch you in time. My fault. Bad management.'

Suddenly the spotlights were off. Side lamps in the corner replaced them. The manacles holding down his hands automatically loosened. Clem shivered and squinted. Hollingworth threw over a blanket and handed him a cup of hot coffee.

He pulled up a stool: 'I reckon we've got a couple of hours to sort this before the FBI, the Californian police and Christ knows who else come knocking at this door to get a slice of the action.'

Mike McKillop melted into the darkness and came out on Nanjing Road where he bought a new shirt from a street stall and a pair of denim jeans. He caught a cab to another side of the city and ordered a beer in a bar called No More Tears, where girls hung around playing dice and a Japanese guitarist sang Bob Dylan.

He looked at the airline ticket still in his pocket. Tommy had got him a first class window seat with a connecting flight from Heathrow to Inverness and eighteen holes at the Royal Dornoch Golf Club. McKillop slapped the ticket down on the bar, choking with tears.

He ordered a double Scotch, drank it in one and made a phone call to Hong Kong, anonymous and coded, knowing it would reach Stephen Cranley immediately.

The clothes were smart enough for the Portman. He crossed the foyer and walked over the ornamental bridge to the coffee shop, just to look around, to feel more at home, then back to the house phones where he called up to Carol Li. Ling had taken a suite. She was in the bathroom, water running and she gave him the room number.

When he arrived, her hair was wet and she had wrapped herself in a towelling robe. She smiled, looking straight at him.

She took the briefcase from him and that was when Mike crumpled. His legs just gave away and he stumbled forward and collapsed on a chair, his head shooting with pain from the fight and the sight of Tommy Lai's body on the esplanade.

She poured him a whisky, led him to the sofa by the window and propped up his head with pillows.

'We're safe for the moment,' she said. 'Druk knows we're here. His men are around.'

She wiped his face with a warm, scented flannel, squeezing water into a bowl and dampening it again.

He was staring blankly out at the Shanghai night. Ling unbuttoned his shirt, carefully removing the cotton around his shoulder so it didn't tear the wound. 'Close your eyes,' she said.

'Tommy's dead,' he whispered.

She didn't answer him. She took a new flannel, wetted it, opened it and spread it over his face, leaving it there, while he absorbed its weight and warmth.

'The briefcase? Tony's stuff. Was it worth it?'

'Yes. I'm sorry Tommy's dead. But it was worth it,' she said. She looked at the wound. The whole of the left shoulder was swollen with bruising. Mike flinched as she cleaned, it, but he let her carry on because it was a different sort of pain, one which would stop if he asked it to. She washed a bruise above his eye, which wasn't so bad and then put on Shanghai FM which played jazz and night music.

'What happened?' he said.

'When?'

'Were you with Tommy before you came into the bar?'

Ling shook her head. 'Tommy was in the lobby. He knew where you were. I don't think he knew where I had been.'

'So you're not . . .' His voice trailed off. His eyes kept opening and closing.

'Let me,' she said. She ran him a bath with oils and salts, undressed him, walked him to it and soaped him. Straight away Mike was relaxed and then aroused. The pain and tiredness didn't matter any more and Ling worked him over, purposefully, knowing what she needed to achieve, soaping and massaging him in the water. She wanted his desire for her to supersede every other disconcerted thought. She wanted to calm him so tomorrow they could fight again.

221

'Whether I'm with the Party or not,' she said teasingly, 'I am still practised in the ancient arts of China.'

The music soothed him. He concentrated on each piano note to bring his muddled and racing thoughts into line. He pressed his hand over his eyes, but his thoughts swirled uncontrollably. When one idea, one obligation, one regret proved too undisciplined to suppress, he summoned the saxophone or drums, even the harmonica – each instrument he used as a sheepdog running round the flock in wild weather on a moor to bring the insubordinate thoughts of his mind into line.

Ling dried him and led him to the master bedroom. The chamber-maid had turned the sheets down on both sides and left orchids and chocolates there. She rolled back the covers and told him to lie face down, naked, while she rubbed him with aromatic oils warmed in the palm of her hands. She started with his legs and moved up over his back and arms. When she kneaded his buttocks and thighs, Mike turned over and slipped off her robe, gazing for a moment at her confident, firm, slender body, astride him, back arched, smiling, her eyes alive, glistening, showing none of the strain of the past few hours. He pulled her down. She responded wildly, both of them wanting it, both alone, hunted, cheated, frightened and confused. Their tongues fought and entwined. Their bodies rolled over and across each other. Their hands went everywhere without invitation and without rejection. They explored savagely. Their limbs were beaten and tired but the pain and pleasure they both gave and received rode over all that. They delved and took with gratitude and curiosity, with the attraction which danger and sadness had created for them. They made love with ferocity and revenge, thinking of the real partners they had cried for and knowing they were gone, but that life in its kindness had supplied another.

Mike woke with the morning light streaming through the window. Ling lay on her side, breathing gently, fast asleep. Quietly, he took the briefcase to the other room, closed the door and fixed himself some coffee.

Mike read and examined each of the documents three times. He made two sets of photocopies, put one in the hotel safe and took the other with him in the briefcase. He walked across to the next door office building and took the lift to the British Consulate where he asked for Stephen Cranley.

He was shown through the security door into the communications room, swept for listening devices and secure for conversations.

Cranley sat alone at an empty desk with just a pad of paper and his initialled Parker fountain pen.

'Well, Superintendent, you used a long-defunct and very secret code to get me down here on the dawn shuttle. So I presume you are not crying wolf,' he began.

Mike pushed a set of documents over to Cranley: 'You can keep these. They are from files in Kang's personal office.'

For the next twenty minutes, without speaking, Cranley read while Mike sipped his coffee. When he had finished, Cranley said: 'And your analysis?'

'It's a secure military complex. The satellite photographs show missile hangars and a railway line on which to transport them. There's a mobile launch pad two miles to the east. The bunkers to the west could be the nuclear waste dump referred to in the files. To the north, it does look like a labour camp, probably with inmates working in the complex. We've had evidence of a camp there for some time. The rows of buildings south of the missile hangars could be anything: residential quarters, laboratories . . .'

'None of that is disputed,' said Cranley. 'The Chinese satellite images are interesting in that we don't see them very often. We have access to the others, of course. The organised crime data is helpful. But I'm not convinced that we're getting anything much that we didn't know already.'

'Have you heard of Lance Picton?' said Mike.

'A former American Chargé d'Affaires to Beijing. Must have been more than ten years ago.'

'Is he still alive?'

'No. He died of cancer at fifty-two. Very quick. He was in the post at the time.'

'He's still getting newspapers delivered to his apartment.'

'Amid the inefficiencies of Communist China and the American State Department, I find that unremarkable.'

Mike remembered now Cranley's idiosyncratic manner and his skills as a runner of agents. He told Cranley about the attack on Clem Watkins in Beijing. 'The men who tried to kill him went back to that apartment,' he said. 'Whenever Tony Zhang wanted to go further on the Heshui file, the computer flashed up the name Lance Picton.'

Cranley laid his pen on the desk, not attempting to conceal his interest: 'OK, Mike, supposing I tell you that the apartment came out of the CIA budget. It wasn't State.'

'Picton was CIA?'

223

'Station chief. After the Hong Kong handover, they moved the post down to Hong Kong.'

'And gave it to Hollingworth?' said McKillop.

'Technically. Although Warren is more senior. He is more a hub co-ordinator for the Asia-Pacific.'

Cranley indicated that McKillop should stay in the room and punched out a number in Washington from memory: 'National Security Adviser, please,' he began.

It was Mackland who picked up the phone. 'Yes, Stephen,' he said, adding, 'you can talk. The line is secure.'

It was just before nine thirty in the evening. Mackland was already in his dressing gown and slippers looking forward to reading the latest issue of *Foreign Affairs* which had arrived that afternoon.

'Is anything about Warren Hollingworth, Clem Watkins, Heshui or Lance Picton crossing your desk at the moment?' said Cranley. It was an unorthodox and blunt question between the security services of two governments, albeit allies. But Stephen Cranley and Peter Mackland had known each other for more than twenty-five years and had worked closely many times before.

'You're calling me because you know something,' said Mackland.

'That is correct, Peter. But at this stage, I don't know what I know.'

'Perhaps you could lead me a bit.'

When Cranley had finished it was almost ten o' clock. He refilled Mike's coffee cup. 'It's been a very long time since you've done anything for us, Mike,' he said. 'Frankly, after you married Sally, we were never sure what pressure the comrades might have brought to bear.'

'Nor was I,' Mike poured his own milk.

Cranley continued. 'But nothing was brought to my notice that you had crossed the golden line. Unfortunate with women, perhaps, but still sound.'

'Thank you, sir,' said Mike.

'So, I'll be franker than I should with you.' Cranley got up, his slight, but tall frame almost too big for the room with its specially lowered ceilings and secure walls. 'We know a bit about Heshui, but not a lot. I don't believe the Chinese have any new missile technology, unless they bought it straight from the Western allies which they didn't. Or unless it was sold to them by a traitor. Their nuclear programme and labour camps, however loathsome, are nothing new. I met Clem Watkins a few times. Sound man, and my instinct tells me there's something up in Heshui which is shaking the comrades to their bones.' Cranley sat down again and drank in one what was left of his coffee: 'How's your Russian?'

'Good,' said Mike. 'Used to be fairly fluent.'

'Do you trust Ling Chen?'

'She saved my life last night.'

'That's never an absolute in our trade.' Cranley spread his hands on the table, pushing down hard and leaning back in his chair. 'I can't give you any equipment, Mike,' he said. 'Too dodgy to bring anything down.'

He paused and brought all four feet of the chair back to the ground: 'They expose in satellite photographs what they want us to see. Missile technology and human rights are the underbelly of China which we have learned to live with. Those evils will be accepted as a given when President Kang goes to Washington. Kang is the urbane internationalist to whom we give support in his attempts to change the system. He is our hope for China. We know it will take time and we don't let it interfere with the other facets of our relationship. What we will see performed during the State visit will be our Ceremony of Innocence.'

Cranley sighed. 'W.B. Yeats. Do you know it? Things fall apart; the Centre cannot hold; Mere anarchy is loosed upon the world, The blood-dimmed tide is loosed, and everywhere the ceremony of innocence is drowned.

'I think, Mike, that we're about to see an end to our absurd innocence in dealing with this country.'

The meeting was over. Cranley stood up and shook McKillop's hand. 'Because something else is up there at Heshui, Mike. Something far more evil. Something which is not a given.'

From where Tony Zhang paid off the taxi, he could hear the music from the Jiangguo Hotel. The fountain in the driveway was running again after being frozen through the winter. Little waterfalls gushed outside the rooms and in one of the first warm early evenings guests sat out on their balconies, looking south over the Avenue of Eternal Peace, with its advertising hoardings and construction sites. No balconies had been built to the north facing onto the alleyways which criss-crossed at the back of the hotel, the railings bundled up with bicycles, the cars bumping along potholes and the street-lamps broken so pedestrians wandered along large stretches in darkness, avoiding the shapes and figures which came towards them.

Tony Zhang had taken his cab as far as he wanted. A line of taxis trying to pass each other jammed the alley. A flower girl, with a handful of single roses wrapped in cellophane, squashed her nose up against his window. Tony pressed money into her hand as he got out. He edged through the traffic jam and walked briskly towards his apartment. The flames of street cooking stalls lit up the end of the alley. The biting smell of burning coal stuck in his throat. Fog and darkness blurred what was happening.

Tony was less than a hundred yards from his compound when a blow from behind hit his kidneys, making his knees buckle and lose his balance. Strong hands caught him as he fell. Nausea swept through him. Vomit came up into his mouth. Another blow struck the small of his back and then he was left to collapse, smashing his shoulder on the road, the attackers gone. No running. No scuffle. No attempt to rob. Nor to kill. Only to frighten him outside the door of his own home.

Dazed and in pain, Tony let himself in and flung himself onto a sofa. Nothing had been touched. His desktop and files were as he had left them. His English-language books remained in the meticulous order in which he kept them. They would have been the first the searchers went to because books and the free thought which accompanies them remained a paranoia of the Party. Tony smoked two cigarettes, lighting one from the other. His stomach churned as his kidneys settled, bruised but undamaged.

That was when Lucy called in a breezy voice, knowing that the listeners might be on the line, so talking as if what she had to say was the least important part, that drinking and sex was really what it was all about and that the news of Alan Zhu's arrest for spying inside Zhongnanhai was a piece of irrelevant gossip.

Tony knew he had perhaps a day, maybe a matter of hours. If they had wanted him, or if they already had the power, they could have got inside his apartment and threatened him there, instead of clumsily on the street. Alan would talk. But Alan didn't know, and right now, less than half an hour from the attack, it meant that Tony still had the power; that Kang was still President.

Tony telephoned the private number of a house in the Western Hills. It rang four times before a gruff voice answered and Tony asked: 'Is that General Yang of Unit 8341?'

'Who wants to know?'

'I am Zhang, personal secretary to the President . . .'

'I retired in 1995,' Yang interrupted.

'Mr Kang told me that if ever the President of China, General Secretary of the Communist Party and Chairman of the Military Commission needed ultimate security, you would provide it.'

There was a pause.

'You were the commander of Unit 8341 which became the Central Guards Regiment?'

'Correct.'

'You protected the leaders of the Motherland with one hundred per cent success since the Revolution.'

The heavy breathing of an elderly man. 'Do you know where I am?'

'Yes, sir,' said Tony.

'Then come and explain.'

Chapter Twenty-Six

Mike and Ling went straight from Beijing airport to Sanlitun and paid off the cab two hundred yards from the diplomatic compound. Mike's white face got him through again, just like it had less than two weeks earlier after Clem had been attacked. He nodded towards Ling and the Diplomatic Security Bureau guard let her through as well.

It was mid-morning and many of the car park spaces were empty. The BMW with its broken rear lights was gone. Workmen with jack-hammers drilled the driveway behind the block. A woman dozed on the glass counter of the shop advertising wine and cigarettes. Mike and Ling were just through the revolving door and in the dreary foyer, when Tony Zhang stepped out. This was how Lucy had arranged it with them and, without speaking, Tony led them into a dismal room, of shelves stacked with files and wooden desks pushed against the wall. The windows were covered with a dirty, cream paint. A single naked overhead bulb provided the light. Four men were there in freshly pressed, green uniforms.

'These men are from unit 8341,' explained Tony in English. 'It was officially disbanded long ago to make way for the Central Guards Regiment. In fact it was kept active for precisely the situation we are now in. They are illiterate, recruited from the mountains, loyal to President Kang and no one else. And deadly.'

He sat on the edge of a desk. He was jumpy and nervous: 'You two go in with three men. They are your ticket into the apartment. Once you're in, I'll leave. Lucy will wait for you in the lobby of the Kempinski Hotel, next to the Lufthansa Centre and get you out safely.'

He looked out of the door. 'I hope just a maid is in there. When she sees 8341, she will let you in without question. If anyone else is around, you will have to bluff. The rest of the platoon is along the corridor if you need help.'

'I hope to hell we don't,' said Mike.

228

*   *   *

They went in through the kitchen door at the back. The unit sergeant showed the maid their identity and a smile spread across her face. For her they represented the certainty of bygone days, before reforms. Hunched and small, she shuffled through to offer tea and show them in. No one from the Embassy was here, she said. There hadn't been since Mr Picton went back in 1995. 'Is he replacing Mr Picton?' she asked Ling, pointing to Mike. No, said Ling. This was Mr Mason who had come from Washington to inspect the standard of Embassy accommodation.

'The handle of the washing machine is broken,' she began, pointing around the kitchen appliances. 'You have to buy a new one in Hong Kong. There are no spare parts in Beijing.'

Ling moved them into the dining area, which spread through adjoining wooden doors into the sitting room and finally a sun balcony adorned with pot plants. There was an echoing emptiness, a musty, un-lived-in smell which the daily visits of the maid were not enough to dispel.

'It's an everlasting dusting job, Beijing is so filthy,' she said. She ran a cloth along the window sill, showing Ling the blackness which had gathered on it. Mike worked quickly and methodically. He opened the mirrored doors of a dark wood cabinet in the dining room. It contained crystal glasses, bottles of brandy and whisky and embroidered linen in the drawers beneath

Two guards took up positions on the back door and on the front entrance with security locks on its double doors. The third moved around the apartment with them. Hand towels were laid out by the washbasin in the cloakroom. Winter overcoats hung in the cupboard, together with a down jacket. A pair of ski boots and poles were in one corner, a set of golf clubs in another. Books lined Picton's study in the room opposite: novels on the right, with an unsurprising collection of William Faulkner, Tolstoy, George Orwell and other classics. To the left were his collection on Asia, a shelf on Washington politics and several dozen paperback thrillers squashed into a corner. The desk was clear of papers. A plastic green calculator designed like a golf course was in the right-hand corner. A jar filled with pens was on the left.

'Who was Picton's family?' said Mike to no one in particular, but Ling translated it and the maid said he was a bachelor: 'Every time Mr Picton came back home from work the collar of his shirt would be grey and black with dust because of the pollution,' she went on. 'I had to prepare three or four shirts for him every day.'

The study door opened out into the sitting area, where rugs from Xian and Tibet lay on a light blue Chinese carpet, decorated with birds. Mike checked both cupboards in the hallway leading to the bedrooms. One was filled with linen, the other with spare lightbulbs, vacuum cleaners and brooms.

'Was Mr Picton ill when he left?' Mike asked.

'He was going to America for hospital treatment and never came back,' said the maid as Ling translated.

'No one has lived here since?'

'They always say someone's about to come and for me to just keep it clean.' They were in the bedroom, with a television in the corner and a walk-in wardrobe. Mike ran his hand down the row of hanging suits and checked the pockets of two at random. He examined the shoes underneath: Timberland, Church's and pairs handmade in Hong Kong.

'So many cockroaches,' said the maid. Mike opened drawers of underwear and folded shirts while she spoke: 'You know why. It's because all the cooks throw rubbish down the tube from the kitchen. Cockroaches live in there and breed more quickly than anyone can kill them.'

Quickly, Mike moved against the wall and out of the line of vision. There were voices in the hall, speaking loudly. A visitor confronted the guard, quoting a security code number and password. The guard didn't respond except to bar the visitor from entering. Then there was the distinctive dialling of a mobile telephone. Mike held the bedroom door ajar: 'Does she recognise him?' he whispered to Ling, nodding towards the maid. Ling shook her head.

The visitor made contact and spoke rapidly. 'The President has his own men on the door.' He repeated himself three times: the first, it seemed, to confirm himself, after that because of a bad line. Then the phone cut.

'Let him in,' said Mike in Chinese.

A tall, gangly man with thick black-rimmed spectacles entered the apartment. He peered as if acclimatising to a different light and held his briefcase and the mobile phone clumsily in his right hand with a letter and government pass in his left. Mike flung open the bedroom door and walked out, the guard on his left, Ling just behind him. The maid hovered.

'Geoffrey Mason, Director of Operations Happy Family in Washington,' said Mike in English with an American accent.

The visitor smiled and held out his hand: 'Dai Feng-cheng, statistician,' he said. 'I was taken aback with the new security.'

'The President is taking a personal interest in the project.'

Dai rested his briefcase on the hall table and clipped his phone back onto his belt: 'President Kang is a . . .'

'I am here on behalf of President Zuckerman,' Mike interrupted. He was standing in the doorway to the sitting room, making it clear that Dai would go no further. 'He believes the work you are doing is breaking frontiers.'

Dai adjusted his spectacles. 'I've never seen another person in here before,' he said. 'It is a rule that we work alone.'

'Presidential summits often override existing rules.'

'Yes, yes,' said Dai. 'Your credentials are with your escorts. Only a very few are aware that the unit remains active.' He paused, letting Mike know that he was one of those few. Then he tapped his briefcase and laughed nervously: 'I need to go downstairs to bring in the latest data on pre-embryological screening,' he said.

'The President is thinking of making an announcement about Happy Family during the summit,' said Mike. 'Not everything of course. But there are aspects . . .'

Dai interrupted enthusiastically 'Yes, I'm sure there are. The benefits to medicine are truly wonderful.' He continued, lapsing into technical language with which he was more at home. 'Right now we are finding distinctive patterns of the propensity for Down's Syndrome in Caucasian subjects and we're beginning to see transmission traits of sickle cell anaemia from Negroid to Malay stock through cross-breeding.'

'Can you take us down to take a look? suggested Mike. Dai hesitated, then looked over towards the guard: 'As I said, only the very highest . . .'

'Thank you,' said Mike.

The maid's attention was now on Dai. She had a ring of keys and led the way into a small corridor which ran between the hall and the kitchen. The cellar door itself was unlocked. The maid pulled a piece of string hanging from the ceiling to turn on a naked lightbulb. Discarded files and furniture were piled up against the wall of the stairs. Grey bricks with cement spattered across them showed up shoddy workmanship, hidden from the outside. A bicycle leant against a broken cupboard. An old Christmas tree balanced in the corner where the stairs curved round, giving the whole jumbled mess a smell of old pine.

Dai picked his way down to the bottom. He put his briefcase on a pile of old magazines, moved aside files against the wall, then took out a swipe card. The door opened inwards and a blaze of lights flooded into the cellar. The rooms were mirror images of those in Picton's apartment, except they only took in the kitchen, dining room and second bedroom. A windowless wall divided what had once been an ambassador's residence, with no access through to the other side. Four computer terminals were arranged in a row and behind them were floor-to-ceiling cabinets on rollers, containing documents and microfilm files.

The office was unmanned and Dai, both excited and impatient, showed Mike and Ling the filing cabinets: 'I won't be long,' he said. 'Why don't you look at our marvellous archive while I log on?'

Dai went straight to a keyboard. Mike and Ling read down the file labels. Ling helped with the translation of Chinese characters. The archivist had been meticulous. The section on the far right was labelled *Human Gene Therapy*, with subsections on *positive* and *negative* therapy, and further down detailed files on *Adenosine deaminase, Familial hypercholesterolemia* and other disorders.

Mike pulled the filing cabinet to one side. Behind it was another. One section was entitled *Historical Data*, with sections on *Francis Crick* and *James Watson* credited with discovering DNA, *Gregor Mendel: Breeding experiments with peas in 1860* and *Harry H. Laughlin, superintendent of the Eugenics Records Office, USA.*

A high-speed printer whirred in the other room and Dai was at Mike's side, looking over his shoulder at Laughlin's file. 'He was right-hand man for Albert Johnson, head of the House Committee on Immigration and Naturalisation,' explained Dai. 'He was such a talented statistician who created a politically acceptable environment to stop defective immigrants coming into your country, mainly from Eastern and Southern Europe, the Balkans and Russia. Many were Jewish, but even I know your President won't be talking about that in public.'

Dai broke away to tear his sheets of statistics from the printer and start another set going. 'Laughlin is one of my biggest heroes,' he said, back at Mike's side. 'In fact, I use the English name, Harry after him. Harry Dai. You can call me that.'

Mike turned over pages of the index to the microfilm file. 'The bill was passed after Laughlin cited IQ and prison statistics.' Dai picked up. 'That was only in 1924. Albert Johnston argued that these immigrants were the dregs of humanity, mentally deficient and unable to assimilate. Therefore they should not be allowed to take jobs away from Americans. It was a perfect combination of science and politics.'

He moved in front of Mike and rolled the cabinet back again while he scanned through other titles: *Trait enhancement, Post-humanism, The Rockefeller Foundation, The Pioneer Fund, Nuremberg Laws 1935, Mankind Quarterly*, finally pulling out a file called *Animal Patent Bill, 1988.*

The printer had stopped again, but Dai ignored it, wrapped in his enthusiasm, and continued: 'Look at this, an article in the *Journal of Law and Medicine* defining what a human being is. Walter Fishman wrote it after the Animal Patent Bill was passed to ensure there would be no conflict of definition.'

The article itself was in its original form with the microfilm in an envelope behind. 'He actually writes,' said Dai, 'that a human being can be a genetically altered animal which possesses the ability to reason, argue facts, arrive at a conclusion and so on. Isn't that incredible?'

Dai put the file back and walked back over to his data sheets. As he read down them, he continued talking to Mike as his captive audience: 'You know, Mr Mason, the ideas all came from your country. You were the pioneers in this science, until Germany damaged it irrevocably with the Holocaust. If only you had stopped Hitler earlier, the advances we could have made . . .'

'Unfortunate, yes,' said Mike.

'The fascinating aspect is that Mengele could only have got so far in his time. But today with so many new scientific discoveries we are close not only to breeding a super-race, but to manu-facturing one.'

As Dai talked, Mike found a section on personnel and member-ship. Ling understood immediately what he wanted her to do. He left her there, sliding the cabinet back so she was mostly hidden.

'Many of us agree, Harry,' he said. He stood on the other side of the workstations from Dai, blocking his view of the archive. 'President Zuckerman feels that the public can be re-educated step by step. He telephoned President Kang personally to look for a way forward before asking me to come over.'

Dai was engrossed in his new statistics: 'The African IQ results are in,' he said more to himself than to McKillop. He leafed through the sheets, then acknowledging that Mike was next to him, said: 'We've devised a universal IQ test which we use on children among all races. It takes it much further than your Stanford-Binet test for pre-schools. Our Caucasoid subjects were from Russia. There is a huge supply of Mongoloids, but a paucity of Negroids. Eventually we managed to use subjects from countries friendly to the Motherland.'

'And the findings are here?'

'Oh yes,' enthused Dai, tapping the sheets of paper. 'The argument against genetically inherited intelligence has always been to do with environment and education. Good schooling against harsh living conditions. But we've managed to disprove that. We were able to use the same tests on Korean and African children both affected by famine. And the Korean IQ came out 20 per cent above that of the African. No one else has done that. With the mean of 100, we have already found Caucasoid West Europeans and Americans to have an IQ of around 108. The Japanese have 120 and the African-Negroid has an IQ of 70. The American-Negroid is about 85.'

Dai put the papers on top of a computer terminal and took off his glasses and rubbed his eyes: 'So you see Mr Mason, if we take Fishman's definition of a human being and the disparity of fifty IQ points between a Japanese and African-Negroid, we are blurring the line between human and animal life.'

'The President would find it very difficult . . .'

'I know. I know. We are in a battle between religion and science. Our job is to supply the facts. The politicians do the rest. If we can draw a new line defining animal and human life, the experiments and advances for medical science would be incredible, Mr Mason.'

'That, as you know, is the goal of Happy Family,' responded Mike quietly.

'Is it? Is it really?' Dai moved restlessly with excitement. 'I thought I was alone with my theory. That even here in China, I was not supported.'

Only then did both men notice Ling arguing with the guard. Increasingly it was becoming heated, but within a few seconds Mike realised what was happening. A sudden order had come through on for Unit 3841 to withdraw from the assignment. Dai heard it too. His eyes moved quickly back and forth from Ling to Mike.

'You stay until we have finished,' Ling screamed at the guard. But the guard was already at the door, shouting to Dai: 'Comrade, open up for me, please.'

'Why are you leaving?' asked Dai, gathering up his documents and putting his glasses back on.

'It's OK, Harry,' said Mike, his arm on Dai's shoulder. 'We were told their time was strictly limited. We've been talking . . .'

'Comrade, the assignment was not authorised at the right level,' interrupted the guard. 'Your exit card, please.'

Mike's hand crashed down onto the back of the guard's neck,

then into his left temple. He fell unconscious between the cabinets. Without speaking, Ling found wire and tape in a storeroom next to the filing cabinets. She tied his arms behind his back and taped his mouth. Mike had Dai in a full neck lock and frog-marched him into a chair at the far end of the room.

'The other side of this wall,' he snapped, yanking the pressure onto Dai's shoulders. 'What's there?'

'The Burmese ambassador's residence,' Dai blurted out.

'The door?'

'Only one. The way we came in.'

Mike pushed Dai roughly down in the chair. The briefcase fell noisily to the floor. Ling was taking files from the personnel section and dropping them into a plastic rubbish bag. Dai shouted out to her in Chinese, but Mike shouted: 'If you speak again, I'll kill you,' said Mike.

'Who are you?' pressed Dai, ignoring the threat.

Mike hit him, the back of his hand across the face, and answered in Russian: 'Mind your own business.'

Dai's nose was bleeding. Tears welled up in his eyes. Ling was at the door, the bag, slung over her shoulder. 'The card,' said Mike in Mandarin again, his hand raised again over Dai's head. Shakingly, the statistician handed him the swipe card. 'Tie him up,' said Mike to Ling. Briefly, he scanned the files, wishing he could deliver the whole room to Cranley, wishing he could deliver up Dai to the Embassy.

Upstairs, Picton's flat, untouched since 1995, was quiet, abandoned it seemed by the maid. At the dining-room window, Mike saw that the compound was clear, noting the low-rise wall and the Indonesian Embassy compound behind it. Noise from the continuing jack-hammer dominated any other sound. From the sun balcony, Mike watched office staff leaving the building for lunch. Diplomatic Service Bureau guards remained on the gates. A Latin American diplomat walked a pair of mastiff hounds around the compound. Ling pulled a small suitcase from the cupboard near the bedroom and packed in the files.

'The stairs?' said Ling.

Mike nodded. They were in the kitchen. He opened the door. Children played table tennis upstairs. The sound of the ball echoed down the stairwell. Building staff shouted down a corridor to each other. A drill started up in a nearby apartment. Mike went down the first flight, while Ling waited, then he beckoned her on, flight by flight, stopping, checking every time. He tried to work out the time-scale of the unit being recalled and new security sent in. Anything from simultaneous to nothing. This was China. They were on the ground floor, the same foyer that Mike had visited the night he met Clem. Mike stopped sharply. Three police jeeps were outside the front door. Barrels of AK-47 automatic rifles were visible in the back of the front one. Two policemen sat there crouched under the low roof. The engines were running. The drivers were at the wheels.

'It's Tony,' whispered Ling. And they pulled him out, Tony struggling, but held in place by two men pinning his arms to his torso, marching him down the small flight of steps and pushing him through the revolving door. His mobile phone fell to the floor. Then sheets of paper he had in his right hand, together with the laminated pass which gave him access to Zhongnanhai. Mike held Ling back in case she wanted to go out. But she stayed absolutely steady, only watching as Tony was pushed into the back of the second jeep. Once he was incarcerated there a pistol was put to the back of his head. A hand slapped him across the face wrenching his head round. They could see him clearly, dread in his eyes and tears as well from the pain and the terror of what happens to a man who crosses the line of China's political system.

Mike waited a full five minutes after the jeeps pulled out. From the interruption of Tony's arrest, the whole compound returned to its daily routine. The knocking back and forth of the ping pong ball; the drilling; the whirring of pumps and air-conditioners.

Mike indicated his plan to Ling. They turned right into the corridor, walking quickly but without panic.

A military truck, troops packed into the back, facing outwards and armed, swept through the gate. Four motorcycles with sidecars came in from the other side. Mike froze, holding Ling's hand, halfway down the corridor. On their right was a blank wall. On their left, the doors to the offices of foreign news organisations. They were trapped in a lethal line of fire which could cut them down from either side, listening to army boots on the concrete outside, then on the polished granite in the foyer.

Mike hurled himself against the nearest door, breaking the lock and crashing into an office. Television equipment with dust covers was stacked up by the windows which were frosted over and closed with no view of the outside. Videotapes filled shelves on all the free walls. A television on a stand in the corner was tuned to China Central Television. To the left was a cloakroom, separated only by a thick red velvet curtain. Tripods, reflectors, batteries and lights were stacked up around the lavatory and sink.

Mike closed the door. Shouting in the corridor got louder. Footsteps were coming towards them and then a calm American voice: 'OK, we'll just get the gear and walk out there like it was any other job . . .'

The speaker walked in and came face to face with Mike who held his finger to his lips, pleading silence.

'And who the fuck are you?' whispered the American, as if continuing his conversation with his Chinese assistant who was just behind him.

'I'm British,' said Mike. 'She's Canadian. If they catch us, they'll kill us.'

'That's about as bluntly factual as anyone can get.' He smiled and held out his hand: 'David Donald, Reuters. Glad to be of service.'

He spoke first to Ling: 'Take the battery belt and strap it round your waist. The spares bag is on the floor by the john. Carry that on your shoulder.' Then he turned to Mike: 'You carry the sound mixer. Put on the headphones and take the tripod as well. I'm going to walk out of this office and turn right, shooting these fuckers handheld, until they tell us to stop. You will go out and turn left.'

He handed Mike a set of keys. 'The van is marked with the Reuters logo. Get in the back. Close the doors and wait.' He smiled and held out his hand: 'I'll see you there, get you out of the compound and then you can tell me what the hell this is all about.'

Donald opened the door to leave, but stopped, taken aback by the two soldiers outside, their automatic rifles pointing into the room towards the ceiling.

He held up a laminated blue press card, straight in the faces of the soldiers. He switched off the telltale red light which showed he was filming, but kept the tape running. He balanced the camera loosely on his shoulder. He moved forward, pushing away their weapons with his free hand. 'They won't shoot,' he said softly in English to Ling who was right behind him. 'Not an American journalist. Not here in Sanlitun. Not just before the summit.'

The soldiers backed away, on the radio to their commanding officer, but Donald was walking in that direction anyway, towards the lifts and the foyer, alone now because his terrified Chinese assistant stayed back in the room. Mike and Ling moved out to the left, like Donald had told them, not looking behind, weighed down with television equipment while the soldiers concentrated on Donald. He was yelling at the troops, making noise, pointing at the commanding officer, knowing that, however insignificant in the Party web, he would have to account for the disturbance.

Donald bawled them out, mixing his Chinese and English, screaming about them wrecking the relationship between China and America. Yet the noise was bringing more people out of their offices; the Italian news agency, Swedish television, *The Times* of London and more photographers. Donald kept going, swinging round to face them, walking backwards, rock steady with the camera, his hand out to push the revolving door. He got the shot of them from outside through the glass, strong pictures of military weapons in a civilian environment. He filmed the truck, reserve troops on the back, alert, ready for action. Donald moved away, walking backwards again to get a long shot and a wide and when they were far enough, no longer harassing him, he stopped to put the camera on the ground and film from there the wheels of the truck, the driver in the cab and close-up of a soldier, his helmet and his gun.

The front door to the Reuters van was open and Mike had started the engine. Donald drove out and right again, deliberately in the mess of traffic and people, very slow with a Wujing People's Armed Police car following, then out in the clear past the South Korean Embassy and up to the Capital Club, where he turned right towards the Lufthansa Centre.

'I'll lose the tail on the airport expressway,' he said. 'Then I'm heading back to CCTV to feed this stuff, so let me know where you want to be dropped.'

Chapter Twenty-Seven

They fell into each other's arms, kissing and running their hands around each other's bodies, Mike fresh from a shower, Ling, her face and mouth caked with the grime of her journey, but neither caring. Mike undressed her while she was standing up, unbuttoning and slipping off her jacket and shirt, leaving her half-naked, his hands stroking, the air-conditioning and the excitement stimulating her with goose pimples and making her nipples erect. He unbuttoned her jeans, kneeling and kissing her stomach, removing her shoes, easing off her jeans together with her panties, lifting one leg out after the other, his hands moving all over her as he made her naked. He lifted her up in both arms and carried her through the bathroom where he filled the bath and they made love, slowly this time, sensitively, washed down with warm water and herbal soaps and not speaking at all about what had happened that day and what lay ahead of them.

Mike let her sleep and when she woke he fixed her some coffee before he told her what he had found. When Donald dropped them at the train station, they split the documents into two briefcases, went to separate airports and flew back to Shanghai on different flights. Mike flew Air Macau from Beijing, calling Stephen Cranley from a payphone at the airport, but saying nothing except to alert Druk that they were coming back. Ling took a three-hour taxi ride to the port city of Tianjin, catching Virgin Shanghai Airlines. By the time she knocked on the door of the suite at the Portman, Mike had the documents spread over the floor and had been given a glimpse into the network which made up Happy Family.

'You met McKillop a few hours before the conference,' said Hollingworth. 'Yet you knew he no longer had security clearance.'

Clem Watkins stared straight at him. The air-conditioning had chilled the room again. Hollingworth had taken away Clem's blanket and turned the lights up to full glare.

'You travelled with your full American government ID, armed, on enemy territory. You had no permission to be in Beijing. You were in contact with Win Kyi, a known terrorist who was planning to blow up the Great Hall of the People. Christ, Watkins, I have enough here to put you away in solitary for life.'

'You have shit in your mouth,' said Clem.

'And I could take you out of here tonight to a place where I would beat the shit out of you until you pleaded with me to stuff it back down your throat.'

The telephone by the door was ringing, but Hollingworth only picked it up when it persisted. 'This interrogation is not to be disturbed,' he shouted angrily.

'The National Security Adviser is on his way down, Mr Hollingworth,' the officer paused. 'We already had word that this is a presidential intervention.'

Clem Watkins' hair was still wet from his shower and they had only been able to find him a tracksuit and a pair of trainers before driving across town to the White House. He followed Peter Mackland into the Oval Office where Donald Zuckerman was sitting at his desk with his Chief of Staff, Charles Murphy, on the other side and a pot of coffee between them.

'I hope, Mr Watkins, you can fill in some gaps to a mess we appear to be in,' said Zuckerman. 'Peter, you called this meeting and if President Kang wasn't due here next week, our evening would not have been interrupted at all.'

Zuckerman paused to drink his coffee, then he stood up, waving his hand for them to use the sofas and armchairs. 'Peter received a call from Stephen Cranley of British intelligence in Hong Kong, which frankly scares the shit out of me.'

'In a private capacity, it should be stressed,' intervened Mackland. 'This is not a government to government issue.'

'Taken on board,' said the President. 'And can you note that point, Charles, in case – or I should say when – this whole thing leaks out. Peter, go on.'

'The British believe the Chinese are running a secret operation at a place call Heshui in north-east China which has American government involvement. Clem Watkins has been posted there for the past year and that is why he is here.'

'Clem,' said the President. 'Fill us in.'

As soon as Mackland had said he was going to the White House to brief the President, Clem had worked out what he was going to say. He had no doubt that Hollingworth was a desperate man, but he was unsure as to whether he was betraying his country or simply protecting his turf. Most field agents had been trained in the cold room, and Hollingworth's accusations against Clem were at least as powerful as any Clem had against him. As he had shivered, almost naked, under the glare of Hollingworth's interrogation, he had realised he had hardly any evidence at all. Just strands, experience and instinct.

'My work in Heshui, Mr President, was highly classified. I reported only to Warren Hollingworth. The project is a Sino-American weapons research facility set up just over ten years ago under an agency operating out of Santa Monica. I know the Russians and Japanese are also involved, but I was never able to ascertain exactly how. My brief was to keep a watch and report back the Chinese technological advances. Just over a week ago, I noticed a change in the military units posted to Heshui. The activity was unusual and Hollingworth ordered me out to a new job in India.'

'Did we know about Heshui, Peter? said Zuckerman.

'It's a blurred line, sir. Our multi-faceted relationship with China means there is co-operation in many areas.'

Clem continued: 'I didn't catch the plane to India. An American who did with a similar name was murdered. In Beijing, gunmen tried to kill me in a drive-by shooting.'

'I'm not getting your strands, Watkins,' interrupted the President.

'I'm sorry, sir,' said Clem. 'It's been a long few days. And it's not every day that a field agent is brought in to brief the President of the United States.'

'OK. Slow down and tell us what you think in your own time.'

'Sir, I believe that General Li Tuo, the military official in charge of security in Hong Kong, is making a play for power in China. I believe Hollingworth knows this and is covering it up and that Heshui is an element of what's happening.'

Mackland contributed: 'Li Tuo, Mr President, made his money in the heroin trade in the early Nineties. Politically, he is a militarist, a nationalist and very anti-American.'

241

'Whereas we classify Kang as a globalist and a reformer?' said Zuckerman.

'Correct, sir.'

'And where does Li's support come from?'

'Substantial throughout the junior officer ranks of the PLA. The colonels are split. Increasing support from Party academics who genuinely believe that any form of democracy will lead to a Soviet-style collapse of China.'

'The general public?'

'In a one-party state, sir, there is no such element to be taken into account.'

'And what is Hollingworth's role?'

'He's been involved with Heshui for a long time,' said Clem. 'Maybe he's covering up an operation which has got out of hand. We do it all the time.'

'That's what worries me about this,' said Zuckerman. 'We do joint military exercises with the Chinese, for Christ's sake. Our aircraft carriers go into Hong Kong and Shanghai. We're building their transport system, their telecommunications and God knows what else.' Zuckerman turned to his Chief of Staff: 'Charles, what's your reading on Hollingworth?'

Charles Murphy had a précis of the file on his lap: 'The records show him to be about the most skilled field operator we have. He was even considered for Director. But he's too impatient with procedure and was best left where he is. He's a highly talented individualist.'

There was a silence between the four men for a moment, then Zuckerman spoke to Clem: 'You told Andrew Carter that you knew who killed his son?'

'Not the individual, sir,' said Clem. 'But I am convinced that Scott Carter was killed because he was about to receive information about Heshui.'

'Go on,' said the President.

'Martin Hewlitt, my predecessor at Heshui, tried to hack into the Heshui file here. He was killed last week, sir, but his wife told me that another hacker had also been into the file from Korea. Scott's meeting was with a Korean agent.'

'Highly circumstantial . . .'

'As is everything at the moment, Mr President,' said Clem. 'But I am convinced that Scott was killed on the highest orders of the Communist Party of China.'

*   *   *

Ling Chen spread her documents on the floor in the suite. Mike sat next to her, feeling better than he had in years. The freshness of Ling mingled with the danger and the discoveries of Heshui. After they had first made love, barely a day ago, in that wild and uncontrolled way of basic desire, Ling had treated him with an intimate affection. She touched his wrist to see what the time was and pushed his hair off his forehead when it was falling in his eyes.

They hadn't properly talked about it and now in the excitement of sorting through the documents he started calling her Sally by mistake. He checked himself: 'Sorry,' he explained with a short smile. 'I'll take you to Bali when it's all over.'

She looked up at him, their faces only inches from each other: 'No way,' she said laughing loudly. 'You told me you had taken Sally there and played her jazz piano. Take me somewhere you love. Somewhere which you're as passionate about saving as I am about China.'

She kissed him quickly on the lips then returned to sorting through the documents, separating those in English from those in Chinese. Even if it was just for physical release, he admired her pragmatism and intelligence: to forget Scott and take him, because he was there, the room was there, the danger was there, and it would be stupid not to. The question floated past him as to whether she would have gone to bed with anybody as long as she was mildly attracted to them. He answered to himself that she would, because that was the character of her spirit and he envied her. Mike was different. Apart from a one-night stand of revenge the week Sally had left, he hadn't had an affair at all. Now with Ling he lived the relationship hour by hour expecting this unusual mix of circumstances to melt away soon and leave him eaten by the same anger and frustration she had found when she arrived.

She slipped her arms around Mike's shoulders, kissed him on the neck from behind and ran her hands down his chest, careful to avoid his shoulder wound. Mike was kneeling on the floor with the papers arranged around him like a card game. Bit by bit he was piecing together the character of Heshui and when he looked round to face her his eyes were grave. 'This is worse than anything the Nazis attempted,' he said.

'What do you mean?' she said.

Mike pointed to the documents closest to him: 'Look here. There's a wafer-thin line between those involved in the weapons research and those working on the eugenics programmes. Warren

Hollingworth and Li Tuo are both down here as representing their governments. He ran his hand down a list: 'Look here.'

'That's Japan,' said Ling, reading the Chinese characters on the list.

'Right,' said Mike. 'Ishii Kajiyama is Hollingworth's counterpart for Japanese intelligence in Hong Kong. Teo Kong is the head of the Singaporean secret service. Victor Chubais was veteran KGB, moved out to Vladivostok to run the Russian Far East. Mohammed Fahid is one of the most senior defence guys in Pakistan's missile programme.'

'You know all these people?' said Ling with surprise.

'From the old days. After the Cold War my work was narcotics and weapons proliferation. The Pakistanis, for example, get a lot of technology from the Chinese.'

'This guy looks Middle Eastern,' said Ling.

'Iranian. But I don't know him. And this one's very interesting. Yun Choi is meant to be the mastermind behind the old North Korea's mobile missile launching programme.'

'Now that Korea's unified he could well have stayed involved.'

'Right,' said Mike. 'And according to Tommy a Korean agent was also killed the night of Scott's death.'

They were quiet, Ling's hand on Mike's knee as they read through the documents describing the dual role of Happy Family: 'Clem told me that Happy Family was a top secret operation between Washington and Beijing,' he said.

'My government is very good at making people think they're the only ones involved.'

'They've been getting input from just about every ally they have.'

'And right under this umbrella, they are running experiments to create a Chinese super-race,' said Ling. 'Probably quite legally, too.'

'What the hell do you mean by that?'

She spoke with impatience, reflecting the dismay at what her country had created. 'Did you not know the Chinese government passed a eugenics law in 1995?' she said, picking up another sheet of paper and reading from the Chinese. 'It looks as if they're using the concept of the law to justify this. Here . . .' She underscored a series of Chinese characters with her fingernail: 'It's using the same wording: '. . . to prevent stupid, idiotic and slow-witted people from having children.'

'Therefore encourage intelligent, healthy and beautiful children,' said Mike.

'Precisely,' said Ling.

Ling watched as McKillop arranged the papers in piles, reading out loud as he came across interesting sections. 'Doctors and scientists pushing to lift the restrictions on genetic and medical experiments in order to improve global health care.'

She was on her knees helping Mike sort through. 'All drawn together by secrecy,' she said. 'A hallmark of the Communist system.'

'Anyone whose name is attached to the Happy Family would have to be associated to both. You sign up to overseeing a weapons programme and end up implicated in something which would be condemned by any decent person anywhere in the world.'

Mike paused mid-thought.

'What are you saying?' prompted Ling.

'If involvement in Heshui is as secret as Clem made out, then each of those men would be wide open to blackmail and that might explain Warren Hollingworth's very strange behaviour in pulling Clem out.'

'And in my interrogation.'

'For sure,' said Mike. 'Framing you is a small price to pay to keep himself clean. Cranley was right,' said Mike.

Mike took a batch of documents to another part of the room and spread them separately on the carpet. Only when they had sifted through the data for nearly three hours did Mike find Happy Family's inauguration certificate. It was a bright embossed document, illustrated by a map of the world with China in the middle. Each of the main countries was marked by two children and their parents, representing the pure race of a perfect family. One of the slogans advocated racial *Balance not Blend*. A separate document, stapled to the back, listed the founding members.

He began reading them off to Ling: 'Ishii Kajiyama for Japan,' he said. 'Here's Li Tuo for China, no surprise . . .'

But Ling was reading over his shoulder and ahead of him. 'My God,' she said. 'Look at this.'

She got up and walked around the suite. Mike kept reading, and when he saw it he put the certificate down in front of him. He got up and took both of Ling's hands, drawing her towards him and holding her while they absorbed what they had found out.

The man who had pledged to support the goals of Happy Family at its inception was not Warren Hollingworth, as they had thought, but Andrew Carter, Chairman and Chief Executive of American Global Communications.

*   *   *

Ling touched his elbow: 'These lists here show how the Chinese run the project. There's no translation.'

She separated the top sheet from the pile and tapped it to make her point: 'I'm almost certain this is the list of prisoners working there. Some of the names are well-known in dissident circles. Qian Ziying got fifteen years for hanging a democracy poster out of his apartment during the funeral of Deng Xiao-ping. Dai Li-teh wrote multi-fax letters advocating independence for Hong Kong.'

She ran her finger down the sheet: 'Here,' she continued excitedly. 'Paul Chu, a Catholic bishop. People thought he was dead. He was arrested more than ten years ago when he held an open-air Mass in Hebei and a quarter of a million people turned up.'

'Anyone who's interested in China has heard of Chu,' said Mike. 'We always had him alive on our file. They often proclaim people dead when they're not.'

'That's what I'm terrified they did to . . .' Ling began, but broke off in mid-sentence.

'What?' said Mike.

'Nothing,' she said softly. 'Except I was never allowed to see my father before he died.'

They were both quiet, because Ling had told Mike about her father and no words were needed to understand the implication of what they were finding out together.

'Are the prisoners actually working or are they Dai's guinea pigs?' said Mike after a while.

'Doesn't say,' said Ling. 'It talks about building work. I imagine they do both.'

There was a knock at the door. Mike brought out the automatic machine pistol he had taken from Tommy, took off the safety catch and stood to the right of the door as Ling opened it, using the door as cover. Stephen Cranley walked in first wearing a three-piece Irish tweed suit, followed by Henry Druk, who had on a maroon golfing shirt and a pair of chequered slacks. Mike spotted another man who stayed outside the door.

'You're the odd bloody couple,' said Mike. He brought both men over to the table, where Ling ran through what they had pieced together so far.

'It's not unusual for Her Majesty's Government to forge odd alliances in the national interest,' explained Cranley, walking straight over to the window and sitting in an armchair there. 'The President's backing Hollingworth,' he said.

'Not when he sees this,' said Mike, handing him a pile of documents. Cranley leafed through them in silence, then passed some sheets on to Druk who held them up to the light. 'I could have had these forged these in an afternoon,' the gangster said curtly. 'I think you'll have to better than that to convince the President of the United States that something is amiss.'

'And that will take time we haven't got,' said Cranley. 'Mackland's put himself behind Hollingworth and I would have done the same in his position.'

Druk opened the mini-bar, took out a beer and drank from the can. 'This sort of thing will eventually lead to China's destruction, as it did in Germany and Japan and as it has in countless other communities which people have forgotten: Cambodia, Rwanda, Bosnia. If Li Tuo succeeds, his arrogance will destroy my business. He will put his men in and cart me away. In the long term, my life is just as much at risk as yours.'

'It is not the first time nor will it be the last that the British intelligence services have worked closely with the underworld,' said Cranley.

'What are you saying?' said McKillop.

Druk took up the cue: 'I've made up identity cards for you both to get into the outer perimeter of Heshui which houses missile development,' he said, pulling an envelope out of his pocket. 'They are high enough quality to get you that far. But to go further, to the biological and chemical weapons plants or to the eugenics laboratories, you're on your own. You're a Russian, Mike. Dr Sergei Akayev. You're Chinese,' he said to Ling. 'Dr Wu Po.'

'You don't have to come, Ling,' said Mike.

'We've already discussed it,' she said, with a pause. 'I have to go because what is up there killed Scott and has tried to kill me.'

'But . . .'

Ling moved over to him and touched him on the shoulder: 'Don't say anything,' she whispered. 'It is in my culture.'

'I have nobody around Heshui itself,' continued Druk, ignoring their sudden public intimacy. 'When you get out, don't come back to Beijing. Head towards Tumen, the Chinese border town. A bridge runs from there to the Korean town of Nanyang. The bridge is heavily guarded, but a mile outside the town would be safe to cross. The river is shallow. You can get over at night and I'll have people in Nanyang to take care of you.'

247

'The American military advisers are up there, too with Korean troops,' said Cranley. 'If you find Bishop Chu, bring him out with you. He could be the Nelson Mandela of China if they haven't broken him. Once he makes a statement, Hollingworth will be discredited. Zuckerman will be free to back us. The tedious grey which has confused our China policy will be polarised into brilliant clarity.'

Chapter Twenty-Eight

'Biological weapons, Mr President,' said Warren Hollingworth. He was sitting directly in front of Zuckerman who had called a full meeting of his security staff. He chaired it from behind his desk. Peter Mackland, Charles Murphy and a few had found seats. Others, including Secret Service agents, assigned to handle President Kang's visit, leant against walls at the back of the Oval Office.

'And you have not reported this?'

'We've known about it for years. Their intention. Their achievements. Their delivery capabilities.'

'What sort of biological weapons?'

'They've been experimenting with 0–157 E-coli bacteria, with anthrax of course which is a terrible weapon. My new concern is EBV or Ebstrien-Barr virus which they are trying to cultivate to be genetically discriminatory in its targets. It could, for example, cause an epidemic of glandular fever among Caucasians but not affect Africans or Asians.'

'Why, Mr Hollingworth, have we allowed the Chinese to continue with this programme?'

'Because, sir, we knew where it was and what they were doing. Because of the Happy Family joint weapon research project, we even had access to the site, although not to the laboratories themselves. We only know something's happening up there because agent Watkins was in place. When I ordered him out two weeks ago, to save his own skin, he blatantly disobeyed orders and went missing.'

'And the classification secrecy of this project was with whom?' prodded Mackland.

'In this meeting, Mr President, I am not at liberty to discuss that.'

'You gave us no warnings of this even though Kang was coming over for the summit,' said Zuckerman.

'The policy of this government is to constructively engage and not confront China. If the policy is successful the weapons plant will eventually be closed through persuasion and negotiation. If we make an issue of it like in Iraq or in a worst-case scenario take out Heshui Libyan-style, the Chinese could simply set it up somewhere else. There have been presidential summits before with distasteful elements unresolved.'

'Where does Scott Carter fit in?' said Murphy.

'Zero,' Hollingworth lied. 'The Koreans had low-level HUMINT, that's intelligence from field agents, on Beijing's long-term military strategy towards Japan. Our use of agents in China is limited because of the control of the Party and the structure of the system. We can't slip people in like we did in the Soviet Union because our best people don't look Chinese.' Hollingworth paused for a ripple of laughter around the room.

'So we have a sharing arrangement with friendly governments, Taiwan and Korea being the closest. It was a routine exchange. We do it all the time. I'm still waiting for an explanation from Seoul as to why Scott and the Korean were attacked and how the exchange was leaked out. I suspect there were problems on the Korean side.'

'Who does the Chinese government accuse?'

'His girlfriend, Ling Chen,' said Mackland.

'Is that credible, Mr Hollingworth?' said Zuckerman.

'At this stage, sir, if it wasn't the Koreans, Ling Chen is very much in my frame.'

A new voice came in from the left of the President's desk. Larry Harper was one of Zuckerman's young personal advisers, only thirty-two years old but charged with long-term image-making of the presidency. 'Excuse me, Mr Hollingworth,' he said, his hand going up like a schoolboy in a class: 'I am not exactly clear of our complicity in Heshui, but strictly from an image perspective would not now be the right time to confront the Chinese, on the eve of the summit, to show the American people that we are able to stand up to China and force her to change her evil ways?

'These are just ideas, Mr President,' he continued, looking at Zuckerman. 'You can turn this situation to your advantage.'

'President Kang wouldn't know about Heshui,' interrupted Hollingworth. 'If you ask him to close it, he wouldn't have the power. You would weaken his position and we'll lose all knowledge of it. The Chinese military will cordon it off.'

'Peter?' said Zuckerman, requesting an assessment from Mackland.

'Kang's position is fragile at the best of times,' said Mackland. 'His reform and anti-corruption programmes have done nothing to strengthen him. Yet ultimately, he is the Chinese leader with whom we can do business. I wonder, like Warren, whether we should not let a sleeping dog lie at least to get the summit out of the way and tackle it with less of a knee-jerk reaction when time is our ally.'

Hollingworth leant forward: 'Heshui, Mr President, is best described as a controlled and humane version of the Japanese project Unit 731. No one is getting killed and we are monitoring.'

'I'm sorry,' said Charles Murphy. '731?'

'The Geneva Convention in 1925 banned the use of biological weapons during war. Japan refused to sign,' said Hollingworth. 'Seven years later, Japan invaded Manchuria in north-east China and set up unit 731, a biological warfare unit disguised as a water-purification plant just outside of Harbin. It was not unlike Heshui: 150 buildings covering six square kilometres and top secret.

'Those killed in the Japanese experiments included American servicemen captured in the Pacific theatre. Bubonic plague, anthrax, cholera and other diseases. In the final days of the war, Japan blew up 731.'

'I'm not sure of your point,' said Murphy.

'The point,' said Hollingworth, 'is that we, the American government, struck a deal. The captured Japanese scientists were given immunity against prosecution for war crimes in exchange for the findings of the 731 experiments – even though American citizens were among their guinea-pigs.'

Hollingworth fell silent. 'Are you saying that our government's complicity with evil is with precedent?' said Mackland.

'Complicity, if we should even call it that, does not begin or end in Heshui. What I have been trying to do is manage an evil which we will eventually destroy, rather than as with 731 have that evil grow unchecked without our knowledge or any ability to stop it. China, sir, is at present more an American ally than an enemy. If we keep it like that, the world will be a safer place.'

An uneasy silence fell on the room as Hollingworth finished. Zuckerman was the first to speak: 'Where does Clem Watkins fit in?'

'I kept him up there too long, sir,' said Hollingworth. 'It happens in the field. The fault is mine.'

*　　*　　*

251

Zuckerman asked Mackland to stay behind as the others filed out of the room: 'How many people in government know about this?'

'As far as I can tell, Hollingworth and the agents, like Watkins whom he runs. Everyone else involved with it has retired or died.'

'So what do we do with him?'

'At the end of the day, Mr President, we have to go with the senior man. Watkins disobeyed orders. Hollingworth has acted by the book. If we back Watkins it will set a precedent for insubordination which would weaken the security services.' The National Security Adviser paused: 'Unless, sir, your instincts strongly disagree.'

'You're right, Peter,' said the President. 'My instincts are chafing at the bit.'

'How sound is McKillop?' asked Mackland in a telephone call from his home.

'Completely,' said Cranley.

'And you believe . . .'

'His material is genuine, yes, Peter. I have seen the certificate with Carter's name on it.'

'Hollingworth has the high ground,' said Mackland.

'McKillop and Ling Chen are on their way up to Heshui,' explained Cranley. 'McKillop has a Russian pass and if the place is in as much turmoil as it seems, he speaks it well enough to bluff his way in. If they get evidence of what is in the documents, it will coincide with or come out just before the summit.'

'I'm reading you,' said Mackland.

'What will the President do?'

'It depends how bad it is. His options range from inactivity to a missile strike.'

'And the chances of that?'

'Very privately, Stephen, he's asked for a plan on his desk.'

'The UN?'

'With China as a permanent member, it would have to be outside the UN.'

'There are labour camps there, political prisoners.'

'Watkins has been working with our planners.' Mackland paused for long enough for Cranley to realise he was about to say something else.

'And, Peter.'

'I'm only telling you because your man will be up there too. I've sent Watkins back just for that reason; to give us the green light to order a strike if it's necessary.'

'Alone?'

'We've moved Delta Force units to northern Korea on the Chinese border. But in Heshui, Watkins is by himself. If he's caught, none of this ever happened.'

'General Li Tuo has flag-marched a platoon from the Central Guards Unit through Zhongnanhai,' said President Kang.

'There is nothing I can do to help you,' said the man who controlled the unit, General Yang Zhongyu. 'We cannot afford a rebellion.'

'Even if it overthrows the President of China?'

'Chinese leaders come and go, Comrade,' said the old man from his farmhouse in the Western Hills.

'Your loyalty . . .'

'Loyalty is a luxury in the situation in which we find ourselves. China has been here before and she will survive.' Yang paused and the President heard his heavy, irregular breathing. 'I can, though, give you some advice from an old and experienced man.'

Kang waited.

'Your support in the south is strong. If you contact General Liu Xuding in Nanjing he will supply men and an aircraft. He is not convinced that the isolation the Motherland will inevitably find herself in is a good thing. He cannot stop a march of folly, as none of us can. But at this stage Comrade Li will not cross him and he will do everything he can to save you and your family.'

'Thank you,' said Kang.

'And, Guo-feng,' he said, referring to Kang by his given name. 'For many years you were like a son to me, and you gave me the affection and regard a son gives to his father. Tony Zhang is like a son to you. Unlike you, his life is at risk and I am trying to save him.'

As Tony was being led out of the barracks, he saw Alan Zhu being marched into the courtyard, his hands in cuffs behind his back, his legs in ankle chains that clattered on the concrete around him. Tony looked behind him to see more, but the guard yelled for him to keep moving ahead. Bruises covered Tony Zhang's face. His right eye was swollen and closed and he limped badly as he walked to the van which drove out onto the Avenue of Eternal Peace and across Tiananmen Square towards the airport.

He walked across the runway with a limp. The evening had brought a sudden chill and Tony shivered, wearing only his shirt which was stained with blood. They hadn't cared any more when they hit him. It wasn't like outside his apartment when they did it so they didn't leave a mark. A British Aerospace 146 with Chinese military markings taxied down to stop outside the small terminal building. Wendy Zhou, Jeremy Tang and John Jiang from Kang's private office were in the small group that waited as the steps came down. Only Alan was missing.

President Kang was the last to board. The aircraft taxied for take-off while the engineer secured the door. In the cockpit, the pilot said they would be flying to Shanghai, where a 747 was waiting for the flight to Los Angeles. Tony lay bloodied. Kang took off his own suit jacket and wrapped it around Tony's shoulders. He wiped his face clean with an airline towel.

Druk gave them an Air Macau Boeing 737 to go direct from Shanghai to Yanji in the north-east. China North Eastern and Air China had cancelled their flights citing military exercises, but there had been no official announcement. Instead, Druk heard that troops were moving into the Heshui area from Shenyang and Jilin.

Ling first saw Sally's name on the Heshui list while they were waiting to take off. She and Mike sat in first class with the plane to themselves. The Australian pilot snapped open two cans of Coke for them, then shut the door. Ling was starting to make sense of the lists of Chinese personnel when she turned to Mike: 'What's Sally's Chinese name in full?' she asked.

'Wong, Wai-lok,' he said. 'Why?' Then he saw her mark the paper with a pen. She passed it over to him. There was no English, but he knew the Chinese characters of his wife's name. Figures of a unit and hut number were logged next to it. Her statistics were crammed together with at least a thousand others. Why should anyone notice it? Except him. It cited her career at Hong Kong Number One Hospital, as a gynaecological fertility specialist. She had been posted to Heshui to conduct experiments in genetically engineered In Vitro Fertilisation. She had been given the rank of colonel and senior Party level accommodation.

Mike felt himself shake with nervousness. He felt numb and wanted to cry at his own stupidity. What was it Cranley had called it? A ceremony of innocence. That's what he had been performing for the past year with his memories of Sally, Charlotte and Matthew. Anger swept over him, then grief, then an hysterical urge to laugh it away. Except his eyes were watering and he turned his head away from Ling to the window as the runway rushed past and the plane lifted off the ground.

He was still looking out as it banked down, beginning its descent. Beneath him was a beautiful windswept wasteland where the frontiers of Russia, North Korea, Mongolia and China met. He could see the Tumen River flowing shallow and fast on a plateau surrounded by small, green hills. The roads were uncrowded and lined with willow trees. An old steam train ran across the border into northern Korea.

The pilot told them to fasten their seatbelts for the landing. Mike handed the sheet of paper back to Ling who clipped it back into the bundle. She looked at him, her eyes filled with sympathy, and touched him on the cheek. He held her hand against him, harder and harder, as the plane hit low-level clouds and jolted in the turbulence.

A calm Australian voice came over the public address system: 'We've been denied permission to land,' said the pilot. 'The Koreans are allowing us down at Ranjin Sombong which is fifty miles to the south-east.'

The aircraft bounced and banked steeply to the right, the sun turning with it and streaming in through the windows across their faces. Then the pilot added thrust to the engines as if they were taking off again. The nose came up and extra speed pushed them back into their seats. The plane went into a fast, steep climb. They bumped back up through clouds and, before levelling off, Mike watched a squadron of Chinese MiG fighters land in quick succession at Yanji one after the other, their parachutes unfurling to slow them down as soon as their wheels hit the runway.

The free-trade zone airport of Ranjin Sombong had been turned into a crisis facility, partly handling military transport and partly huge cargo planes of international aid in preparation for the refugees who might come in from China.

The 737 taxied to a remote corner of the airfield where a jeep was waiting to pick them up. Two men simply identified themselves as Air Macau officials, meaning they worked for Druk. There were no immigration or customs formalities. Mike and Ling climbed into the jeep. The driver took them away quickly, cutting through a gap in the perimeter fence behind a disused Air Koryo Tupolev TU-154 and then onto the road.

After nightfall, Druk's men drove them to the Tumen River on the other side of which was China. They gave them an inflatable boat, wet-weather gear, a change of clothes, waterproof pouches for their passes and documents, and a Korean army issue defence kit, belts of ammunition, with grenades and machine pistols.

They were driven to a bridge where at low tide the Tumen River ran narrow like a gorge. In the moonlight, they could see old men squatting by the guardhouse on the Chinese side playing chess. Cows grazed on both banks where the barbed wire had rusted and farmers ignored the border.

Mike pushed out the boat, the water icy around his ankles. He jumped in and Ling was at the front paddling hard. They had blackened their faces and their clothes were dark. They let the current carry them to midstream, pushing themselves off the shingle banks in the middle. Then they guided the boat into the Chinese side, as Mike had done with Clem at Maekok, carrying their weapons in two bags.

The river path followed the road. They changed into civilian clothes and walked north along it, watching but hidden from the road, for about a mile until they came to an empty, newly built town. There was no sign of life. The street lights were off. No light shone in the buildings. No television flickered. No tired voice crooned Karaoke. Apart from the howl of wind, there was no noise.

The first houses stood on a hill, unfinished and abandoned, with land dug out for a swimming pool and the first landscaping made for a golf course. Further on polythene flapped around half-built office blocks. Wide roads like airport runways criss-crossed between buildings with advertisements for hotels and shops which only existed in a planner's fantasy. Cranes brought in to build them were static and rusting. Scaffolding had come loose and banged bamboo against bamboo in the gales which roared across the barren, flat landscape.

They walked, the two of them in the middle of deserted streets, exposed but sensing they were alone, that some order from the Party had closed down the town of Hunchun and that its inhabitants had left. The closest real city was Vladivostok about 130 miles to the west. Pyongyang in Korea was four hundred miles south and Beijing was eight hundred miles away. This axis of three countries lay in one of the most isolated places on earth, and Heshui was more than sixty miles to the north. Once they had left the river basin, they would climb steeply. The road was difficult and winter was still up there. The moon lit up snowfall on the tops of the mountains around them.

At what should have been a central crossroads, a sign pointed towards the Russian border, and when they got there, sovereignty was marked by an unmanned concrete guard-house, its windows smashed. The Chinese flag flew strongly. The Russian flag was torn. Its white, red and blue flapped like a severed arm, unreplaced because the Russians couldn't afford a new one. The road between two great empires disappeared through high grass and forest into Russia like a country lane. Watchtowers were set starkly against the night sky. But no guard was in them. There was no need. This was the free-trade zone of the northern Pacific governed by the laws of the Tumen Trust Secretariat. It was an open, unwanted frontier, protected by the UN. No one cared who crossed it.

To the left of the unoccupied customs house were four mini-vans, a Toyota Crown and a Nissan truck. Mike checked the tyres of the Crown. They needed air but the car was drive-able. The door was open. Mike was under the dashboard, look-ing to wire it, when he heard a rumble of vehicles from the Russian side. Lights illuminated the trees and, before he could move away, Mike was caught in the high beams, squinting in the glare.

Ling hid in the shadows. The lead truck stopped. Troops jumped off the back. Mike threw his arms above his head and shouted at them in Russian, walking slowly out towards them. He pulled his Heshui pass out of his pocket and held it up to torchlight which was dancing on his face.

The sergeant asked him what he was doing, but helicopter rotor blades drowned out the sound. The aircraft with Russian markings flew with spotlights searching the border area. The troops raised their weapons and cheered.

'They seem to have evacuated Hunchun,' yelled Mike. 'My driver got scared. Apparently, there's chaos at Heshui, and I need to get there to save the Russian research data.'

The sergeant shone his torch on the pass, then enthusiastically he grabbed Mike's hand. 'Dr Akayev, we will do anything we can to help you. I am Sergeant Victor Panov,' he said. 'We are deployed to rescue Russian nationals from that place. They're evacuating all non-essential staff.'

'We never realised such a catastrophe was going on.' Mike

gestured for Ling to come out. 'I came in to save Russian scientific documents. This is my Chinese colleague, Dr Wu.'

Mike and Ling crammed into the heated cabin. Temperatures dropped with the higher altitude. The trucks heaved their way along the mountain roads. Headlights showed up landslides and sheer drops where the soil had eroded and the mountainside had fallen away. Piles of filthy snow lined both sides of the road.

Ling snuggled up to Mike, squeezing his hand, and Mike thought of Sally somewhere in the shivering environment ahead. His emotions swung violently, wondering how involved she was with the experiments. Wondering how much of a volunteer she had been. Jolting around on the mountain road, he felt a dismal sense of emptiness when he remembered the children. They would be gone. Marched away so he would never see them again. Given new names, and the memory of their father defaced at the best, or erased altogether so that Mike McKillop had never really existed at all. Yet as they grew up and their Eurasian features developed, what would happen to them in such an evil society, striving for racial purity?

'Don't think about it,' said Ling in Chinese, seeming to know his thoughts. 'You were coming here anyway.'

The watchtowers were manned and reinforced with sandbags and armoured plating, and searchlights swept round the compound. A red banner of five stars rising stretched across the gate which was open. High walls, made more secure by rows of razor wire, stretched back into the darkness, then suddenly hundreds of yards away they became visible again as the searchlights did their rounds. Military helicopters circled in a landing pattern to get down to the helipad. At the gate, the Russian drivers handed over papers and the convoy was waved in, as if the presence of armed foreign troops on Chinese soil meant nothing.

Just as Clem had said, the road improved straight away to a well-marked four-lane highway. Smaller roads cut across it at right angles, lined with rows of two-storey ferrous concrete buildings. Half a mile on, there was an anti-aircraft position on top of a roundabout, the men on duty covered by green netting. Chinese troops halted the convoy at a road block there. On each side of the road was a white armoured personnel carrier. A pattern of machine gun emplacements covered the area. People, rugged up against the freezing temperatures, queued at desks set up on grass verges. They stamped their feet and moved around to keep warm. Guards, fingers poking through woollen gloves, ticked off names from lists.

On the other side of the road block was another military convoy. The Japanese flag of the red sun on white cloth flew from the bonnet of a Toyota Landcruiser.

'We let them transit Russia to get here,' said Sergeant Panov. 'Just us and the Japanese have been allowed in.'

Panov jumped out of the cab. Ling handed Mike the bags of weapons, then got out herself. The Russian troops were on the ground too, backs to the vehicles, taking up positions. The driver of the Japanese Landcruiser flashed his lights. The Russians flashed back in recognition. A Chinese captain let Panov and his men through the road block on foot. Mike and Ling followed.

Panov led them for three blocks until they came to a fluorescent light shining through a window. There was a huddled group of people inside and a sign in Russian on the door. A lone, cold Chinese soldier was outside, smoking. Panov banged on the window and went in. The Chinese soldier followed, but Mike stayed back.

'We're going over to the laboratories,' he told a Russian private, who just nodded. They watched the Russian troops file into the building and then melted away.

Ling went in front, reading Chinese signs in the darkness, heading further away from the noise and activity, deeper through parts of the compound from which Clem had been banned during the years he had lived here. Mike recognised missile hangars from the satellite photographs, huge silent buildings of corrugated iron with a railway line running out from beneath cumbersome doors. Further in, Ling read the sign to the nuclear waste dump, the entrance watched by a guardhouse, with lights on, troops inside and vehicles outside with their engines running.

The road was getting busier. People were walking, some riding bicycles, mostly going in the opposite direction where in the distance lights darted around the road block where the Russian vehicles were. Ling grabbed his coat and pulled him to the side of the road. They were two hundred yards past the entrance to the nuclear site. Another hundred yards ahead a banner was illuminated across the road, red with the Chinese rising stars again like at the gate to the whole compound, but smaller.

Ling translated slowly, checking each character as she went: 'This is it,' she said. 'Centre for the Improvement of the Human Race.' Ling went in front, showing her pass, but the guard was too bored to give it more than a quick glance. He didn't even take his hands out of his pockets. He was no more than twenty, his cheeks reddened with the cold.

'Russian?' he asked, looking towards Mike. Ling nodded. The guard continued: 'In the morning, you have to go first to register at the project office.'

The road split into a circular driveway with a snow-covered lawn stretching towards a sprawling one-storey building, a monolithic structure which appeared to have no out-houses or extensions. Ling pushed through swing doors. Staff milled around in corridors. Groups of doctors and scientists carried clipboards and stethoscopes. Military officials in olive-green uniforms were armed with pistols in their holsters. Some carried machine guns. No one took any notice of them. Music was piped through the building, and straight in front of them was a wall filled from floor to ceiling with slogans and posters.

The predominant language was Chinese. But many of the slogans were repeated in Russian, Japanese, Arabic and English.

'*Purge society of imbeciles and criminals*', said one of the posters in English. '*Weed out idiots before birth to avoid pain and cost in life*', said another. A cartoon picture of a farming couple working among their animals with a son and daughter had a caption: '*Enhance beauty and enhance the economy. Your child's pedigree is as important as your animals'. Create your own well-born child.*' More detailed rallying cries for genetic self-improvement scrolled down television screens banked along the wall.

'We can create for you a custom-designed child selected from our very own gene catalogue,' began one, citing examples as the text moved up of how Britain had been examining the genes which made a perfect fighting soldier for its elite regiment the Special Air Service. Japan had preliminary results on aggressiveness among the workforce to cut down on strikes. China had rudimentary results on personal curiosity and aspiration, human characteristics, it said, which, bred dissent and subversion. Studies in the United States had determined that continuing cross-fertilisation would make social control far more difficult. 'After three generations of mixed breeding between Negroid, Caucasian and Mongoloid,' said the report, 'it will be impossible to know as a given which genetic categories are in a mixed-race subject. Therefore such practices must be discouraged with the utmost persuasion.'

Ling turned over the back page which carried a final, succinct message: 'Societies all over the world will eventually applaud our scientific courage for making the masses more controllable. Governments will be more stable and the world a safer place in which to live.'

Chapter Twenty-Nine

Armed troops, under the command of a Major Hu Zhongli, were at the foot of the steps of BAe 146 as it came to a standstill at Jiang Zemin International Airport in Shanghai. President Kang stepped off first. Major Hu saluted, shook his hand and pointed towards a Toyota Hi-Ace minibus and a stretch Mercedes Elegance 230 parked near the nose of the plane. Tony came down slowly, holding the handrail and helped by Wendy Zhou. A sergeant held open the back door of the limousine for Kang to get in. Four people were already inside. Kang's wife smiled grimly as her husband got in beside her. She gripped his hand: 'The children have left already,' she said in a whisper. 'They are on their way to the States.' The Mercedes drove quickly across the tarmac to a Chinese Air Force 747.

But the minibus carrying Kang's private staff headed straight for the airport terminal. In the ride which lasted less than a minute, all four were handcuffed. Tony Zhang was hit directly on his wounded eye. He screamed out and blood dripped onto the seat.

'Your bank accounts have been reorganised,' said Li Tuo. 'The movements of money are untraceable.'

'Thank you,' said Hollingworth. He was walking by the Potomac River, using a mobile phone he had hired in a false name.

'Now clarify. You told them about the biological element, but not everything else?'

'That is correct.'

'And they accepted your explanation?'

'At least for the period of the summit.'

'Good. Then we have time.' Li Tuo looked at the digital time display on his telephone. 'The next stage is that you must convince your government of the following. An unauthorised Chinese military aircraft is taking off about now for the United States. The pilot will claim that the Chinese presidential delegation is on board.

But this is a blatant lie in order to get through American airspace. The aircraft is in fact carrying biological weapons warheads which could kill hundreds of thousands of Americans. The pilot is a madman whose grandfather was killed in the Korean War and has a long-standing grudge against the United States. The Chinese government will request the United States Air Force to shoot down this plane.'

'Jesus,' said Hollingworth. 'What the hell are you playing at?'

'Grow up, Warren.' Li Tuo's voice was particularly confident. 'If we are to succeed, Kang will have to die. And what better way than for the Americans to shoot down his plane?'

'No. Count me out.'

'But why do you think I'm telling you, Warren?' asked Li Tuo. 'You are in this up to your neck. If you back out now, you are just another American traitor who's going to rot in jail until death.'

'Fuck you.'

'Remember Tiananmen Square in 1989? You tell me how long it took for you so-called Western democracies to shake hands with the Chinese dictators begging for our trade contracts. After this, Zuckerman's officials will be beating a path to Beijing within a few months. What are you going to do, Warren? Watch it all from a prison cell?'

Clem Watkins' twin engine Cessna light aircraft took off from Pyongyang military airfield in northern Korea, climbing through the buffeting cross-wind. It settled just below 250 feet in a highly dangerous night-time operation. The pilot knew the mountain ranges that were lit up by moonlight and he stayed low enough to remain undetected by Chinese radar.

The seats at the back had been removed to install extra fuel tanks. Clem Watkins sat behind the two pilots, facing inwards across the small fuselage, checking his equipment. He kept the pack small because he didn't know the terrain where he would land or how far it would be from Heshui itself. Food supplies and ammunition were crucial. He stripped the first aid kit to phials of morphine and bandages. He strapped his machine pistol around his chest, with ammunition clips in his pouch, together with his communications equipment and Global Positioning System.

'Can you do the drop from four hundred feet?' asked the pilot. 'Any higher, I'll have a squadron of MiGs on my ass as soon as you've gone.'

Clem nodded.

263

'Signals Intelligence is reporting unscheduled military aircraft movements in a two hundred-mile radius and dozens of rotary aircraft directly over Heshui itself.'

As soon as the co-pilot pulled back the aircraft door, a wall of icy, streaking air filled the fuselage. Clem gasped to acclimatise. Outside, he could see nothing except a black swirl of cold blinding mist. He turned to give a thumbs-up, then jumped, pulling the cord immediately. His body jerked as the chute opened. Clem's supplies hung fifteen feet below him. His weapon was by his side. He scanned the terrain through infra-red night glasses. He saw the lights of Heshui to the north and watched the irregular and dark landscape rush towards him.

At four hundred feet, Clem had fifteen seconds to identify a landfall area that wouldn't break his ankles.

Door by door, they moved through the building. They read the signs at the side of each entrance. Their scruffiness and unfamiliarity caused no concern among anyone else around. In some rooms, the doors were ajar. Staff packed files onto portable cabinets. Computer data was being copied onto CD-Rom. Specimens preserved in jars of alcohol were being wrapped in polythene bubble protection. Some rooms had just two or three desks of drab government-issue furniture. Other doors opened onto rows of laboratory benches, floodlit from the ceilings.

They worked their way through, watching evidence of the terrifying medical experiments being boxed, crated, packed and disappearing before their eyes.

Deep inside the building there were the smells and equipment of a hospital. They passed by three operating theatres, empty and spotlessly clean, a chill in the room where the central heating had been closed down. Cloth, tissue, disinfectant, robes and towels were stored and ready for the next patient. They walked through wards where nurses were stripping off linen, taking down identification tags above beds and removing clipboards. The sister in charge was a thick-set woman of about forty. Her uniform was freshly laundered, with a bright red buckle belt and a tiny watch showing the face of Mao Tsetung pinned to her lapel. Ling showed them her pass and asked where the patients were.

'They went in the afternoon transfer,' said the sister in charge. 'The most normal are going first,' she added.

'Who's that?' said Ling.

'People here,' said the nurse, ripping up a sheet from under a mattress. 'The musicians, athletes and engineers are staying for the ceremonies tomorrow.'

She stopped work for a moment, the dirty sheet bundled in her arms, and looked enthusiastically at Ling, her eyes shining with pride. 'The Motherland has honoured our work unit by ordering us to stay.'

Further ahead, they heard the sounds of violins, distant and disjointed notes. The route from the hospital ward ran into an atrium with a glassed skylight. Lights flashed from a helicopter coming in to land. An empty podium was set up in the middle, with a lectern at the front and chairs with music stands for a small chamber orchestra behind. There were seats for an audience of about two hundred. Pamphlets were laid on each and banners stretched around the walls with slogans.

Music was coming from individual practice rooms, with each player concentrating on a particular piece. A chart attached to the wall showed the practice, eating and sleeping shifts of the musicians. The rooms were in use round the clock.

Ling took out the documents from Sanlitun, running her finger down the categories to see if any of the names matched those on the lists here. One by one, Mike looked in the glass window of each door. The scenes were duplicated room by room. The only light was a single desk lamp shining on the instrument. The walls were painted with identical murals of China, blending mountains, lakes and wildlife with scenes from industry, technology, and commerce, interspersed with missiles and warships.

Through the first window, Mike saw a lone musician, a boy of about ten, struggling with a cello. Through the second, a boy and a girl were practising a duet with a violin and piano. Another was practising the clarinet.

Then, when he came to the fourth window, he saw Charlotte.

His hand shook on the door handle. No. He wasn't mistaken. He was tired. God, was he tired. He thought he had seen Charlotte a thousand times before: getting onto a bus, walking away from him, her school satchel bouncing; through the window with a family in a restaurant. He had gone up to her and she had turned to look at him with a mixture of surprise and fear. And he had seen a little thing in her mannerisms which proved he had made a mistake, so he said sorry and left. A father gets to know the ways of his daughter. the way she tilts her head; how she screws up her forehead in concentration; the manner in which she rests her left foot on top of the right when sitting down; the movement of the fingers on the neck of the violin.

Charlotte was wearing a white smock, staring obsessively at the music sheet. Electrodes were attacked to the back of her head and she was on a drip. A floor polisher started up in the atrium and he heard Ling talking to the cleaner. Another aircraft flew overhead. Far away were the sounds of crates being moved, scraping over the floors. Mike knocked first. Charlotte looked up, her eyes flickering, faced with the prospect of the unknown. Perhaps because her shift wasn't over and a teacher was coming in. On the knock she had missed a note and her fingers slipped causing a discord. Mike pushed the door, just gently, but as soon as Charlotte saw it opening she lowered the violin, holding it at her side like a rifle. She stood up, staring dead in front of her, head back, the wires of the electrodes and the drip hanging from her.

For a few seconds she looked at him without expression, without recognition, without moving at all. Music came in from the rooms around them. The light from the corridor lit her so Mike could see her more clearly. She was taller. Of course she would be, he thought. She was just as pretty, with her sharp confident jaw against which she rested the body of the violin. Her hair was long, except for two tiny patches which they had shaved for the electrodes. Her fingernails were filed short and now that she was standing up, he knew that this time he was right. It was his daughter because he saw the brown birthmark just below her left knee.

He whispered more than spoke her name. But nothing registered because he had called her Charlotte and not Wai King, her Chinese name meaning infinite energy. Then he said Wai King and her eyes moved, hesitantly, as if she wasn't usually called that either. He wasn't planning. He never did. Clem had been the planner. Sally had been the planner. He acted without thinking of what might happen next, five seconds from now, even five years from now. Mike put down his bag so he had both hands free to embrace her. He stepped towards her, saying her name again both in Chinese and English. Then he added the surname: 'Charlotte Wai King McKillop,' he said gently. 'This is your father.'

He leant to touch her and that was when she screamed, a horrifying, piercing sound. That was when Mike saw the mask strip from her face and the stages of recognition take hold of her. First that he was not a music teacher. Then that he was the man who claimed to be her father. Then that he was her father, but the father who was evil, the one she had been told to forget.

Charlotte shook uncontrollably. She turned to point at him:

'Colonial murderer. Colonial murderer,' she yelled. She banged the violin like an alarm to attract attention.

'You are a family impostor,' she shouted. He tried to quieten her by putting his hand over her mouth. But she struck out at him, slapping him with anger and crying out for help. Then Mike felt a hand grab his wrist and jerk him backwards towards the door.

'Out,' snapped Ling.

'It's Charlotte . . .'

She had picked up his bag: 'I know. She's on the register.' Her eyes moved from the room to the passageway outside. Mike tore himself out of Ling's grip and looked straight at his daughter: 'Charlotte . . .' he shouted.

'Violator,' she screamed back.

'Where's Matthew? for Christ's sake, where's . . .'

'You are not our father,' yelled Charlotte. Light shone on the tears in her eyes. She was shouting and crying, wildly tearing at her medical smock, frustrated but, as if in chains, confined by the tubes and wires which were attached to her healthy young body.

Ling wrenched Mike out of the room. A sharp burst of small-arms fire cut into the concrete around their feet. A light shattered at the end of the corridor and chunks of plaster flew out of the walls. They were trapped in a deadly line of fire. Mike hit the ground near the door of Charlotte's room. Ling ran ahead to the end of the corridor and threw herself to the left. The attacker shouted for her to stop. She broke her fall with the bag, at the same time freeing the machine pistol. A second burst opened up, but this time Ling broke cover, rolling out low and firing back, three single controlled shots. The clatter of the dead man's weapon in the empty passageway echoed loudly. The violins and pianos kept playing.

'He's alone,' shouted Mike, joining Ling up ahead. He took out his own weapon, putting a grenade and four magazines of ammunition into his pockets. They sat on the floor, their backs against the wall, listening for the enemy. Ling put her hand on his arm. 'I'm sorry,' she said simply.

'Thanks,' said Mike. He tried not to think about it, to focus on the physical danger and not the shaking emotions which were gripping him now. But to see his lost daughter like this. He grasped his weapon, grateful there was an enemy out there, a lucidity in which he could forget his anger, his failures. The image of Charlotte flashed recurrently in front of him.

At the end of the passageway there was a door with an Exit sign in Chinese and a metal bar, like in a theatre, to push and release the lock. They came out into a large quadrangle, covered with ice, but with red and blue lights shining up from the ground in the shape of an H, to guide in a helicopter.

Mike went out first, weapon ready to fire, Ling held back. It was snowing heavily, driving in a swirl of wind and coming up in drifts against the walls of buildings.

Ling held back, her foot in the door as Mike went out. Spotlights from watchtowers at the edge of the building passed over every few seconds. At the far end, lights shone through curtainless windows and figures, blurred by condensation on the glass, moved around inside. The square appeared to be empty. They ran around, not straight across, but keeping to the walls so they didn't get caught in the searchlight. Wind tore across at them, taking the chill factor to far below zero. They stumbled on the freshly fallen snow. Once closer, they could make out the beds of hospital wards.

Mike tested the door, but it could be opened only from inside. On the other side, where they had been attacked, there was silence. They were both flat against the wall, breathing heavily, the cold air catching in their throats.

The door rattled. A man stepped half out, holding it open as Ling had. Ash blew off from a cigarette he was keeping cupped in his hand. The collar of his greatcoat was pulled up round his neck. He wore a green military issue hat with flaps which came over his ears.

Ling held her weapon on him. Mike slipped his gun back into the bag and stepped out of the darkness straight in front of him, in light thrown out through the windows. He showed his pass. 'I'm Dr Sergei Akayev from Vladivostok,' he said, offering the guard a 555 cigarette. 'There was shooting over there. I got frightened . . .'

'There's been a lot of shooting lately,' the guard said gruffly. He lit Mike's cigarette from the butt of his own and looked at the pass. 'Frightened and locked yourself out, eh?' he said. He shone a torch in Mike's face. 'At least you look Russian, not like the traitors we're getting in the Motherland now.' He turned off the torch. 'You'd better come in, or you'll end up a frozen corpse.' He laughed. 'Only came out because I thought I heard another helicopter coming down.'

Mike turned towards Ling: 'This is Dr Wu . . .'

He shone the torch on Ling, then switched it off and held open the door for them. 'They say that's why some are having to move,' he continued. He was a rugged man, probably only twenty-five, although he could have passed for forty. 'Subversives don't want strength in nationhood,' he said. 'That's what they tell us.'

He let the door slam shut. The warmth enveloped them. Unlike the last ward, this had the atmosphere of a slow hospital night shift. There were no crates, no trolleys being wheeled away. The beds had patients sleeping in them.

'We're pulling out in the morning,' he said. 'But these subjects are staying.'

'We're looking for Russian subjects among the mentally ill,' said Mike, using a polite translation.

'He means the imbeciles and idiots,' snapped Ling.

'Don't know about Russians because you look like us out in the East, here,' he said. 'You're welcome to look.' He pointed to the left. 'Up this corridor to the end, turn right, keep going and you'll see the sign for idiots. I'd come with you, but . . .'

Mike pressed the whole packet of cigarettes into the guard's hand.

They tried not to look while he was still watching them, but the horrible scenes in the rooms to their left and right made it impossible. There was an extreme drop in temperature as soon as they turned out of the main corridor. The beds had no linen. Patients lay on planks, warmed only by the thin clothes they were in. Some were sleeveless, with skeletal arms poking out and their hands shackled to the metal bedposts.

Their heads were shaved, lying awkwardly without pillows. Their eyes were mostly expressionless, just looking ahead of them, but some moving around maniacally. They shivered automatically. There was a smell of urine, decaying food and human waste.

'Keep going,' said Mike.

'Here,' said Ling, pointing to a sign hanging from the ceiling. Automatically, they both broke into a run, bringing out their weapons, opening doors which were closed, pausing for fractions of a second at open entrances to assess. Quickly, the appalling scenes became familiar. Living, chained skeletons of men and women. Eyes sunken. Scarred, emaciated bodies. The stench of disease.

They kept moving. This was the ghastly evidence of the documents they had found in Sanlitun. Rows of men and women, almost naked, shivered from the fever. Bruises and welts covered their pathetically sick bodies. Their eyes and noses ran. They reached out like dying animals. Some called out.

'They've been induced with biological weapons,' said Mike.

'How could anyone . . .'

Ling choked. Mike had to stop himself from vomiting. Somewhere far away an alarm went off. But it seemed distant and too sophisticated for the terrible place they were in.

'The children are to the right,' shouted Ling, taking in another sign. They worked their way down the corridor. Ling stopped at the entrance of a darkened ward and turned on the light. 'Mike,' she yelled. 'Come, here. Quick.'

Mike ran to her side. He squinted as his eyes got used to the brighter light in the room. All the beds were empty, their bedclothes stripped off, except for one right at the end.

'Is that Matthew?' said Ling.

Mike went into the ward, while Ling kept watch outside.

'It's him,' said Mike. He ran across the room to his son. Matthew's bed was next to a door and with a torn, grubby curtain pulled around it. Unlike the deadened horror of the other wards, he was kept warm with sheets and pillows and a colourful duvet. There was a plate of food, untouched on a table at the end of the bed, and at his bedside was a collection of crayons and drawing papers.

Ling stood in the doorway, looking left and right. Mike touched Matthew's shoulder and the boy opened his eyes. He blinked and shook his head. Almost from birth, they had known he had some permanent brain damage because of Sally's difficult delivery. He had learned his first words when he was nearly four. His walking difficulties became apparent even earlier. The doctors talked of stiffening of the lower limbs and spasticity. Mike remembered a therapist describing him as a sociable little boy. Sometimes, after the medical pronouncements, it became too much for them. Either it was Sally or Mike who broke down wondering what place there was in this rotten world for such a vulnerable, sick and innocent child.

Now Matthew looked at him, sleepy but not with the fear that Charlotte had shown. Mike did not need to prove to himself that this was his son because when Matthew's eyes registered, he sat up shakily, losing his balance a bit, but correcting himself.

At first his face was blank. No fear. Yet no recognition. Then suddenly, Matthew's face lit up and he threw himself at his father: 'Daddy,' he squealed. 'Daddy.'

He locked his arms round Mike's neck, clinging to him and pulling him down: 'Yes,' whispered Mike, quivering. 'Yes. It's me. It's Daddy.'

Matthew was crying wildly, his little arms holding him harder and harder against his father. They hugged each other, as hard as Mike could remember and he let the tears stream down, wetting Matthew's hair which was pressed against his chest. 'I've missed you so much,' screamed Matthew.

'You said it.' Mike moved away a few inches so he could see

Matthew's tear-soaked face. His hands trembled as he held him. Furious emotions tumbled around him in a kind of love and happiness he had never known. He put Matthew down and wiped his face with a towel, then used the same towel for his own eyes.

'Why did you leave us?' whispered Matthew.

'I'm back now,' said Mike. He couldn't control himself and he held his son again, pressing his face into his chest. 'All that matters is that I'll never leave you again.'

Chapter Thirty

'Visitors,' said Ling sharply, her voice cutting across the room. She turned off the lights, slipped inside, and closed the ward door. She crouched, taking cover behind a bed, hidden, but her weapon up and ready to fire if they were seen.

A door opened at the end of the corridor. Mike carried Matthew gently to the floor, pulling the duvet with them to keep him warm and sliding under the bed. They heard footsteps of military boots; men running; rifle butts against doors; then banging against their door. A face in the window, the edges of the helmet visible.

A torch beam darted in and around the beds. There were two soldiers. First she would take out the one on the left, whose finger was inside the trigger guard. Then the one behind.

'Looks empty,' said the one in front.

'They've been spotted in the east unit,' said a woman's voice from further up the corridor. The torch went off. Ling relaxed. They left the door open and Ling edged out across the floor to Mike.

'We're taking him,' Mike whispered.

'Of course,' said Ling. 'Can he walk?'

'Course I can,' Matthew said confidently. He pushed himself to his feet, unsteady at first, balancing on the bed. He had done this before, mustering every cell of his damaged brain to tell his limbs and muscles what to do. 'I can get dressed, too,' he added, cheekily.

With a limp, he went to a cupboard and put on a jersey, jacket and trousers straight over his pyjamas. Mike knelt down to help him tie his shoelaces. 'Did you come to find me, Daddy?' Matthew asked.

Mike nodded. 'Mummy said you were never coming back and she said I should forget about you.'

'Mummy probably didn't know,' said Mike.

'Who's this?' He looked up at Ling.

'A friend,' said Mike.

'A girlfriend,' said Matthew. 'Mummy said you had lots of girlfriends.'

'More urgently, how we get out of the building?' said Ling.

Matthew pointed in the direction the troops had gone. Mike took his hand and Ling led the way. She heard the same voice again and stopped at the door. Then another torch, this time shining straight in her face.

Ling's reaction was instant. One hand smashed down on the torch, the other brought the machine pistol up into the face. Mike's hand was on the shoulder, pulling the person right back inside, and closing the door.

Sally looked just as she had in the hospital wards in Hong Kong. Not a day older. Her skin smooth and unwrinkled. Her face confident and sensitive. Her hair short, like she always insisted on wearing it. Her coat was clean and pressed and her features unruffled, despite Mike's hard grip on her shoulder, Ling following her into the room with the gun, and Matthew's soft exclamation of 'Mummy.'

'Are you alone?' said Ling.

Sally nodded. She looked at her without fear and then at Mike with the astonishment of unexpected recognition. He thought he detected a happiness in her disciplined eyes. But perhaps not. Too much. Too quickly. *Sally wants to see you. The kids adore you*, had been Elton's refrain. Now Elton was dead and Sally was here. The weapon the Party had used for so long to persuade him to betray his values.

She shook herself loose from his grip and stepped back. 'They told me you had killed an American in Hong Kong.'

Mike shook his head.

'You can put the gun down,' said Sally. 'I'm not armed.' Matthew stood silent, holding Mike's hand. Ling kept the gun on her. She looked out through the window in the door.

'They wanted Charlotte for her musical talent,' said Sally in English. She sat down on the bed; any aggression was drained out of her. 'They would have killed Matthew because of his disability. I managed to save him, made a scientific excuse to keep him alive. I told them he had sickle cell anaemia, you know, that genetic blood disease.'

'Why?' said Mike, almost in a whisper.

Sally didn't answer. 'Just so they would keep him alive for tests. Otherwise they would have . . .' She remembered Matthew was there and stopped. His eyes moved from one parent to the other.

273

'He knows,' added Sally.

'You. All this.' Mike trailed off and swept his hand around the room. 'You were part of this?'

'I know. I know. You don't realise the pressure.'

Mike felt Matthew let go of his hand. He ran jerkily over to Sally and pressed his head into her lap. She held him, then lifted his head up. 'The Koreans found out what was happening here,' she said. 'There are so many stories. They've built another one. Everything's being moved to Sichuan.'

'And we had better move out of here,' said Ling.

But Sally ignored her. 'You never knew what it was like being Chinese in a place ruled by foreigners. What it was like to be part of a race which had been conquered, which had fled its homeland, which had been overtaken in medicine, technology, engineering by the civilisations that colonised it.'

'So you create this to make up for it?' said Mike, his voice too loud. 'And subject our own children to it.'

Sally shook her head: 'I didn't know. I didn't . . .'

A new louder siren started up. Ling levelled her weapon at Sally: 'How do we get out?'

'You take him,' said Sally, looking at Matthew. 'They're moving Charlotte to Sichuan. But not the ones like Matthew.'

Sally went in front. She put on a coat, then pushed open the door and stepped into the cold outside. Mountains loomed straight ahead of them. Snow fell mixed with hailstones. Ten yards from the door was a wire fence.

'What's there?' said Mike.

'The labour camp,' said Sally. To the left her torchlight picked up a line of military jeeps. Mike tested the doors of the first three. The fourth opened.

'Shine it here,' he told Sally. With the beam lighting up the wiring under the dashboard he started the engine. It coughed, jumped, then took with a cloud of exhaust smoke spewing out of the back.

Ling helped Matthew into the back. Mike was in the driver's seat. Sally stood next to him the snow falling on her hair and face where it melted. She wiped away the water.

'Li Tuo's coming up tomorrow,' she said. He thought she might say something else. But discipline had returned to her eyes and suddenly there was a roar of engines as a helicopter took off and another came in to land. Sally turned to go back inside. Mike let in the clutch and drove away.

It was Matthew who heard the phone ringing inside Mike's

weapons bag. He rummaged for it and proudly passed it to Mike, who was driving lights off, one hand on the wheel weaving to avoid the potholes in the road.

'Clem here,' said the familiar voice on a clear line. 'I was asked to drop by to see if you need some help.'

Lights flashed up ahead at them. Mike turned on his lights. Another jeep was parked halfway across the road. Two soldiers waved red flags as a sign for Mike to stop. Immediately beyond them was darkness again and in the distance were the lights of the complex where they had entered. Spotlights from helicopters showed up queues waiting to fly out.

'Get down. Hide,' he whispered. He looked at Ling, but there was no need to speak, as he changed down gear, slowing the jeep. The soldiers lowered their flags and stepped away from the centre of the road to the side. Mike kept the jeep going at a crawl, in first gear using the clutch.

'Dr Sergei Akayev from Vladivostok,' he said, a torch shining right in his face.

'We have orders to detain all traffic from this sector,' said the soldier. Ling shot him in the head.

She fired two more shots. The soldier collapsed on the ground, rolling and crying out. Mike revved the engine, then let in the clutch. The uniform of the first soldier had got caught on the wing mirror. The man's head bumped along on top of the bonnet as Mike gathered speed. The eyes of the dead man stared grotesquely at him through the windscreen. Mike tried to push it away, then they hit a pothole. The jeep bounced. The weight of the man tore off the wing mirror. It fell with him, rolling on the road and the jeep roared away.

Small arms fire hit the back window. Ling turned in her seat and let off a long burst. 'Stay down, Matthew. Don't move,' she whispered urgently. Matthew crouched by her feet, head on his knees, like a baby rabbit.

Suddenly it was quiet. But in less than a minute they would be back where the Russian had dropped them. More road blocks. More hostile weapons.

'What in the hell's going on?' said Clem's voice on the phone.

'We're on an empty stretch of road about half a mile from a main helipad,' said Mike quickly. 'How in God's name do we get out of here?'

'Are you east of the missile hangars?'

'Yes.'

275

'What's behind you?'

'The labour camp.'

'Good. The nuclear dump is to your right?'

'Correct.'

'OK,' said Clem. 'There might be a way out.'

It took Lucy Yu less than half an hour to catch the eye of Peter Wilson, a young American banker spending a lonely evening in the China World Hotel. She went there after waiting more than six hours at the Kempinski Hotel for Mike and Ling. She hadn't asked Tony what the operation was about. She never did. Tony knew how to get hold of her, but as it got later and later she sensed that something had gone horribly wrong. At seven thirty she walked out through the shopping centre and called Tony's office and his apartment, but there was no answer. His mobile had been turned off since the early afternoon. Then she caught a taxi to the China World.

Cosmopolitan and beautifully dressed, Lucy turned heads in the lobby. She had done this dozens of times before. She enjoyed new sex and watching the pleasure Western men seemed to get from her agile and promiscuous Chinese body. When they offered money she took it. But that was never the issue and she liked peeling off their clothes and escaping from the drabness of China into the luxury of a five star hotel room.

But tonight, she was doing it for survival. Like all Chinese, she knew that anyone who had crossed the Party would be hunted down and ever since seeing Tony in the Lost Oasis she had sensed that her friend was living on the edge of that invisible line.

She liked Wilson and showed it. By nine o'clock he had taken her to Le Fleur restaurant and an hour later they were in his suite on the executive floor. He came out of the shower, towelling himself, and poured them both a glass of champagne when her mobile rang. Lucy answered it quickly.

'Who is this?' shouted a coarse voice on the other end. There were office sounds in the background and Lucy hurriedly cut the line. She keyed in the recall code to check the incoming number. Immediately, she recognised it as a Ministry of State Security number, probably the offices behind the Beijing Grand Hotel near Tiananmen Square.

She was unable to hide her tension from Peter Wilson yet she knew from experience how a man's hospitality could suddenly switch to irritation if she did not give him the attention he craved. Right now, the hotel room was the only sanctuary she had.

She unwrapped his towel and told him to lose his inhibitions, which he did. With his skilled, adventurous and enthusiastic love-making, she too managed to forget about the danger, until they had finished and he fell asleep while Lucy stared out of the window at the Beijing night, making a plan for the morning.

Li Tuo had asked to be left alone in the Presidential suite in Zhongnanhei. He inspected himself in the long mirror on the door of Kang's wardrobe. Nothing hung inside the cupboard. All traces of Kang had been moved out. Li had always had power. But this was different because it was absolute. He was the most powerful man in the most populous country in the world.

Li smoothed down his uniform and arranged his medals. He flicked a speck of fluff off the right-hand shoulder and dabbed make-up powder on his forehead and cheeks to soak up moisture.

When Tony Zhang was led in, Li remained in front of the mirror. He told his guards to leave them alone. Tony's wounds were untreated. He could only see through one eye. The blood from his beatings had dried on his shirt.

'You are an intellectual, are you not?' said Li Tuo. Tony didn't answer. He watched the eyes in the mirror shift from the uniform to himself and back to the uniform.

'You are not a soldier, are you?'

'No, sir,' said Tony weakly.

Li closed the cupboard door and turned to face him.

'Sir? You called me sir?' snapped Li. 'I am your comrade. We are compatriots of the Motherland.'

'Yes, comrade,' said Tony.

'Do you believe in the policies of Comrade Kang Guo-feng?'

Tony coughed. His lungs and chest hurt. He thought a rib had been broken. 'The policies of the fourth generation leadership have been excellent for the development of China,' he replied, retreating into rhetoric.

'Was Comrade Kang loyal to the leadership?' Li sat on the edge of his desk. He drummed his finger on top of the folder. 'Was he right?'

There were footsteps in the corridor. A horn blared in the car park below. The remaining bulbs in the chandelier flickered as the power fluctuated. Li moved back behind his desk and sat down.

'Sit,' he said. He indicated a chair in front.

Tony sat. The silence continued as Li opened and leafed through

277

the folder. 'You once had a girlfriend, comrade,' he said. 'She moved to Hong Kong. Aged twenty-seven. Works for an American company as a trade consultant.' He turned to the next page. 'She did well in the Travel Orientation Course and has reported back regularly. She's a good agent by all accounts. Did you encourage her to go to Hong Kong, comrade?'

'No, she found the position through her study unit.'

'Yes, yes. Of course. Why not Shanghai, I wonder? Or Taipei?' Through the window, the horn started up again. Voices shouted on the tarmac. 'The American company is called Prime Coasts. It develops luxury resorts along China's coastline. This report sent up to me says it has hotels, golf courses, horse riding stables, yacht clubs. The money is paid in American dollars in Hong Kong and then transferred out to Bermuda. It is never circulated within our economy. Is that a good policy? Is that right?'

Li's voice was raised. He swung his feet to the floor and slammed his open hand down on the desktop.

'I don't know, comrade,' said Tony.

Li walked round from the back of the desk and smashed his fist into Tony's face. 'Don't know. Don't know.' Li straightened his tunic and swept his hand back through his hair. 'For an intellectual there is a lot you don't know. What is the difference between Prime Coasts and the Colonial traders who exploited our cities before the Revolution?'

Tony's head lolled. His breathing was irregular: 'I didn't . . .' he whispered.

Li was back at the front of his desk, speaking more calmly: 'But she reports back. She tells us everything. Her information is of high quality. Her loyalty to the Party is without question.'

From the corridor, there was the sound of the door opening to another room. Tony heard the voice of an American global television announcer, reminding him that always there is another world outside the madness that sometimes afflicts China.

'We know everything about your visit to Sanlitun. We thought it was Alan Zhu. But all the time it was you who was betraying the Motherland.'

'Where is Alan?' Tony managed.

'He's dead. It was a mistake. It should have been you.' Li tipped a pile of photographs out of an envelope onto the desk. 'Look at them,' he said.

They were pictures of Tony ten years ago. Tony giving his speech comparing Mao to Hitler. Tony boating in the Summer Palace with

Lucy. Tony seducing Ling in the tiny hotel room they had managed to rent for the afternoon.

Li pushed another set across the desk. These were the same pictures Tom Elton had shown to Mike, shot through the window of Scott Carter's flat in Hong Kong. The focus was so sharp that Tony could make out the separate strands of Ling's hair falling down her naked back. The same back. The same nudity. Different place. Different lover. But Ling standing. Ling's hands drifting down Scott's body. Ling holding him. Kissing. Ling kneeling, arched back. Ling guiding his hands. Tony's first girlfriend in naked profile, in the lens of the camera of the Party.

'She had orders to sleep with you, an intellectual, with an American spy and with dozens in between. She told us all about your political beliefs and that Scott Carter was about to be told about Heshui. So we had to kill him.'

This time it was his fist striking Tony underneath the chin, throwing him off the chair onto the floor. The heel of Li's boot dug into his neck.

'But you know all about Heshui, don't you?' A door closed outside and the voice of the television announcer faded. A car drove off below and, in the sudden silence, cicadas started up in the trees like a distant roar of water. 'Comrade Ling told us all about your visit to see the late Mr Picton at Sanlitun. You called in Unit 8341, didn't you? You let the McKillop traitor into the sanctuary of the Motherland.'

'What is it you want from me, Comrade General?'

'I want you to know that we know,' said Li. He kicked him in the chest. Tony coughed, tasting blood. 'Comrade Ling is to receive the highest patriotic honour on Motherland Day. I want you to know that she betrayed you. You are a despicable traitor to your country.'

Tony tried to get up, but collapsed. Li Tuo opened the drawer to the desk and brought out a gun belt with two pistols in their holsters. He buckled them up, then called for his escort.

The colonel in charge of the unit walked in. 'American fighters have been scrambled from Okinawa, Comrade President,' he said. 'The aircraft carrying the subversive elements has been declared hostile. And your helicopter is ready to go to Heshui.'

The door closed. Tony coughed again, choking violently. Then he lost consciousness.

Clem stayed on the line until they were through the perimeter fence. He guided them right round the edge of the camp to join the mainstream traffic again at the main gate, where he was waiting for them. He took them to a Daewoo ski-resort which was still operating as normal, ninety minutes away.

For the last five miles, they had come up the mountain with a Korean military escort. 'The Koreans have brought in mobile anti-aircraft guns, tanks, armoured vehicles, an infantry battalion and special forces units to safeguard Korean investment,' said Clem. 'The Chinese won't dare touch us here.'

They parked the jeep on the other side of the wooden bridge. Clem led them through the hard-packed snow and Mike carried Matthew, who was asleep with exhaustion. To the left was a forest and the surge and roar of a waterfall within the trees. Most of the fall was frozen into heavy icicles. The water pushed itself under the ice and fell out into the stream below. A Korean colonel was expecting Clem and came out to welcome him. They checked in as if they were guests on a package tour from Seoul. A bellboy wheeled their bags to their chalets. They made no attempt to conceal their weapons. But other governments had sent people in as well, and journalists had begun arriving.

Fires were lit in their rooms and the chambermaid brought clean towels. Clem spoke directly to Mackland in Washington where it was mid-afternoon and when he had finished Mike told him he was going back to get Charlotte. Ling would stay with Matthew.

'Mackland's guys have seen the list,' said Clem. 'They say if we can get anyone out, make it Bishop Chu. They want to hold him up as the Nelson Mandela of China.'

'Then we'll do that as well,' said Mike, working through the weapons and arranging the ammunition.

'We've got about six hours,' said Clem with a grin. 'They're talking about missile strikes and want me to show them how not to kill the good guys. There seems to be a bigger flap in the White House than the one here.'

Mike saw Matthew to bed and within an hour, he and Clem had eaten, re-armed and set off back again to Heshui.

Donald Zuckerman's private secretary was blunt when Peter Mackland arrived at the Oval Office unannounced: 'I'm sorry, sir. The President is in a meeting,' she said quickly.

Mackland was equally abrupt: 'Well, get him the hell out of the meeting,' he snapped.

When Zuckerman appeared, the two men talked in low voices

in the outer room. 'A Chinese military 747 has taken off from Shanghai,' said Mackland. 'Our intercepts in Okinawa report that the pilot is heading for Los Angeles with the Chinese president and his delegation.'

'They're not due for another four days,' said Zuckerman.

'Hollingworth rang me directly two minutes ago. He said he has reports of mayhem up at the Heshui complex and unauthorised troop movements around Beijing. He doesn't know exactly what's going on.'

'Did he know about the 747?'

'Yes, sir. He says a 747 has been stolen by a rogue pilot. And it could be armed with biological weapons stolen from Heshui.'

'Heading for the United States?'

'If it is, the aircraft it will be here in about fifteen hours.'

Peter Mackland opened a map of the Pacific and spread it out on the top of the President's desk. 'A few minutes ago, the Chinese aircraft was six hundred miles east of the North Mariana Islands in the Pacific Ocean, Mr President,' said Mackland.

Zuckerman had called an emergency meeting with the senior defence and intelligence staff, including Hollingworth and Mackland.

'The Chinese military command has now told us officially that the aircraft has been stolen by a rogue pilot,' Mackland continued, sitting down at one of the two chairs in front of the desk. Warren Hollingworth took the other chair. 'The aircraft captain still insists he has President Kang and his wife on board.'

'Can't you get a firm identification, then?' said Zuckerman.

'The digital voice match didn't check out, sir.'

'Which means?'

'Because of signal interference and the inferior Chinese communications equipment the result is not conclusive.'

Zuckerman got up from his chair, leant over his desk and looked at the map. The concept of ordering American aircraft to shoot down any civilian airliner filled him dismay. Yet the spectre of just one American community ravaged with a disease created by biological weapons weighed so heavily against that. In six years of office, he had never been faced with such a choice.

'OK, Mr Hollingworth,' he said slowly. 'If they've admitted to the rogue pilot, why not to the weapons? Why not come clean if they know we know they have them?'

'Having them sitting up in some remote mountain is different to having them in a plane heading for American soil,' answered Hollingworth.

He turned to Hollingworth. 'Do we know anyone who can tell us something about Kang that no one except him would know. An incident, an anecdote with which he could identify himself . . .'

'I'm reading you, Mr President. But China is a very impersonal place.'

Zuckerman pointed to an area on the map: 'All right. Get the F-16s in the air. Bring in the in-flight refuelling tankers. If we're going to eliminate this threat, it'll be just after it passes Johnston Island and before Hawaii. That gives them about seven hours to prove who they are.'

He spoke directly to Mackland: 'Whatever the hell is in this Heshui place, I think we've got to neutralise it. Peter, the *Harry S. Truman* carrier group is in the Sea of Japan. Notify the Koreans and Japanese that we might need their airstrips. And get me the plans from the Joint Chiefs for the bombing strike.'

Downstairs in her hotel suite, the fire burnt, crackling beneath her bedroom with logs freshly dried from the wetness of the snow.

Upstairs, Ling's eyes were wide open. She stared at the ceiling and sometimes moved them across towards the window, looking at the snow piled high on the window-sill by her head. Exhaustion ran through her.

Matthew slept deeply in the bed next to her. She heard John, the Korean bodyguard Mike had insisted on leaving with them. He was awake on the sofa, warmed by the fire, the radio softly on with a night music show playing Bach. He turned the cards in a stud poker game with himself, keeping himself alert.

Ling heard sounds outside. At first she associated them with the danger of the last few days. But they were the sounds of life. The creaking of a tree; the crunching of tyres on the snow; a door opening; voices from another room; a conversation on a doorstep. A gust of wind on the panes frightened her. She opened her eyes and concentrated on the writing table at the top of the stairs. She tried to memorise the articles on top. Three pens, a telephone pad, two magazines, the room key, her check-in card, the documents about Heshui. As she took it all in, fatigue took over again, crying out for her to sleep. She let her mind play the rhythms of the Bach. Her eyes closed.

Three minutes later her sanctuary blew apart. A draught shot through the room. The window panes shook. Cold wind hit her face. She heard John shout. The temperature dropped. She shouted for him. She heard the breaking of wood. The door smashed open. She didn't hear the shot from the silenced pistol, only the breaking of the still of the night, the noise replacing the quiet. The fear.

The force of the bullet knocked John's body back. His blood sprayed the wall and, before he died, the killer was up the stairs, black ski-mask, thin leather gloves. He slapped Ling. She felt the pain, the shock and her neck cracking. He slapped her again. He took her wrist and dragged her out of bed, the covers tangled in her legs.

Matthew woke up and screamed.

The gun was in her back, hard and hurting. He pushed her forward down the stairs. The killer spun her around, so that she fell on the floor. Ling felt herself sobbing. He pointed the pistol at a coat hanging on the back of the door, her boots in the corner. He watched her putting on the coat, sitting on the floor, shaking, pulling on her boots.

Matthew appeared at the top of the stairs and screamed again. He clung to keep his balance at the top of the banister. The gunman turned with the pistol aimed straight at him.

'Don't,' screamed Ling. She uncoiled herself and leapt at him. He struck her face and pushed her down, and pressed the gun against her neck: 'Comrade Li wants you in Beijing,' he said softly.

The telephone, so close, so normal, so lethal if she tried to reach for it. The weapons hidden out of reach and useless.

'And the documents on Heshui,' said the gunman.

Amid her fear, her voice was calm and gentle: 'There,' she said, pointing to an envelope on the coffee table next to John's deck of cards.

The gunman pushed it inside his jacket. He took her by the arm and pulled her out of the door. There was no light outside. The cold stung her cheeks.

Then she turned and smashed her boot into his groin. Her fist crashed into his nose, and she ran.

He was close behind her. She saw his pistol arm coming down towards her. She struck his face again, enough to throw him off balance so she could roll away from him.

In two steps she was on the path. The bridge was there. She remembered it. She heard the river. She saw a sign, lit up: 'Scenic walk to water-fall.'

She cut into the trees. The moon lit up the path a bit. As she ran on, stumbling in the snow, the roar of the river became louder, frozen over with the water running fast under the ice.

He turned down the path after her, clumsily, knocking the branches so that snow fell off them in clumps. She moved back into the trees, but the snow crunched and he heard her. A bullet cut through the branch just above her head. She lay on the ground, pretending to be hit, quietly, waiting for him to get closer. Then she scooped up the snow, flinging it into his face like sand and heaved herself at him, knocking him down.

He threw her back hard and she hit a tree, winded. She rolled and he fired again. She picked herself up. Snow sprayed around her.

She slipped down the steep river bank. There were different sounds now. Dogs in kennels, tearing at their leashes; the running of water over rocks; music from a room somewhere. But no cries, no rescue. She was at the edge of the river, where the snow on the bank and the ice over the water was indistinguishable.

He came down towards her, his hands steadying his descent. He fired. She rolled again. But she had nowhere else to go and he stood steady in front of her, confident. The gun at her chest as she lay in the snow. His breath exhaled in a cloud. They both panted. She watched the barrel and waited for him to fire.

Then there was another crack. But different. A groaning boom – breaking ice. A splash of water and he swore, losing balance, one foot caught in ice. Ling pushed herself up and grabbed his other, twisted it and threw him on his back. The weight of his body smashed through. He gasped in the freezing water and the gun fell away. The current pulled and tore him under the ice, over the waterfall and she watched until his body emerged in a pocket of water in the stream below.

Ling scrambled down. She pulled up the ski-mask. It was a cruel face – cut-up, bruised. But it was the same face she had seen through the window in Scott's apartment; the same returning horror which had been chasing her and was now gone.

She plunged her hand into his torn jacket and found the sodden documents, clasping the envelope in her numb fingers. She shivered.

Suddenly everything was tranquil. Above her were the lights of the hotel, lamps on the path to the car park, where the Korean armoured vehicles were under the cover of pine trees. Ling staggered up the river bank.

The light on the bridge shone on the tyre tracks which were grey-white, mud mixed with snow, hard-packed and slippery.

284

Through the cover of the pine trees, Ling moved on. The hall of the main building came into sight. She saw a night porter, old and hunched in his chair, his head lolling.

In her suite, the door was ajar as she had left it. The fire still flickered. John's body lay where it had fallen. The Bach had changed to Chopin's *Nocturnes*. Ling pushed the door closed and went automatically to the fire; the flames had settled and the logs were full of heat, throwing it out, enveloping and warming her.

Then she heard footsteps on the stairs and remembered Matthew. He had dressed and holding the banister with both hands made his way down carefully. Ling went to help him and took him in her arms. He hugged her hard, his arms clinging around her neck. 'It's not safe here, is it?' he asked gently and Ling shook her head.

Chapter Thirty-One

M ike cut the wire, ready for an alarm, but nothing happened. They ran across the open ground just as the sun was coming up, Mike first, fast with just a light bag, then Clem slower with more gear and Mike covering. They got through the second fence of rusting barbed wire and came to the high walls of the prison. The watch-towers were empty. No searchlights shone through the dawn. There was no movement in the compound either. They moved through empty dormitories, the beds empty. The coal fire in the canteen was still hot. They were checking the washroom, the water frozen in buckets, when they first heard the violins tuning up. It was a distant and clear sound in the quiet of the dawn.

Mike thought of Charlotte there, hating him, and him loving her. He remembered Sally's confused, angry and conflicting signals in her eyes. The discipline and the despair. He didn't love her any more, though, not like he did Charlotte and not as he had thought he would. However long he had waited, he could never have predicted his emotions when he saw her then. All the way back, after leaving Ling, he had thought about it. Probably, it had never been love. More a sense that he had failed to keep her. A determination to defy his own inadequacies and win her back. But her doctor's coat, her clipboard, her role with the Party proved that he could never have kept her. A man can be jealous of his wife's affair with another man, but an obsession with anything else is out of his control. *Don't think about her*, Ling had said. *You were coming here anyway*. Or maybe it was because he had had Ling for a few days while the danger lasted. Then she would drift away and he would pine for Sally again because that was what he had always done.

'Li Tuo's chopper's coming in,' said Clem quietly. He was pressed up against the window of the washroom with a clear view across the prison compound into Heshui. 'It has his markings.'

It became clear then why the prison was empty. The prisoners had gone for the big farewell ceremony for Heshui. Red and green lights flashed on the helicopter. Its search-light cut through the dawn as it hovered over the complex. The crew of four attack helicopters kept watch above it. While Clem maintained his cover, Mike ran up to the heavy gate of the prison compound. He pressed plastic explosives over the lock, inserted an aluminium blasting cap and set the timer for thirty seconds.

The noise of the explosion was drowned by activity from Heshui. They fixed double magazines to their machine pistols. Mike went first. The rotary blades of Li Tuo's helicopter were disappearing behind the walls of the quadrangle. The Chinese flag flew on each corner of the building. As the noise of the aircraft diminished, the violins came through again, this time playing properly as an orchestra, an emotional Communist Party song. Then there was cheering, loud and intense, relayed through speakers and into the empty prison as well.

Mike laid another charge and blew the door which Sally had brought them through a few hours earlier. It swung open so casually that it could have been caught by the wind. Mike waited back flat to the wall. Clem was twenty yards away in cover by the prison gate. A guard shouted from down the corridor. They heard his footsteps walking towards them, then his hand came out to close the door, but he drew it away sharply when he saw the damage. He began to shout, but it turned into a yelp and then silence as Clem shot him twice in the neck. Mike pulled the body outside and they went in, closing the door behind them.

Screens hoisted up along the corridor showed the scene inside the quadrangle as the helicopter touched down. The prisoners were arranged in units around the helipad. They squatted, hands behind their backs. Like the patients in the hospital, their heads were shaved and they wore whatever cloth they could find to keep them warm. Some who tried to balance by resting their hands on the ground were hit with rifle butts. Others who had collapsed from the cold or disease were picked up and carried away. The prisoners shuffled around to fill the gap.

They shivered in the windchill from the helicopter blades, then when Li Tuo got out, they stood up all at once and cheered. A small podium, draped with the Chinese flag, was set up just in front of the helicopter.

Li Tuo stood there and held up his hands to speak: 'You are criminals,' he said. 'But you are criminals of the Motherland.'

There was more cheering. 'You are serving the Motherland with your patriotism and your dedication . . .'

They moved into the safety of an empty ward and, with Mike watching at the door, Clem called Mackland at the White House on his mobile.

'Mackland's still keen to get Bishop Chu,' said Clem when he had finished.

'He's right,' said McKillop. 'The world wouldn't believe two villains like us. But they would believe Chu.' Clem moved over to the door. He smiled grimly: 'Permission to kill Li Tuo has been denied.'

'Denied to you. I answer to no man,' said Mike.

'And they want us to let them know if the prisoners move from where they are now.'

'Why?'

'I've given them an all clear for the missile hangars.' Clem looked at his watch. 'Starting in about twelve minutes.'

In the Sea of Japan, American fighter aircraft took off from the USS *Harry S. Truman* to join B2 Stealth bombers from bases in Seoul and Okinawa. Three Los Angeles-class submarines prepared for cruise missile launches.

The voice of the F-16 pilot came through clearly into the headset of the captain of the 747: 'We have orders to open fire when you cross 170 degrees, unless you turn back from your route towards the United States or we have positive identification of the Chinese President. At your present speed, you are 182 minutes from 170.'

'I am speaking to you from the cockpit,' said Kang. 'I am the President of China flying on the invitation of President Zuckerman.'

'We have information you are a hostile aircraft,' replied the F-16 pilot.

Ling Chen tucked Matthew under bedclothes in the back seat of a jeep parked in a deserted spot under pine trees. She lit a match to examine the wires under the dashboard and had the engine running within seconds. On the passenger seat, she arranged the weapons which Mike and Clem had left with her: a 9mm Browning pistol and four American M26 Grenades. In the euphoria only a few hours earlier of getting safely to the hotel, she had said she didn't need them. Now she wished she had asked for more. She kept the headlights off and drove with her left hand, leaving her right free to use the Browning pistol. She looked behind her and Matthew's eyes stared out at her silently, awake and, like her, afraid. The hotel guard at the main gate briefly shone a torch in her face and waved her on. Then the lights stopped and she was on the winding, descending road.

Druk had told them to head towards Tumen and cross over to safety at night. But that was how they had come in, thought Ling, as she changed down gear for the steep descent. And besides she would be there in daylight hours. The road narrowed for a series of hairpin bends. She hugged the mountainside, keeping clear of the sharp drop to her left. As she came out of an almost 180-degree turn a searchlight snapped on. A voice through a tannoy in Chinese and then Korean ordered her to stop. There was gunfire, three distinct explosions, Matthew cried out and the searchlight went dead.

Mike had a clear view of Charlotte. She was a lead violinist right at the front in the atrium. Snow was falling heavily with strong, cold winds blowing it against the windows. About three hundred prisoners squatted outside in rows in the quadrangle acting as a guard for the helicopter. As the temperature dropped, prisoners fell over, shivering violently. Now that Li Tuo was inside, the guards just left them. They huddled in groups, many of them inside the building and not keeping watch. Mike and Clem shuffled across the courtyard hardly visible in the blizzard. Their heads were lowered and their collars were up.

Charlotte drew her bow across the string just as Li Tuo walked into the atrium, a lone, single note which hung and created the atmosphere before the other instruments struck up to accompany her. Her eyes flickered nervously on the music sheet. The hospital staff stood up, applauding. Sally was there, three rows from the front, clapping and holding the Happy Family pamphlet which had been left on the seat. Mike saw she had a similar watch on her tunic to the nurse they had met the day before, with Mao Tse-tung's face. Then he noticed everybody had it.

Li Tuo kissed Charlotte on the forehead first, then the other lead violinists. He shook the hand of the conductor and walked to the podium. Outside were the sounds of aircraft and of the wind howling around the building.

'Comrades,' Li began. 'China has today been purged of the enemy within. But that enemy betrayed Happy Family and the achievements here have been told to foreigners. When Mao Tse-tung was at war with the Imperialist powers nearly fifty years ago, he created the defences of the Third Line in Sichuan Province out of range of foreign bombs and missiles. It is behind those defences that your work will continue. You are the few who have been chosen to re-create Happy Family.'

The applause had only just begun when it stopped abruptly. An explosion from a laser-guided bomb ripped through a missile hangar half a mile away. There were two more explosions in quick succession, one starting a fire which ignited a fuel tank, sending out high flames and burning debris which blew off in the wind to other parts of the complex.

Li Tuo's face tightened. His bodyguards moved to take him down from the podium. The audience rushed to windows to see what was happening. Sally ran over to Charlotte and hugged her. Clem was by a window, covering Mike. The prisoners remained hunched against the cold. The helicopter pilot ran across the quadrangle, weaving around them, slipping once on the ice, but getting to his aircraft. The rotor blades started up.

Mike broke cover and ran through the prisoners towards it. Li Tuo, flanked by four men, stumbled out of the atrium. The next bombs fell closer, hitting the eugenics complex itself. Inside, Mike heard screams and he stopped dead, turned round, running back towards Clem. He had come not to kill a man, but for Charlotte. Clem caught him by the lapels, his mouth right up against Mike's ear shouting above the explosions and the helicopter engine: 'Charlotte will be safe,' he yelled. 'Get him.'

But Li was on board. The pilot was lifting the aircraft up, hovering it inches from the ground. A massive explosion ripped into the mountainside behind them. The helicopter skewed and Mike sprinted towards it, pulling a pin from a fragmentation grenade. A line of sub machine gun fire cut across the ice in front of him. Then the commando at the trigger fell forward out of the helicopter into the snow, caught in covering fire from Clem.

Mike saw Li Tuo at the door holding onto a strap, both pistols out this time, just like he had at Maekok. They bucked one after another, but Mike was moving too fast for him. He threw the grenade, fell on the ground, pulled the pin from a second one, got up and hurled that as well. The first bounced on the side of the door, but went inside the aircraft. The second missed by inches and fell underneath. The pilot took the helicopter straight up. Li Tuo kicked the first grenade out and it exploded mid-air. Shrapnel from the second grenade ripped through the tail. The helicopter, barely twenty feet in the air, began to spin wildly.

The rotor blades dipped. The pilot struggled with the controls.

Mike took cover among the prisoners who grouped around him, not knowing who he was, what he was doing. The pilot had the machine back on the level, trying to bring it up again and over the roof of the two-storey building. Mike watched Li Tuo so close to escape. The man who had killed Jimmy Lai, who had taken his wife, his children, who had ultimately killed Tommy Lai as well, so alone on the Bund in Shanghai.

Mike ran forward across the empty quadrangle. There was firing, but he kept going. He jumped up, grabbing hold of the skid, in a ridiculous attempt to hold the aircraft down. Pain tore through his shoulder with his own weight. The helicopter swayed, but then the pilot adjusted and brought it up, fighting inch by inch to gain height. Mike's legs flailed helplessly in the air as the helicopter rose up, then down again. Then up. He had to calculate the millisecond difference between the altitude of a drop to safety and a jump to death. He hoped for another explosion to throw the aircraft out of control again, for something which would make this desperate act worth the risk. He thought of the stupidity of making his mission so personal. Of Matthew safely with Ling, of Charlotte, safely with Clem. Perhaps, all was for the best. Then he heard a cheering, like a football crowd, behind him. He saw reckless wild eyes. Desperate hands clawed up with his. Scarred, gnarled people, their bodies wrecked but their spirits alive with a last strength for revenge as they grasped the freezing metal of the helicopter skids. Prisoner after prisoner hung on to bring down the man they hated so much.

The pilot tried to shake them off by turning in mid-air. But it was no good. The sheer weight of the men pulled the machine towards the ground. In a final burst of power he brought the aircraft up, but she lurched across the quadrangle like a wounded elephant. The tip of the rotor blade caught the roof, twisting the metal and hurling the machine onto its side. The cries of men crushed underneath were lost in the chaos of the crash. Mike was hurled in the air, thrown clear and landed heavily on ice. Oil and fire streaked across the snow from the wrecked aircraft.

A burst of machine gun fire tore across the quadrangle. Li Tuo's bodyguards had the door of the helicopter open and were shooting their way out, cutting down prisoners in a vicious field of fire. Mike was on the ground. Li Tuo stumbled out with them, shooting wildly himself, edging into the protection of the Heshui guards who bundled him inside the building. The pilot slouched dead in the cockpit.

*   *   *

Peter Wilson had to check out early to catch the first flight down to Hong Kong. Lucy left before him, accepting an offer of payment, but asking if he would get her a hotel limousine and put it on his account. She walked from the lobby straight into the car and, speaking in English, asked the driver to take her on a sight-seeing tour: Tiananmen Square, the Temple of Heaven and Beihai Park.

She sat back in the seat and, using the limousine phone, called Tony's numbers again and again: there were no replies. She did the same for President Kang's other advisers, all of whom she had met, either at university or through Tony. For Wendy Zhou, Alan Zhu and Jeremy Tang. When she called John Jiang's home, however, his mother answered.

'He's been arrested,' she said when Lucy told her who she was.

'They took him from his office yesterday afternoon.' She was crying. 'They came back here to search afterwards.'

Lucy cut the line and asked the driver to turn round and take her to back to the Jianguomenwai diplomatic area. There was nowhere to hide if the Party turned against you; nowhere except a foreign embassy. She got the driver to drop her outside the International Club on the Avenue of Eternal Peace and walked quickly back to a fuel station just one street down from the American Embassy. She remembered it had recently installed a payphone and dialled the Embassy number.

'You are fourteen minutes from 170 degrees,' said the F-16 pilot. 'I repeat you will be shot down if you cross that line. You will be shot down.'

President Zuckerman and his advisers had moved down to the war operations room in the White House. The warning was relayed on loudspeakers in the room. This was the time when the American President became the Commander-in-Chief. His split-second decisions, right or wrong, could affect world affairs for years to come.

'Fire a cannon warning,' said the President.

The command was repeated to the F-16 pilot who was lining up the central fuselage of the Boeing 747 in his head-up cockpit display and confirming the lock-on of the target with the aircraft's central computer.

'A warning?'

'Affirmative.'

The pilot fired a stream of cannon in front of the Boeing's cockpit, but the plane continued on course.

Zuckerman waited a further minute. 'Fire an air-to-air missile,' he ordered.

'A warning?'

'Affirmative,' said the President.

As soon as the missile shot out from under the fighter's wing, the Boeing 747 lurched to the left and lost height. Its automatic defence mechanism sent out silver chaff to lure the missile away from its target.

'The damn plane has electronic decoys,' said Mackland excitedly.

'It's a presidential jet,' replied Zuckerman calmly. 'If Air Force One has them, I suspect this one has.'

'He's slowing,' said the F-16 pilot. 'He's now ten minutes from target. If he loses any more speed he'll stall. If he turns round, he'll run out of fuel.'

'And if he's got biological weapons on board, he'll kill the population of Hawaii,' muttered Zuckerman.

They lay with their faces pressed into the ice, bracing for more fire. But instead there was an unexpected quiet and cries of pain from the wounded. The bombing appeared to have ended. The helicopter engine was silent. There was no gunfire and the guards seemed to have gone, more concerned with protecting Li Tuo than holding the quadrangle. At least twenty prisoners had been hit and, in a manner of self-containment which is necessary in Chinese labour camps, others got to their feet, slowly and cautiously, and began to help the wounded because no one else would.

Mike felt a tap on his shoulder. The prisoner had a skeletal face and scars down both cheeks, but unlike most, there was an intelligence in his eyes and he spoke in fluent English: 'I'm Bishop Paul Chu from Hebei Province,' he said. 'I don't know who you are but thank you.'

Mike recognised him, even from file photographs ten years old of Chu in his bishop's surplice.

'Thank you for fighting evil,' said Chu with such gentleness that Mike felt in awe of being with someone of such courage.

Clem was running towards them, kneeling down, checking Mike was unhurt, then recognising Paul Chu and helping him to his feet. 'They're abandoning Heshui completely,' he shouted. 'There's no more resistance.'

*   *   *

Sally and Charlotte sat in the middle of the of the atrium. Charlotte gripped the neck of her violin and held Sally's hand. Clem stayed back with Paul Chu and as soon as Sally saw Mike, she went over to him. Charlotte put both hands on the violin and stared ahead of her.

'Take her with you,' said Sally. She held both his hands and her eyes were alive with their old passion and magic. She spoke with the intimacy of a wife, as if he was going for a walk around the Peak on a rainy Sunday afternoon. Mike felt himself squeeze her hand and she squeezed back. Suddenly, her head was on his chest, her arms were round him, clawing at his back as she had when they used to make love. She was crying without shame or control. He held her, feeling her shoulders, her rib cage, her body through her uniform. Feeling the familiarity for which he had craved, re-living the emotional innocence which had tortured him since she had left; the innocence that his family would one day return.

'We'll take you, too,' he whispered. Her hands opened, splayed across his back like she used to when she said she wanted to touch as much of him as possible. She lifted her head and looked at him, her eyes red now, her cheeks wet with tears.

'You can't,' she said.

'We'll get you out,' said Mike. A lump swelled up his throat and he felt himself beginning to cry. 'Come with your family,' he managed.

Sally loosened her grip and held his hands again, looking directly at him: 'I have to go to Sichuan.'

'Why?'

She looked up at him and suddenly he realised that she was tormented by the same grief as him. She was crying now as a gift, to tell him he had not suffered alone, to offer him back his daughter and to show him the pain of a mother torn from her family.

'They tried to take Matthew away after the first month.' She paused and swallowed hard. 'I had to offer them both up for experiments or they would have got rid of him.' She clasped her hands in front of her and stared at the floor. Mike stepped back and began to answer. But he had nothing to say. He just nodded his head.

Sally took his hand again. 'Mike, please take Charlotte,' she said. 'I'm sorry.'

She was telling him she wished it had never happened. Mike drew her back towards him, kissed her on the lips and held her

294

head against him. She responded as she had when their relationship had worked flawlessly, when neither of them had to make an effort to keep it on track.

'Then come with us,' he whispered. It was the only way in this public place, with their meeting punctuated by time and danger, that he could tell her he forgave her and that he loved her.

She shook her head. 'I have no life outside of this,' she said, holding his cheek and turning his face so they were looking straight at each other. Mike recognised the hardness in her tone; that he should know what she was talking about. A steel façade which would see her through the separation from Charlotte.

Mike put his finger to her lips and she bit it gently. 'I'll see you out of the compound,' she said.

The cruise missiles came down on the eastern side hitting two rocket hangars with precision and smashing open their protective concrete bunkers. The blast shook the building. The queues had broken up with the first attacks and now, with fires burning throughout the complex and more explosions, Heshui was gripped with panic. The Chinese troops had lost control. Prisoners, doctors, patients and soldiers ran to find the best way out. Chinese fighter aircraft screamed overhead. Anti-aircraft positions opened up on the incoming missiles. Sirens wailed at different pitches and fire hydrants burst open with water gushing onto the snow and ice.

Sally appeared to know where she was going. She held Charlotte's hand and Paul Chu held the other. Mike stayed just ahead of her, stopping to watch as the corridor turned or spawned another passageway exposing them. Clem was at the rear, running in bursts, looking behind him all the time. Sally led them towards the entrance to the complex, keeping inside as much as possible. In some places, fires had broken out, so they had to go out and run across freezing courtyards. Once, Mike blew open a door with plastic explosives. Paul Chu limped weakly along, gaunt and malnourished. He talked to Charlotte all the time in a soft voice in a mixture of Chinese and English to stop her from looking too much at the appalling things they were seeing.

Chinese guards were shooting hospital patients before they fled. In one ward, their skeletal and diseased bodies lay inert and bloodied, bed after bed. At the corner of a corridor, four prisoners had tried to escape and met a hail of gunfire. Their bodies were piled so that Sally had to step over them. Outside, more bodies lay in the snow, caught up in fires or collapsed from exhaustion. Paul Chu muttered their names when he recognised them.

They skirted round the destroyed missile hangars, keeping their distance to avoid debris from sudden explosions. Mike recognised the roundabout where they had arrived with the Russian convoy. The anti-aircraft position was abandoned. The roof of the Russian accommodation quarters had been torn off. Sally took cover behind two jeeps which had been blown on their sides. The dead drivers were still in them. Clem pointed up to a helicopter flying low and fast over the complex, then its nose tipping down as it gained altitude and disappeared over the mountains. No one spoke about it. They just watched, silently. The aircraft was the same model as the one which had been wrecked and it bore the markings of Li Tuo.

Sally pointed to a line of vehicles by the entrance of the complex and explained that they had been reserved for Li Tuo's delegation to tour the camp. So far they were undamaged. One driver had kept to his post. The rest had gone.

There were two hundred yards of open ground. Blackened holes were burnt into the snow where hot debris had fallen. Sally and Mike ran over to the vehicles: three Audi saloons and a Dodge van and a Toyota Landcruiser. Sally spoke to the driver in the front vehicle, telling him that Li Tuo had just left in a helicopter. He shrugged, threw his cigarette to the ground and got out of the vehicle leaving the keys in the ignition. Clem and Paul Chu came over with Charlotte. Clem turned his back to the vehicle keeping watch. Mike was at the wheel.

Paul Chu tilted the passenger seat forward for Charlotte to get in, but she was clinging on to Sally's hand, not letting go. Sally leant forward and kissed her on the forehead: 'Go with your father,' she said.

'He's not my father,' said Charlotte.

'He is,' said Sally. 'And he loves you the most.'

Charlotte let go of her mother's hand and stared at Sally in confusion. The reversal of years of brainwashing had begun. Mike reached out from the driver's seat to help her in, but she shivered and didn't move.

'Come with me then,' said Paul Chu. 'In a way I am also a father to you.'

'I'm not going with any of you,' Charlotte screamed. She ducked under Sally's arm, running across the snow back the way they had come. Sally chased her. Mike jumped out but was a few seconds behind.

The explosion must have been the start of another bombing raid. There was a flash of yellow flame some way away. The two vehicles behind which they had taken cover were thrown up and one of the fuel tanks exploded in mid-air. Charlotte was running straight towards it as the flames were coming straight towards her. Sally was almost at her side, her hand reaching out to take her shoulder and hold her back. The other jeep blew up on landing. Glass and twisted metal flew out in all directions like shrapnel. A line of spilt fuel lit up on the snow.

Charlotte fell first, her hands failing to come up to break her fall. Sally twisted as she went down. Her head jack-knifed back and her legs buckled under her. Mike kept going, although he knew he should have stopped for the effect of the blast to finish. Sally was lying face-up, blood streaming from her left arm and leg, turning the snow deep red around her. Her pulse was weak, but she was breathing and her eyes rolled to the whites then came back and flickered as if registering what was happening around her. She grimaced with pain and moved her right arm to take hold of Mike's hand. Her face was wet and dirty with snow and grit. He lifted her up slightly by the shoulders, letting the head tilt back and open the air passage.

Mike saw Clem come in front of him, checking the same with Charlotte – pulse, breathing, bleeding, limbs. Without speaking he pushed a first aid kit towards Mike, then lifted up Charlotte's light and limp body up in his arms and ran back with her to the vehicle.

'Can you hear me, Sally?' said Mike. 'I'm lifting you out.'

He felt a weak squeeze on his hand. Her colourless eyes livened up for just a moment, mocking him, playfully almost, like she used to when he switched the washing machine onto the wrong cycle. *Don't be stupid, I'm dying*, she was saying, but she only managed to get out: 'Don't.'

'We'll fix you up,' whispered Mike. 'Get you . . .'

'Is Charlotte . . .'

'She'll be fine,' said Clem.

Sally went limp and she managed a smile. Her eyes were rolling back again. Her heart palpitated, looking to pump blood which wasn't there. She flinched with a pain which gripped her body. She could hear him, he knew that, and he said: 'You are my wife. I love you.' He felt the muscles go in her neck, but he thought he heard her answer before she lost consciousness; he thought he saw her smile at him.

Another explosion tore through a building.

Clem laid Charlotte across the seat by the door, Paul Chu rested his hand on her forehead. Clem opened the side door of the Dodge van. Mike stood holding Sally's body.

'Leave her, Mike,' Clem ordered. 'She's dead.' Clem helped lower Sally's body to the ground. Mike kissed Sally's forehead and got into the jeep.

He let off the handbrake and drove out of the gate. Clem clipped a new thirty-round magazine into his sub machine gun. A blast of freezing air swept in as he wound down the window to give him a clearer field of fire.

Chapter Thirty-Two

'The State Department on the line, Mr President,' said Zuckerman's Chief of Staff, Charles Murphy. 'Our Embassy in Beijing has received a called from a Lucy Yu, out of nowhere, saying that all five of President Kang's personal advisers have disappeared or been arrested.'

'One minute to 170,' came the voice of the pilot, although from the message screens in the operations room everyone knew that the President was within seconds of making his decision.

'If it's nothing to do with this, hold it,' said Zuckerman.

'Requesting clarification of orders,' continued the pilot. 'Is the Chinese aircraft hostile? Should I prepare to take it out?'

'Halfway through the call, sir,' pressed Murphy, 'the phone was taken from her. She screamed and she was told she was under arrest. On the tape recording there are sounds of scuffles.'

'Names?' said Zuckerman.

'Wendy Zhou, Jeremy Tang, John Jiang, Alan Zhu and Tony Zhang. Tony Zhang is her friend.'

'Tell that pilot to hold his fire,' responded Zuckerman. 'Get me the man who calls himself Kang.'

'Thirty seconds to 170.'

'This is President Kang,' said a shaky voice from the Chinese Boeing. 'I am speaking from the cockpit. Your pilots should be able to see me.'

'Who is Tony Zhang?' said Zuckerman.

'He is my personal adviser.'

'Where is he now?'

'He has been arrested. He was badly beaten when I last saw him.'

'Doesn't tell us anything,' said Charles Murphy, unaware that the radio link was left on. 'Anyone going to attack us would know this sort of stuff.'

'Fifteen seconds to 170,' said the F-16 squadron leader.

'How far can we stretch this?' asked Zuckerman.

'Mr President, if that aircraft flies for more than five minutes, and is armed, American civilian lives will be in severe danger,' said a senior general.

'Answer my question, damn it,' snapped Zuckerman.

'Ninety seconds maximum, sir.'

President Kang began speaking again: 'Perhaps I can help,' he said, his voice shaking. 'Only Tony Zhang and myself knew about my meeting next week with Microsoft in Seattle . . .'

Zuckerman interrupted: 'Repeat that.'

'Tony Zhang had arranged for me to spend a night at the Microsoft log cabin . . .'

'Stand down the F-16s,' shouted Zuckerman. 'Why the hell didn't we think of that,' he asked to just about everyone in the room. All but a few had blank faces.

'I'm furious I didn't remember that before,' Kang was saying. 'Mr President, I am asking for asylum until I can return safely to my country.'

The squadron of F-16 aircraft split away and tipped their wings as the Chinese Boeing 747 began its final descent into Hawaii. Donald Zuckerman watched the live coverage on television in the Oval Office: 'Charles,' he told his Chief of Staff. 'Make sure Kang gets the finest treatment of any head of state who has visited this country and of any man who has sought refuge on American soil.'

'Sure will, Mr President,' said Peck.

Zuckerman waited until the early evening to call Andrew Carter, when he knew his friend would probably be in his study.

'I wanted to do this personally,' Zuckerman began. 'One of the documents which has come out of the Heshui project has your name on it as a founding member.'

The President described to Carter the copy of the certificate.

'Yes,' said Carter after a pause.

'Did you know we were funding a biological and chemical weapons factory?'

'No, Donald, I didn't . . .'

'And we're hearing right now that it was also a centre for medical and eugenic experiments which make Auschwitz look like a kindergarten.'

'How bad is it?' said Carter almost in a whisper.

'It's a death camp, Andrew.' Zuckerman was failing to control his anger. 'It's a place where innocent people are used as scientific guinea-pigs and then left to die. It's everything the American people have fought against.' His tone dropped. 'Everything my own race and religion has suffered.'

'I didn't . . . I didn't have any idea . . .'

'Then you should have done,' snapped Zuckerman.

'I must have my name on dozens of committees and organis-ations . . .' Carter interrupted himself. 'Sorry, I'm not thinking straight. I'm not making excuses.' He paused. 'And Scott?'

'Yes,' said the President, calming down. 'That's why Scott died. He was about to get documents revealing . . .'

'I take full responsibility,' said Carter, putting down the phone.

He sat in his study all night with a picture of Scott graduating from Harvard in front of him on the desk. Susan slept upstairs. Geoffrey was in California and Madelaine had gone back to New York. In the morning, just before dawn, he walked quietly out of the house, careful not to disturb Susan. He walked down towards the river front, putting to flight the pigeons nesting in the trees by the path. He went on past the old, hollow trees and mooring stakes exposed by the low tide on the muddy banks. It was a chilly, damp and invigorating morning.

Andrew Carter opened the small green gate into the churchyard. He had his own key and let himself into the church, where the statues and vaults showed the Carter ancestry and contributions to civilising America. His father, grandfather and great-grandfather were buried here. Members of the Carter family had been flown back from all over the world, killed in war, by disease, accident and occasionally old age. Two of Carter's brothers had been buried here, their coffins draped in the American flag, their bodies riddled with Soviet-made bullets fired by Communist Vietnamese guerrillas. Happy Family in its genesis had been created to stop a repeat of rogue ideologies threatening Christian democracies. Andrew Carter had half forgotten about it, half wished it away with the Republican presidential victory. But whatever he had done, his negligence had killed his son.

He knelt at the altar and prayed. Then he went outside where the soil was still fresh on Scott's grave. It was marked with a simple wooden cross and flowers, waiting for the headstone. Carter knelt on the wet grass and prayed there as well.

'Sorry, Scott,' he whispered to himself. 'It was never to be like this.'

301

He took a pistol from his jacket pocket and put the cold metal barrel into his mouth.

Then a hand rested on his shoulder, not gripping it, not pulling him back, allowing him to pull the trigger if he wished. Without turning around, he knew Susan was there. She had followed him out in her night clothes. 'There's been enough death for the moment,' she said softly, breathing in long and deep. 'And besides, it's a beautiful morning,' she added.

Hollingworth was in his hotel room looking at the television broadcast from Hawaii, when FBI agents carried out the arrest. He offered no resistance and was taken straight to an FBI apartment in Washington where Peter Mackland was waiting behind a desk. He ordered the handcuffs to be taken off. 'We did a forensic investigation of your bank accounts,' Mackland began, as Hollingworth sat down in an upright chair in front of him.

'And they didn't add up?'

'The latest credits from stock sales . . .'

'I fucked up, didn't I?'

'Understatement doesn't become you, Warren,' said Mackland. 'You betrayed your country. What's more you didn't do it for any ideological motive, you did it for pure greed.'

'No,' said Hollingworth. 'Don't go down that line. If you want to know the truth, hear me out.'

'I heard you and I backed you against Watkins and we ended up nearly shooting down the President of China,' snapped back Mackland.

'Happy Family was authorised at the highest level . . .'

'I will remind you, Warren, that however distasteful it might seem to you, we operate a multi-party democratic system in this country. And if the President or any member of his cabinet didn't know about your sleazy deals, then as far as I'm concerned they're illegal.'

'You know that's bullshit,' said Hollingworth quietly. The two men had worked together so many times in the secret world that Mackland couldn't help acknowledging Hollingworth's blunt truth. They were quiet for a moment, then Mackland said: 'All right, I'll hear you. Then I'm going to hand you over to the American judicial system.'

'We set up Happy Family in the Nineties as a missile research project,' said Hollingworth. 'It was a natural progression from regular military exchanges. But alongside it, basically in the same complex, they set up a biological and chemical weapons facility. Bit by bit they let us find out about the weapons, using them as a bargaining chip in our general relationship. Basically they were saying be nice to us and we'll wind it down eventually. Just like we'll bring in democracy, lower tariff barriers and all that. Confront us with it and we'll spray your cities with death.'

'So that's as you told the President?'

'Correct. But what none of us knew was that behind the weapons of mass destruction were the eugenic laboratories. And on the Chinese files anyone who signed to Happy Family signed up to the whole thing.'

'I don't buy it,' said Mackland.

'I haven't finished.'

'All right.'

Hollingworth paused: 'I was blackmailed.'

'That's better. For what?'

'Getting rich. Taking stock market tips. Rigged horse races. Share options in the latest missile announcement which you found in my accounts.'

'How long for?'

'Years, Peter. Fucking years, I took it and nothing happened, nothing happened, then they turn round last week and say betray your country or we'll expose you.'

'Who?'

'Li Tuo. The guy who started out as a dope dealer and is going to end up as the leader of China.'

'He blackmailed you into getting Scott Carter killed?'

Hollingworth stood up and paced to the side of the room. The door immediately opened and an FBI agent came in, weapon drawn. But Mackland nodded that he could withdraw.

'The Koreans had something for us. I thought it was a regular drop, something Scott could easily have handled. Now I reckon it must have been data on Heshui.'

'Who ordered the killing, Warren?'

'My guess is Li Tuo. But I really don't know.' Hollingworth sat down again, hesitating before he spoke again. 'Can you get me off the hook, Peter?' he said softly. 'For old times' sake?'

Mackland took time to answer, then shook his head. 'If you knew President Kang was on that plane, then the first rap they'll be putting on you is attempted murder. After that, they'll be asking about Martin Hewlitt, Henry Fordham, Christopher Watson, Win Kyi. Don't give me off the hook.'

*   *   *

Ling Chen shot out the searchlight, then fired off three rounds directly to her right, to her left and behind her, accelerating at the same time with her lights on full beam. She heard the distinct thud of a grenade launcher and an explosion on the mountainside in front of her. She skidded, the back wheels flying loose on the ice, as the road made a sudden turn to the left, then bringing the vehicle back onto a long straight run down before the next tight turn. Two more grenades exploded to her right, but harmlessly over the mountainside. She drove in a low gear, afraid of the ice and afraid of what was behind her. But nothing followed, just quietness from behind. She turned back quickly to look at Matthew and he was lying perfectly still, being jolted around in the seat, but as if he was asleep. She screamed to ask whether he was all right and Matthew didn't answer.

Like the helicopter, the Dodge had the markings of Li Tuo. The barrier at the two surviving road blocks on the way down was up anyway and troops waved them straight through. They drove mostly in silence, Mike concentrating on the hazardous road. Paul Chu kept a watch on Charlotte, whose pulse was strengthening. Every so often she regained consciousness, and amid the jolts Paul Chu was able to get some water into her mouth.

Once Clem was convinced they were clear of the camp, he called the Daewoo resort and asked to be put through to Ling's room. The phone rang three times before it was answered in Korean by the same colonel who had shown them in. Clem identified himself and the colonel paused for a moment: 'I am sorry, Mr Watkins,' he said. 'There has been an attack. One of our men, the bodyguard, is dead.'

'And Ling Chen?' Clem spoke softly so that Mike wouldn't hear above the noise of the engine. 'She is missing, together with the boy.'

Clem didn't say anything to Paul Chu or Mike. There was no point. Instead he called Washington and asked to speak directly to Peter Mackland:

'The border's abandoned. China appears to have no government,' said Mackland. 'Give me your co-ordinates and we'll send a chopper in to get you out.'

Clem reeled off a map reference then said: 'We've got Paul Chu.'

Mackland was unable to hide his excitement. 'Then we've won!' he shouted. 'We need to get him on the breakfast shows.'

'The White House congratulates us,' said Clem to Mike, when he had finished. 'They're sending a helicopter.'

'OK,' said Mike. 'We get Paul and Charlotte into Korea. Then we chopper back to the hotel to get Ling and Matthew.'

Clem said nothing.

The deep throb of the American Super Cobra helicopter got louder and louder. In the middle of the day, it was strangely empty on the road by the Tumen River, warm again on the plain with the sun high in a clear sky and the wind blowing strong across from Korea. The land sloped gently down to the river and farmers were working there as if nothing unusual was happening. The rice fields gave way to high grass and across the road the land stretched back flat, then suddenly rose into the range of mountains which had led them to Heshui.

The odd military vehicle passed them by and disappeared down towards the Russian border or to Ranjin Sombong just across in Korea itself. Mike had pulled the van off the road in a sheltered spot a hundred yards from where Clem had called in the helicopter.

Clem scooped Charlotte up in his arms. Mike and Paul Chu waved as the aircraft twisted in the sky, the crew spotting from one side, the door open and the machine gun ready on the other.

The wind from the rotor blades cut through the high grass by the river. Mike noticed the flash from a Chinese gun position in the mountains, then the crump of a shell, but by then the helicopter had been hit. There was a shattering blast as the aircraft twisted and turned over, then exploded with fireballs shooting out and plummeted into the river. The grass caught light, but only for seconds before dampness killed the flames. Burning debris was flung down, blackening the snow and hissing in the sudden cold.

An American airforce band was on the tarmac. A red carpet stretched from the aircraft stairs to the terminal building where the head of the Pacific Command, the governor of Hawaii and a dance group waited for the touchdown. As President Kang Guo-feng appeared at the aircraft doorway, he waved unsteadily, but his defiance to arrive as the President of China prompted spontaneous cheering. An American marine guard fired off a twenty-one-gun salute. As soon as Kang was inside the terminal, Donald Zuckerman called.

'Mr President,' he said. 'Your state visit will continue as scheduled. After that you and your wife are welcome to stay in the United States as long as it takes to get this problem sorted out.'

'I apologise for the inconvenience,' Kang answered.

'The road to democracy is bumpy for all nations. America has had first-hand experience and the people give you their full support.'

'Thank you.'

'I'm sending Air Force One over now to bring you safely to Washington.'

Within seconds of his finishing the call, the live television broadcast switched to an announcer in Beijing, reading from a sheet of paper. A map of China was behind her and the camera kept moving between her and scenes in Tiananmen Square where military units were gathering in disciplined formations.

'The Standing Committee of the Chinese Communist Party politburo has found Kang Guo-feng guilty of acts of treachery,' the announcer said. 'Comrade General Li Tuo has been appointed to head a caretaker government.'

Pictures of Li Tuo were superimposed on the images from Tiananmen Square.

'Hegemonous powers are taking advantage of our internal problems and are threatening our northern borders. Extra units have been deployed on the Korean border where a blatant presence of foreign troops is breaking all international agreements. The border has been declared a war zone.'

Against a backdrop of Party music, the announcer read out the names of those who stood accused with Kang and finished with those who had already been punished. The last names to be listed were Wendy Zhou, Jeremy Tang, John Jiang, Alan Zhu and Tony Zhang.

'They confessed to their crimes and have been executed by lethal injection,' she said. 'According to Chinese tradition, their families thanked the Communist Party and agreed to pay for the drugs which killed them.'

'President Kang is on his way to Washington,' said Zuckerman in the White House press room. 'And as far as the Free World is concerned, he is the President of China.'

Hands shot up to ask questions, but Zuckerman continued: 'You and I have just seen on Chinese television that a man called General Li Tuo claims to have taken power in China. He was quoted in the broadcast as wanting to open diplomatic negotiations with friendly countries. He has asked that China be given time to solve its internal problems.'

Zuckerman paused: 'I want to make clear right now, that the United States does not recognise and will not negotiate with this illegal regime. It does not cut deals with leaders of coups d'état or terrorists.'

'Mr President, is this the beginning of a Cold War with China?' came a question from the back.

'Cold war, hot war, call it what it you like. But as sure as hell, right now the United States is not at peace with the thugs who control China.'

After the appalling noise of the explosion, there was a deathly quiet over the Tumen River, apart from small sounds of the metal in the water, cooling, and the fires going out. They waited for the debris to settle; Mike judged they were about four hundred yards from where he and Ling had left the inflatable. As they edged down to the river, a heavy machine gun opened up from the position on the mountains. Seconds later there came the crump and flash of an artillery shell from the Korean side. Clem's phone rang and an American voice was the other end: 'Colonel Watkins, I'm Captain James Crawford. We have instructions to give you covering fire while you try to get out.'

'Since when was I a fucking colonel?' Clem answered. The machine gun raked the riverside again, but off-target, testing their position more than knowing it.

'I'm told my orders come straight from the White House, sir.'

'All right, Captain. We're going to come across in an inflatable about four hundred yards downstream. Do you have any boats . . .' The line crackled, The battery was running low. Clem heard Crawford say he was ordering an artillery barrage and that boats were on their way. Then it went dead. Crawford's shells exploded right along the mountain and heavy machine guns opened up high above their heads, hitting targets more than a mile away. Mike took up the rear. Charlotte made her way with Paul Chu and Clem went up ahead, running through the grass and finally down to the river where he saw a rope, discarded cartridges and a pistol lying on a shingle beach.

He leapt down the bank and as soon as he was on the shingle he lay on the ground, weapon ready, facing the road and the enemy. Within seconds the others were with him.

'It was here,' said Mike.

'Not any more,' said Clem.

'Then we'll walk it.'

The water was icy and the shingle moved dangerously under their feet with the fast-flowing current. Paul Chu went first, holding tightly onto Charlotte. Clem and Mike waded, keeping watch on the river bank. They had got over the first shingle bank. Suddenly the river became deeper, with the water sweeping around their thighs and up to Charlotte's waist.

A convoy of five military trucks, with troops on the back, came around the corner and pulled up less than two hundred yards away. The Chinese troops set up positions with heavy machine guns and mortars and opened fire at first above their heads at the incoming fire from the Korean side. Then Mike heard a shout from the Chinese that they had been spotted.

McKillop hoped to hell that Captain Crawford had seen them as well. The first burst hit the choppy water around them. Mike turned, dropping down into the fast-running water, using the river itself as cover as he let off tight bursts in the direction of the Chinese. A mortar exploded a few yards ahead of them. The water was still deep, but it became shallow quickly with the shingle on the other side. Charlotte was ahead of them, on all fours, scrambling up the bank. A Chinese platoon raced through the high grass towards the river. Clem and Mike stayed in the middle, firing accurate, controlled bursts as the soldiers came into range. Paul Chu was halfway onto the bank, struggling in the fast water, weakened by years of hunger.

Crawford sent a hail of machine gun fire over their heads towards the Chinese. Then two rocket-propelled grenades broke their formation. For a few seconds, all firing stopped. Charlotte pulled herself up and ran, the water just over her ankles, then she was out, sprinting through the grass and out of sight.

A Chinese heavy machine gun, mounted on one of the trucks, opened up on her, hitting areas of the bank. Lines of bullets cut up the ground around Paul Chu. He clawed onto the earth, pulling himself up, and then Charlotte was back again, giving him her hand. Three more rocket-propelled grenades from the American positions and a series of mortars fired in quick succession exploded around the Chinese trucks.

Mike and Clem edged further across the river. Mike saw Korean troops break cover, lift up his daughter and help Paul Chu to safety.

'You're clear,' yelled Crawford. Mike and Clem scrambled across the bank.

Captain Crawford's men bundled them through the river undergrowth into military jeeps. They drove half a mile to the road and five miles further on where the Korean and American forces had set up a base camp in another tourist hotel.

An army nurse was waiting for Charlotte and, before she left, holding the nurse's hand, she didn't say anything to Mike and he didn't push it. The process could take years. No one knew what terrible damage might have been done to her. Charlotte turned and looked over her shoulder at him, but it was a searching look which told him nothing except that to become her father again would take time.

'We've got to get back,' said Mike turning towards Clem who was sorting through the weapons bags to see what was left. Clem kept working for a few seconds before he looked up. 'There was an attack at the Daewoo Hotel,' he said softly. 'Ling and Matthew are missing.'

Crawford strode over towards where Mike and Clem were talking: 'Colonel Watkins, I've been instructed to put you on an aircraft to Washington. Apparently, the President would like to see you.'

Mike was beginning to ask about Ling, but Crawford kept speaking: 'And my apologies to both you gentlemen for not knowing this earlier. Apparently your inflatable was taken by one of its rightful owners, a Miss Ling Chen, and your son, Superintendent McKillop. I understand Matthew has been in our communications tent giving a full account of his ordeal for the lunchtime shows back home.'

Over Crawford's shoulder, Mike saw a child walking determinedly and uneasily towards him. Matthew broke into an awkward run and stretched out his arms. Mike picked him up and Matthew began talking non-stop about being on American television: 'They were shining lights in my eyes,' Matthew was saying, 'and putting microphones on me and telling me not to look at them but to look at the camera . . .'

Clem came up. 'They're putting Bishop Chu on in five minutes,' he said. 'To talk live to the President.'

Mike lowered Matthew to the ground. Clem clasped Mike's hand: 'It's been good fighting with you again, Superintendent,' he said with a huge smile across his face.

'You too,' said Mike, adding drily: 'I suppose we must have done the right thing.'

'Chu says those bunkers which were meant to be nuclear waste dumps were where they killed and burnt the prisoners.'

'My God,' said Mike.

'And that's what he's about to tell the networks.'

Crawford was back holding a sheet of paper from a telephone message. 'Superintendent, I understand that the British Prime Minister has asked to see you as well. So we have booked seats for you and your family . . .'

On the word family, Mike was swept with emotion. He hugged Matthew so hard that he squealed. 'I have orders that neither you nor Colonel Watkins can appear on television or give any interviews, but I have a personal message from Miss Ling Chen.'

Mike saw Ling in the distance, noticing how attractive she looked even in ill-fitting military fatigues. 'She says your suggestion of Bali is ridiculous because it is now in enemy hands.'

Ling was smiling and walking towards him.

'But if you were planning to go sailing round a Scottish place called Islay she would be happy to join you.'

*   *   *